"I don't really ⟨ W9-CDE-739 said.
"Not really, not anymore. And yet
there *is* some connection still.
Do you feel it too?"

"Yes," he said hoarsely.

Eliza held her breath as his fingers traced that heartbeat, the swell of her breast through the thin silk dressing gown.

His other hand grasped her waist, drawing her up against him until there was not even a breath between them. Their bodies were pressed together, hard angles against soft curves, fitting perfectly as if they were made to be just so. She felt dizzy. As if she were falling, falling, into him, where she would vanish completely.

His tongue touched hers, and she tasted wine, mint—oh, yes, she remembered the taste of him well. But their younger selves had never kissed like this. There was nothing tentative, careful, or artful about their kiss. It was frantic, hungry, and passionate, full of the dreams of years, of adult need, of fear and darkness and the force of life itself.

"An unforgettable love story."
    —**LORRAINE HEATH**, *New York Times* bestselling
    author of *Midnight Pleasures with a Scoundrel*

more . . .

Countess
of
Scandal

LAUREL McKEE

FOREVER

NEW YORK   BOSTON

Cover design by Christine Foltzer
Cover art by Alan Ayers
Handlettering by Kate Forrester
Book design by Giorgetta Bell McRee

Forever
Hachette Book Group
237 Park Avenue
New York, NY 10017
Visit our website at www.HachetteBookGroup.com.

Forever is an imprint of Grand Central Publishing. The Forever name and logo is a trademark of Hachette Book Group, Inc.

Printed in the United States of America

First Printing: February 2010

10 9 8 7 6 5 4 3 2 1

Countess
of
Scandal

Prologue

County Kildare, Ireland, 1790

Lady Eliza Blacknall slipped through the front doors of her home, Killinan Castle, easing them shut behind her. The drive was quiet, the length of white gravel gleaming under the moonlight. Her slippers whispered over the stone, her muslin skirts held close to still their rustle as she ran toward a small walled garden. Free at last! Her parents' dull party, and the dull fiancé they intended for her, were left behind.

The evening was still and clear but cool, and she wrapped her arms tightly around herself as she sat down on a marble bench. The moon was a fat, silvery crescent set in the purple-black velvet sky, outlined in twinkling stars.

Certainly that must be a magical Irish moon, Eliza fancied, thinking of old tales her nanny once told her, tales of nights when all the humans were gone home to their beds and everything was silent. That was when tiny battalions of fairies would creep out from their hiding places and hold their own gatherings in magical circles beneath that moon. No dull *Macbeth* for them, oh no. No tea and minuets. Pipes and harps, wild jigs, laughter that went on until dawn. Eliza closed her eyes, picturing tiny wings shimmering like diamonds. . . .

Suddenly, a gentle touch interrupted her whimsical musings. Strong, warm fingers slid over her eyes, and the light scent of soap and new wool tickled her nose. Her heart skipped, then pounded in her breast, so hard she was sure everyone could hear it. She couldn't breathe. Her blood ran hot, yet she shivered.

"Penny for your thoughts," a low, rough voice whispered, his breath cool against the nape of her neck.

Eliza reached up and caught those hands in her own, holding them tightly as she twisted around on the bench. Their owner smiled down at her, all golden hair and gleaming blue-green eyes.

"Will!" she cried out, too loudly. Lowering her voice, she leaned closer and whispered, "Will, what are you doing here? We might be seen." And yet hadn't she hoped, deep down, that he would be waiting here? Wasn't that why she slipped away from the party?

"Seen by whom? The moon? The stars?" As he spoke, a puffy cloud slid in front of the moon, leaving them in the haven of darkness.

Will sat down beside her, twining his fingers tightly with hers. She knew she should pull away, move apart from him, or, better yet, leave altogether. She should go back inside, where she couldn't feel him, smell him, see his golden hair and laughing eyes.

But she could not leave him. "My mother might come looking for me."

Will shook his head, his bright hair gleaming under the stars. Surely he was only part of a dream, for he was too lovely for every day. Too lovely for her. "When I last looked, your mother was deep in conversation with her friend Mrs. Franklin." He raised her hand to his lips, pressing a soft kiss to her fingers before cradling her palm against his cheek.

She felt the smooth heat of his skin and the sharp line of his cheekbones. How she longed to be even closer! To crawl inside his being and stay near him forever, warm and safe. To never lose that crackling excitement he brought with him whenever he walked into a room.

How had she—tall, plain, dark Elizabeth Blacknall—ever been so fortunate to find him? To have him for her friend? She lifted her other hand to his long, tied-back hair, stroking the satiny length with the tips of her fingers. "We must not stay here too long. If my mother sees us, she and my father will lock me in my room for a month." Or marry her to Frederick Mount Clare, posthaste.

Will laughed, the sound deliciously deep, reverberating against her hand. It seemed to echo all through her, to the very core of her heart. "Then you would have to let down your hair so I could climb up to rescue you. Like in a fairy story."

Eliza laughed, too, picturing such a thing. "I don't think my hair is long enough."

"No?" He released her hand to twine one curl around his finger. Usually dark brown, her hair was ebony in the night. It caught and clung to his skin. "Then I shall have to remember to bring a very tall ladder."

If only he could. A very, very tall ladder, to lift her

from her real life into a world with only him. Where she would never be apart from him and the way he made her feel—so very alive, as if all her fifteen years before had merely been a waiting slumber.

"Can you come riding tomorrow?" he murmured, still toying with her hair.

She could scarcely think straight when he did that. "I don't think so," she said reluctantly. "I have to have tea with my mother and Lady Mount Clare." And Frederick. "But the next day I can."

"It'll seem like ten years until then." He pressed a gentle kiss to her hair, then gently released the curl to rest it on her shoulder.

"My parents are going to the village after luncheon to inspect the new school that day," she said. "Will you wait for me in our secret place?"

"Always, Eliza."

She nodded, swallowing hard past the dry longing in her throat at the way he spoke her name. "I should probably go back to the house now."

As she spoke, the clouds slid from the moon, and its chalky light streamed down over their hidden garden. That was when she saw it.

Will wore the scarlet coat, faced in yellow and trimmed with narrow gold lace and brass buttons, of the Thirteenth Regiment of Foot. An *English* regiment. After she had told him how she felt about Ireland and all it stood for! After she poured out all her passion to him.

A cold wave seemed to break over her at the sight of that hated coat, washing away the warm, giddy haze of unreality that always wrapped around her when he was near. Her skin turned to ice, and she dropped his hand, leaping up from the bench to move away from him.

She had known this might happen. He was, as her mother pointed out, a younger son, and younger sons had to make their own way. But an English regiment!

"You . . . you purchased your commission?" she said, her voice strained.

Will frowned, tucking his hands behind his back as if he, too, felt the sudden chill. The slow snapping of their friendship. "Of course. My family has long intended me for the army."

"Yes, but surely the Kildare militia would—"

He laughed humorlessly. "An Irish militia would offer few chances for advancement, I fear."

"Advancement in London, you mean? You would rather be an English officer, sent away from here? From Ireland?"

"Eliza," he said, shaking his head. "Are we not English ourselves? We owe our allegiance to the king, the same as anyone in London. This is the best way for me to make my way in the world. Surely you see that?"

All Eliza could really see was that he was leaving, going into a world that she had never really understood. But he was part of it, as was her own family. Protestant Ascendancy families like the Dentons and the Blacknalls had come from England decades ago to claim estates as prizes from the king for their loyalty. They lived in Ireland, derived their fortunes from it, but were still *English* in their hearts. They were the rulers; the Irish who had been there for centuries before had no power.

Eliza had only ever wanted to be *Irish,* but no one else

in her world felt that way. Not even Will. And now he was leaving her behind.

He took her hand again, holding it tightly in his warm embrace. Eliza stared down at their joined fingers, at the touch that had so thrilled her. Now . . . now she just felt cold numbness. Will, and the dream of their friendship, was gone. Captain William Denton was the reality, and the future she had not wanted to face was upon her.

Perhaps her mother was right after all. Love didn't last. Position and responsibility were forever.

"Eliza," he said coaxingly, "the regiment is being sent to the West Indies, but surely it won't be there for long. When I return, we will be older, and I will have made money of my own. May I write to you?"

His eyes, as blue-green as the deepest sea, stared down at her, full of wary questions. She could not read them. Yet, for an instant, it was as if they galloped over the fields together, laughing again. Or when he kissed her in the woods and all time stood utterly still. They were the only two people in the world, bound together by a shimmering, unbreakable bond.

Then the moonlight glinted off one of those newly minted buttons.

"I don't think my parents would allow that," she said.

"When have you ever cared what your parents allowed?" he said with a puzzled laugh.

True enough. Her parents seemed to lecture all the time about proper behavior and family honor, and she seldom listened. She was too caught up in her own fancies. But maybe it was time—past time—she started paying heed.

"You are thinking of your future," she said. "I must think of mine. And mine is here, in Ireland."

"So you still feel the English officers are oppressors?" he asked, disbelieving. "You think I . . ."

She gently extracted her hand from his clasp and went up on tiptoe to kiss his cheek. Even though she was tall, he was taller. The perfect handsome officer. His skin was so warm and smooth under her lips, his clean scent so alluring. An ineffable sadness seized her heart, and she longed to stay just where she was, to wrap her arms around him so tightly he could not escape.

But she stepped away and said, "I wish you fair prospects, Will. I'll think of you often, I promise."

And she turned and walked quickly away from him, hurrying toward the lit edifice of Killinan Castle. It looked just the same as ever—sturdy gray-white stone, Palladian columns, all the many windows glowing with welcome. Yet, even though she had been gone only half an hour, *she* felt completely changed.

As she entered the foyer, she could hear the hum of voices and laughter from behind the drawing room door. The play had not yet resumed, and hopefully that meant her mother was still too busy playing hostess to have missed Eliza.

She paused before a tall, gilt-framed looking glass to smooth her dress and hair. Was it only her imagination or did she even *look* older than before? She had certainly been a fool to think she could marry Will Denton. It was time for new plans.

"Psst! Eliza!" she heard someone hiss. She turned toward the grand staircase to find her two sisters perched there, peering through the carved banisters. Anna, who at nine was becoming the golden-haired beauty of the family, always cried about not being allowed to join the parties. And seven-year-old Caroline, dark like Eliza, would rather hunt for tadpoles in the pond. It was she who had spoken.

"You two are supposed to be abed," Eliza said, hurrying to the foot of the stairs.

"We wanted to see the gowns," Anna answered. "And watch the party!"

"It's not much to see," said Eliza. "Quite dull, in fact. I wish I could be upstairs with you!"

"I don't think Mama would allow that," Caroline said. "She was out here looking for you."

Eliza was afraid of that. "When?"

"Not ten minutes ago. The Mount Clares have arrived."

"I had best go in, then," Eliza sighed. She turned away, smoothing her skirts again.

"Eliza," Anna called. "Why were you outside for so long?"

"I think she was meeting an admirer," Caroline sang. "He was reading her poetry in the moonlight."

"No such thing," Eliza said sternly. "I just needed some fresh air."

Caroline seemed convinced, more interested now in persuading Eliza to bring her refreshments from the party. But Anna, the Blacknall sister most addicted to romantic novels and sad songs, watched her solemnly, as if she knew what Eliza had been doing in the garden.

Eliza hurried into the drawing room. Everyone still milled about, sipping wine and negus as they chatted, waiting for the play to resume. Her parents stood near the stage, her mother's silvery-blond hair and pale blue brocade gown shimmering in the crowd like a stylish beacon. With them were the Mount Clares, and their son.

Katherine saw Eliza the moment she stepped into the room and beckoned her closer with a bejeweled hand. Eliza pasted on a polite smile and stepped forward into the future—whatever it might hold.

Chapter One

Dublin, December 1797

Isn't that Mount Clare's widow?" a man asked as Eliza passed by him in the crowded, palatial assembly rooms of Rutland Square. It was Lord Morely, secretary at Dublin Castle. He raised his quizzing glass to his eye, watching her closely.

"Indeed, it is," said his portly companion, Mr. Pelham. "Poor Mount Clare. He was a friend of mine, y'know. We hunted together. Lucky he can't see what his wife's been up to since he died."

"Formed one of those blasted teapot societies, I've heard," Lord Morely answered.

"Sedition over the tea table and embroidery hoop. My wife tells me she entertains teachers, poets, female radicals, even *Catholics*. Shocking."

"Those damnable United Irishmen. They prey on the gullible peasants, persuading them to do their filthy, treasonous work. Lord Camden has been a weak Lord

Lieutenant, indeed. He does little to stop them. He should be sent back to England."

Eliza ignored them, passing serenely on her way, though she longed to burst out laughing. If they only knew! Mount Clare had never cared what she did when he was alive, as long as she left him alone with his cards, horses, and mistresses. It left her plenty of time to travel and study, to read and form "shocking" friendships of all sorts.

Now that he was gone, she finally had the funds to put some of her ideas into action. Ideas that narrow, cruel men like Morely could never understand.

Eliza sighed as she edged her way around the crowded dance floor, the blur of bright silks, velvets, and sparkling jewels, and the thunder of stamping feet and claps. Men so rarely understood her. Certainly not her husband or her poor late father! They had always looked at her as if she were a Chinese puzzle box, an exotic stranger in their midst.

Eliza paused before one of the floor-length mirrors that lined the green silk walls of the assembly rooms. She didn't *look* like a puzzle, she thought. She wore a fine gown of silver-lilac silk, embroidered with silver thread and beads, proper half-mourning that went well with her grandmother's diamonds. Her dark hair was carefully curled and piled high and pinned with pearl combs, not tucked up "croppy" style, as Lucy Fitzgerald and her wild sister-in-law Pamela liked to effect. They were easily reckoned to be "democratical" and thus not danced with.

Eliza preferred to keep her convictions hidden, or at least as hidden as they could be, where they could do the most good. Silks and diamonds were as good a mask as any, though her disguise was slipping, if Morely and Pelham's conversation was any indication. Soon she would have to come out into the open—as they all would.

She closed her eyes against the lavish party. Ever since she was a girl, she had been keenly aware of the difference between her family's comfortable life and those of the Irish farmers and workers. She saw the gulf between the privileged Anglo-Irish few and the suffering many. As she grew older and her marriage gave her independence, she learned how the government in Dublin truly worked; she often went to Parliament to sit in the gallery and listen to the debates. Whenever any politician actually showed some compassion and tried to help the Irish people, tried to lessen the harsh Penal Laws or improve the lot of the Catholics, they were shouted down by the Ascendancy landowners who were protecting their exclusive powers and privileges.

She had tried to follow her mother's fine example of charity and compassion but quickly saw that would never go far enough to really improve anyone's life. It could never lessen the weight that prevented real prosperity and happiness. The land she loved so much was dying under oppression.

So, when Lord Edward Fitzgerald, the son of her mother's friends the Duke and Duchess of Leinster, came and asked for her help to make true changes in Ireland, to throw off British rule as America had done and move forward as an independent nation, it seemed the work she waited for. The work she was meant to do.

She would not turn away from it.

Eliza turned her back to the mirror to study the room behind her. That kaleidoscope of dancers, the spiraling music and laughter, grew ever louder and wilder as the punch poured on. This Christmas season had been like none other she could remember. Irish holidays were always lavish and merry, but this year there was a knife-sharp edge to it all, a frantic decadence, as if they could all go tumbling down into dark oblivion at any moment.

"Après moi, le deluge," she heard someone say behind her. She turned to find her sister Anna standing just beyond the edge of the glass's reflection. Anna's beauty had only grown over the years, and now she was all gold and ivory and roses, a bright, brilliant goddess in her white and pink gown.

Too bright, perhaps? Eliza examined Anna's shining blue eyes, her tumbled blond curls—the champagne glass in her hand.

Anna laughed. "You see, sister, I can read your mind. We dance while Rome, or Dublin, burns."

Eliza shook her head and took the glass away from her sister. "Were you in the card room?"

"Of course. I must have my share of fun while I can, since I'm to be shipped back to Mama at Killinan after Christmas! She is shockingly strict these days, Eliza. You would think I was still in the schoolroom with Caroline."

That wouldn't be such a bad thing, Eliza thought as she tasted the champagne that was left. Anna was as wild and frantic as everyone else in Dublin, and that could be very dangerous in the days to come. "How much did you lose?"

Anna waved her lace fan in a dismissive gesture. "The merest amount, Eliza, I promise. Mostly to Peter Carstairs, too, and he won't press to be paid."

"Because he is violently in love with you. Like all the other young men in Dublin."

Anna laughed, her cheeks bright pink. "Well, I am not

in love with any of them, I assure you! Silly puppies, all of them."

"One day, sister dear, someone shall capture your heart, and then you shall have to eat your words."

"I could say the same thing to you, Eliza. Where will all your talk of independence go when you meet someone you could truly love?" Anna took a lobster tart from a footman's tray, munching on it thoughtfully before saying, "Someone dashing and smart, not like Mount Clare. Someone handsome, too . . ."

Eliza laughed. "You have been reading too many romantic novels, Anna! I must lend you some more improving volumes."

"Not if it's going to make me sound like I'm reading from *Fordyce's Sermons*. We have to make merry while we're young—while we can."

"So, you will leave sermons until you're an old, gray widow like me?"

"Oh, Eliza dearest! Widow you may be; old and gray you are not. You can still find romance." Anna pointed with her folded fan at the dance floor. "What of Walter Fitzwilliam? He cuts a fine leg."

"And he is a terrible drunk. He fell into the gutter on Sackville Street last week, they say."

"That does not bode well for the bedchamber, then," Anna muttered. "I have heard things about men who imbibe too freely. It, er, disables certain vital parts."

"Anna Blacknall!"

"There *are* benefits in reading novels, sister. Especially French ones. What of Lord Aldington . . ."

At that moment, the assembly room doors opened to admit a group of latecomers. As was becoming more frequent in Dublin, as regiments newly arrived from London sought amusement, they were officers. Young ones, too, not old and portly colonels in too-tight red tunics. These men seemed tall and strong, their bright gazes keen as they swept over the noisy throng.

"Well, now," Anna said. "This is more like it."

"Anna, I am hardly likely to take up with some newly arrived officer," Eliza said.

"No one said you have to 'take up' with one! A dance would make a fine start." Anna tapped her fan against her chin as she examined the new arrivals. "What about that one there? He is quite a beauty, I must say, and even taller than you."

Eliza couldn't help laughing. It felt as if they were at a horse fair, and Anna was a shrewd Arab trader evaluating fillies. "Which one?"

"That one, of course. He doesn't appear a drunkard at all, does he?"

Eliza followed the pointing line of Anna's fan to a man who was half turned away from them, greeting Mr. Neilsen, the Master of Ceremonies. From that angle, he *did* seem a beauty, she had to admit. Very tall, with broad shoulders, a tight backside, and his long dark golden hair tied back with a black ribbon. If only those fine shoulders weren't encased in a red coat!

Green would suit them so much better.

Then he turned toward her, the flickering light of dozens of candles falling over the chiseled angles of his lean face.

Eliza gasped. She was surely imagining things! Anna's romantic nonsense was infecting her senses.

She closed her eyes, gulping down the last of the champagne. When she looked again, though, nothing had changed. He was still there. Bigger than life. Bigger even than the dreams that had come to her, unbidden, over the years.

Will Denton was back in Ireland. *Major* Denton, to judge by the decorations on his uniform. Time had carved his face into a hard, elegant sculpture, like a statue of a Roman god colored bronze by a harsh West Indies sun.

From across the room, his eyes, those intense blue-green eyes she had imagined so often over the years, seemed to touch her very heart. The noise and movement of the room all faded away, and she saw only him. For an instant, she was fifteen again, so full of yearning and romantic hope.

Her hand tightened on the glass until it bit into her rings and dragged her back down to earth. To cold reality.

"Good heavens!" Anna exclaimed. "Isn't that Viscount Moreton's younger son? The one who's been gone so long?"

"I believe so," Eliza said hoarsely. Her throat felt so dry and tight. Where was that champagne when it was needed? "I'm surprised you remember."

"Oh, I never forget a face. Especially one like that. Was he not your friend back then?"

"I wouldn't call him a friend. Just a neighbor and acquaintance."

"Did you sneak out to go riding with all your acquaintances, then?"

Eliza shouldn't be surprised, really. Despite her careless, party-loving facade, Anna had always been a shockingly sharp observer. Which meant having her in Dublin, now of all times, was not very wise. "That was a long time ago."

"The years have certainly been kind to our old neighbor.

We should renew our acquaintance. It's surely the polite thing to do."

Before Eliza could protest, Anna seized her by the hand and drew her across the room, through the knots of laughing people. Will watched their approach, his expression utterly unreadable, as if he had become a Roman statue in truth. As she drew closer to him, she suddenly recalled every minute they had spent together. Every single stolen kiss.

She tried to breathe, but her stays were too tight. Only Anna's firm clasp on her arm held her fast, not allowing her to run away. She had to keep moving forward, ever forward—toward Will, and the past that was suddenly all tangled up in the present.

Mr. Neilsen bowed to them as they drew near. "Lady Mount Clare, Lady Anna. May I present—"

"No need, Mr. Neilsen, for we are old friends! Are we not, Mr. Denton?" Anna said gaily. "Or should I say Major Denton, yes?"

"I am most pleased to meet with you again, Lady Anna," Will answered. Eliza thought she saw a flashing glint in his eyes, as if he would smile at them. But he merely bowed politely.

"I'm surprised you recognize me. Have I not grown much taller?" Anna said. "Yet my sister, Lady Mount Clare, has grown only more beautiful. Would you not agree, Major?"

Will looked directly at Eliza, his gaze steady and as dark blue and unreadable as the deepest sea. Eliza clutched at her folded fan, as if its carved ivory could keep her from drowning. "Most beautiful, of course—Lady Mount Clare. Then, you always were. Lord Mount Clare is most fortunate."

"He would be if he wasn't dead!" Anna said brightly.

"Anna!" Eliza admonished.

Far from being repentant, Anna took Mr. Neilsen's arm and smoothly led him away, saying, "Mr. Neilsen, there is something I absolutely must ask you about next week's reception . . ."

And Eliza was left quite alone with Will.

Well, alone in a room with dozens of other people— people who always watched each other's behavior with the most avid interest. Yet it felt as if there was only the two of them, cast round by a spell of glittering silence. All the years of her unsatisfactory marriage, her work, everything, just . . . disappeared.

"You look well," she said, finding her voice at last. "The islands must have agreed with you."

That lurking smile touched the corner of his lips. A mere shadow, but it sufficed. "Can they agree with any man? The heat, the hurricanes . . ."

"Those recalcitrant natives?"

"Them, too."

"And now you are brought back to Ireland to subdue a different set of natives?"

Will laughed. She remembered well his old laugh, that merry, carefree sound that would burst forth like sunshine. This laugh was different, harsher somehow. Rougher and darker. "Do *you* need subduing, Eliza?"

"Not by the likes of you, Will Denton. *Major* Denton."

"Ah, yes, I remember—not by a man in an English coat."

"That was a long time ago."

"And things change, do they?" His gaze swept over her, her silk gown and diamonds, the gold ring on her finger. "How long has Lord Mount Clare been gone?"

"Over a year now."

"You look surprised as you say that."

In truth, she was a bit surprised. It seemed longer than a year; he had been so often away from home, from her—and she from him. An arrangement that suited everyone most admirably.

Once, she could have said that to Will. Said anything, really. But the sun-bronzed, hardened man who stood before her was a stranger, and she had learned caution. Keeping one's own counsel these days was essential.

"Shall we take a turn about the room?" she said. People were beginning to watch them, no doubt to whisper about their long conversation.

"Certainly, Lady Mount Clare," Will answered, politely offering his arm. She slipped her fingers over the fine woolen sleeve, feeling the hard, taut muscle beneath. His hand flexed at her touch, sending the shift and ripple of it into her fingertips, and she realized that his laughter wasn't the only thing that had roughened in the West Indies. He was not the boy she had once felt a foolish infatuation for. He was a man now, a man of mysterious depths and unreadable purpose.

"Have you been to see your mother yet?" she asked, keeping her voice and expression carefully pleasant. Neutral. Polite.

"Not yet, but they say we are to be posted to Kildare soon," he said.

Posted to Kildare. Very interesting. "She will surely be most happy to see you. Your father has been in London for many months. My mother tells me they have grown quite solitary at Moreton Manor." And also that Lady Moreton lived in such terror of her tenants killing her in the night that she slept in the attic with a loaded pistol at her side.

"I trust your mother is in good health? And Lady Caroline? For I see that Lady Anna is doing fine," he said.

Eliza glanced over to see that Anna had joined the dance and was leaping about and laughing with immense vigor. Eliza laughed, too, and said, "Anna enjoys . . . What is the phrase? Rude health. She is to return to Kildare after Christmas and is not happy at the prospect. Though my family is all very well, thank you."

"And you, Lady Mount Clare?" His voice lowered to a murmur, close to her ear. So close his cool breath stirred her curls, and she shivered. "How do *you* occupy your days in Dublin?"

Eliza's steps slowed, but she refused to let her polite smile waver. "Oh, Major Denton, my days are very full. I chaperone my sister, write letters to my mother, embroider cushions . . ."

"A full day, indeed. Are your letters only to your mother, then?"

"I have many friends I correspond with."

"So I have heard," he said in a hard voice.

Eliza stopped, so quickly that her hand tugged hard at his sleeve. "Are you insinuating I have a clandestine lover, Major? How terribly ungallant."

She tried to pull free, but he held her fast. Ahead of them was a set of tall glass doors leading to a narrow terrace. He tightened his grip on her arm, bearing her forward to the door so swiftly she hardly realized what he was doing. Before she could protest, she found herself outside with him in the night. Alone.

It was too cold for any fresh-air seekers or secretive lovers, and the street below was eerily silent. No one wandered the lanes of Dublin at night these days, for fear of encountering the patrols. It was just her and Will—or rather, the hard stranger Will had become.

"If only a lover *was* the rumor I heard," he said, quiet and fierce. His stare never wavered from her face, as if he could read her secrets, read her very soul. Eliza backed up until she felt the hard edge of the stone balustrade through her skirts. Will followed, relentless, resting his hands on the balustrade so she was caught.

They were as close as if they embraced, the warmth of his body wrapping all around her. But the hard glint in his eyes was far from affectionate.

Eliza tried to laugh, to edge past him, yet she was truly caught. "I am just a respectable widow."

"A respectable widow who consorts with radical pamphlet writers and Catholic lawyers? With the likes of Lord Edward Fitzgerald and his French wife?"

"My friends are my own business."

"You choose some dangerous friends in these uncertain times, Lady Mount Clare. And perhaps *friendship* is not all you offer them." He leaned even closer, so close she could scarcely tell where he ended and she began. And, despite the peril of her situation, she felt some of the old stirring within her, the excitement of just being close to him again.

"Are you *up,* Lady Mount Clare?" he whispered.

And the hot excitement was swept away in a cold tide at those words. The words that asked if she signed the United Irish petition. If she gave aid to traitors to that red coat he wore.

She turned her head, staring blindly at the street below.

"Whatever do you mean, Major Denton? La, such odd things you say! Did you learn them in the West Indies?"

"Blast it, Eliza, listen to me!" Will grabbed her by the arms, holding her close, refusing to let her go. "You are as stubborn as ever. But you must listen to me now. This is a most perilous path you tread, and I would not see you hurt."

Eliza stared up at him, at his golden beauty limned in the reflected light from the assembly room beyond. He was beautiful, indeed—but so distant from her now. "What do you know?" she asked tightly.

"I know all is not as it should be here," he said. "That we dance tonight on a powder keg. And the most surprising people hold the match to set it alight."

"I have taken no oaths. You cannot arrest me simply for my friendships."

"Don't be a fool, Eliza. Your 'friends' cannot win, and treason is a deadly game to play. Even for a countess."

Hot anger flowed through her, giving her a new strength. She twisted away from him, ducking past his confusing embrace. "I do not play the traitor here. And I believe this conversation is at an end."

She whirled toward the doors, but he caught her arm, reeling her back toward him. She collided with his chest, grabbing at his shoulders to hold herself steady. He wouldn't let her go this time, holding her pinned to his hard body.

"We were friends once, Eliza," he said roughly. "Please, for the sake of that old friendship, listen to me now."

He hardly gave her a choice! She could not move, trapped by all his heat and strength, by the sudden weakness in her legs, the pounding of her heart. She said nothing.

"Go stay with your mother at Killinan Castle," he said,

seeming to take her silence as acquiescence. "Or, better still, take your mother and sisters and go to England, while you still can. You'll be safer there."

"You are right, Will. We *were* friends once," she said. "And surely you remember that 'safety' was never my first concern."

"I remember you rode your horse like a madwoman," he said with grudging admiration. "You had no fear of any obstacle then, and I'm sure you have none now. But I'm also sure you care about your family. You don't want them caught up in whatever your friends are planning."

Eliza stared up at him. "What do you know?" she asked again.

"Not nearly enough at present. But I will find out, never fear."

"That's what you were sent for?"

A tiny, bitter smile quirked the corner of his lips. "Do you really think I would tell *you* why I'm here—Lady Democratical?"

Eliza shoved him away, dashing past him to the welcoming light and noise of the party. This time he let her go, but she felt his penetrating stare against the back of her neck.

Once in the ballroom, she drew in a deep breath, trying to calm herself and cool the hectic heat she felt on her cheeks. She realized she had lost her fan on the terrace, but she certainly was not going back to retrieve it.

It was time for her to go home. She had had enough of this assembly, of those people and their stares and whispers. She had had enough of Major William Denton and his "warnings"!

She found Anna in one of the antechambers, laughing with some of her young friends. Her cheeks, too, were flushed, but that was probably due to the almost-empty punch glass in her hand. Eliza took it away and grasped her sister's hand, leading her toward the front doors that opened out to Rutland Square.

"It grows late, sister," she said. "We must go home."

"Oh no!" Anna protested. "It is scarcely two, Eliza. Surely there is much dancing left to be done."

"I am sure there is, but not by us." Dublin had been one nonstop gala for weeks. Useful for gathering information, but wearying, indeed. "Old widows like myself need their rest."

Anna pouted but climbed into their carriage meekly enough. That was all to the good, as Eliza knew she could not face another quarrel. She felt exhausted and drained from her encounter with Will.

Eliza leaned her head back on the velvet squabs, closing her eyes as she listened to the clatter of the wheels bearing her back to the Henrietta Street house. Will knew something, something vital. Or he was very close to it. Would he ruin everything? Now, when they were so very close to their goal?

Yet, even as she longed for Will to be gone again, to go back to the islands and cease making everything so very complicated, she remembered the feel of his touch. His breath against her skin. And how she didn't really want him to let her go . . .

Complicated, indeed.

"My heavens, but William Denton has grown mightily handsome," Anna said, interrupting the whirl of Eliza's thoughts.

She opened her eyes to find her sister gazing pensively out the window, her hood thrown back from her pale curls. "I remember he was quite good-looking when I was a child," Anna continued, "but nothing like now. And he seems to admire you as much as ever."

"We were childhood friends, perhaps," Eliza said. "But that was a very long time ago. I would scarcely say he *admires* me."

"Oh? Then why were you on the terrace with him for so long?" Anna smiled teasingly. "Reminiscing, were you?"

The carriage jolted to a halt, saving Eliza from answering. Anna hopped down and hurried into the house, while Eliza slowly followed. By the time Eliza reached the foyer, her sister was already skipping up the grand staircase. A footman stepped forward to take her cloak, Anna's already draped over his arm. He gave Eliza a lit taper.

Eliza followed her sister up the stairs and turned at the top as if to go on to her bedchamber. And, indeed, she did long for nothing so much as the haven of her own bed, a warm fire, a soothing tisane concocted by her maid, Mary, and the oblivion of dreams. But she had one more thing to do before she retired.

Instead of going to her chamber, she turned and went back down via the narrow servants' stairs. Aside from Mary, who waited in Eliza's room, and the footman, everyone was already retired. The back stairs were echoingly silent, lit only by her flickering taper, which cast deep shadows on the walls. Eliza hurried ever downward, holding up her skirts with her free hand to still their rustle.

Once, she had not enjoyed this vast house on its fashionable street, had thought it too large and unwieldy and cold. But after it became her own, her inheritance from her husband, she found great use for it, indeed.

At the kitchen, she went down yet more stairs, into the

chilly wine cellar below the butler's pantry. She paid no mind to the dusty rows of bottles, hurrying past them until she found what she sought—a door half hidden in the corner, tucked behind stacks of barrels.

She knocked on it, two short raps, a pause, then three more. For a moment, she heard nothing, and her heart pounded with apprehension. The house *seemed* peaceful and secure, but what if something had happened in her absence?

What if Will Denton really did know?

At last, she heard the metallic scrape of the lock, and the heavy door swung open. A man stood there, outlined by the glow from the lamps set amid the jumbled books and papers on a table. He wore a loose banyan coat over his shirt and breeches, his brown hair tumbled as if from sleep. But his smile was full of relief.

"Mr. O'Connor," Eliza said. She slipped into the room, closing the door behind her. "I'm sorry to interrupt your rest. I know you need it after such a long journey."

"Not at all, Lady Mount Clare," he answered. "I've been waiting for what feels like ages! Tell me, what news from the outside? What is happening?"

Eliza sighed. How could she tell him, poor man, that she bore no good tidings as of yet? That Major Denton and his regiment had come to Ireland.

Chapter Two

Blast all women! Will pounded his fist on the cold, un-yielding stone of the balustrade, frustration and anger and unwelcome lust all tangled up inside of him.

Blast Elizabeth Blacknall above all.

He braced his hands on the balustrade, closing his eyes against the force of his emotions. Emotions were useless; they only got in the way when there was a job to be done. Just as women with flashing dark eyes and deep secrets were a fatal distraction.

He opened his eyes, staring down at the street below. Yet, he did not see the few passing carriages, didn't hear the music and laughter from the bright ballroom behind him. He could see only Eliza.

She had been a pretty girl. Now she was a beautiful woman, far beyond any vision of her he had cherished over the years. Oh, she was not beautiful like the society misses his mother kept pressing him to wed. Not soft and pale and sweet, with blond ringlets and pink cheeks. Eliza was dark, with glossy hair and those eyes—those eyes so black and unreadable, hiding and promising so much. She was as slim as a reed in her fine gown, almost delicate-seeming, yet he well remembered how she could ride and run faster and farther than anyone.

That spirit that drew him to her, even as he knew well he should stay away, still burned within her. That daring and quickness, and that independence. Marriage had not doused her flame. But did she use all that spirit now for treason?

"Damn it, Eliza," he muttered. "Why will you not listen to me?" She had never listened to him when they were young, never wanted to hear his reasons for going into the army. Not so much had changed over the years after all.

He frowned, thinking back to those long-ago days. Eliza had been enthralled by the idea of "Ireland" back then, had avidly read books on Celtic history and culture, even corresponded with members of the Dublin Society. Now he heard tell she belonged to the Society herself, read the *Hibernian Journal* and received a most strange assortment of visitors at her grand Henrietta Street house. Radicals, artists, Catholics. Rebels?

So much had changed in Dublin since he left. He felt it everywhere he went, in the very air he breathed. People stared at his uniform in either barely concealed distaste or in awe, as if he was a savior. A protector from the howling masses. Everywhere there was an atmosphere of hectic gaiety, a sense that a conflagration was about to burst out and burn them all to ashes.

Broadsheets and green streamers were torn down from walls only to appear again. Bodies were fished from the river. Terrified landowners barricaded themselves in their houses. Rumors raced of French invasions and innocents killed in their beds.

His home, whose cool green fields he had dreamed of on sun-blasted tropical days, teetered on the edge of blood-soaked oblivion. Could Eliza really be part of it?

He feared she very well could. Eliza was a girl no longer. She was a widow, a rich one, who was free to indulge her passions. One of those passions could be that idea of Ireland. She had never done things halfheartedly; she always threw herself fully into any cause she chose, no matter how misguided and dangerous.

His time in the city was short. His regiment had been sent to Ireland to quell any unrest, and soon they would be sent to Kildare and then to points north, where there were already rumors of fighting. He had to make Eliza listen, to make her see the foolishness of any rebellious path she might be on. He had left her all those years ago and had not tried hard enough to persuade her to see that he did right in joining the army.

But, by Jove, she *would* listen now! For the sake of that old friendship, her family, her own life, he had to persuade her. No matter what it took.

Resolute, he turned back toward the assembly rooms. As he strode to the half-open doors, a ray of candlelight fell on a shimmering object discarded on the stone floor. It was a fan, its carved ivory sticks spread open to reveal delicate lilac silk.

The exact color of Eliza's gown. Will knelt down to scoop it up, balancing the delicate bauble on his sun-roughened hand. A faint whiff of Eliza's rosewater perfume drifted from the folds.

Well, well. Surely she would soon be missing such a pretty trifle. It would be only polite to return it.

Eliza shut the cellar door behind her, listening for the grate of the lock turning before she made her way back up the stairs. She was exhausted after the party and her long talk with Mr. O'Connor. Her steps felt leaden in their satin slippers as she hurried up to her own chamber; her gown surely weighed a hundred pounds now. And she still had letters to write before she could at last crawl into bed and pray for sleep!

Yet, Eliza well knew it was not just the dancing and the letters that preyed on her mind. It was not even the man hidden in her cellar. No, it was quite another man altogether. Will Denton.

She pressed her hand to her whirling, aching head. She had thought never to see him again, and to find him suddenly there before her was . . . dizzying.

The years away, long years across the sea in foreign lands, had obviously honed and hardened him. He was even more handsome than in her cherished memories, with a whipcord strength barely hidden by his dashing red coat. But the kindness she remembered in his blue-green eyes, that warm light of understanding and laughter, was quite gone. He stared at her with a hard determination to discover all her secrets. As if he knew what she was doing and would put a stop to it, however he could.

Treason is a deadly game to play, she remembered him saying.

Once, she had fancied she could love him. Now he was one more obstacle to overcome. Perhaps the most formidable obstacle of all. If only she could overcome her own lust for him, too!

Eliza paused outside Anna's room, where all was silent. Her sister had a propensity to stay up all hours reading novels, but hopefully all the dancing and card-playing tonight had worn her out at last. Eliza sighed and continued down the corridor to her own chamber. She did love Anna, but she would be glad to send her back to their mother's care after Christmas. Truly, Eliza was only one woman— she could either write revolutionary pamphlets or watch after a willful teenaged girl. Not, it seemed, both.

"Did you have a good evening, my lady?" her maid, Mary said as Eliza entered her own room at last.

"Yes, thank you, Mary," she answered. "The assembly rooms are so lively at this time of year." She breathed in deeply with relief as Mary unfastened her heavy jewels and the elaborate gown. Those fashionable trappings always felt like a mask, a confining disguise. Surely she could think more clearly when they were gone and she was just herself. Not the scandalous countess Dublin whispered about.

"I have to admit I will be very glad indeed when the holiday festivities are done with," Eliza said. Her silks divested, she wrapped herself in her dressing gown and sat down before the mirror as Mary brushed out her coiffure. "I am too old for Dublin parties, Mary."

"Oh, come now, my lady! You're not a bit old. Now, Lady Dunmore, she's three hundred if she's a day, I vow!"

"Don't be cheeky, Mary," Eliza said, but she still laughed. Lady Dunmore *was* quite venerable. She even had an ear trumpet.

"But she still gets about in that Bath chair of hers, does

old Lady Dunmore," Mary went on. "They say her son is quite terrified of her."

"Hmm, and him all of *two* hundred years old, too," Eliza said. Then a thought struck. Mary, and all the servants, so often seemed to know so much. Eliza heard more gossip from Mary than she did over any aristocratic tea table, and it made her doubly cautious with her own words and her correspondence. "Mary, had you heard that the younger son of Viscount Moreton was back from the West Indies?"

"Major Denton, you mean? Oh yes, my lady. He's taken rooms on Castleton Street, and my cousin is a footman in that part of town." Mary sighed as she plied her brush. "He's ever so handsome, is Major Denton."

"Indeed. I saw him at the assembly."

"Did you, my lady? How lucky! Did you dance with him?"

Eliza laughed. "I'm also too old for dancing, I fear. Is his whole regiment in Dublin?"

"So I've heard, but they're soon to go north, more is the pity." Mary's eyes grew wide in the mirror. "When they leave, will the city be unprotected, my lady?"

"Certainly not. We are quite safe, with or without Major Denton's regiment." She smiled at Mary. "It will be a shame to lose such a handsome face, though. He could brighten this dull town considerably, I think."

Mary giggled. "That he could, my lady."

"But perhaps we will soon be gone ourselves. I've been thinking of going back to Kildare for the winter. And before you ask, Mary, I'm sure traveling will be just as safe as staying in town." There—let Will think she heard his warning and was decamping.

"Yes, my lady," Mary said uncertainly.

Eliza was silent for a moment as Mary finished her hair. "You will tell me if you hear anything else of interest about the handsome major?"

"Of course, my lady." Mary grinned, and Eliza could tell she thought her employer was thinking of taking a lover at last. Well, better that than the truth. "I left a tisane for you on the bedside table. Is there anything else you need, my lady?"

"No, thank you, Mary. That will be all tonight."

Mary curtsied and left the room, and Eliza was alone at last. Alone but for her thoughts, and they were always far too much company.

She studied herself in the mirror. With her hair down over her shoulders, brushed free of their elaborate curls and divested of jewels and combs, she looked so young. Young . . . and frightened?

Never! This was not a time for fear; this was a time for action. All her hard work would soon come to fruition. She could not waver, not when liberty and justice were at last within sight.

It was Will making her feel this way. But she couldn't, *wouldn't,* let him.

Eliza opened her top dressing table drawer, feeling along the edge with her fingertips until she could pop free the false back. There, tucked behind lacy handkerchiefs and silk garters was a small, round badge bound in green ribbon. On it was embroidered an Irish harp and the words I AM NEW STRUNG AND SHALL BE HEARD.

She traced the motto carefully, the image that always gave her courage. Tonight, though, it kept blurring, overlaid with the picture of Will Denton's sky-blue eyes.

There was a rustling behind her, so soft as to be almost inaudible. Yet, Eliza had been on edge for weeks, months, and all her senses went on high alert at the noise. She shoved the badge back into the drawer, sliding it closed. She grasped the handle of a sharp penknife, holding it up as she whirled around.

She gasped aloud in disbelief at the image that greeted her. Will Denton sat on the floor, where he had emerged from under her bed. His red coat was gone, replaced by a rough black wool jacket and a knitted cap over his golden hair.

Eliza was certain she must be dreaming. Her obsessive thoughts had surely conjured him up out of nothing! He couldn't be here in her bedchamber.

But the bite of the knife handle against her palm was all too real. As was the smile he gave her as he swung lightly to his feet. It was a wide, almost piratical grin, just like the ones he used to flash when they carried off some youthful mischief.

But they were not so young now. And mischief could surely be deadly.

"So, Eliza my dear," he said. "You think me handsome?"

Chapter Three

Eliza leaned back against the drawer, staring at Will in half-comprehending shock.

He took a step closer, and she waved the knife about. "How did you get in here?" she demanded, cursing that quiver in her voice. This was no time to let her fear show, to be vulnerable. Once, Will had known her all too well. The glint in his blue-green eyes said he surely could again.

He held out his hands as if in surrender, but Eliza knew better than to be fooled. He had been nearly eight years in the British Army now; surely he had been taught to *never* surrender.

"Nothing easier, I fear, Eliza," he said affably. "You should have more care with your house. Such a fine dwelling is a tempting target for villains."

"So I see. What did you do, then, bribe my servants?"

"I didn't have to go to such trouble. I climbed the ivy vines that cling to those columns outside your portico. You've neglected them too long, and they're prodigiously thick. Any thief could have made off with your jewels and plate by now." He gestured toward her grandmother's diamonds in the open case on her dressing table.

Despite herself, Eliza felt a grudging admiration thinking of Will climbing those vines. Thinking of the powerful shift of his muscles under that rough wool. His years in the hot islands had obviously not weakened him, as they did some men.

"I have had too many things to think of to remember to cut back the vines," she said.

"So I've heard."

"What? Are you a Castle spy now, too, Major Denton? In the pay of Lord Camden?"

"Don't be ridiculous, Eliza."

"Am I being ridiculous? I hear tell that spies and informants are everywhere in Dublin these days. That we should not trust our servants or our own families."

"You can trust me."

"Can I?" She studied him carefully, his elegant, handsome face outlined by the flickering candlelight. He looked hardened, darkened by that island sun, by whatever he had seen there. Or by whatever he had come here to do.

His regiment, the Thirteenth, had a reputation for ruthless adherence to duty and fierce loyalty to the Crown. That was certainly why they were here in Ireland now—to stamp out the fires of dissent by whatever means necessary.

Was the old Will under there somewhere? Was her laughing, lighthearted friend hidden beneath the uniform?

She wanted to drop the knife, to run into his arms and hold him so tightly he could never escape her again. To feel his lips on hers again and meet him as a woman now and not a foolish girl.

But even as tears pricked at her eyes, she knew she

could not. He was her enemy now, and she would not sacrifice her work, the freedom of a whole country, for lust.

"We cannot trust anyone these days," she said, thinking of the brittle, frantic fear that overhung all of Dublin like a smoky pall. "Why have you come here, Will?"

"I don't think I can speak rationally with a knife pointed at me," he answered. "Even if it *is* a penknife."

Eliza glanced down at the blade in her hand, half surprised she still held it. It *was* a puny thing, and he could surely wrest it from her in an instant.

"I merely came to return this," he said, holding out the fan she lost at the assembly. "That is all. See, I'll just put it down right here . . ."

He made a move to place the fan on her desk—the desk where the notes for her newest "seditious" pamphlets were piled. He could not see *those*! Eliza dropped the paper knife as she dove for the fan, snatching it from his hand as she landed hard atop the desk, sitting on those incriminating papers.

"Very well," she said breathlessly, trying to cross her legs as if she hadn't a care in the world. "You have fulfilled your errand."

He gave her a coaxing smile. "Aren't you even going to thank me?"

"Thank you."

She studied him carefully in the firelight, the sudden glow in his eyes, the warming of his smile. He looked more like the old Will now, and she didn't want to think about that at all. Why would he not just go?

"Oh, Eliza," he said softly, as if speaking to a skittish horse. "Can we not sit down and talk, just for a moment? For old times' sake?"

Suddenly weary of acting, of her armor, she pushed back those papers before stalking over to the brocade chairs grouped by the fireplace. The flames flickered weakly against the cold night outside.

She wrapped her dressing gown closer, not looking directly at him but at the orange simmer of the fire. Yet she was achingly aware of him as he sat down across from her, resting his elbows on his knees as he leaned toward her.

"Well?" she said again. "Why are you really here?"

His smile dropped. "I came because you would not listen to me at the assembly rooms," he said, his voice low and solemn. "You were quite right, of course. A crowded party is not the place to speak of such things."

Eliza curled her fingers over the arm of her chair, grasping so tightly the gilded wood bit into her palm, pressing her wedding ring deep into her finger. "What sort of things?" she said dismissively. "Here in Dublin, we don't have the social delicacy of London. I hear people discussing such things as birching their servants, starving out tenants' children when they don't make the rent, nailing up the doors of Catholic chapels—right in the middle of fine banquets."

Will slumped back in his chair, shaking his head in exasperation. His dark gold hair, streaked almost white in places by the tropical sun, gleamed in the firelight. It all made her ache with sadness for what could have been—for what could never be.

"Eliza, you are more stubborn than ever," he said. "But I fear your stubbornness can't save you from what is coming. You play a dangerous game, and people know about it."

She grasped the chair's arm even tighter. "So you *are* a Castle spy."

"I am a spy for no man!" he scoffed.

"Then what 'people' do you speak of? What do you think is coming that I must be protected from?"

"Eliza, please, don't play games. Not with me. You and your friends the Fitzgeralds may enjoy playing at revolution. Maybe you both think your family and position will protect you. But nothing can protect you, or anyone, if Ireland explodes."

"I do not play games, Will." She stood up, unable to sit still any longer, and leaned against the carved fireplace mantel. She stared down into the dying fire, but what she saw was her beloved country in flames, the green fields scorched. Herself, her family and friends, Will—all of them consumed.

She feared it, yes. How could she not? She lived and breathed for Ireland, for what it meant and what it could be. She worked so hard for change and for justice. She had to keep believing, no matter what Will said.

"Then you should secure your house better, Lady Mount Clare," he said, coming to stand beside her. He stood very close to her, the warmth of his body, the clean scent of him, and the memories of his touch reaching out to wrap around her senses like an alluring caress.

She closed her eyes against it, but it just made the longing worse. She had been alone for so long—for always, it seemed. She had missed Will for so long, and now he was here, so close she could reach out and touch him.

But they were different people now, and she had to remember that. Forgetting could be fatal.

"Anyone could climb up that ivy, just as I did," he went on, leaning closer. His sleeve brushed her arm, and she opened her eyes to stare at him. He did not look at her, though; he studied her mantel and the objects clustered there. A Sevres clock flanked by a shepherd and shepherdess, a pastel portrait of her and her sisters, and a pile of books.

He ran his fingertips over the leather bindings. "But they might not be after your jewels, either."

"What would they be after, then?" she whispered.

"Your papers and letters, Lady Mount Clare. Fugitives. Seditious books."

Eliza frowned, thinking of Mr. O'Connor in the cellar. "They will find nothing of the sort."

"Are you quite sure of that?" He plucked a slim volume from the stack of books, turning it over in his hand. "Priestley's *An Essay on the First Principles of Government, and the Nature of Political, Civil, and Religious Liberty.* Interesting reading indeed for a countess. Where did you get it?"

She snatched it away from him. "Perhaps you think I should confine myself to romantic novels, like Anna."

"Not at all. You were never the novel-reading sort, were you, Eliza?" He reached out to trace the line of a dark curl that lay against her neck, twining it around his finger to gently tug her closer. "It was what I always liked about you."

She stared up at him warily, poised to break away. "What was that?"

"Your intelligence. Your independence. That wondrous, fiery spirit. You *believed* in things, really believed in them to the core of your heart. I had never known anyone like that." His fist closed on her curl, holding it fast, holding her trapped against him. "I don't think that has changed, countess or not."

"It hasn't changed," Eliza said, staring up at him. His eyes were so dark in the encroaching night; she could not read them at all. "I do not abandon what I care about."

"And do you still care about me? Just a little?"

God help her, but she did. This handsome, hard-faced stranger, all entangled with her memories of her sweet Will. Here, now, when he did not wear his hated red uniform, she could almost forget what lay just outside their firelit circle.

But maybe, just maybe, the two *could* be separate worlds, just for a moment. They could be Eliza and Will, not Lady Mount Clare and Major Denton.

She reached up and caught his hand in hers. His skin was rough, but it could not disguise the elegance of his long fingers. She kissed them, one after the other, before pressing them to her heartbeat.

His gaze grew hooded and intent as he stared down at her. She just smiled at him.

"I don't really know you, Will," she said. "Not really, not anymore. Too much has happened. And yet . . . yes, there *is* some connection still, I confess. Do you feel it, too?"

Surely he could. Her heart was pounding, a thunder beat in her ears loud enough to drown out all else. To drown out any fears or misgivings, as long as they touched each other.

"Yes," he said hoarsely.

Eliza held her breath as his fingers traced that heartbeat, the swell of her breast through the thin silk dressing gown. The soft fabric rubbed against her nipple, a delicious friction as he circled it with his fingertip.

His other hand grasped her waist, drawing her up against him until there was not even a breath between them. Their bodies were pressed together, hard angles against soft curves, fitting perfectly as if they were made to be just so. She felt the hard, heavy press of his erection against her belly, and it made her dizzy. As if she were falling, falling into him, where she would vanish completely.

His lips covered hers, open, hungry, and Eliza clutched at his shoulders to keep from falling.

His tongue touched hers, and she tasted wine, mint—and that sweetness that was only Will, like the darkest, richest, rarest chocolate. Oh yes, she remembered the taste of him well. But their younger selves had never kissed like *this*. There was nothing tentative, careful, or artful about their kiss. It was frantic, hungry, and passionate, full of the dreams of years, of adult need, of fear and darkness and the force of life itself.

Through the hot, humid blur, Eliza shoved his coat back from his shoulders, letting it fall to the floor as she reached for the fastenings of his shirt. In her haste, she tangled the lacings, breaking them, but at last she could reach between the linen edges and touch him.

His skin was hot, like heated satin over iron-hard muscles, roughened by a crisp sprinkling of hair. She touched the arc of his ribs, the line of his lean waist, greedy for more of him.

She traced the flat disc of his nipple, feeling it pucker under her caress.

"Eliza," he groaned against her mouth. His lips trailed to her cheek, her jaw, the sensitive little hollow just below her ear. His tongue swirled there, his breath hot against her, and she shivered.

"Will," she protested, shaken to the core by the force of her desire. She had never felt like this before, had never been so close to losing all her hard-won control. She half pushed him away, but he would have no mercy on her. His open mouth kissed the curve of her shoulder, and he eased away her dressing gown, the neckline of her thin chemise, until her breasts were bare to him.

"Eliza," he breathed. "So beautiful. I dreamed of this, so many nights in the islands." Lightly, enticingly, he traced the curve of her breast, the soft skin, moving closer and closer to her aching, erect nipple, but never quite touching. Never quite giving her what she wanted.

"You dreamed of *this*?" she said, laughing shakily. "With all the dark beauties there?"

"No one has ever been more beautiful than you, Eliza Blacknall," he said, just before his mouth closed over her nipple at last.

She cried out from the pleasure of it, the hot rush of desire flowing through her. She collapsed to the floor, but he caught her, falling with her as they kissed, again and again. A wild tangle of clothes, arms, lips . . .

A crash sounded from outside the window, a loud, metallic clang followed by a burst of drunken laughter. It was like a sudden blast of cold rain, a storm dousing the flames of passion.

Eliza pulled away from Will, covering her face with her hands. She trembled as if in a winter wind, her mind whirling. She felt like such a great fool. All her hard work, her years of caution! Gone in a moment, because she turned back into an infatuated fifteen-year-old at the sight of Will Denton's handsome face.

But he was *not* her Will anymore, not really. That young man who had once made her feel so alive, so bursting with joy, was gone. This man before her was a veritable stranger. An English stranger, in a red coat.

Eliza's hands slid from her eyes, and she stared at him, still amazed at her wild folly. But then, perhaps it was not so amazing after all. He was a handsome man, with his golden hair and golden skin, with his lean, hard body. And she had been alone for a long time.

He stared back at her, his eyes midnight blue, his lips parted as he caught his breath. His unlaced shirt hung from his shoulders, with his skin gilded in the firelight, like some ancient pagan idol.

Yes, her feelings were natural. It was only lust—desire and memory, all tangled up in the strain of all the endless, tense waiting. But she had to be careful—very careful—from this moment on.

Will leaned back on his elbows, sprawling on her carpet as his hair spilled over his shoulders. An unreadable little smile touched his lips as he watched her. A pagan god, indeed. A heroic legendary warrior, Cuchulainn, returning victorious from his cattle raids and waiting for his reward.

Well, he could wait until Morrigan, the death goddess, came along and snatched him away! Eliza pulled her dressing gown tightly around her and scrambled to her feet.

Will's grin widened as he gazed up at her. "Now, *that* is what I call a grand welcome home, Eliza."

"Oh, do get up!" she cried, her head still spinning. She hurried to the window, parting the curtains to stare at the street below, to see what the crash was. It looked like a confrontation in the middle of the quiet neighborhood, two soldiers and a roughly clad man whose cart had crashed, spilling out a pile of dried-up potatoes.

"Perhaps you should go down and see to your duty," she said. "Help out your comrades in confronting a man with purloined potatoes. As long as no one sees you leaving here, that is . . ."

Eliza heard the rustle of wool as he rose to his feet, straightening his clothes. She felt him move to stand just behind her, close but not touching as he stared down at the street. He still smelled of clean soap, leather, and that faint citrus cologne, but it was blended with salty sweat and her own rose perfume.

And that seemed even more intimate, more frightening, than the overwhelming passion of their kiss.

"Your reputation is safe, Lady Mount Clare," he murmured close to her ear. "No one knows I'm here."

Her reputation? Eliza laughed. What reputation would that be? "I hardly care what those clucking Castle hens have to say," she said.

"I'm sure you do not." Will rested his chin on her shoulder, his breath stirring her rumpled curls. "But what of people like Emmett and Fitzgerald? What would they say if a British officer was seen leaving your bedroom? Would you be drummed out of the United Irish, Lady Democratical?"

Eliza tore herself away from him, from the allure of his touch, and sat down heavily at her dressing table. "So you did break in here to spy on me. To try to find information I do not have."

Will scooped up his black coat, angrily pulling it on. "I am not a fool, Eliza, no matter how forgetful your pretty bosom makes me for a moment. I know you are over your head with these plots. But I have no interest in playing spy, not for Dublin Castle or anyone else."

"Is that so, Major Denton?" she said. She picked up her silver-backed brush only to drop it again. "Then why are you here? Why has your regiment been so hastily summoned back to Ireland, if not to harass innocent citizens like your comrades in Belfast do?"

Will laughed humorlessly. "As if I would tell you. I have no desire to see my words passed around in some United Irish dispatch."

"I am no spy, either!"

"Eliza, I don't care what you are. I only care what you were, what we once were to each other." He let out an exasperated groan, and suddenly Eliza felt his hands grasping her waist, spinning her around on the bench so fast she could not protest or pull away. His arms went around her waist, holding her still.

"You would not listen to me at the assembly rooms," he said. "So I had to come here."

"To warn me," she whispered.

"Yes, to warn you. I don't want to see your neck in the noose when Lord Lieutenant Camden and his generals unleash their forces."

Did he think she had not thought of that? That doubts and fears did not wake her in the middle of the night? She was only human. But . . . "Some things are too important to abandon."

"Exactly." He took her hand in his, raising it to his lips for a lingering kiss. Over their joined hands, his gaze met hers. "That is why I am here."

Eliza opened her mouth, but she could not reply. She didn't know what to say. Will let go of her hand, striding toward the window. She watched, stunned, as he opened the casement and leaped up lightly to the sill as if he were a jungle cat.

"You can't go that way again," she said hoarsely.

He smiled back at her. "Are you offering to escort me out the front door, Lady Democratical? I doubt that's a good idea, even as that little altercation seems to be ended," he said. He gestured toward the now-deserted street, and then he vanished.

She ran to the window, leaning out to stare as he lithely climbed down the tangled vines until he could leap to the roof of her portico and swing to the street. The light had turned pearl gray now, and a cold wind swept down the street like an angry ghost. The cart and the men were gone, a minor skirmish in a bigger war.

Will tugged his cap down over his bright hair and gave her a jaunty salute. "We will meet again soon, my lady, I promise. Try not to miss me too desperately."

Despite herself, Eliza wanted to laugh as he ran off, disappearing into the shadows. Perhaps, deep down inside, there *was* a spark of her old Will. The one who always made her laugh, teased her out of her seriousness. The one who made the dark world brighter. And she feared it was that spark that could be her undoing.

She shut the window, locking it securely and pulling the curtains tightly against the growing light. Then she turned back to her silent room, her gaze alighting on the secret drawer of her dressing table. The one where the United Irish badge hid, its green ribbons glowing.

"I am new-strung," she whispered, "and shall be heard."

That was when she realized the papers on her desk were gone.

Will made his stealthy way through the deserted Dublin streets. It was eerily silent; even the hardiest of merrymakers had gone home, leaving the elegant lanes empty. The sharp whistle of cold winter wind was the only sound. That, and the sound of his own blood in his ears.

He felt tautly alert, as just before a battle, that moment when every sense was heightened, the very air crystalline and sharp around him. The instant when the world grew still—just before it exploded.

It was a battle about to be joined by a formidable foe, indeed—Eliza Blacknall.

Will shook his head, kicking out at a broken bottle with his scuffed boot. He wasn't entirely sure what he had expected when he broke into her bedchamber, climbing up the ivy to slither in the window and hide under her very bed. Such poor security for the house of a rumored United Irish partisan.

Perhaps he thought that once they were alone he could finally make her listen to reason. To his warnings. Make her see the danger and folly of the path she had chosen. But *he* proved to be the fool, for once he was near Eliza, he forgot all but her. His Eliza—the girl who had taught him the ecstasy and pain of love.

Was he now in danger of remembering those old lessons all over again? He feared he was. The old clumsy, youthful, wild passion between them was still there, sharpened and honed by the years and ready to catch fire again.

Yet, he had to face a conflagration of a far different sort now—the fires of rebellion and war. They threatened to consume Ireland, the country he loved, and Eliza with it. Worse, it seemed she fed those flames herself.

If he did not stop her, he would lose her again—forever this time. He would not let that happen. Even if he had to fight her every step of the way.

He had come to the embankment along the Liffey, and he stopped to stare down into the night-black waters. They looked thick and inky, lit only by the reflected gleam of a few faded stars. Boats were moored there, more than usual at that time of year, waiting to carry the frightened populace to safety in England.

If only he could just kidnap Eliza and toss her in the hold of one of those vessels! Send her to safety whether she would have it or not. But he knew that would never work. She would swim all the way back across the Irish Sea if she had to.

Thus, he needed a new strategy. A new battle plan.

He took the paper from his coat pocket, the scrap he had snatched off Eliza's desk while her back was turned. It seemed to be a scribble, but for a mere scribble it was dangerous, indeed—a page labeled for the *Northern Star,* the United Irish newspaper printed secretly somewhere in Belfast and passed around the country.

. . . call for an equal and just distribution of the benefits of our country, this particular article said. *An equal and full representation of all Ireland's people and an end to absentee landlords who care nothing for our traditions and our populace.* It was accompanied by a pencil cartoon of a fat landlord grinding tenants under his boot.

And the article was signed *By A Lady.*

Will crumpled the scrap in his fist, tossing it into the river. There were many ladies in Ireland who thought to aid the United Irish and their allies, the Defenders, by hosting salons where sedition was the conversation of the day. By controlling gossip and rumor and by passing messages. But those words seemed to have one specific lady's stamp. And if he realized that, so would others.

"Oh, Eliza," he muttered. "My dear girl. What must I do to stop you once and for all?"

Chapter Four

Y ou're very quiet today, Eliza," Anna said, spreading marmalade on her breakfast toast.

Eliza gave her a weak smile. How could she tell her sister she had not slept at all last night, because first she hid a fugitive in the cellar, and then she kissed her childhood love until she collapsed with foolish lust? Just remembering it made her feel faintly uneasy as she watched Anna attack her meal with gusto.

"I'm a bit tired, I confess," Eliza said. She reached for the teapot, hoping the Indian brew would soothe her stomach. "Perhaps that is because *someone* kept me at the assembly rooms all hours."

"Oh, pooh!" Anna protested, licking a drop of sticky marmalade from her finger. "We left before the party even started."

"It was after two in the morning!"

"You sound like Mama. What is the use of living in Dublin if one can't fully enjoy its delicious diversions? One might as well be buried at Killinan, a fate you seem determined to consign me to."

Eliza sipped at her tea, remembering how frantic and frightened everyone seemed of late. How uncertainty hung in the air like the sword of Damocles. "You will be safer there."

Anna frowned, her pretty face suddenly solemn. "Is something *really* going to happen here, Eliza? Just like they say?"

"Like who says?"

"Just . . . everyone. Lord Morely was telling me last night that there's a plot to burn the city and all the great houses nearby. That we'll all be murdered in our beds."

"Morely is a great fool, and he must have been a drunk one to tell such tales to impressionable young ladies."

"Impressionable, *stupid* young women who read too many horrid novels, you mean?" Anna said in a strained voice.

"My dear, you are certainly not stupid," Eliza protested. And, indeed, her sister was not. But she *was* sensitive and romantic. "Far from it. It just seems that everyone has forgotten any rules of civility of late, and reactionaries like Morely are the worst."

"He was foxed, to be sure," Anna said. "Everyone was last night, I think. Yet I don't remember you being so mightily concerned with civility, Eliza."

"What do you mean?" Eliza asked stiffly, pouring out more tea.

"Back home at Killinan, before you married Mount Clare, you used to ride hell-for-leather all over the county. Traipsing through mud, drinking ale in tenants' cottages—Mama was in despair over you."

Eliza had to laugh. "Poor Mama! She did try so hard with me, disgrace that I was."

"And you became a countess!"

"I became a countess," Eliza murmured. She stirred idly at her tea, remembering those lovely days of running free, listening to tales of old gods and goddesses and great Irish heroes by crofters' peat fires.

Kissing Will Denton in the woods.

"Well," said Anna, "I don't think we should stay trapped in here, no matter if rebels are waiting to pike us in the streets. The sun is out for once, and we need fresh air. Shall we walk on St. Stephen's Green? Maybe do a bit of shopping?"

Eliza bit her lip. It *did* sound tempting, a breath of air to clear her head after last night. But she had work to do, a pamphlet she had promised to finish writing. She had to start it all over again now, thanks to her carelessness with Will. "I am not sure that is such a good idea, Anna. There is so much to do. . . ."

"Oh, come now!" Anna cried, jumping up from her chair to run around the table and grab Eliza's hand. "Whatever there is to do can wait. The sun will certainly not last, and if I must go back to Killinan, I want to enjoy every moment in town. Besides, I promised Mama I would bring her the newest music from London."

Eliza laughed. "Oh, very well. A morning walk, and work this afternoon."

"And dancing tonight!"

An hour later, Eliza found herself dressed in a woolen walking gown and her warmest fur-lined cloak, strolling with her sister along Grafton Street toward St. Stephen's Green. She had long ago learned that going against Anna was futile, and in truth, she relished the exercise. City life was making her soft; she doubted she could ride hell-for-leather or walk all over the countryside now.

St. Stephen's Green was the favorite site in Dublin for strolling and riding or for just being seen, and the rare winter sunshine had lured everyone out. As Eliza and Anna turned through the gates into the park, they saw they were not alone. The graveled pathways were crowded with chattering, laughing groups and their barking lapdogs.

Yet, even here there was some measure of peace, Eliza thought, linking arms with her sister as they strolled along. The watery pale light gleamed on the elegant buildings lining the square, making the gray stones shimmer. Frost still overlay the grass, but there seemed the promise of warmth in the breeze. The promise of new beginnings.

Eliza smiled, feeling quite absurdly optimistic as she listened to Anna's bright chatter. Until suddenly, in the distance, she heard the unmistakable sound of drumbeats. Everyone near them fell silent, tensely alert as they turned toward that martial echo. Even Anna was quiet, holding tightly to Eliza's arm.

Over the horizon, along the wide, main thoroughfare of the park, came a sight Eliza would vow had come straight up out of Hades. The drummers were followed by standard-bearers, carrying the king's gold lion on red, and the regimental colors of the Thirteenth Regiment of Foot. And behind them was the regiment itself, perfectly aligned ranks of marching red coats with glinting gold lace.

St. Stephen's Green was often the site of military show, but usually it was the slightly clumsy maneuvers of local militia and Volunteers. It was a chance to show off their specially designed uniforms and flirt with the pretty girls, a lighthearted indulgence of the Irish love of show.

But this was different. This was a real British regiment of real soldiers, their gleaming new weapons on obvious display, their faces hard, etched with focus. They would not be easily dismissed or defeated.

Their appearance, on the main parade ground of Dublin, was meant to show the intent of the Crown and its vessel, Dublin Castle. The hammer blow was coming, and the United Irish had to be prepared.

And at the head of those neat red columns, mounted on a jet-black horse equally caparisoned for war, was Major William Denton.

Eliza studied him as he rode by, the lean, sharp lines of his face shadowed by the brim of his helmet. He stared straight ahead, unsmiling, and in that armor of red wool, he was not at all Will.

The grim parade seemed to go on and on, an endless barrier between them and a free Ireland. Even Anna, who could usually be counted on for a comment about handsome officers, was silent as she leaned on Eliza's arm.

"At last," a man growled behind them. "It seemed like the king and Prime Minister Pitt had deserted us to defend ourselves against the rabble!"

"Better late than never, I suppose," another man said. "Though I hear the Thirteenth is to be sent north."

"And leave the streets of Dublin open to murderers!" a woman said shrilly.

"If the north continues to burn, Dublin will certainly be next, my dear," the first man said. "Perhaps when the regiment leaves, we should, too?"

"And go where?" the woman said, panic in her words. "No place is safe at all."

"Are they right, Eliza?" Anna whispered.

Before Eliza could answer, someone at the edge of the growing crowd started singing. "'Oh, croppies, ye'd better be quiet and still. Ye shan't have your liberty, do what ye will. As long as salt water is formed in the deep, a foot on the neck of the croppy we'll keep.'" "Croppies Lie Down"—the worst of the latest round of British songs— was about killing "croppies," men who cut their hair short in sympathy with the United Irishmen.

Eliza felt the gathering, so quiet and solemn when the regiment appeared, now growing restive and angry. What was it Will said at the assembly rooms? That they were all dancing on a powder keg, and it took only one match to set it alight.

And she grew angry at these people who cared only for their own privilege and not for the suffering and injustice of others.

She took Anna's hand and drew her through the crowd. They pushed their way past until they were out of sight of the regiment, who now set up their maneuvers on the frosty grass. Near the gates, she glimpsed the man who sang that hateful song. He was a beardless youth who would doubtless run and hide at the first sign of any real fight.

Even as she considered marching over there to push him to the ground, she knew he was not the real enemy. He had no power. It was that well-trained, relentless regiment they had to beware of.

But Anna had no such restraint. She snatched her hand from Eliza's, hurrying toward the singer with fire in her blue eyes. A crowd had gathered, some to cheer him on, some with angry expressions, and she shoved her way past them.

Eliza dashed after her sister, her heart pounding. This

was not the moment to call attention to themselves! Timing was everything these days, and any trouble could ruin it all. The tiniest misstep could be their last.

"How dare you?" Anna's voice rang out, clear and indignant over the out-of-tune song. "Such vulgarity, and in a public place!"

For an instant, the man's song faltered at the sight of Anna's blond beauty and her fiery anger. Then his face flushed red, and he sang out louder, others joining in.

Anna opened her mouth again, just as Eliza caught the edge of her cloak. Over her sister's head, she glimpsed a familiar face at the edge of the crowd. Mr. Boyle, her go-between to the hidden *Northern Star* printing press.

Oh, that was *all* she needed, she thought. Double the trouble. How could she tell anyone a British officer stole her pamphlet notes from her desk?

"Anna, this is not the time," Eliza whispered quickly. "Just ignore him."

Anna looked at her with startled eyes. "How can I ignore a song about killing Irishmen?"

Mr. Boyle vanished into the crowd, obviously deciding this was not the moment for any messages.

"The moment will come, sister," Eliza said. "But not now. Not over something so trivial."

"Trivial?" Before Anna could say more, there was a new vibration in the air, a new murmuring as the thick crowds parted.

Still holding on to her sister's cloak, Eliza twisted around to see a flash of red from the corner of her eye as Will made his determined way on foot through the crowd. They all parted before him immediately, a hush falling. He strode directly to the man who led the singing and grabbed him by the front of his coat. Eliza saw the flash of an orange badge pinned there, the sign of the Loyalist Orangemen.

"There are ordinances against disturbing the peace here," Will said firmly, giving the man a shake. "I must ask you to depart immediately."

The formerly arrogant man turned pale at the sight of an officer, but he muttered, "I break no laws by singing, surely."

"You incite violence in a public place, which is against the Insurrection Act." Will gave a humorless smile that made even Eliza shiver as he shoved the man toward the gates. "Go sing your drunken ditties in a tavern somewhere, boy. This is not the time or place."

The man backed away. "Perhaps not. But soon enough it will be, yes, Major? Soon you'll make the Liffey run with croppy blood."

Will turned on his heel, not deigning to answer. He didn't even seem to notice the onlookers. His grim stare landed on Eliza, and there was no mercy there.

She felt cold, icy cold, under that pitiless blue-green gaze, and she tugged her cloak closer around her as he marched away.

She rushed toward the gates, pulling her sister with her. The man's song had faded down the street, but the memory of it was too vivid. And Mr. Boyle waited at the gates.

"Lady Mount Clare," he said with a bow, his craggy face hidden by the broad brim of his hat. "Quite the spectacle, is it not?"

Eliza glanced back over her shoulder. No one paid them any heed, but they could not be too careful. Even work as seemingly innocuous as writing and printing pamphlets could lead to arrest and death.

"Anna," she said, trying to keep her tone light, "why don't you go ahead to the bookshop? It is not far, and I will be right behind you."

Anna gave her a doubtful frown, but she did go, quietly for once. *Quiet* was never a good sign with her sister, but Eliza had no time to worry about that now. She had only a moment to hear whatever Boyle's message might be.

"Indeed, it is a spectacle, Mr. Boyle," Eliza said softly.

"One we will see much more of in coming days," Boyle answered. He reached inside his coat, bringing out a small, sealed paper. "Will you be so kind as to deliver this to our friend Fitzgerald?"

"Of course," Eliza said, sliding the note into the fur muff over her arm. "Is that all?"

"For the moment. Your latest work has been a great success."

"I will have more in a few days."

"After the queen's birthday ball?"

"If all goes well." And if she could stay out of Will's way . . .

"Let us hope." He gave her another bow. "Good day, Lady Mount Clare."

As he left, disappearing into the milling crowd, Eliza tried to take a deep breath. She felt a sudden burning on the back of her neck and whirled around to find Will staring at her. His eyes fairly glowed with anger, even across the distance of the park. Had he seen the exchange, then? Did he know the significance of it from her stolen papers?

Her fist closed over the note in her muff, crushing it as she hurried away. She could still feel him watching, though, suspecting her as she turned the corner and headed for the bookshop.

Anna waited for her in the doorway, and at first, Eliza was relieved for the distraction of her presence. But Anna's lips were set in a stubborn line, and it was soon clear she would be yet more trouble.

"When I go back to Killinan," Anna said, "will you not come with me, Eliza?"

Eliza shook her head. "I can't yet leave Dublin."

"But what if it's true?" Anna said stubbornly. It was obvious she had a thought in her head, one that would not be shaken free. "What if there are battles in the streets, houses burned? Blood in the river?"

"That won't happen," Eliza said, hurrying her sister into the shop. The note was like a rock in her hand. "You can stay with me until after the queen's birthday celebration next month. Then I'll join you at Killinan in the spring. In the meantime, I'm sure it will be more peaceful here than with Mama."

Anna ducked into a quiet aisle. "Then why can I not stay with you until the spring?"

"Mama has written that she needs you at home, to help with Caroline."

"I don't know why. Caro is always buried in her dull history books. She thinks I am quite the featherbrain."

The more fool Caro, then, Eliza thought wryly. Anna saw so much behind that façade of golden curls and silken gowns—things others might wish she did not.

"Perhaps that is why they need you," she said. "To drag Caro out of her books and teach her some social graces. I'm sure Mama will want to marry her off soon enough, along with you."

"Shall we catch earls like you, Eliza?"

"I hope not," Eliza muttered.

"Of course not. My heart is set on a duke, at the very least."

"Then you will have to go to London, for dukes are thin on the ground here."

"Or perhaps I will go to St. Petersburg and find a Russian prince. They are quite plentiful there, or so I hear." They had come to a window, and Anna gazed at the carriages rattling by. "Where shall we go this evening?"

"I hardly know. Not St. Petersburg, though," Eliza said. After the spectacle of military might, and seeing Will such a part of it all, she felt all turned around.

"Do you need to deliver that note?"

She glanced sharply at her sister. "Note?"

Anna gave her an innocent smile. "The one the man waiting at the gate gave you. Is it terribly important?"

"He is courting one of the housemaids," Eliza said carelessly. Why, oh why, couldn't she have been born with finer acting skills?

"How romantic!"

"But not urgent. Shall we go by the milliner's shop before we go home?"

"Oh yes! After I collect all the latest Minerva Press novels."

"Perhaps you could buy some gifts for Caro, too," Eliza said. "To soften the blow of dance and deportment lessons."

"Quite right. And an etiquette book for Mama! She always wants to be so sure she is absolutely correct."

As they turned toward the bookshelves, Eliza decided not to mention what was in the rest of their mother's latest letter. One of the tenants at Killinan had been arrested for hiding pikes in his barn, another for allegedly taking the

United Irish oath—both capital offenses. Katherine was worried what else might be behind the ordered little kingdom she had painstakingly built on her estate.

Eliza was sending Anna home thinking it was safer than Dublin. But was Will right? Should she send her family to London? Or was anyplace at all really safe?

Chapter Five

Lady Smythson's ball looked to be what in London would be called a "great crush," Eliza thought as she peered out the carriage window. They crept minutely forward toward the great house, which was near the assembly rooms on Rutland Square, hemmed in by other vehicles and by a flock of richly dressed pedestrians who had lost patience with the waiting.

Eliza rested her chin on her gloved hand, in no hurry to follow them. Dublin society was always in a vast hurry to get to their amusements, to dancing, cards, quarrels, flirtations. No more so than of late, when those amusements were life's best distractions. But Eliza felt strangely distant from it all, as if more than window glass separated her from the glittering desperation.

Even Anna seemed subdued. She had been quiet ever since their excursion on St. Stephen's Green, retreating to her chamber with her new books as soon as they returned to Henrietta Street. Now she sat on the carriage seat next to Eliza, twisting her fan in her fingers.

Eliza caught sight of her own reflection in the window.

Her face was pale in the frame of her fur-lined hood, her eyes wide and shadowed with worry. No wonder Anna was so quiet.

She turned back to her sister with a determined smile. "Tell me, Anna, which of your ardent suitors will you dance with first?"

A faint answering smile touched Anna's lips, but she still twisted her fan around and around. "Whoever asks me, I suppose."

"Even Mr. Andrews, the ever-preaching curate?" Eliza teased. "Or perhaps Lord Simonson, who mashed your slippers to shreds last time?"

"I heard Lord Simonson gave up dancing entirely, much to every young lady's great relief. And this hardly looks like Mr. Andrews's sort of gathering. Too crowded and loud, too fast." Anna paused as the carriage lurched ahead a few feet. "What about you, Eliza?"

"Me? I never danced with Mr. Andrews in my life. I frighten him, I think."

"I mean, will you dance with Will Denton, if he's here?"

Eliza felt a sharp pang in the region of her heart at the mention of his name. "Ah, now, *he* frightens *me*."

"I doubt anyone frightens you, Eliza! You are so very brave. But I see what you mean."

"Do you?"

"Yes. After seeing him today, so severe and stern, so . . ."

"Military?" Eliza murmured.

"He was so different from when we knew him at Killinan."

"He *is* different," **Eliza** said. And she should not forget that.

"Still, he stopped that man from singing that ghastly song."

"Only because he did not want to have to quell a riot there on St. Stephen's Green."

"Perhaps, but it still should be worth something, I think."

"Worth a dance?"

The carriage finally came to a halt at the front doors, Lady Smythson's whole house blazing with light in welcome. Before the footmen helped them alight, Anna suddenly grasped Eliza's hand. "If he does ask you to dance, you should say yes. Now, sister, while you still can."

Before Eliza could say anything, Anna leaped down in a flurry of golden curls and pale blue muslin. Eliza followed slowly, going up the steps and into the crowded foyer, where servants waited to take their winter wraps.

Like most grand Dublin houses, the Smythson structure boasted a severe classical facade of gray stone, unornamented except for a leaded glass fanlight over the door. But inside, all was sweeping grand staircases, polished marble floors, ornate white cakelike plaster work, and shimmering brocade draperies.

"Isn't it strange, Eliza?" Anna said as they joined the long line snaking its bejeweled way up the curving staircase toward the ballroom.

"Isn't what strange?" Eliza answered, thinking all of life was strange, indeed. Especially since Will had come back into it.

"How well our houses reflect our whole little Dublin world." Anna waved her fan around the glittering, soaring space. "Such austerity and decorum outside, such barbaric emotion and showiness inside."

A loud burst of laughter from above rang out, along with a violent shout, as if to prove her words. It was true enough, Eliza thought. They seemed to have all the stuffiness of London, the "elegance and decorum" of their English cousins. But inside . . .

Inside they were Irish, whether they liked it or not. But was Will still Irish inside, too?

The line finally reached the doors of the ballroom, flowing into the vast space like a river of diamonds and satin. Lady Smythson greeted Eliza politely enough, but with caution etched around her eyes thicker than the rice powder she wore. No one would deny a countess an invitation, especially one who was born a Blacknall of Killinan, yet there were always the rumors of Eliza's "unfortunate" friendships and inclinations.

"I think I will just go play a hand or two of whist," Anna said.

"Don't lose too much," Eliza warned.

"I never do! Or at least, not very often." Anna quickly kissed her cheek. "You look very pretty tonight, sister. Remember what I said—dance while you can."

Eliza shook her head as her sister skipped away. She knew she did not look "very pretty" in her somber dark blue satin trimmed with black velvet bows and only one strand of pearls at her throat. Not beside Anna or the other young ladies in their bright gowns and ribbons. And she did not intend to dance at all, not with Will or anyone else. But it was nice of her sister to care.

"Champagne, Lady Mount Clare?" a familiar voice

said, a lean, sun-browned hand holding a glass of bubbling pale-gold liquid before her.

Eliza slowly took the glass, slowly turning to face Will. "Were you lurking here in wait for me, Major Denton?"

He gave her a smile, charming but cautious, much like Lady Smythson's. What did they all expect? She wondered. That she would hike up her skirts and launch into a jig? Jump onto a chair and shout, "Erin go bragh!"?

That might be enjoyable, if only to see Will's reaction.

"Of course I was," he said cheerfully. "I thought you might be thirsty after your arduous voyage across town."

"I am much obliged," she said, taking a long, fortifying sip. Perhaps it would erase the memory of him marching on the green. "Champagne is always a welcome offering."

"I must remember that. Nothing else about me seems terribly 'welcome' to you, my lady."

"Oh, I wouldn't necessarily say that," Eliza murmured. "I saw you today at St. Stephen's Green. Everyone seemed most impressed with your . . . strong military bearing."

"That is what we're meant to do. Show everyone our strength, our determination to keep the peace."

"Is that why you stopped that man singing?"

"We won't stand for anyone starting a riot," he said tightly.

"Even an Orangeman?"

"Anyone. We are all Irish, all in this together; we must act as such. For the good of our country."

Eliza studied him over the edge of her glass. His face was set in most determined lines, his blue eyes dark. "Do you really think that? That we are all Irish?"

He gave her a surprised glance. "Of course. Was I not

born here, the same as you? My family has been here for over a hundred years. What else would I be?"

Her gaze slid over his red coat. "You have been away a long time. Perhaps you have forgotten."

He leaned closer to her, his eyes intense as he watched her. That warm strength of his seemed to reach out and surround her again, luring her ever closer and closer. "A man never forgets the things most important to him, however long he is parted from them."

Eliza swallowed hard, her throat suddenly dry, her heart pounding. She gulped down the last of her champagne, remembering Anna's words. *Do it now—while you can.* But she had other work now, no matter how tempted she was to dance with him, to feel his arms around her again.

"I think I would like a breath of fresh air," she said. "It is very crowded in here."

Indeed, even more people had pushed into the ballroom during the dancing, a great horde seeking punch and lobster patties—and news. The buzz of it was like a flock of frenzied birds, flying around the treetops as the sharp-clawed cats drew near.

"I could use some air myself," Will said. "Let me go with you."

"Are you quite sure you want to be seen in my company?" And Eliza feared she could not trust herself with him.

"A British officer in the company of Lady Democratical, you mean?" He grinned at her teasingly. "Someone needs to keep an eye on you. It might as well be me."

Eliza laughed. "Good fortune with that, Major. I move very quickly."

"Oh yes. I know."

The long, narrow picture gallery, lined with paintings on one side and tall windows on the other, was filled with only a few couples, murmuring quietly together in the shadows. Starlight shimmered through those windows, etched with the cold brightness of winter. It was lovely after the heat and noise of the ballroom, but as Eliza walked along with Will close at her side, she wondered if she was not safer in the crowd after all.

She paused before a landscape, a scene of pastoral idyll with haystacks and pretty shepherds and shepherdesses, and sipped at the last of her champagne. It was warm now, but at least it steadied her nerves.

"You no longer care to dance, then?" Will asked. "I remember when you loved it."

"I fear I am quite out of practice."

"Lord Mount Clare was not fond of a reel, then?"

Eliza laughed. "If it did not involve hunting or shooting, Mount Clare wasn't interested at all. Rest his soul."

"A countryman, was he?"

"To his core. Horses, dogs, and guns were his life."

"He didn't care for books?"

"Not unless it was a treatise on horse breeding. We didn't have a great deal in common, as you see." She smiled up at him. "But we rubbed along well enough. Especially when I was in Dublin and he was in the country."

He smiled at her, too, yet it seemed somehow . . . sad. "I've thought of you so often over these years, Eliza. Wondered what you were doing, what your life was like."

"Dull, indeed, compared to yours, I am sure."

"I doubt it. Nothing is duller than the life of a regiment on a faraway island."

"Oh yes. Warm sunshine, stretches of sandy shore,

fresh, sweet fruit all year round—it sounds dreadful. I, on the other hand, trudged my way along through long Irish winters, with only my books to keep me warm."

Will laughed. "If you only knew how I dreamed of cold winters sometimes! Dreamed of . . ."

"Of what?" Eliza asked softly, finding she longed to know his dreams.

"Of home, of course."

"Of course." But whose home? Whose version of Ireland? She drifted toward the window, staring out at the street below, dotted with lights from the house, then at the night sky, stretching on and on, forever it seemed. The moon hung suspended in that purple-black sky, like a perfect luminescent pearl.

"I can see why you would think of home," she said. "Surely there can be no other moon like that in all the world."

"Indeed, there cannot," he said, standing close behind her as they watched the night.

"When I was a child, one of my nursemaids told me tales of such a moon," she said. "Such a moon is a *sidhe,* or faerie moon, and all the woodland faeries come out to dance under its lights."

"It sounds a grand party."

"Yes. After that, I read every Irish tale I could find, stories of the faerie folk, gods, heroes. I was sure that a land that birthed such glorious beings must be the finest on Earth. The one most worth defending and fighting for."

"And nothing has ever changed your mind."

"No." She turned to face him, studying his features, etched in the chalky moonlight. How beautiful he was, just like those heroes of her tales. At times, she felt closer to him than to anyone else in the world. From the time they were young, it seemed they were two halves of the same ancient coin.

"I love Ireland," she went on. "It is a part of me, and I belong to it. You say you love it, too."

"Of course I do. I have dedicated my life to protecting it."

Eliza shook her head sadly. Did he truly not see? He gave himself to the forces that would erase Ireland, her true self, forever. Forces that would always subject it to the iron weight of a foreign will and keep her people crushed beneath it.

"I fear we shall be forever at odds," she said.

He caught her hand in his, bringing it to his lips for a kiss. His mouth was warm through the thin kid. Eliza swayed toward him, mesmerized by that heat, by the sensual curve of his lips. She caught herself just in time, trying to disentangle her fingers from his.

"We shouldn't do this here," she whispered. "Someone will see."

His hand tightened. "And tell your United Irish friends you were in an intimate tête-à-tête with an officer?"

She pulled away. "And tell Lord Lieutenant Camden you were seen with me."

"Point taken, Lady Mount Clare. Shall I test the ivy outside your window again tonight?"

"I knew I should have told the servants to cut those vines away."

"But you did not. Because you know how useful it is."

"You are just as impossible as ever, William Denton."

"Yes, I know. But don't you like it?" He grinned at her, unrepentant.

She did like it—far too much. "I am taking Anna to the theater tomorrow night. Mrs. Crosby is performing in *Romeo and Juliet*. Perhaps we shall see you there?"

"Yes, you will see me there. General Hardwick and his wife have invited me to sit in their box, as a matter of fact. Now, should we go back to the ballroom? Perhaps we could even attempt a dance."

"But I fear I have given up on dancing. We should go back, though, before Anna has time to lose her allowance again."

"She seems a high-spirited girl."

Eliza laughed as they walked back down the length of the deserted gallery. "To say the least! My mother thought she was bored in the country and that a time in town would do her some good. I am not sure that has been the case."

"She takes after her sister, then, I think. Full of energy and life."

Eliza glanced at him, surprised. Full of life? Nay, of late she had felt weighed down by seriousness. Until she saw him again.

But there was no time to say anything else. They had returned to the ballroom doors, to all the overly bright sparkle of crystal chandeliers and frantic laughter. Will bowed to her and disappeared back into the crowd.

Eliza rubbed at her bare upper arms, shivering despite the overly warm room.

"Eliza, dear? Are you unwell?" she heard Anna say, and turned to find that she didn't have to seek out her sister after all. Anna's trail of admirers hovered in the background, but she paid them no mind.

Their mother had sent Anna to Dublin not just because she was bored at Killinan, of course, but also in hopes she would find a suitable husband. Perhaps not the duke or prince Anna teased about, but someone who could control her and her "high spirits" and not let her independence fly out of control, as Eliza's had. It seemed that plan would meet with no success, for she cared for none of her respectable suitors.

"I am just a bit tired," Eliza said. "I think it is time we departed."

For once, her sister made no protest at leaving so early. "Of course," she said, going along quietly as they reclaimed their wraps and sent for the carriage.

As they jostled through the empty streets, Eliza gazed out the window, wrapped up in thoughts of Will, just as when they had arrived. She could feel their old bond tightening again. Something in their hearts still called out to each other, a soft, irresistible whisper.

But it was too late. They had chosen their paths, and they were separate ones, indeed.

"It was good to see you smile again tonight, Eliza," Anna said.

Eliza took her sister's hand. "Have I been so dour of late?"

"Perhaps just a bit. But it is hardly a wonder. Everyone behaves so oddly these days. Yet, Will Denton made you smile."

Was it so obvious, then, that irresistible seed of old happiness she felt when she was with him? She would have to be much more careful in the future.

"It is pleasant to see him again after so long," she admitted.

"Yes. I am sure that is all there is to it."

Was that *sarcasm* in Anna's voice? Eliza studied her sister's angelic face in the moonlight, but Anna just smiled.

The carriage halted at their own front door, light shining faintly from the fanlight. The house seemed quiet, almost deserted. Mr. O'Connor had gone, slipping away from the cellar before dawn to head for France to avoid arrest and plead for French allies. One task accomplished. Yet, another always awaited.

"You go ahead, Anna," Eliza said. "I have a quick errand."

"At this time of night?" her sister cried.

"I shan't be gone long," Eliza answered soothingly.

"But the patrols!"

"They won't bother me, not while I'm in my own carriage."

She could see that her sister wanted to argue, maybe insist on coming along. Finally, Anna nodded and let the footman help her from the carriage. "Be careful, Eliza."

"Of course I will," Eliza said, blowing her a kiss. Once the front door was safely shut and the house quiet again, she told the coachman, "One twenty Green Street, please, John."

Green Street was the site of a respectable-looking coffeehouse. Eliza left the servants with the carriage a few doors down, drawing her cloak's hood close around her face as she hurried past the sparsely filled tables, through the warm coffee- and spice-scented air. The proprietor behind the counter paid her no mind.

She went through a door at the back and up a narrow, creaking flight of stairs. At the top was a landing with one door made of stout wooden planks with sturdy new iron fittings. It smelled of coffee even there—coffee, lilac perfume, and fear.

She knocked twice in quick succession, then twice

slowly. She held her breath as she listened carefully to any sign of movement behind that door.

At last there was a thump, a squeal as the lock was peeled back. The door was opened a crack, and a woman's pale face, framed with a cloud of dark hair, peeked out cautiously.

"Eliza!" she cried, her voice heavy with a French accent. "You are here."

She opened the door wider, letting Eliza slip inside before shutting and locking it again. The chamber was small, windowless, and cold, lit only with a branch of candles on the one table, which also held wine bottles and the remains of supper. An open traveling case spilled clothes and papers onto the floor, and on the bed slept a little girl under a pile of quilts.

"Of course I am here," Eliza said, embracing the woman, who was heavily pregnant under her black muslin gown, her pretty oval face shadowed with exhaustion. Pamela Fitzgerald looked like she would give birth any day—without her husband nearby and no family. Her husband, Lord Edward Fitzgerald, son of the Duke and Duchess of Leinster and leader of the United Irishmen of Dublin, had been on the run from the British for months. Eliza had helped him find hiding places, and she had promised she would help Pamela if she could. She always kept her promises.

Pamela sat down carefully on the edge of the bed, tucking the quilts closer around her daughter. "How has it been for you, *petite amie*?" she said. "Have you been much harassed?"

Eliza smiled at the sparrowlike Pamela calling *her* "petite." "I have not been harassed at all, so far. No one dares accuse a countess of sedition, not without solid proof. And I am careful."

"I'm glad for that at least."

"But you, Pamela—I was surprised to hear you were here in Dublin. You should have stayed at your home at Kilrush or gone to Edward's family. They are powerful; they can protect you."

Pamela shook her head. "Edward's *maman, la duchesse,* is in London. She has my little Eddy with her. She and her Mr. Ogilvie are trying to get Edward out of the country, I think, though he will never go."

"You could go to Castletown, then. No one would dare bother you there."

A wry smile touched Pamela's pale lips. "Lady Louisa would not want me there. She might be Edward's *tante,* but she and Mr. Conolly are Ascendancy through and through. *Vraiment?*"

Eliza had to admit that was true, indeed. "It's not safe here. And this stuffy little room cannot be healthy for you."

Pamela shrugged. "I am strong, Eliza, don't worry, and so are my *bébés.* We are here just for a few days, to see my husband. Then we will go back to Kilrush. It is safe for us there, even if it is not for Edward."

Eliza reached into her reticule and drew out the object of her visit—Mr. Boyle's note, pressed into her hand as they watched the regiment on St. Stephen's Green. "You will give him this when you see him? He must receive it as soon as possible so he will know where to go next, and I do not know when I will see him again."

"*Certainment.* He will be happy to hear you are well and that your own work progresses."

"And you? Do you need anything? Food or milk for little Pam?"

Pamela looked down at her sleeping daughter. "*Non,* nothing. Lady Lucy sends things. She looks after her brother's family well."

Eliza stayed a while longer, telling Pamela what meager news she had. Then she reluctantly left the little family to their sparse lodgings, with Pamela's assurances they would move elsewhere the very next night.

As Eliza climbed into her carriage, she thought she glimpsed a shifting shadow across the street. She peered closer, her shoulders stiffening, but she saw only a bit of windblown debris and the cast of the moon in a shop window.

Feeling foolish, she laughed at herself and turned toward home.

Will stared after Eliza's departing carriage, pressed tight to the stone wall deep in the shadows. Only after he was sure she was gone, the coach rattling back toward Henrietta Street, did he turn his attention to the building she emerged from.

A coffeehouse, one of several in this respectable neighborhood. Small, quiet, half full of genteel-looking patrons, but distinctly mercantile class. What was a countess doing there, slipping inside in the middle of the night with her cloak hood drawn up?

He would wager it was not just for their blend of coffee.

As soon as Eliza's coach was gone, a shadow detached

itself from a wall across the way and followed at a fast pace. The man was not tall, but he was quick and muffled in a black coat and wide-brimmed hat. At the corner, he glanced back and held up his hand as if to signal someone else.

So Will was not alone in watching Eliza at the coffee-house. He wasn't the only one tracing her movements, keeping track of where she went and who she talked to. But who sent this man? What did they hope to gain?

Will, in turn, followed the follower, keeping the man in his sights as they made their way through the quiet streets. He would not let anyone hurt Eliza.

Will trailed him at a discreet distance, but the man did not go to Eliza's house on Henrietta Street. He went toward the Castle, dark and ominous in the night. Before he could reach the locked gates, he stumbled on the paving stones.

"Blast it all," he muttered in a rough accent, the words unnaturally loud in the dark silence. A twist of paper and a few coins fell from his pocket. For a flashing instant, Will wanted to grab the man, to hit him viciously until he confessed his mission, confessed who sent him to watch Eliza. To beat him bloody for daring to threaten her in any way. But cold reason held him back. He could not help her at all if he was in prison for attacking a Castle lackey.

And he would learn nothing behind bars, either.

A guard let the man in through the gates, so obviously he was expected. Once all was quiet again, Will scooped up the twist of paper left behind when the man collected his dropped coins. It was probably nothing, but who knew what could be useful.

Will unrolled the scrap, his blood freezing as he saw

what it was—another seditious pamphlet from By A Lady. The Castle knew about her writing, then.

Stuffing the paper into his own pocket, he turned back toward the coffeehouse, intent on discovering what led Eliza there in the first place. What sort of secret meeting had she attended there? What was she up to now? And who exactly at the Castle ordered her followed?

He was determined to find out—and to stop her from destroying herself.

Chapter Six

"But, soft! What light through yonder window breaks? It is the east, and Juliet is the sun. Arise, fair sun, and kill the envious moon . . .'"

Eliza peered down at the stage through her opera glasses, watching Romeo gaze up at Juliet on her balcony. She leaned her elbow on the gilded balustrade of the box, wrapped up in that little dreamworld.

It hardly mattered that the painted backdrop behind the balcony depicted the solid bulk of the Dublin Parliament building, pale gray against a blue sky, where there was no evidence of a moon, envious or otherwise. The carved allegorical figures of Theater and Music to either side of the stage looked on stolidly, unmoved by this or any other spectacle they beheld here at the Crow Street Theater.

But the audience was not so hard-hearted. Usually Dublin theatergoers were loud and rowdy, conversing between themselves, shouting at the actors, even causing riots, as Edward Fitzgerald had several months ago when one of those actors shouted too enthusiastically, "Damn France!" and he took it as an insult to his French wife. The new decorum of London theaters had not yet found its way across the Irish Sea. Tonight, though, everyone, from the glittering gold and blue boxes down to the rough benches of the pit, was transfixed by the romance unfolding onstage.

As was Eliza. It had certainly been a long time since she was a teenaged girl, giddy with first love for Will Denton. And the actors, too, looked as if it had been some time since they saw fifteen. But none of that mattered. Their acting skills and the eternal power of Shakespeare's beautiful words made her remember it all. The soaring highs of love; the dark despair when it was over.

Except she feared it was *not* over. Not yet.

She raised her glass from the stage to a box just across the U shape of the theater. Will sat there with General Hardwick and Mrs. Hardwick, along with their pretty daughter Lydia. His gaze was focused on the stage. He looked handsome as always in his red and gold coat, his bright hair tied back in a queue that shimmered in the house lights. But a frown etched his brow as if he, too, remembered those sunlit days of their infatuated youth.

" 'I take thee at thy word,' " Romeo declared, climbing up the ivy-covered stones of Juliet's tower. " 'Call me but love and I'll be new baptized . . .' "

" 'What man art thou, that thus bescreened in night so stumblest on my counsel?' " Juliet protested, modestly gathering close the neck of her gauzy night rail.

Eliza reluctantly smiled, remembering Will climbing the ivy up her own wall. Perhaps they were not past such youthful follies after all.

" 'By a name I know not how to tell thee who I am,' " said Romeo. " 'My name, dear saint, is hateful to myself because it is an enemy to thee.' "

An enemy to thee. Eliza lowered her glass. Romeo and Juliet's deep-seated enmity, through no fault of their own but part of their essential natures, led to their doom. What would happen here and now?

Next to her, Anna sat perched on the edge of her seat, her eyes wide and shining with tears as she watched the lovers embrace. Anna was young and so romantic, so fragile. Eliza feared so much for her, as she did for all who felt so deeply.

She raised her glass again, glancing back across the theater to find Will watching her. That frown was gone, but his face was smoothly expressionless. Utterly unreadable.

Eliza feared she would cry. She felt the ache of tears behind her eyes, a new, sharp sadness for what could not be. She *did* have feelings for Will; she had to admit that to herself. The old feelings had never quite gone away, even over the years of his absence, and now that he was back, they, too, returned. Deeper, fuller—a woman's desire.

But she could not be turned from her course. Irish independence was just and true, far bigger than herself and her desires. And she was sure Will would not be turned from *his* course, either. One of them would be defeated in the end.

Yet, for this moment, it was the calm before the storm. Just like Romeo and Juliet's moonlit balcony.

The blue velvet curtain dropped over the lovers' futile plans, signaling the interval. The audience stirred back to life, stretching and laughing as the girls selling oranges and sugared almonds took to the aisles.

Anna dabbed at her eyes with her lace handkerchief. "It's so beautiful, Eliza. I'm glad we came here tonight."

Eliza laughed, despite the tight lump in her own throat,

and squeezed her sister's hand. "I am wondering if a comic opera might not have been better for you, my dear."

"Oh no! What can be *better* than love, love against all odds? It is glorious."

Glorious until the wrenching end. "Mama would say a sensible marriage, based on parents' good advice, would be far better."

Anna shook her head. "Did your sensible marriage make you happy, Eliza?"

"Mama would say happiness is irrelevant. Duty is all," Eliza said carefully.

"So she would. But would *you*?"

"My marriage was no Romeo and Juliet tale, to be sure. But it was not so very bad." It gave her the independence to pursue her own work, to find out who she really was. That was more than most women had.

"I don't want 'not so very bad,'" Anna said stubbornly. "I want passion and joy! I want someone who makes my soul sing. Mount Clare didn't make your soul sing, did he?"

Eliza laughed. "Not at all. I am not sure that would be such a pleasant sensation."

"Oh, sister, always so sensible. Haven't you ever met anyone who made you feel like Romeo and Juliet, just a bit?"

Oh yes. She certainly had. And he sat right across the theater, making her feel those things all over again.

Or he *had* been there. When Eliza peeked over at the Hardwicks' box, she saw that Will was gone.

"Mama would say such things are unimportant, and even dangerous," Eliza murmured. "They disrupt the natural order of things."

Anna sighed. "I know what Mama would say. She lectures endlessly at Killinan. But what do *you* say, Eliza?"

"I say . . . I am thirsty, and I need to stretch my legs. I shall go and find someone to procure us some negus."

"By yourself?" Anna said. "Now, Mama would say that is most unwise."

Eliza laughed. "I will be gone for only a moment. Surely you can behave yourself without me for that long, sister dear."

"Perhaps," Anna said teasingly. "But can *you* behave yourself without *me*?"

Eliza left the box, still laughing, her gray silk skirts rustling. The corridor outside was crowded with others seeking refreshment and gossip. Eliza eased around them, headed toward the staircase to seek out a footman to send for the drinks.

She found Will instead.

He was just coming up the stairs, a look of intent concentration on his face, as if he thought of something far away. They nearly collided on the dimly lit landing, and his hand shot out to clasp her arm, steadying her.

"In a hurry for an appointment, Lady Mount Clare?" he said. A half-smile curved his lips, but his gaze studied her intently.

"Yes, indeed," she answered. "An appointment with a glass of negus. I am perishing of thirst."

"How appalling. We certainly cannot have that. Come, let me be of assistance."

He held out his arm to her. Eliza glanced over her shoulder, but no one seemed to be paying them any attention. "Are you sure you should, Major Denton?"

"Fetching refreshments in a theater is shocking, I know,

Lady Mount Clare. But I think my reputation can bear the strain."

"But can *mine*?" She slid her hand through the crook of his elbow, just as she had at the ball, letting him lead her downward. The blue-carpeted stairs were narrow, lined with framed sketches from past plays. As the stairs turned on a landing, she and Will were momentarily alone, caught in a second of silence.

"I need to see you, Eliza," he whispered in her ear.

She stared at him in surprise. "You *are* seeing me."

"Alone. Please, I need to speak to you alone."

An enemy to thee. Eliza wanted to refuse, for she was not sure what would happen when they were alone. What emotions would flare up, burning away caution and sense and . . . everything. Yet he looked so very serious, she feared he would just climb up the ivy and hide under her bed again if she refused.

"Very well," she said. "Tonight, after my household has gone to bed."

He arched his brow questioningly. "Shall I climb to the window again?"

"I think the play has too much influenced you, Romeo. I shall let you in by the kitchen door." That should be safe enough, because her cellar was empty now.

He quickly kissed her hand as they neared the foot of the stairs. "'Tis twenty years till then.'"

Eliza tiptoed down the back stairs of her house, the si-lence of deepest night crowding around her. Everyone was asleep, even Anna, and the cavernous kitchens seemed to echo like a cave.

Was she being foolish, agreeing to meet Will like this? She very much feared she was. His eyes, so blue, so quiet, calm, and watchful—angel's eyes—sought out all her secrets. But she wanted to talk to him and had to know what he would say to her.

She remembered his words about how he, too, was Irish, his family planted here for decades, as was hers. Why could he not, then, see things as she did? There had to be a way.

She gathered the high swansdown collar of her dressing gown closer about her neck, shivering as the cold of the flagstone floor seeped up through her slippers. The fires were banked for the night, but she still smelled the residue of smoke, of cooking meat and boiled vegetables. It made her think of the kitchens at Killinan, of how she would dash through their bustling activity to snatch a picnic lunch of bread and cheese on her way to meet Will in the woods.

Not much had really changed, and yet everything had.

Eliza leaned against the locked door, listening for any sound outside. Her heart pounded so loud in her ears that she could scarcely hear, but then at last it came. A knock.

She went up on tiptoe, peering through the tiny barred window. It *was* Will, dressed again in his rough black clothes, his cap pulled low over his brow. She unlocked the door, drawing it open just enough for him to slip inside.

Without a word, he caught her in his arms, his mouth coming down on hers in a desperate kiss. He touched her tongue with his, tasting, seeking, and it was as if she were struck by a sizzling, blue-white bolt of lightning. Enveloped by fiery heat that burned away everything else.

She curled her fists into the coarse cloth of his coat, dragging him closer, closer. Yet still it was not enough. The desperate tension of life in Dublin combined with her desire for Will, creating an explosion of sheer need, of the necessity to feel alive again, as if for the last time.

But from along one of the snaking corridors, she heard a sound, a rustle, reminding her of where they were. She tore her mouth from his, leaning away from the heat of his body.

"Come with me," she whispered.

Wordlessly, he took her hand, letting her lead him up the stairs and into her bedchamber. A smoldering fire crackled in the grate, providing the only light. The bed, with its turned-back blankets, was in blessed, forgetful shadows.

Will closed the door, leaning back against it as he studied her from under the concealing brim of his cap.

Eliza studied him, too, unsure of what to do next. She still trembled with the force of their kiss. But was he still Will, her Will, or was he Major Denton?

He swept off that cap, dropping it to the floor as he shook his long hair free. He smiled at her and held out his hand, and she knew—he was Will, if only for tonight.

She took his hand, letting him draw her closer until he took her in his arms again. He kissed her hair, her brow, the pulse that beat at her temples. Eliza closed her eyes, losing herself in the sensation of his lips against her skin.

"I missed you, Eliza," he muttered.

"I missed you, too," she answered, and knew the terrible truth of it. She *had* missed him over all these years, even as she tried to deny it, tried to lose herself in the routines of her own life. Whenever she was at Killinan and they called on Will's mother at Moreton Manor, she tried to stay indifferent to Lady Moreton's news of him in the West Indies. But those tidbits had been like precious pearls, hoarded by her against lonely days. Laid away with her memories of him.

And now here he was, in her arms.

She buried her fingers in the rough silk of his hair, pulling his lips down to hers for another kiss. She closed her eyes tightly, savoring each taste and texture, the slant of his lips over hers, the soft moan deep in his throat that made her melt. He tasted of mint and wine, of Will.

She parted her lips, twining her tongue with his, and it was as if that lightning blast enveloped him as well. He groaned again, his hands seizing her waist to swing her back against the door, lifting her high.

She was braced between the polished wood and his lean, muscled body, surrounded by the scent and heat of him—by the humid blur of sexual need that dragged her down into a boiling whirlpool. She held him closer as their kiss slid into desperation, into frantic need.

The skirts of her dressing gown and chemise fell back as she wrapped her bare legs around his hips, the coarse wool chafing the soft skin of her thighs. She felt his erect penis, hot and as hard as iron through his trousers, as he rocked into the curve of her body.

His hand slid from her waist to her bare leg, sliding up and up, slowly, his callous palm a delicious friction on her skin as he pushed the fabric out of his way until she was completely bare to him. Spread wide, vulnerable, open to any desire he possessed.

Eliza's head fell back against the door, her eyes drifting

closed as his lips trailed from hers and along the column of her throat. In that whirling darkness, she couldn't think at all. Only feel. Need.

His tongue delicately touched the hollow at the base of her throat, tracing the arc of her collarbone, nudging her chemise away until it fell from her shoulder. He kissed that naked skin, the soft slope of her breast where her heart pounded. His hand slid to the top of her thigh, drawing her up even higher against him.

His thumb pressed to the wet seam of her womanhood, sliding just barely inside. Eliza moaned at the flood of raw sensation, the rough friction of his touch on that delicate skin.

"Do you want me?" he gasped against her breast. "Do you want me, Eliza?"

Want him? She had never felt anything like this terrible, desperate, primitive need, that ache of urgent desire deep inside her, at her very core. Surely the world would shatter into sizzling little shards if she could not have him.

He nipped at the soft skin just above her aching nipple, soothing the little sting with the tip of his tongue. "Do you want me?" he said again.

"Yes," she whispered. "I always have."

His mouth came back to hers in a frantic kiss, and he swung her away from the door, her legs still wrapped around his hips. They fell onto her bed, sinking deep into the feather mattress.

Will rose above her, tearing off his coat, pulling his shirt over his head and tossing the clothes away. His muscled chest, taut, bronzed skin rippling over his ribs, was lightly dusted with pale blond hair, which turned him to molten gold in the dying firelight.

Eliza discarded her own garments, the dressing gown and chemise landing atop his shirt. She never took her eyes from him as she lay back, naked, parting her legs in silent invitation.

"Do you want *me*, Will?" she whispered.

In answer, he kissed her again and again, his body falling into the arch of hers as she wrapped her legs around him, holding him as her prisoner. The strength and weight of him on her, around her, was delicious, wondrous. Her rare fumblings with her husband, even her dreams of Will over the years, could not compare with this burning, desperate forgetfulness.

She reached between them, unfastening his breeches and peeling them away until she could feel him. She traced her fingertips along the veined length of his penis, the iron under hot velvet of his erection. It leaped under her touch, and he moaned against her mouth.

He did want her! Eliza longed to shout out with exultation, with triumph. But then she moaned, too, as he parted her legs wider and sank deep inside of her, to her very core. And they were joined together at long last.

She clutched at his sweat-damp shoulders, closing her eyes as she felt the slide and press of him against her. There, in that darkness again, she could hear his breath, the pounding of his heartbeat that echoed her own. He went still, and she dug in her nails, holding him to her.

"Eliza," he gasped, sliding out of her and then plunging back again, deeper and faster. He caught her mouth with his, mingling their gasps, their incoherent words.

She slid her palms down the groove of his spine, feeling the powerful shift of his muscles under her touch. A glorious sensation expanded inside of her like a sunrise, all hot color and burning emotion. It danced up from her very toes, over her whole body until it exploded into a hundred brilliant fireworks.

"Eliza!" Will cried, his body rigid above hers, his back as taut as a bow. Then he collapsed beside her, their arms and legs entwined.

She slowly, slowly caught her breath, the world still twirling around her. She turned her head to kiss Will's brow, his closed eyes. She stroked his damp hair, whispering soft, wordless murmurings as his own breath grew even and slow.

She edged up onto the pillows as he rested his head on her abdomen, his arms around her waist. They said nothing—what could there be to say? What words could solve their terrible dilemma now?

They were as close as two people could be, their bodies twined together in the lassitude of sex. Yet the Irish Sea might just as well lie between them.

I have this moment, she thought, spreading the length of his golden hair over her stomach, listening as his breath slipped into sleep. The moment would have to be enough.

Chapter Seven

Will sat straight up in the bed, jolted from sleep by some half-remembered dream. Some twisted nightmare of battles, blood, and cold drowning waves. *Blood flowing on the Liffey.*

He rubbed his hand hard over his face, trying to erase the hazy, horrifying images. It was still night outside the window, and the fire in the grate was burned down to embers, leaving the chamber cold.

He looked down at Eliza, still sleeping amid the rumpled bedclothes. Her dark hair was tangled around her face, her bruised pink lips parted on a breath. How young she looked asleep, he thought sadly, young and carefree, like the girl he remembered from Kildare. The girl who would ride and run and kiss with abandon, with no fear. Who would tell him tales of ancient Irish kings and gods, her brown eyes shining with the wonder of it.

Perhaps, deep down inside, they *were* still that Eliza and Will, and they had found each other again all too briefly tonight. But when morning came, Lady Mount Clare and Major Denton would still be waiting. And he still did not know how to stop her headlong tumble into the dangers of rebellion.

Eliza murmured in her sleep, turning restlessly as if seeking warmth in the cold winter night. Will lay back down beside her, gathering her gently in his arms. She settled against his shoulder with a soft sigh.

He pressed a kiss to her rumpled hair, inhaling deeply of her scent of roses and salt, of clean linen sheets. Her tall body curled into him, as if she felt safe with him.

"I *will* keep you safe, Eliza," he whispered, thinking of her follower at the coffeehouse. "Whether you like it or not."

She stirred at the sound of his words, her eyes slowly blinking open, as if she, too, surfaced from deep dreams. For a moment, she gazed at him with puzzlement, as if she could not quite recall who he was or why he was there. Then she remembered, and a wide smile broke across her face.

"You're really here," she cried, sitting up beside him as the sheet fell away from her bare breasts. She kissed his cheek, his nose, his mouth. "It was not a dream!"

"I hope not," Will answered, laughing as she rolled atop him, her legs straddling his hips. He felt himself stirring to life again at the warmth of her body, his penis hardening. He arched up against her. "Does this feel like a dream?"

"Not at all." She leaned down, her lips finding his for a lingering, exploring kiss. It wasn't desperate, lustful, like their kisses of the night, but full of wonder and welcome. He caressed her shoulders, feeling the fall of her hair over his hands, curling around him to hold him her willing prisoner.

"It is just . . . sometimes I did dream of this, while you

were gone," she said. She sat up, staring down at him as she traced his features with her fingertips, as if to memorize him. He caught her finger between his lips, suckling at it until she gasped.

"I dreamed of you, too," he answered, cradling her hand against his cheek. "It was a lonely life in the islands, and at night I would lie awake and stare up at the stars in that hot sky. I would think of you, imagine kissing you by a cold Irish stream. I wondered so often what you did, how you fared."

She smiled teasingly, sliding her palm along his rough, whiskered cheek, down his neck, tracing a light pattern over his chest. "Were dreams of me all the romance you had, Will? I would vow not."

He laughed hoarsely, remembering the bored English wives, the French plantation owner's widow, and the pretty milliner. None of them had been able to turn him from his memories, no matter how hard he—or they—tried.

"There has never been anyone like you, Eliza," he answered truthfully. There never could be anyone like her, with her wild Irish spirit.

She leaned down to press light, alluring kisses over his skin, her tongue tracing the flat, brown disc of his nipple. "And was it worth the wait?" she whispered.

"Assuredly so," he muttered tightly.

"Good. I would hate to think you were disappointed." Her mouth slowly trailed lower, over his chest and the sharp arc of his hip, until she reached out to caress his now achingly hard erection. Delicately, teasingly, her fingertips slid down and up again.

"Eliza . . ." He groaned, threading his fingers through her hair.

"Shhh," she whispered. "I want to try something. . . ."

And then—oh, by the saints!—her mouth closed over him, her tongue tasting him.

His hips jerked at the hot waves of pleasure, his hands instinctively pressing her closer. It was unlike anything he had ever known, a rush of primitive sensation blended with an almost unbearable intimacy.

And that intimacy, that bond of trust that made them engage in such an act, was too much. He gently tugged at her hair, drawing her up to him again.

She stared down at him, her glistening lips parted, her eyes as dark as the night outside. He clasped her hips, spinning her down to the mattress as he drove inside of her.

They watched each other as they moved together, finding each other's rhythm, learning what brought pleasure. Will felt he would drown in her eyes, fall into that darkness and be lost forever.

Their fingers entwined, pressed flat to the bed as their movements grew faster and faster, their breath ragged. Eliza cried out, her body writhing beneath him, her legs tight around him, holding him to her, in her.

And he, too, cried out in his release, the blood roaring in his head. He knew only her, her scent, her body, and the desperate pleasure of their joining.

He fell to the pillows beside her, his head on her shoulder. He pressed his face to the curve of her neck, inhaling the essence of her. Her breath whispered over him as she wrapped her arms around him tightly.

How very *alive* she was, his Eliza. Alive and vibrant, as wild as the Irish land she loved so much. But he so much feared that in the stormy days to come, one—or both—of them was doomed.

As if she read his dark thoughts, her arms tightened even more, pulling him into her as she kissed his cheek softly. At the window, the black light had softened at the edges, heralding the dawn.

" 'It was the nightingale, and not the lark, that pierced the fearful hollow of thine ear,' " she whispered.

Will smiled at her, twining one of her long, dark curls around his finger. " 'It was the lark, the herald of the morn. . . .' "

" 'More light and light it grows.' "

" 'More dark and dark our woes.' "

He kissed her once more, lingeringly, gently, before climbing from the warm haven of her bed. He gathered up his discarded clothes as she watched him, sitting up and wrapping the sheet around her.

"I warned Anna against reading too many romantic novels," she said. "But perhaps Shakespeare is the real danger."

Will laughed roughly, pulling on his shirt. "I don't think we needed poetry to inflame our passion."

"No. We needed only to see each other again."

"Speaking of which . . ." He paused in reaching for his coat. "Can I see you tonight?"

She hesitated, her gaze sliding away from his. "Not tonight."

"You have a previous engagement, I'm sure."

"Yes."

"Lady Mount Clare's schedule is no doubt busy, indeed. A ball, the opera?"

"My schedule is not so *busy* as all that! But I am engaged with friends tonight."

"Friends," he said slowly. He could imagine what sort of "friends"—United Irishmen.

Eliza bit her lip. "And tomorrow I promised Anna I would take her to the draper's to shop for feathers for the queen's birthday at Dublin Castle. No doubt I will see you there. All of Dublin must be seen to attend the birthday."

"That is not the sort of 'see' I meant," he said, leaning over the bed to kiss her lingeringly. To remind her of the storm of their passion just barely spent.

She smiled, gently touching his cheek. "Perhaps tomorrow night. I will send you word. Are you at your family's town house in Merrion Square?"

"Nay, I moved to lodgings in Castleton Street. My family's house is far too gloomy for me, I fear. Good night, Eliza."

"Good morning, Will."

He hurried to the window, unlocking the casement and lowering himself down to grasp the thick growth of ivy clinging there.

"I grow too old for this," he muttered as his well-exercised muscles gave a twinge. Too old, indeed, especially after a night of passion. But it was thrilling, too, he had to admit. The subterfuge of being Eliza's lover at last.

Thrilling—and dangerous.

Chapter Eight

A nd I call this meeting to order," Mr. Boyle announced, banging on the table with his gavel.

Eliza took her place at the table, her notebook open before her as she studied the men gathered around. Boyle, O'Malley, Jameson, and a hard-faced man named Duson from the islands. But not her old friend from home at Kildare, Lord Edward Fitzgerald, who was still deep in hiding.

And they should all be in hiding really, she thought wryly, twirling her pencil nervously between her fingers. With watchful military men like Will back in Dublin, they had to be doubly careful.

She frowned, tapping the pencil against the table. *She* should be the one most careful. It had been three weeks now since she and Will became lovers, three days since she last saw him at a card party. Then he vanished from Dublin. They said his regiment was sent on patrol to Queen's County, so she agreed to attend this hidden meeting.

Where *was* he? Was he only biding his time until he caught her out?

"Lady Mount Clare has generously agreed to act as secretary, in Mr. O'Connor's absence," Boyle said, dragging her out of her whirlwind thoughts. "We will keep this meeting as short as possible."

"Aye, the longer we stay, the greater the chance of a raid," Jameson, the delegate from Munster, said harshly.

Eliza glanced around the windowless room, a cellar far beneath a bookshop. All seemed quiet outside, but the very air in the stuffy little chamber seemed to shimmer with tension. The usual civility of an executive committee meeting, as opposed to the rowdier general meetings, seemed strained.

"Then perhaps you will give us the news from Munster, Mr. Jameson," Boyle said, nodding to Eliza.

She jotted down the reports as each man spoke, using the code she would translate into dispatches to send around the country. If she was caught with the notes now, they would merely look like a lady's rambling diary of gowns and tea parties. In reality, they were words of arms, troops, hiding places, strategy.

The island delegate finished up the reports with tales of caves that could be used to hide guns from France—if they ever showed up as promised. So much depended on that, and Eliza didn't like that at all. Surely the uprising should depend on the Irish alone now.

She studied each man's face, their expressions written with grim determination in the faint lamplight. What was writ on her own face when Will looked at her? What did he read there with his too-perceptive gaze?

She took a deep breath, setting thoughts of Will aside for the moment. "Gentlemen," she said. "It sounds as if the work in the counties is progressing much as planned. Now it is Dublin's turn."

Boyle frowned, leaning forward in his chair. "In what way, Lady Mount Clare?"

"Tomorrow night is the queen's birthday ball at the Castle," Eliza said. "All members of the Irish Parliament, all the nobility, will be there."

"Are you suggesting we mount an attack on the Castle?" Jameson said. "On a day's notice?"

Eliza laughed. "I would hardly say we are ready for *that*. No, our cause can be served in a much . . . quieter fashion, I think."

A ripple of interest went around the table. "What do you suggest, Lady Mount Clare?" O'Malley asked.

"I suggest," Eliza answered, "that people such as Lord Lieutenant Camden will be much preoccupied with the festivities. His offices will be empty, and guards are often easily bypassed in a party atmosphere. Especially by tipsy ladies . . ."

Boyle laughed. "You *are* bold, my lady."

"Taking a little peek at papers left carelessly lying about is not as bold as going into pitched battle," Eliza said, starting to gather up her own papers—and trying not to think of battles that would surely involve Will. "But we all do what we can. I suggest you all watch for a new dispatch soon, gentlemen."

"Troop numbers?" O'Malley asked. "Regimental movements into the counties?"

"If we're fortunate," Eliza answered. She thought of Will and the Thirteenth marching on St. Stephen's Green. But this was what she had set out to do; she would finish it.

"Now, if there is no more business, I must go before I am missed. Good night, gentlemen. And *Erin go bragh.*"

Will stared down at Eliza as she slept in his arms, her naked body as pale and perfect as marble in the darkness. Their lovemaking that night had a strange edge to it, almost frantic as she grabbed him in her arms as soon as he climbed in her window. He had been gone for a few days on patrol and just returned, not sure of his reception in her house. Not that he minded her haste in the least—making love with Eliza made him feel intoxicated, drunk on her scent and feel, her kiss. But still, he wondered what came over her tonight.

He leaned over, kissing her collarbone, the curve of her shoulder.

"Will," she murmured, her breath cool against him in the shadows of their bed. "It's late; we shouldn't—"

"Shh." He pressed his lips to that soft, sensitive little spot just below her ear, the one that always made her sigh and moan. And wriggle against him, as she did now. His body hardened as her skin slid against his, his pulse thrumming in his veins.

"We have a little time," he said. He pressed his open palm against her hip, sliding it up, up, over her slender waist and her ribs. At last he brushed the underside of her breast and balanced its weight on his hand, feeling her heart beat frantically.

"I'm afraid a *little* time won't be enough," she said, her words fading to a moan as he stroked her nipple.

She rolled over in his arms, arching up to kiss him. It

was a frantic, wild kiss, full of need. A kiss that said all they could not in words. Their tongues touched, wet and hot.

Will pressed her down into the rumpled sheets, covering her with his body. She smelled of roses still, of cold night air, the salt of sweat and sex. Her legs wrapped around his waist, pulling him even closer, skin to skin. He felt her hands on his shoulders, the nails digging into his back as if she would hold him her prisoner, would never let him go.

And he was more than willing to be chained to her. But he was determined to hold on to *her* in turn, to make her his own forever.

His kissed her jaw, her neck, sliding his lips along the soft inside of her arm. He reveled in the moaning sigh she made as his teeth grazed her breast. Her fingers tangled in his hair, drawing him to her. He was happy to oblige. Lightly, he bit down on her erect, rosy nipple, flicking it with his tongue.

"Will!" she cried. "You make me insane."

"That's two of us, then." He stared up at her, their eyes meeting for one long moment. "Let's never be sane again."

She laughed hoarsely, tugging at his hair until he slid back up her body. "At least until the morning," she whispered against his lips.

Until the morning. At the taste of her, he forgot everything that waited outside this room. Ireland, England, duty, family—all gone. There was only Eliza and Will, the way he felt when he held her in his arms.

He clasped her hands in his, entwining their fingers as he held her to the bed and pressed deep into her body, into the warmth and heat of her. He threw his head back, his jaw clenched with the rush of raw, primal pleasure.

She tightened her legs around his hips, drawing him even deeper until he couldn't tell where his body ended and hers began. They were like two halves of the same whole, as they always had been.

Would they be ripped apart in the morning? Even that didn't matter now, not with her wrapped around him, the sound of her voice in his ear.

"Will, Will," she sobbed as he drew back and plunged forward again, deeper, faster. The pressure built and built until he exploded with it.

"Eliza!" he shouted, feeling her body go taut beneath his with her own release. "Eliza."

He collapsed to the bed beside her, quivering as he pressed his face into her hair. She whispered soft endearments, holding on to his shoulders as if she, too, feared to fall. And morning was rushing upon them much too quickly.

Chapter Nine

"Will you wear the diamonds, my lady?"

"Hmm?" Eliza said, distracted. Diamonds were the furthest thing from her mind. She was far too busy thinking of Will. Would he be there tonight at the Castle? Would he discover what she was planning?

She did a fine enough job concealing her intentions last night. But those eyes of his sometimes seemed as if they could see into her very soul.

She pushed away those worries. "I'm sorry, Mary," she said, turning to her maid. "I fear I was woolgathering. What did you say?"

"I asked if you'll wear the diamonds, my lady. They'll look so well with your new gown."

Eliza held up her arm, examining the satin sleeve. "White, of course. Why must it always be white for the queen's birthday? I'm too old to be a bride or a debutante."

"White looks well on you, my lady," Mary said soothingly, putting the final touches on Eliza's coiffure, the upswept dark curls fastened with pearl combs.

"It makes me look like a silly miss in her first Season. But, yes, the diamonds will do very well."

As Mary fastened the heavy necklace and earrings, Eliza reached for her pot of rice powder, dusting it over those freckles. Another queen's birthday ball at the Castle. And no plans for the uprising yet, despite the fact that Kilmainham Gaol was filling up with United Irish from the north, and delegates from the counties arrived daily with reports. Surely they were doomed to always live in this limbo, she thought with a sigh. Maybe what she found tonight could change all that.

"How is your family, Mary?" she asked.

"Well enough, my lady," Mary said. "My mum thanks you for the ham you sent for Boxing Day, and my brother Billy took us out for a sail on his fishing boat. It was ever so cold in the bay, but the fresh air did my mum some good, as did seeing Billy. He's been away so much of late."

As so many young men were. "The British frigates gave you no trouble on your pleasure cruise, then?"

Mary shook her head. "Mum always acts so stern and respectable; I'm sure they would have let us go at once if they dared board us and listen to her lectures! I daresay it's not so easy for Billy in his work now, my lady, having to get up before dawn and try to get the fish and avoid the patrols, too. They seem to stop everyone not in regimentals now."

"I can imagine," Eliza murmured, remembering what she had learned at last night's secret meeting. No one was safe any longer.

"Speaking of regimentals, my lady . . . ," Mary said, gathering up the feather fan and reticule and tucking a handkerchief in its beaded depths. "I saw Major Denton marching in St. Stephen's Green this morning."

Eliza felt her cheeks turn foolishly warm at the mention of his name. Anyone would think she *was* a silly miss in her first Season! "Indeed?" she said, hoping she sounded quite indifferent. She covered her blush by reaching for her scent bottle and dabbing a drop of rose perfume at the base of her throat.

Just at that spot he liked to kiss, to taste with his tongue . . .

"Oh yes, my lady. He drew quite a crowd of gawking females. Such a lot of silliness over a handsome face and a red coat! As if they had never seen one before."

"Do you not care for handsome faces and red coats, Mary?"

"The coat I can do without, my lady. But if the face looked like the major's . . ."

Eliza laughed despite herself. "I would not know. Major Denton has not shown himself at a gathering for some days." He had only shown himself in her bedroom, as soon as he returned to Dublin.

"I hear tell the Thirteenth was sent out on patrol, my lady. Quiet like."

"Patrol?" Eliza asked, pretending no knowledge at all.

"There was some rumor of unrest at Prosperous Town, my lady," Mary said. "They say there was some thought of reinforcing the barracks there, but it came to nothing. A few pikes found and a hay rick burned, that was all. So, back the Thirteenth came. But I don't think they will be sent north after all. We're going to need them here."

Prosperous Town—that was not so far from Killinan.

"I'm sure the young ladies are glad of that. There will be no lack of dancing partners tonight."

"Shall you dance, too, my lady?"

Eliza laughed. "You and Anna, always trying to get me to dance! I suppose I might, depending on who asks me. If anyone *does* ask me."

"I don't think you need worry about that, my lady. You look grand."

Eliza stood up from her dressing table to face the full-length mirror. Her white gown was trimmed with black velvet and pearl beadwork. Black plumes, fastened by her pearl combs, nodded in her hair.

"I would not say grand," she said. "But certainly presentable, entirely thanks to you, Mary."

The maid handed her the fan and reticule along with a pair of gloves. As Eliza drew the thin kid over her hands, she noticed the gold glint of her wedding ring. It had been over a year since Mount Clare died. Why did she still wear it? Sentiment? A sort of armor? Certainly not in memory of some undying flame of love.

She had the sudden flashing image of Will in her bed, their bodies entwined as they rolled through the sheets, all that heat and need in the darkness. And she slid the ring off her finger, handing it to Mary before pulling on her gloves.

"Put that in my jewel case, please, Mary," she said. "We probably won't be gone late; Castle events are rarely raucous, dance-until-dawn affairs."

"No, my lady," Mary said, staring down at the ring with wide eyes.

Eliza hurried down to the foyer, where Anna already waited. She, too, wore white satin, her gown trimmed not with black but with pale pink and glistening silver embroidery. Pink plumes nodded in her blond curls, secured with their mother's diamond tiara.

"Mama entrusted you with *that*?" Eliza teased her sister as the footman assisted her with her heavy cloak. "You must have made a concerted effort to be very good indeed before you left Killinan!"

"I *can* behave, when I so choose," Anna said airily, touching the delicate floral loops of diamonds and small pearls. "And when there is a reward for it. Mama says it is only on loan for the birthday, though, then back it goes."

"It suits you very well. Much better than it did me."

"Is that why you have not worn it since your wedding?"

"Exactly so. Plus it is so monstrously heavy. I wager you will not be able to dance at all!"

"Oh, I can always dance, even if I wore leaden boots." Anna swept out the door and down to the carriage with Eliza close behind. Perhaps Anna would marry a duke after all—tiaras and sweeping parades became her so well.

"And you will have no shortage of eager partners," Eliza said, settling herself on the seat with all her heavy skirts and feathers. "Mary tells me the Thirteenth is back in Dublin."

"Indeed? That is good news for you, Eliza."

"For me?"

"Oh yes. Now you can cease pacing about the house so restlessly and dance all you like with Major Denton."

Eliza stared out the window at the passing houses. It was a good thing indeed that Anna was going home soon. "I do not pace."

"Certainly not," Anna said, obviously not at all convinced.

"And I will not dance tonight, either. Staid Castle minuets are hardly worth the trouble."

Anna smiled smugly. "If you say so, sister."

"Major Denton. How very pleasant to see you again," Mrs. Hardwick, General Hardwick's wife, said, holding out her hand to Will as he stepped under the columned portico of the Castle.

The Hardwicks' pretty blond daughter, Lydia, who had sat next to him at the theater, stood behind her mother. She smiled at him shyly from beneath her white plumes.

Will bowed over Mrs. Hardwick's hand. "And pleasant to see you as well, Mrs. Hardwick. Miss Hardwick. You are both looking splendid this evening."

"We were not sure you would return to Dublin in time for the festivities," said Mrs. Hardwick. "My husband told me the Thirteenth was dispatched to keep the peace in some horrid little village."

Will thought of the town of Prosperous, so near to Moreton Manor and to Eliza's family at Killinan. While Queen's County just to the south was in a state of insurrection, Kildare County had been eerily quiet. The streets of Prosperous had been nearly deserted, suspicious eyes peering from behind shutters. Green streamers fluttering from flagposts had been torn down and trampled by the soldiers.

"It is quite fearsome that the rebellion draws so

close," Lydia whispered. "I have the most frightful night-mares. . . ."

"I should not worry, Miss Hardwick," Will said reas-suringly. "We found the town, and all of Kildare, to be quite peaceful. And Dublin is well fortified."

Mrs. Hardwick gave him an approving smile. "And we have fine men such as Major Denton to protect us, do we not, Lydia dear?"

Lydia smiled and blushed. "Indeed, Mama. I see we need not fear at all."

"Though perhaps the major, having been away, has not enjoyed a dance in many days?"

Will could take a hint. "I have not, Mrs. Hardwick, sadly enough. Perhaps Miss Hardwick will honor me with the first dance, if she is not otherwise engaged?"

"Thank you," Lydia breathed. "I am not otherwise engaged."

"My dears!" General Hardwick boomed, emerging from a door hidden to the left in the dark gray stone wall. He was followed by two other men in brightly decorated regimentals. "Are you importuning the poor young man for dances already? He has scarcely arrived! I vow, Major Denton, facing our fair Dublin ladies is far more hazard-ous than any pack of rebels."

They all laughed as Mrs. Hardwick tapped her hus-band's arm with her folded fan.

"Papa!" Lydia cried, blushing again. "You will give Major Denton entirely the wrong idea."

"Indeed, General, Miss Hardwick has given me the honor of a dance," Will said. "I daresay a minuet is prefer-able to rebels, when it is with such a charming partner."

Miss Hardwick's blush flared even pinker, and her

father affectionately pinched her cheek. They were the very image of a contented family, and as Will watched them, he felt a pang that felt strangely like . . . longing.

His own family was not particularly close, each of them preferring to go their own way—his father to London and his mother to Moreton Manor. If there was any affection, it was for his older brother Henry, but he was always in sunny Italy with his mistress. Will often wondered what a home, a family, of his own would feel like. A place of warmth, welcome, acceptance, and love.

He thought of Eliza, of her soft smile as she rested in his arms. Of her fingertips tracing lazy patterns on his skin, the two of them bound in the greatest of intimacy. Once, long ago, he thought his true home could be with her. But these dangerous days were no time for peaceful dreams.

"Run along now, my dears," General Hardwick said, kissing his wife's cheek. "I want to have a word with Major Denton."

Mrs. Hardwick whispered something in his ear, and he nodded. As the two ladies hurried toward the doors to the state apartments, the general led Will to a bench near the stone wall.

"Colonel Brandeis tells us you behaved in an exemplary fashion these last few days," the general said. "You kept your men calm in a very tense situation."

"I was only doing my duty, sir," Will answered.

"Indeed, and doing it very well. We are in the midst of strange times, Major. We're threatened with the horrors of civil war, and everyone is on edge, are they not? There have already been some unfortunate actions in the north, I fear. It would only take one foolish movement, one misfired shot, to blow up this whole country. We cannot have things happen in Kildare that we've heard of in Queen's, not so near to Dublin."

Will's jaw tightened. "Pitchcapping and flogging?"

"Yes, indeed. Terror is not the way to make people disarm and listen to reason. Instead it only drives them closer to those damned United Irishmen and away from what is good for them. Cool heads are what we need now, Major. Like your own."

"I hope I can be of service, General. My own family is in Kildare."

"Ah, yes. At Moreton Manor, is it not? A fine estate, so I hear. You have been commended, and I am sure you will be again. But we must all be very cautious these days. It would be fatal to trust the wrong people, have the wrong friends."

Will frowned. "What do you mean, General Hardwick?"

"Oh, nothing to concern a fine young man such as you, Major Denton. After so long in the West Indies, you surely know how small societies like to gossip. Lady Mount Clare has long been a favorite topic here in Dublin."

So that was it. He had been seen talking with Eliza and was being warned off. "Lady Mount Clare was a childhood friend. Moreton Manor is very near to Killinan."

"And Lady Killinan is, of course, above any suspicion. Her daughter, though—she is one to watch. Too clever and independent by half, a most unnatural woman." General Hardwick glanced toward the doors, where the hum of conversation grew louder. "I have been thinking of sending my wife and daughter to England for a time, merely as a precaution."

"Dublin would certainly miss their presence greatly," Will said absently, still thinking of Eliza.

"And I fear my Lydia would miss *you,* Major. She has talked of little else since our theater excursion."

Will looked at him, startled. He had been so preoccupied with Eliza, with their blossoming affair, that he had not thought of anyone else at all. Of looking to his future, as he must. "General Hardwick?"

The older man smiled at him. "A word of advice, if I may. The right wife, a lady who knows the ways of Society and the Army, can be of great value to a young man rising in the world. And a great comfort at home. I have been content with my Hester these twenty years, and it is a blessing I would certainly wish for our dear daughter."

The general clapped Will on the shoulder before strolling to the doors. The green-liveried footmen leaped forward to open them, and Will was momentarily alone in the cool stone portico.

He rubbed his hand over his eyes. This was surely not the time to think of marriage! But if it was, Lydia Hardwick would be perfectly suitable. Young, pretty, well connected. Just what would satisfy his family and aid his career.

And it would erase any suspicions of a dangerous friendship with the democratical Lady Mount Clare. He could not let his family name down, could not cause a scandal and leave the Army.

It would be sensible, pragmatic—and entirely out of the question. A moment on the cusp of war was not one for practical betrothals. And he found he could not give up his stolen nights with Eliza. Could not give up the desperate chance to hold her, kiss her, and be near to her, just for a moment longer.

Eliza made him feel alive, as nothing ever had. Made the colors and light of the world brighter and more intense, made him feel things as he never had before. It was as if he were frozen, until she touched him again, and then winter blazed into burning summer.

The doors to the courtyard opened on a blast of cold wind, and a laughing group hurried in, wrapped in their cloaks and scarves. One of them was Eliza.

She did not yet see him as she swirled off her cloak to reveal a gleaming gown of white satin and black velvet with the sparkle of diamonds. She shimmered like a goddess of light, a beacon luring him along a dark, stormy shore. Whether to salvation or doom on the rocky shoals, he did not yet know.

"I fear my plumes are entirely crushed," Anna cried. "Why must Queen Charlotte have her birthday in January when we all have to muffle up so tightly just to go out? It ruins our finery."

"Oh, Anna," Eliza said, laughing. "The queen can be blamed for many things, perhaps, but not for when she was born. At least there is no danger of being overheated in these drafty state apartments, yes?"

Then she turned and saw him, her smile freezing on her lips. She curtsied slowly, her lashes sweeping down to cover any secrets in those dark eyes. "Major Denton. You have returned to Dublin, I see."

"Indeed I have, Lady Mount Clare, Lady Anna," Will said. He moved closer to her, reaching out to take her hand and raise it to his lips. Her fingers trembled in the thin kid gloves.

Ah-ha, he thought. She had missed him after all.

"We missed you here in Dublin," Anna said, her gaze darting between them. "There has been a lack of fine dance partners, I fear."

"Then perhaps you would both honor me with a dance this evening," he said.

Eliza shook her head, smoothing the lace on her sleeve so she did not look at him. "I do not care to dance at these Castle affairs."

Perhaps she was right, he had to admit, despite his disappointment. It would do neither of them any good to have their "friendship" gossiped of even more. She would gather more attention, and he would disgrace his family and the Army. "Then maybe Lady Anna would dance with me."

"I am not so choosy as my sister as to where I dance, Major Denton, as long as I do dance," Anna said.

"I look forward to it, then." Will bowed to them once more before leaving them for the now-crowded gathering. He was soon surrounded by fellow officers and acquaintances, yet in his mind he still saw Eliza.

Eliza made her way through the gallery with her sister, their heeled shoes echoing on the cold floor of green Connemara marble. All the ladies' satin and silk gowns rustled like a forest of spring leaves, their laughter and chatter as loud as birds.

She murmured replies to greetings, even laughed at Anna's wry comments, but she could think of only one thing—Will had returned. She would have to be very careful in carrying out her plans tonight with him there watching her.

They emerged into the vast ballroom, which was lit by the blaze of Waterford crystal chandeliers set between the gilt-framed mirrors and the speckled marble pillars. High above, soaring above the musicians' gallery and the gilded moldings, the ceiling was elaborately painted in incongruous scenes of the coronation of George III and St. Patrick introducing Christianity to Ireland.

And below was a great, courtly crush of satin, plumes, and pearls, velvet and diamonds, packed together to celebrate a faraway monarchy that cared little for this barbaric colony.

"Now I know I shall lose my feathers utterly," Anna said, straightening her tiara.

"Better that than your foot," Eliza said, snatching her toes away just before they could be crushed by an officer's pump. "There are some chairs over there by the wall. Quick, Anna, let's claim them before someone else does!"

They rushed toward the last two empty gilt chairs, diving into them just before two other disgruntled ladies.

"Why ever do you keep coming to these things, Eliza?" Anna said breathlessly, fluffing at her skirts.

"If you want to find a husband to please Mama," Eliza answered, "we must come to Dublin Castle."

"I do not *want* to find a husband. Especially not one who comes here."

"No? To be sure, there are seldom any Russian princes, but I fear you may have to lower your sights just a hair, my dear. What sort of husband would you like?" Eliza scanned the crowd, seeking out each red coat and moving along when she found it was not Will. He had certainly seemed healthy and whole, but she had to be sure.

Lud, but she was a fool. He had merely been out on a marching drill. What would happen, how would she feel, when it came to a real battle?

Anna seemed unaware of her sister's inner turmoil, fanning herself languidly. "A handsome husband, of course. A man of sensitivity and passion! Of poetry."

"Mama would not like you marrying a poet."

"He would not have to be an actual poet, I suppose. Merely have poetry in his soul. Be open to life and all its wondrous possibilities."

Before Eliza could answer, Lord Lieutenant Camden and his wife made their entrance, a wide pathway cleared for them along the center of the ballroom. His henchmen and generals were in procession behind them as they took their places beneath the portraits of the king and queen, and the musicians launched into "God Save the King."

Everyone rose to their feet, Eliza and Anna staying close to their hard-won chairs. When the song was mercifully done, the figures formed for the opening minuet, led by the Camdens.

That was when Eliza saw the red coat that belonged to Will. Young Miss Hardwick was on his arm, smiling up at him and blushing prettily as he escorted her to their place in the dance. General Hardwick and his wife looked on with approving smiles.

Eliza froze as she watched them, the whole crowded, glittering room fading to a blur around Will and his dance partner. They were crystalline bright, illuminating one startling realization—what a terrible romantic fool she was.

"How insipid Miss Hardwick looks," Anna said. "How horrid for Will that he must do his duty and dance with her."

Eliza glanced at her sister, to find Anna frowning as if concerned. She gave her a reassuring smile. "I am sure it cannot be so irksome as all that. Miss Hardwick is said to be quite the belle of Dublin."

"Nonetheless, I am quite sure he would much rather be elsewhere. As I would." Anna vigorously wafted her fan through the miasma of candle smoke and perfume. "I thought the birthday ball would be merry and fun."

Eliza laughed, watching as the dancers processed through the last patterns of the stately music. She feared Miss Hardwick did not look "insipid" at all. She looked young and pretty and innocent, while Eliza herself felt a hundred years old with all the tensions of the past months. Had Dublin ever been fun?

And this was not the night it would start, either. She had her errand to perform and could not be distracted by Will and his pretty dance partners. She had no right to be jealous of anything he did at all.

Anna was claimed for the next dance, leaving Eliza alone. She abandoned her preciously won chair, making her slow way out of the jammed ballroom and back to the gallery.

The marble floors and walls and the tall windows made the space cold, but a few people still strolled there for a breath of air or a quiet word. Eliza went to one of the windows, peering out at the courtyard and the grim tower of Kilmainham Gaol.

That forbidding place was dark tonight, no screams of terror echoing. But in the distance, somewhere near the river, a few sparks like stars flew up into the black sky.

"Damned United Irish bonfires," a man across the gallery said, his stern voice echoing on the stone. "They light them out by the river, and if you happen to pass them, they seize you and make you sing French songs—or they slit your throat."

"Dreadful," his companion answered, her tone quavering. "Can't the patrols stop them?"

"By the time they get there, the villains have vanished. My sister sees the sparks and is convinced we'll all be dead before morning. The Lord Lieutenant is a bloody useless fool, I say!"

Eliza spun around and hurried back toward the doors leading to the ballroom, as if to rejoin the dance. But she veered away at the last moment, turning instead toward a narrow staircase at the end of the corridor.

Slowly, the hum of the crowd faded behind her, and the shadows grew thicker and darker. This was not one of the grand public corridors, designed to awe and amaze visitors with the grandeur of Anglo Ireland. It was utilitarian, serviceable, and cold, a way to move quickly from one place to another behind the scenes.

Even with its quiet isolation, though, she had to hurry. Guards surely patrolled everywhere in the Castle, and Anna would notice if she did not return soon.

Holding her heavy skirts close, Eliza dashed along the carpeted corridor. She listened carefully for any sound, any footfall or cough, but she heard only the excited rush of her own breath.

Hurry, hurry, she thought. At the end of the hall was the door she sought, locked and guarded. But at least there was only one guard, a young man who looked terribly bored as he leaned back against the wall.

Eliza pressed her hand to the nervous flutter in her stomach, thinking quickly. How could she get him away from the door just long enough to carry out her task and be on her way?

"Excuse me!" she called, rushing forward to the doorway. The guard immediately stood up straight, his eyes brightening with interest.

"I am terribly sorry," she said, "but there seems to be some sort of trouble in the kitchens. An intruder, I think." She had no need to feign breathless urgency, for she felt it all too keenly. "I happened to be nearby, so I was sent to ask if you could come right away and assist."

"Oh yes, ma'am, at once!" He was so eager to be away from his dull duty that he did not even ask why a lady would be sent with such a message. The kitchens were at a far distance; she would be finished and gone before he came back.

He ran off down the corridor, leaving Eliza alone in the silence. As soon as he was gone, she drew one of the long, pointed hairpins from her coiffure, kneeling down to slide it into the keyhole. Learning to pick locks was just one of the useful things she had learned from the United Irishmen. She jiggled it around carefully until she fit it in below the mechanism and twisted upward. One of the plumes dropped down over her eye, its black feathery bits tearing.

"Damn all fashion!" she muttered, shoving it back. "Such a nuisance."

At last the lock gave way, and she ducked into the room, shutting the door carefully behind her. The one window let in the torchlight from the courtyard below, illuminating a small office.

The Lord Lieutenant had his grand office below, where he received guests amid marble and mahogany splendor. This private office was very far from that, a space set with a simple desk, straight-backed wooden chairs, and bookshelves lined with documents. But glitter certainly wasn't what was important.

The papers were neatly stacked on the desk, just where the United Irish agent said they would be.

Not daring even to breathe, Eliza sifted through them, her jeweled bracelets flashing in the torchlight. Copies of letters from Lord Lieutenant Camden to Prime Minister Pitt begging for more men and more guns. Replies from Pitt—he did not seem so concerned about the situation yet. That was good. They were not about to be overrun with yet more soldiers fresh from England.

But Eliza knew that good fortune would not hold for long.

She hastily studied the maps and the orders to move regiments, memorizing the scraps of information. It was quite useful to know where the enemy thought trouble would be—and then give it to them where they least expected it. She would send the information to the United generals tomorrow so they could move their men accordingly.

As she moved onto another stack of papers, she heard a noise out in the corridor. A mere footstep, just a whisper over the carpet, but her mouth turned dry. Her pulse beat hard, warning of danger. Had she overstayed her time, even when trying to be so very quick?

She fell to her knees, heedless of the fine satin skirt, and slid under the shelter of the desk. She huddled there, watching through the tiny gap below the edge of the desk as the door opened and a pair of polished shoes appeared. They moved across the floor with steady, measured, silent steps. In the tense quiet, she could hear a man's soft breath.

She pressed her hand hard to her mouth to keep from making any sound at all.

Suddenly, in a heart-poundingly swift move, he knelt on the other side of the desk. His hand shot under the gap, holding a tiny shred of black plume that had fallen from her headdress in the corridor.

"You can come out, Eliza," Will said tonelessly.

Eliza fell forward onto her hands, her breath rushing out of her lungs. In relief, or even greater terror? She wasn't at all sure.

"No, I don't think so," she answered.

"You prefer to stay concealed under there, then?" he said. "Very well, I will join you."

Before she could even move an inch, he swung over the desk, crawling into her hiding place. He blocked her exit and most of the light, his shoulders wide as he reached up to brace his hands on the wooden ledge.

"What the devil are you doing, Eliza?" he demanded. "Trying to get yourself arrested right in front of your sister and half of Dublin?"

Eliza tilted back her chin. "I thought this was the ladies' necessary," she said. "I was mistaken."

"Oh, I don't think you were *mistaken* at all," he said tightly. "You knew exactly what you were doing. How did you know this office was here?"

"I didn't—that is, I was not entirely certain."

"But now you are?" He reached out, grabbing her wrists to drag her near. "Eliza, what did you find? Tell me now!"

"I didn't have time to find anything at all," she managed to gasp. His arms came around her like steel bands, so tight she could hardly breathe. "You came in here too soon, damn you."

"Eliza, I swear . . ." Suddenly there was another sound from the corridor outside. Footsteps, louder than Will's stealthy progress had been, voices, and laughter. Will's head went up, his eyes narrowed like a forest cat sensing danger.

"Who is it?" Eliza whispered. Someone he had alerted? Someone he was in league with? That did not seem to be the case, though, for his jaw tightened in surprised anger.

"Shh," he answered. "Perhaps they will just pass by."

But they did not. The footsteps stopped outside the door, and there was the metallic scrape of a key. It seemed Will had had the foresight to lock the door behind him.

Eliza curled her fists into his uniform coat, holding on as if to keep from drowning. She had a flashing thought of Anna, dancing innocently below, of her family. The great scandal of her arrest.

The information that would never get where it needed to go.

". . . this way, Lord Averley," a man said. "The maps are here. It should take only a moment to look at the planned route."

"Excellent. Lady Averley will be most unhappy if I don't dance with her at least once this evening."

"Lord Camden is most eager to hear your opinion," the first man said. Their voices were louder now, thunderous in Eliza's ears, and they were almost to the desk. There was no way she could stay concealed there, because the space was too small.

She would go down for certain, and Will with her.

But then Will seized her by the waist. "Don't fight me," he whispered against her ear.

"What . . ." Her gasp was drowned out by his mouth crashing down on hers, hard and hot. He laid her down flat on her back, covering her body with his. They were tucked under the desk, her skirts spread around them in concealing white billows.

Despite the great danger—or perhaps because of it—

Eliza felt something hot and desperate bubble up inside of her at his kiss. Something she could not push away or deny. She clutched at his shoulders, arching up against him, holding tightly to keep from falling into the darkness.

"Well," she heard the man say, a murmur that seemed to come from very far away. "Perhaps we should return in just a moment, Lord Averley. We do so hate to . . . interrupt a private moment."

Eliza glanced past Will's shoulder in time to catch a glimpse of two smirking men turning away—and her slippered foot sticking out from the desk, giving away their hiding place.

They hastily departed the room, the door clicking shut behind them. Will sat up, pulling her with him as he crawled out from the shelter of the desk and rose to his feet.

"You should get into trouble more often," he muttered, sounding almost as dazed as she felt.

"I can probably oblige you on that score," she said, shaking out her skirts and smoothing her hair. That telltale feather drooped again.

"That is what I'm afraid of. And I won't be here to rescue you next time."

"I've been rescuing myself for a long time now!" she said indignantly, suddenly embarrassed to remember exactly how much in need of rescue she just was.

"And doing a marvelous job of it, I see." Will tugged his coat into place.

She opened her mouth to argue again, but he pressed his fingertips to her lips. "We have to go now. They'll be back at any moment."

"Do you think they know who we are?" she whispered.

"Me, probably. I will surely be reprimanded for it in the

morning. But I think you were, shall we say, concealed. And every lady here tonight is wearing white."

Concealed beneath his body, he meant. "Surely this is not the first time a tryst was interrupted at a dull Castle reception."

A tiny, reluctant smile touched his lips, but it vanished into a stern frown. "Nor will it be the last. Come, we need to return to the ball before we're missed. I promised to dance with your sister."

Eliza nodded. She had the troop plans anyway, and much more besides.

Will suddenly dragged her close to him again, whispering in her ear in a hard, unyielding voice. "This is not finished, Eliza. You will tell me what you were after here."

She stared up at him, at the determined gleam in his eyes and the hard, shadowed angles of his face that matched his tone. And she thought of the sparks from the bonfire and of Will's own words. *We are all Irish.* An idea formed deep in her mind, with the potential to be even more dangerous than breaking into the office.

He wanted a battle of wills, did he? Fine—she would oblige.

"Then meet me later tonight," she whispered. "But be sure and change your coat first. . . ."

Chapter Ten

E liza, where are you taking me?"

Eliza laughed, tugging at Will's hand as she led him down the narrow, silent lane. Quickly, before he could find time to lecture her about the scene in the office. "You will see in good time!"

She met him outside her kitchen door, she dressed in a plain black dress and thick knit shawl, and he in his coarse coat and cap. They took a hansom to the southern edge of town, beyond the patrols. Now they were in the district known as Porto Bello, a neighborhood of small houses that lined the canals off the road leading to Rathmines. During the day, the muddy, grimy hamlet was busy with the passage of coal barges. By night, it seemed deserted.

Will stopped in his tracks, pulling her into his arms. "Are you luring me into an ambush, my little spy?" He laughed, but there was suspicion in his voice. Yes, of course he would expect more espionage. But she was done with that for the night.

She wound her arms around his waist, feeling the imprint of the pistol and the dagger concealed under his coat.

"I would not do that, Will. Do you trust me—as I trust you?"

He studied her silently, his face a hard, beautiful mask. "God help me, but I do, though I certainly have no reason to."

"You and I must not be enemies," she said, her throat tight. "No matter what happens."

"I could never be your enemy." He kissed her, his lips finding hers in the dark, tender and perfect. It made her ache with longing, with the wild wish that she could hold on to him forever and never see this one fleeting moment end. The taste and feel of him, the way his kiss surrounded all her senses—it was transcendent.

But it did have to end, of course, as all perfect moments must. Will rested his forehead against hers while his hands caressed her shoulders.

"You did not say where we are going," he said.

Eliza smiled. "That is because it is a surprise. And we will be late!"

She took his hand again, leading him down another narrow street beyond the canal where the bulk of barges slept. The houses, too, seemed to sleep, the windows shuttered and the doors barred. The cold air smelled of cabbage, coal dust, and peat smoke from that bonfire.

They were a long way from plush Henrietta Street and the stifling opulence of Dublin Castle.

"This is it," she said, stopping at a dwelling at the end of the lane, at the very edge of town.

Will looked up, frowning at the whitewashed walls. "Are you sure? It looks as deserted as the others. Do you go knocking on random doors now?"

"Of course I am sure." Then she did proceed to knock

on the door, which opened a crack. A gloved hand appeared.

"I am new strung and shall be heard," Eliza whispered, pressing a coin into that hand as she repeated the United Irish motto.

"Come in," the doorkeeper said, and Eliza slipped inside, drawing Will with her even as she felt his muscles tense and saw his hand moving slowly toward that hidden dagger.

The small foyer was almost empty of furniture except for a small, rickety table holding a lamp. Its flickering light illuminated peeling wallpaper and a scuffed wooden floor. But they did not stay there long; the doorkeeper led them through a trapdoor at the back, where a flight of steep stairs led down to the cellars.

Will's sharp, blue gaze darted through the shadows. One hand held hers, but the other flexed. He said he trusted her, yet that could not come easily to either of them. This was a great leap of faith for them both.

"Are you planning to buy this place?" he muttered in her ear. "Because I think it would be a poor investment."

"Shh!" Eliza said, trying not to laugh. At the end of the stone cellar corridor, another door opened, and they stepped into a different world. A world of light and noise and bright, whirling merriment.

Countless lamps and candles burned on a scene of dancing, one so very different from the staid Castle minuets that it seemed like a different planet. Couples spun down the length of the room, skipping and leaping, their feet beating out a thunderous pattern on the stone floor. At the far end was a platform where the musicians sat, no fine orchestra but fiddles, flutes, and bodhrans.

" 'I'll tell me ma when I go home, the boys won't leave the girls alone! They pulled my hair, they stole my comb, but that's all right till I go home. She is handsome, she is pretty, she's the belle of Belfast city. She is courting one, two, three, please won't you tell me who is she!' "

Eliza's toes tapped in time to the infectious old song, her spirits rising.

"What is this place?" Will asked, staring out at the raucous scene with narrowed eyes.

"A ceilidh, of course," she answered. She grabbed two pottery goblets of ale from the table of refreshments and handed him one. "Do you not remember them from Killinan?"

"Of course I do. Your mother forbade you to go."

"You know I went anyway," she said cheerfully, sipping at the dark, strong ale.

"Nothing has changed, I see."

"No. I still love this music, these people, above everything else." She nudged him teasingly with her elbow. "Admit it, Will. This is a much better party than any at the bloody Castle!"

Will laughed. "I think that can hardly be denied." He took a cautious drink. "But how did you know where to find it? I'm sure it's not always in the same place."

"Certainly not. I knew because of the bonfire."

"The bonfire?"

"Oh, come, Will, this is a party. I want to see more dancing and less talking!"

"Far be it from me to disappoint a lady." He laid aside their goblets and seized her hands, drawing her into the midst of the dancers.

" 'Let the wind and rain and the hail blow high, and the

snow come tumblin' from the sky! She's as sweet as apple pie, she'll get her own lad by and by . . .' "

He caught her around the waist, lifting her high and twirling her around and around until the lights blurred and she laughed helplessly, her head swimming. He sang along lustily with the chorus. " 'She is handsome, she is pretty, she's the belle of Belfast city! She is courting one, two, three, please won't you tell me who is she.' "

And Eliza saw that, truly, he had *not* forgotten. Like her, he remembered the glorious freedom of those long-ago ceilidhs, when they sneaked out of their houses and ran across the fields at Killinan to some crofter's loft to dance and sing. And she would remember this one, too, in the cold, dark days ahead. He lowered her until her toes touched the floor, only to raise her up again. Eliza clung to his shoulders, throwing back her head in the glory of the movement.

As he spun her again, she stared down into his blue eyes, laughing as he sang in his off-key tenor. " 'Let them all come as they will, for it's Albert Mooney she loves still!' "

The song ended, and he slowly, slowly set her on her feet again, his hands sliding down to her waist to pull her close. "I see this is, indeed, an ambush—a test of my stamina," he said.

"You cannot fail now," Eliza answered, "for I hear another reel coming on."

And they danced on and on, twirling and stomping through reels and jigs and moving instinctively to the old rhythms. As if it had been mere days and not years since they had last danced together like that. Last felt the rhythm of their homeland pounding in their blood, binding them together, tighter and tighter.

She could be young again as they danced, young and hopeful and free.

But the music ended, the jig winding to its inevitable conclusion, and she was no longer the young, romantic Eliza Blacknall but Lady Mount Clare. The scandalous countess rolling the dice of her future.

Yet, for the moment, she had Will's smile, open and happy as he led her from the dance floor. Did the music make him feel young, too? Did it remind him of old hopes and dreams, of that feeling of being Irish, down deep in the blood and bone? She hoped so. Oh, she desperately hoped so.

"I think you have passed the test quite well," she said as they searched for more ale, still hand in hand.

"I'm surprised I remember those steps at all," he answered, seizing two goblets before the thirsty crowds could descend.

"I don't think a person can forget, not once the music is truly inside you."

"Eliza!" someone shouted. "You are here!"

She froze, her goblet at her lips. She glanced at Will, who was peering over her shoulder at the man who hurried toward them. The man who was meant to be in hiding, but it seemed he was as incautious as ever.

Edward Fitzgerald caught her in his arms, lifting her from her feet as he kissed her cheek. His short, dark hair was disheveled, and his green neckcloth was askew from the dancing. His hazel eyes were bright with his love of subterfuge and a good Irish reel.

"I could not miss this grand music," Eliza answered, trying to warn Will with her eyes to say nothing. "How are you keeping, Edward?"

"Well enough, as always," he said, snatching up a goblet. "Pam says she saw you before she went back to Kilrush."

"Indeed. I wanted to be sure she needed nothing, that she was in good health."

"And you found her as big as a house, I'm sure! We'll have another pretty little one soon." He gave Will a curious glance. "You brought a friend, I see."

"Aye, this is Will," she said. "He is a great aficionado of jigs, I think."

"And of beautiful ladies, too," Edward said, offering his hand to Will. "How do you do, sir? Any friend of Eliza Blacknall's is welcome here—and at any other gatherings you might care to attend."

Will slowly shook Edward's hand, solemnly, carefully. Eliza held her breath, thinking of those hidden weapons. "I fear I only have the energy for music and Eliza at the present—Lord Edward."

Edward's gaze narrowed, as if he recognized Will, or was close to it. "We have no 'lords' here, not now. But music—now, that is always welcome, indeed." He suddenly whirled around, pushing his way through the crowd to leap up on the platform.

"My friends!" Edward cried, everyone turning toward him eagerly. Such was his charisma wherever he went— everyone wanted to be near him and hear what he said. Follow him. It was what made him an effective leader.

And his rejection of his own aristocratic privilege was an inspiration to Eliza.

"There is an old Irish custom, or so my mother tells me," Edward said, "that a newcomer to a gathering must grace the company with a song."

He grinned at Eliza mischievously, beckoning. "Perhaps this good man shall lead us in a tune?"

Eliza took Will's hand in hers, not sure what he would do. She knew this was not some sort of a test, some bizarre oath. Singing and music was merely the way of such gatherings, as surely he remembered. But things *were* different now.

His fingers tightened on hers, and he did not look at her. Instead he studied Edward, his body tense. Without a word, he let go of her and strode to the platform, climbing up with the ale-drinking musicians.

"You know 'Cliffs of Doneen'?" he asked roughly.

As if sensing his authority, the musicians immediately took up their instruments again, launching into the plaintive tune.

"'You may travel far from your own native land, far away o'er the mountains and the foam. But of all the fine places that I've ever been, sure there's none can compare with the cliffs of Doneen,'" Will sang, and though his voice was unpracticed, it was deep and pleasant, the words poetic. The jostling crowd grew silent, watching him with rapt faces.

Eliza made her way slowly to the foot of the platform, gazing up at him as he sang those lyrics of leaving home, leaving the place one loved above all others. There was a melancholy to it, a strange beauty that was lacking in more practiced performances. The song seemed to come from somewhere deep inside of him, a secret, hidden well of loneliness.

"'Take a view o'er the mountains, fine sights you'll see there. The high rocky mountains o'er the west coast of Clare. Oh, the town of Kilkee and Kilrush can be seen, from the high rocky slopes round the cliffs of Doneen,' " he sang, and held out his hand to her. She took it, letting him lift her up beside him as her voice rang out to join his.

" 'Fare thee well to Doneen, fare thee well for a while, and to all the dear people I'm leaving behind. To the streams and the meadows where late I have been, and the high rocky slopes round the cliffs of Doneen,' " they sang, and slowly everyone else joined in, first a lone voice here and there, until all the room was alight with song and with tears.

" 'Fare thee well to Doneen, fare thee well for a while . . .' "

And the last notes slowly faded away, like a dying dream that couldn't quite let go. Will stretched out his other hand, gently brushing her cheek with his fingertips. She was shocked to find her skin was damp with tears she didn't even realize she shed. Tears from deep in her heart.

He handed her a handkerchief, and she buried her face in the clean linen folds that smelled of him. She had such sad longings; they threatened to overwhelm her, like a winter storm. She wanted to grab Will, to hold him to her fiercely as the two of them sheltered alone against the howling winds.

Yet there was no shelter to be had. There never had been, not for them.

She wiped away those tears, tucking the handkerchief into her sleeve.

"Come," Will said gently. "Let us go home."

Eliza nodded, letting him put his arm around her waist and lead her through the crowd. Behind them, Edward Fitzgerald launched into "The Wind That Shakes the Barley," but they soon left the sound behind.

They made their way back to the Henrietta Street house in silence, up the back stairs to her dark, cold bedchamber. She had sent Mary to bed hours ago, and the fire had died down.

That room, the one that had been her sanctuary through years of a loveless marriage, hardly seemed any more real than the raucous, rebellious ceilidh, Eliza thought as she locked the door behind them.

But she had no time to think more, as Will caught her hard in his arms, his mouth coming down on hers. He tasted of ale and smoke, and of some bitter, dark anger. Yet she was drawn into him just the same, craved him with a fierce hunger she had never known before.

She arched into his body, wrapping her arms around his neck until she could feel every inch of him against her, every lean muscle, the sharp curve of his hip, the growing erection of his penis through her skirts. Their tongues met, their mouths and sighs melting until she was sure they were one.

As his knee drove between her legs, higher and higher until she straddled him, she buried her fingers in his hair, loosening the queue until it spilled over her hands and she felt his heartbeat against her breast, strong and true.

"Eliza," he muttered, his mouth trailing, open, wet, enticing, along her jaw and her throat. "This is madness. . . ."

"Yes," she gasped. "But I can't end it, can't give you up. Not again. Can you?"

"No. Never."

And in those two words, she heard the fearful echo of all her own pain and sadness. To make love with Will was so very sweet, the consummation of all she had wanted since she was a girl. Of all her dreams as a woman. He was her hero, her beautiful, only love. But this moment was all they had.

So they had to make the most of it.

Eliza stumbled back from him, reaching up to loosen her linen fichu, unfasten the bodice of her simple dress. Watching him the whole time, she shrugged the sleeves down her arms, letting the gown fall to the floor. His eyes were midnight blue and intense, his breath harsh.

She shed her chemise and petticoat, standing before him in only her stockings. Naked in all her desire.

She could hardly breathe, her chest aching with longing and fear. Slowly, trembling, she reached for his hand, drawing it to the vee of her womanhood, damp with her need for him.

His fingertips combed through the curls, teasing, before finally they pressed deep inside of her. The rough friction, the press of his caress just at that one perfect spot, made her cry out. Her head fell back, her knees collapsing as his mouth claimed hers again.

He lifted her high in his arms, twirling her around until they fell across her bed, a tangle of arms and legs, of moans and sweat.

"You are so beautiful, Eliza," he whispered, smoothing her tumbled hair back from her brow. As he stared down at her, tracing the angles of her face with his fingertips, she could almost believe it. Perhaps she *was* beautiful in his eyes, if only for that one passion-blind moment.

"Not as beautiful as you, my Cuchulainn," she said.

He kissed her again, his hands sliding over her shoulders, along her arms, to capture her breasts. She groaned as he plucked at her achingly sensitive nipple, rolling it gently, plucking at it until she could bear it no more. She pushed him away, reaching out desperately to strip away his coat and shirt, tug at the fastenings of his breeches.

And Will let her undress him, lying back against her pillows as he stared up at her, wary and lustfully greedy. Watching her like a gorgeous Celtic god, waiting for his handmaidens to serve him.

Slowly, carefully, she straddled his hips, teasing a light, caressing pattern over his naked, damp skin. She wanted to memorize every inch of him, every curve and angle of his body, so she could remember this always. Remember *him,* when he was gone from her.

She rose up, sliding her cleft along the iron-velvet length of his erection, lowering slowly, slowly, until he was fully sheathed inside her, all heat and friction. Bracing her hands on his shoulders, closing her eyes to fully feel every inch of him, she rose again.

"Eliza!" he shouted, grasping her waist to roll her beneath him in one smooth movement, not breaking their fragile, perfect connection. He picked up her rhythm, the two of them moving faster, desperately.

"Will," she gasped, a hot, sparkling flame rising from her core, spreading over her until she was utterly consumed by it.

His body arched over hers, and he cried out wordlessly.

By the time Eliza floated back into herself, he had drawn the bedclothes over them against the cold night. His arm was draped over her hips, drawing her back against his body as they drowsed, drifting together in a twilight dream world.

Eliza smiled, stretching lazily as she smoothed her fingers down his forearm and back up again, the light blond hairs on his skin tickling her palm. He pressed a kiss to her shoulder.

"Eliza," he whispered. "Why did you take me there tonight?"

Something in his voice made her pleasant lassitude vanish, like clouds sliding away in a dark sky. Her hand stilled on his arm.

"What do you mean?" she said. "You used to enjoy such gatherings in Kildare, the music and the dancing. And especially the ale. Have you left behind us common Irish already?"

"Eliza, how *common* can a countess be?" Gently but inexorably, he turned her in his arms to face him. A bar of moonlight fell across him, turning his tangled hair to gilt. His expression was not angry or violent, but it was quite solemn and implacable. "And this was not a gathering of friends on a country estate, as you well know. Did you know your friend Fitzgerald would be there?"

"Of course I did not." Eliza sat up, drawing the sheet around her. He, too, sat up, leaning against the carved headboard, his arms crossed over his bare chest.

"I did not know Edward would be there," she repeated. "He is meant to be in hiding, of course, but he sometimes takes ill-considered risks."

"He is not the only one," Will muttered.

No, he was certainly not, she thought sadly. It had been foolish of her to break into the office, not realizing he was following her. It had been foolish of her to take Will to the ceilidh, no matter what her hopes or memories were. Such gatherings were always peaceful, a time to dance and sing—and remember what they truly fought for.

But Will was not just *her* Will now; he was Major Denton. And she was fortunate he had not turned in Edward on the spot, and her with him.

"I suppose he is not the only one to take risks," she said. "I should not have put you in such a position, disguised or not. And I am sure General Hardwick and his daughter do not care for you associating with me at all."

Will frowned. "What have the Hardwicks to do with anything?"

"They are your friends. I swear to you, Will, I did not want to get either of us into trouble tonight. I just . . ."

"You just what?"

Eliza sighed, leaning back on the bed so she did not have to look at him. "I thought about what you said, about how we are all Irish. Once, it seemed you loved this country as I do. I just wanted you to remember."

"Oh, Eliza, I *do* remember." He reached down and took her hand, holding it closely, their fingers interlaced. "All those years so far away, I longed for home. For the green, cool wildness of it all. It's a part of me, just as it is of you."

"Then how can you stay in the army? How can you bear to be a part of all that oppresses us, if this is your home? If you love Ireland?" she asked, aching with sadness and confusion. He held her hand, yet it seemed he was even farther away from her than when he had been in the West Indies.

"You have not changed, my dear," he said, his voice heavy with a sadness of his own. "You were always so full of dreams of perfection, of idealism. Of a complete sense of right and wrong and who you are."

"Not with everything," she said. She obviously had no

sense of right and wrong when it came to him. "But for too long, Ireland has been in chains. And they tighten every day."

She climbed out of bed, snatching up her dressing gown from a chair and wrapping it around herself. The velvet and swansdown were not much of an armor, but it would have to serve. Will sat up in bed, watching her warily.

Eliza took up a book from the stack on the mantel. "Paine says, 'All men are born equal and with equal rights.' That surely also means 'equal political rights,' the right to elect an assembly to write a constitution and then govern by it, as the Americans do. Free of the English taking advantage of our resources, burning up our country and leaving us with the dregs."

She stared down at the volume in her hands, the worn leather binding soft. "The Penal Laws, the embargo on exportation, the unjust imprisonments. Absentee landlords who ruin their land and people out of greed—it has gone on too long. Ireland must be free to find her own destiny."

The gold lettering on that cover blurred, and she found to her chagrin that she was crying. That got her nowhere. She had been strong for so long; she had to be so now. Too much was at stake.

Will followed her out of the bed, twisting the sheet around his waist. Slowly, gently, he took the book from her hands. "I, too, have read Paine. His ideas are beautiful simplicity, I admit, and America is enviable in what they have accomplished. There *are* injustices from Westminster and the Castle; I cannot deny it. But violence will not gain what you want."

Eliza impatiently wiped at her cheeks. "I do not advocate violence!"

"Then you agree that to work from within the political system to effect reform is better? Is indeed the only way to bring about change, as your family's Whig friends declare?"

"Only a very small proportion of the Irish are even allowed in Parliament," she protested. "And they are all Ascendancy, Protestant aristocracy. Their interests are served by kowtowing to Westminster, in blocking any expansion of political power. Only a complete change will set Ireland free."

Suddenly deeply weary, her head aching, Eliza sat down, rubbing at her temples. Will knelt beside her, his hands braced on her knees as he gazed up at her steadily, sympathetically. How very calm he was—damn him!

"Complete change of the sort your friend Fitzgerald advocates would come at a very high price," he said. "Indeed, it already has in the north. Murder, burnings, looting—on both sides."

"Once Dublin Castle is emptied and there is a National Convention, a republic—"

"And how can that be without violence? Without the suffering of innocent people—people like Anna and Caroline."

"Oh no." Eliza shook her head, trying to snatch her hands away from him. But he held fast. "You cannot involve my sisters."

"But they *are* involved. We all are, if it comes to rebellion and civil war. I have seen battle, Eliza my dear. The blood and pain, the terrible suffering. It never leaves me, and I would do anything—anything—to save you from those horrors."

Eliza feared she would cry again, weep at the hidden

passion in his words. At what he must have suffered, her beautiful, darling Will.

"It will not be that way," she whispered. "Not here."

"It is always that way—especially here," he said. "Ireland has long been watered with blood and suffering. I could not bear it if even a drop of that blood was yours."

Eliza bent her head to kiss the rumpled silk of his hair, inhaling deeply of his scent, his essence. Trying to memorize everything about him, about this moment. The blood spilled would more likely be his. Warfare was his profession, and he was determined to do his duty.

And she could not bear *that*. Could not bear to think of his bright glow extinguished.

He turned his face up to hers, capturing her lips with his. Their kiss was tender but tinged with desperation and longing. With the terrible knowledge of time and love slipping away.

Will threaded his fingers through her hair, holding her to him as their tongues twined and tasted. He rose up on his knees, leaning into her as if they could become one in truth, could absorb into each other and never be apart.

His kiss slid from her lips and along her arched throat as he parted her dressing gown. The tip of his tongue tasted the soft curve of her breast, flicking over her nipple as she gasped. Her eyes closed, her body falling back in the chair, but he showed no mercy. He pressed his open mouth to her abdomen, to the cluster of pale freckles on her hip.

Then he slid the velvet cloth back from her legs, parting her thighs wider as his finger slid inside of her.

Eliza closed her eyes, every sense focused on that one delicious spot, on his touch. He gently parted her wet, petal-like folds, and she felt the slide of his tongue, tasting her very essence. Teasing her.

"Will!" she cried, clasping his hair to push him away—or to pull him closer.

It seemed even more intimate than their sex had been, his mouth on her, tasting, savoring, giving such wondrous pleasure she could hardly bear it. She had never let anyone do that before, and now she knew why—it bound them together in trust. It was overwhelming.

Her head arched against the cushions of the chair as her release swept over her, wave upon wave of pure, hot pleasure.

He kissed the soft skin of her inner thigh, the sensitive little spot just behind her knee. His hand slid down her leg to her foot, until he could press its arch to his bare chest, staring up at her in a silence that thundered louder than any words.

He pressed his lips to her ankle before letting her go, collapsing back to the floor with his arm over his face. Eliza sank down beside him, drawing him against her as he rested his head on her shoulder. She listened to the rush of his breath, the beat of his heart. He was *alive;* they were alive, and together. It was perfection.

But when she closed her eyes, feeling his hot skin under her touch, she saw blood. Rivers of it, drowning them both in its suffocating tides.

Chapter Eleven

The foyer of the Henrietta Street house had surely never seen such chaos, Eliza thought. Trunks and bandboxes were stacked high, an impenetrable mountain range traversed by hurrying servants striving to carry them all out the door. Outside in the street waited the baggage cart and the carriage to take Anna back to Killinan.

Eliza tried to keep herself busy counting the trunks, tried not to think of how big and echoing the house would be when her sister was gone. She would be alone then, with her fears and hopes and worries. With thoughts of Will.

Anna came clattering down the stairs, tying the ribbons of her cloak over her wool traveling dress. She held a packet of books in the crook of her arm, and her maid followed with the locked box containing Mama's precious tiara.

"Do you have everything, sister?" Eliza asked. "All your new purchases?"

Anna laughed, gesturing to the heaps of trunks. "If I forgot anything, I doubt I shall miss it for days! It will take a fortnight to unpack. But I have Mama's and Caro's gifts in this case here; that's the important thing."

Eliza kissed her cheek, holding her close. Anna hugged her back, and Eliza remembered Will's words. Innocents would suffer. But not her sisters, never that. Eliza would protect them with her own life if need be.

"I have loved having you here with me, Anna," she said.

"Even when I was a nuisance at the gaming tables?"

"Even then."

"Well, I have loved being here. We see too little of you at home, sister, and we miss you."

"That will change soon. I promise." Eliza kissed Anna once more and let her go. "Remember what I said—take care of Mama and Caro."

"I will, always. But what of you, Eliza?"

"I will take care of myself."

"I know you will, but you don't have to. Come back to Killinan with me, please."

Eliza laughed. "There would be no room for me, with all these trunks! I will come in a few weeks, when the Season is over."

Anna's pale blue eyes narrowed. "Because you love the social whirl so very much?" she said doubtfully.

"Something like that."

"Of course." Anna smoothed on her gloves and straightened her hat. "Say good-bye to Will Denton for me. It was lovely to see him again." And then she was gone.

Eliza stood at the window, watching until Anna turned the corner and there was only the usual morning bustle on the street. Then she went back upstairs to her chamber, locking the door securely behind her before going to her desk. There was much work to be done here, indeed, but not on the "social whirl."

She had a task to finish before she could beat any kind of retreat to Killinan.

Anna leaned back on the carriage seat, gazing out the window as the miles bounced by. The grand, wide, pale streets of Dublin had given way to the sooty outskirts and then to open countryside.

Rolling hills, yellow-green under the gray winter sky, seemed to flow on forever, broken up by low black stone walls snaking their way up the slopes. Stands of silvery-pale ash trees and ornate iron gates hinted of homes hidden somewhere beyond those never-ending fields.

Despite the cold, a few hardy cows grazed, almost the only signs of life for miles. She saw no people at all.

It made her think of Dublin late at night, the streets empty and windows darkened. The sounds of patrols in the distance and the echo of that hateful "Croppies Lie Down" song. The fear had been palpable, an acrid odor on the air.

And all her dancing, champagne drinking, and card-playing had not been enough to erase the foreboding, to keep away the rumors of unrest, murder, rape.

She turned to the book lying open on her lap, a Gothic romance of haunted castles and a dark, tormented man, the innocent maiden caught under his terrible spell. How she loved such tales! Loved their images of an enchanted world full of danger and romance. They often kept her awake at night, turning their pages in a feverish haste and then lying awake in the dark imagining all sorts of terrors. Those tales did not seem so wondrous now, with true dangers lurking around every corner.

She shut the book with a snap, tucking it away in her valise. If such dangers came, how would she react? With tears and shrieks and swooning, like those fictional maidens? With courage and fortitude like Eliza?

She feared it would be the former.

Suddenly, the carriage felt so small, so confining, the tufted leather walls closing around her. She lowered the window and called out, "Can we stop for a moment, John? I wish to walk a bit."

Her maid, Rose, peered nervously outside. "Oh, my lady, 'tis perishing cold outside! And no one is about at all."

"It's only for a moment, Rose. I need some fresh air. You can stay here, if you like."

One of the footmen helped her to alight, and she hurried along the edge of the road, back in the direction they came. The wind *was* cold against her face, shocking her out of her nebulous forebodings.

Perhaps Mama was right, she thought. Perhaps novels were a danger, and she should read more history and philosophy. Like Caroline, who never seemed to worry about anything in her calm, scholarly serenity.

Anna dashed along a pathway leading away from the road, through a stile in a rough stone wall. The path twined up a wooded hillside, and from its flat summit she would be able to see for miles.

She took off her hat, letting the wind ruffle her blond hair. There were endless fields, endless expanses of pale green dotted with those dark cows and a few whitewashed cottages. The solid gray hulk of a great house loomed in the distance. It all seemed so quiet, so still, like a painting.

Anna shielded her eyes from the milky light, gazing farther down the road that eventually led to Killinan. At the crossroads was what appeared to be a scaffold, with the dreaded wooden triangle used for flogging suspected United Irishmen. Blessedly, it was empty today, but she still shivered at the sight of it.

"And what do you do here, miss?" a man's deep voice suddenly said, almost making her jump out of her skin.

She spun around to find him standing behind her, just at the edge of the hill's crest. A horse pawed the ground at the foot of the hill, but she had been too preoccupied with the scenery and her own worries to even notice his approach. If the rebellion and civil war *did* come, she would certainly be completely useless.

Anna sucked in a deep breath, steadying herself as she studied the man before her. And what a man he was, like a character in one of her novels—the mysterious, dangerous antihero lurking in a storm-swept castle. He was tall, broad-shouldered, and well muscled under his brown wool riding coat and doeskin breeches. Black hair fell in unruly waves over his brow, his craggy face shadowed by a growth of dark whiskers. Green eyes, so pale they seemed almost silver, burned as they glared at her.

What right did *he* have to glare at *her*? He was the one who crept up on her. Anna stiffened her shoulders, glaring right back. Perhaps if she acted like she was not afraid, she could forget that cold pit of terror in her stomach at the sight of him.

"I was traveling through and wanted a breath of air," she said, with far more bravado than she felt. Her pride would not let her do what she really wanted—to run back down the hill and throw herself into the carriage, far away from those angry green eyes.

"Well, you are breathing the air on *my* property," he said. His voice was deep and rough but touched with the lilt of an Irish accent.

"I saw no sign or locked gate," she said. "And even if it is your property, as you say, I am doing no harm."

"You shouldn't be wandering around the countryside on your own, girl," he said. "'Tis foolish in these days. You never know what villains may be lurking in wait."

If there were any villains lurking, it was surely him, Anna thought with a shiver. He seemed so perfect in the part that he might have been cast from the Crow Street Theater! Dark, powerful, brooding . . .

And handsome, too, she saw in surprise as the wind tossed his hair back from his face. Not conventionally handsome, as her sister's golden Will was, but compelling nonetheless. A dark Donn, the Celtic lord of death.

He was quite right—she should not be wandering about alone. Not with men around who made her feel like this. She was terrified, excited, exhilarated, all at once.

"Who are you, sir?" she said, trying for something of her mother's unshakeable dignity. Lady Killinan's haughtiness always kept the world at bay.

Obviously, it did not work, for he smiled at her in a sudden flash of infuriating amusement. She saw he was not just handsome—he was gorgeous. Alluring, enticing, masculine, in a way all her yapping, puppyish Dublin suitors could not even approach.

Anna struggled to hold on to that flimsy, false dignity, even as she could not quite breathe.

"Who am I?" he said lazily, taking a slow, loose-limbed step toward her. "That's hardly important, miss. The question is, who are you? And why haven't I seen you before?"

"I . . . I hardly think we have any mutual friends, sir," she managed to say. Confused, she turned to run down the hill, away from this strange man and the spell he seemed to cast around her.

But he was a magic being, for he was beside her in a silent flash of movement, grasping her wrist in his hard, ungloved hand. It did not hurt; indeed, he seemed to exert no effort at all, yet she could not escape him. His heat and power surrounded her, burning away the winter day. Anna shuddered.

"I am quite certain we don't move in the same circles, colleen," he muttered, reaching out with his other hand to touch the fine fur edging of her cloak. "I know no English princesses."

"I'm not English!" Anna protested, thinking of Eliza's oft-repeated admonition—the Blacknalls were *Irish* and had been for generations.

"You speak like an Englishwoman," he said, his touch sliding up the soft fur. His gaze followed, his eyes as dark as fine emeralds now. "Are you on your way to Castletown, mayhap? For one of the Conollys' grand parties?"

Anna suddenly wrenched away, unable to bear his nearness another minute. She feared she would faint, like one of those ninny heroines in her novels. "It is none of your business who I am, sir, or where I am going!" she said, running back down the hill. Running away from him and her unladylike feelings.

But his laughter followed her, full of mocking amusement. "You would do well to heed my words, colleen," he called after her. "Go home and bar your doors."

She did not slow down until she threw herself back into the carriage. "Drive on!" she shouted. "Quickly."

Rose stared at her with wide eyes. "Is something amiss, my lady?"

Anna shook her head, trying to catch her breath. "I am just eager to get home." She craned her neck to stare out the window, but the road behind them was empty.

Had the whole scene been nothing but her overly vivid imagination, then?

"Do you know whose land this is, Rose?" she asked, gesturing to the fields and woods outside.

"I think it is the Duke of Adair's land, my lady."

"Adair?" That name seemed familiar. Anna searched her memory of county gossip. Then she remembered—the reclusive Irish Duke of Adair, the last of an ancient line, had been in a dispute with his Protestant cousin over the estate. But that had been years ago. "I thought he lost the estate."

"He got it back, my lady. Though who knows how long that will last, these days. You need to stay away from men like that. They're terribly dangerous."

Anna could well believe that that man wrested back his property, even under the weight of the Penal Laws against Irish landowners. Surely he always fought for, and won, everything he wanted. And she knew he was dangerous.

She leaned her head back with a sigh, closing her eyes. "We'll soon be home," she whispered. And as soon as the doors of Killinan closed behind her, she would surely forget her strange encounter with the enigmatic Duke of Adair.

Chapter Twelve

I think I have the high card! I take this trick," Lady Connemara said. "What of you, Lady Mount Clare? Have you anything higher?"

Eliza glanced up, startled to find herself still at the Connemaras' card party. Her thoughts were still on the proofs of her latest pamphlet, on its way to a secret printing press in a courier's saddlebag.

"Oh no," she said, quickly studying the cards in her hand. "You do win the trick, Lady Connemara. Shall we deal again?"

"It's hardly surprising we are all so distracted," Lady Connemara said as her partner, Lord Banning, nodded. "What with rumors racing through Dublin and preparations for war galloping apace. I'm tempted to barricade myself in my chamber until all is over!"

"My brother, General Hardwick, is in charge of fortifying the old city walls," Mrs. Easton said, shuffling the cards again for another hand of whist. "He says the stones are ancient and crumbling and the mortar full of gaps, especially in the south. How can such a flimsy barricade hold out the French, I ask you?"

"I wouldn't worry, Mrs. Easton," Lord Banning said. "That's what our fine army is for! They won't let any Frenchies or any damned Irish pikemen through. Those cowards will run at the first hint of real battle."

Eliza glanced across the room at Will, who sat by the window playing backgammon with Miss Hardwick. Despite herself, she felt a pang of jealousy at the sight of their blond heads bent near each other.

"I do hope your sister will make it home in safety, Lady Mount Clare," Lady Connemara said. "I vow I would not care to be on the roads these days."

"I'm sure she will be fine," Eliza said.

"In Kildare?" Mrs. Easton asked worriedly. "I have heard the place is full of rebels, hiding in the woods and bogs."

"Perhaps we would all be better off in the country," Lady Connemara said as distant cannon fire boomed like approaching thunder. They had been testing the guns along those crumbling walls all day and now were doing so into the night.

"At least there, in our own homes, we could see to our own fortifications," Lady Connemara went on, gesturing to the footmen to serve more wine to steady everyone's nerves.

"Not if we can't trust our own servants," Mrs. Easton said, watching suspiciously as her glass was filled by one of the footmen.

"I shouldn't worry," Lord Banning said again, drinking heartily. "I hear General Lake will soon be in charge of the entire forces. Now, there is a man who knows how to nip rebellion in the bud!"

Lake—a man who was an utter brute, Eliza thought, remembering tales of his doings in the north, including burnings, floggings, and torture. With such a man in charge, surely these things would spread over the whole country like wildfire.

And would he draw Will into such horrors, too? Even good men could fall into brutality in the red haze of war.

She looked at him again. He smiled gently at Miss Hardwick as the young lady blushed back. No, Eliza could not see such brutality from him; it would destroy him. And destroy her, too, to see it.

"Will you also go back to Kildare, Lady Mount Clare?" Lady Connemara asked, studying her new hand of cards.

"Perhaps," Eliza murmured, shifting the cards in her own hand. "My mother and sisters are quite alone there, and I find I miss them."

"I should go soon, then," Lord Banning said. "Before the roads become quite impassable with the fighting."

The card games ended soon after that, servants setting up refreshment tables as everyone milled about. There was laughter, gossip, and flirtation, as usual, even as the guns boomed in the distance, lighting up the night sky.

Eliza took a cup of tea from one of the tables, standing by the window to watch those red flashes against the darkness. She caught a glimpse of Will's reflection in the glass, standing right behind her as he, too, watched the cannon fire. She did not turn to him, but her every sense was attuned to his presence. To everything about him.

"Can I see you tonight?" he whispered.

Before she could answer, the drawing room door flew open and a dusty messenger hurried in, still wearing his riding boots. Silence fell like a storm cloud over the company as everyone turned to the intruder. Excitement on a dull evening at last!

Lady Connemara rose from her seat, her hand pressed to her throat. "What is this?" she said tightly.

"I beg your pardon, my lady," the butler said, dashing in after the messenger. "He insisted on speaking to his lordship at once."

"Speak to me of what?" Lord Connemara said, taking his wife's arm. "We have guests."

The messenger ignored that, striding forward to hand Lord Connemara a sealed letter. "As a magistrate of Westmeath, you are needed at the Castle at once."

Lord Connemara broke the seal, hastily scanning the message, his face turning white.

"What is it?" Lady Connemara whispered. "The children . . ."

"Nothing like that, Marianne." He did not look at her, just crumpled the paper in his hand. "I will come at once." His gaze swept the startled party. "And I suggest all the officers here return to their homes and wait for their own orders."

As Lord Connemara hurried away with the messenger, leaving a sudden excited clamor behind him, Eliza spun around to face Will. His expression was tight, blank, giving nothing away at all.

"I will come to you later, Eliza," he said quickly. "I know it is probably futile to say this, but please go home. Stay quiet tonight."

She nodded. She *would* go home, but she would send

messages from there, too. She had to find out what was about to happen, one way or another.

Eliza lit the branch of candles on her desk, watching as they flared into bright, flickering light one by one. The rest of the chamber was deep in blackness, as was the night outside her window. Only distant, ominous fires lit the sky at its edges.

As she lit the last taper, she caught sight of her reflection in the mirror. For an instant, she was launched back in time to confront her younger self. Her hair fell over her shoulders in unruly waves, and her eyes were very large, dark, and as frightened as a doe's in her pale face. Will was leaving very soon. She was sure of it. And this time he would not come back.

But she wore a garment her younger self would never have possessed. On a whim, she had purchased the dressing gown on her last shopping expedition with Anna and then immediately regretted it. It was a frivolous bit of sheer, pale blue silk trimmed with lace and white satin rosebuds. It skimmed over her body like a light caress, parting provocatively over the bosom and tied with satin ribbons. Beneath it, she wore nothing at all.

Yet now the gown felt foolish. He had said he would come to her tonight, and he was not there.

"Blast it all," she muttered, reaching for the delicate satin ribbons. She would put on her sensible night rail and go to bed—alone. But as she pulled the first ribbon free, there was a rustle at the open window, the sound of a booted footfall on the floor.

"It would be a shame to waste such a charming gown," Will said.

Eliza whirled around, pressing a hand to her pounding heart. "Will! I thought you weren't coming. After the party—"

"Sorry for my tardy appearance." He closed the window behind him and pulled off his coat and cap. "Ran into a patrol near the river."

"Did they give you trouble?"

"Of course not. I am quite adept now at taking cover when needed." He grinned at her. "And I absolutely must mention again how fetching that gown is."

Eliza laughed, sitting on the edge of the desk, dangling her bare feet above the floor. "I just thought you might."

"It is most . . . charming. I'm glad you listened to me for once and came home after the party." He crossed the chamber in two strides, his eyes dark with intent in the candlelight. He clasped her waist as he stepped between her legs, drawing her close against him as if there was no time to lose.

As their lips met in a welcoming kiss, one of his hands slid up over her ribs to balance her breast on his palm, massaging and squeezing gently through the thin silk. His fingertips circled her nipple, rubbing the cloth against the aching, pebbled skin. Eliza moaned.

"Eliza, Eliza. You are so very beautiful," he whispered, lowering his head to take that swollen nipple into his mouth, wet and hot through the silk.

She buried her fingers in his hair, holding him close to her as the sensations grew deep in her stomach, hotter, tighter, until she feared they would snap and send her spinning off into the night sky.

"I think that you, Major Denton," she gasped, "are entirely overdressed."

She grabbed the hem of his shirt, dragging it up over his head. The cold night air washed over the damp silk of her robe, her breasts, and she trembled as she went about her task.. She unfastened his breeches, easing the rough wool down until his manhood was free, as stiff as iron.

His arms tensed around her as he swung her off the desk. They fell to the floor, still tangled in their kiss, their frantic caresses, as if they were starved for the taste and the feel of each other.

He impatiently tugged the gown from her shoulders, snapping the ribbons as the silk drifted around them in a sky-blue cloud. Through her closed eyes, through that shimmering haze of dreamlike lust, she felt him draw her down, down, until their kiss slid away, and she lay on her elbows and knees against the rough carpet.

She felt his presence behind her, the hunger in his touch as his hands stroked the length of her spine. He traced the soft curve of her backside and then her thighs as he parted them.

He drew her back and up, sliding inside her from that angle, deep and swift. So deep he could surely touch her very core, her soul. He held her still against him, his hands tight on her hips as he pumped into her, his body hot as it arched over hers.

She moaned, curving back into him as she reveled in the tight joining of their bodies, the intense, frightening intimacy of the moment. His sweat mingled with hers, their breath and heartbeats as one.

The pressure built and built inside of her, hotter, tighter, until at last it broke, a shower of intense, unbearable pleasure that erased all else for an instant. Above her, Will shouted out her name, and she felt the warmth of him deep inside her.

She collapsed, weak and sated, to the floor. He fell down next to her, his arms still around her, his shoulders heaving with his ragged breath as he turned his face toward the wall. Eliza caressed his damp shoulder, his back, the tangled length of his hair. *How beautiful he is,* she thought tiredly, exultantly. And he was hers, even if he was leaving soon.

They lay there for long moments as Eliza felt her heartbeat slow. The chamber grew cold around them as the fire in the grate died and the candles sputtered lower. Will sat up beside her, gathering her into his arms and lifting her with him from the floor. He laid her gently on her bed, climbing in beside her as he drew the blankets close around them. She curled into his arms, sighing with sleepy contentment.

"Tell me a story," Will muttered, kissing her tumbled hair.

Eliza laughed. "What sort of story? A naughty one? I fear I don't know any of *those.*"

"Tell me an Irish story, then," he said. "You always knew those."

"There are *Three Sorrowful Tales of Erin,*" she said, remembering those childhood tales she loved. "And the first is the tale of Deirdre of the Sorrows."

"She sounds most unhappy."

"Oh, of course. She was born on the night of a full moon, a sidhe moon, and when her father took her to the druids to be blessed, they said, 'This child will be the cause of much trouble. She will be the most beautiful woman in Ulster, but she will cause the deaths of many men.'

"King Connor heard of this girl and declared that she should be reared far from the kingdom, deep in the forest under the care of an old woman, and when she was of age, he would marry her himself. As foretold, Deirdre grew to be very beautiful, but very lonely. One night she dreamed of a handsome, fearless warrior, and she could never forget him. When she met her dream warrior in truth, she found he was named Naoise, one of the sons of Uisneach, and they fell in love with each other at once. Deirdre knew she could never marry Connor, and she and Naoise fled. No one in Ireland would take them in, fearing the wrath of the king, and finally they set sail for a foreign shore. They made their home on a Scottish island and lived happily there together for five years. Until a message arrived from the king."

"Never a good sign," Will said.

"Shh," Eliza said, laughing. "I am the one telling this story. Anyway, the king's messenger conveyed forgiveness and asked Deirdre and Naoise to return home to Ulster. Deirdre did not believe the king and wanted to stay in their new home, but Naoise, being a trusting man, insisted they go back."

"I think perhaps Naoise is foolish."

"Indeed. For no sooner did they enter the king's fortress than they were surrounded by an army. Naoise and his brothers fought bravely, but they were outnumbered. Poor Naoise had his head cut off, and so vast was Deirdre's sorrow that she fell upon his body and joined him in death."

Eliza glanced down to find that Will had fallen asleep in her arms. She kissed his forehead softly. "I wish you would not go into the realm of King Connor tomorrow," she whispered. But she knew that, even as Deirdre could not stop Naoise from obeying his king, she could not stop Will. They both had to do what they must, even when sorrows abounded around them.

Chapter Thirteen

Will paced the length of the Castle corridor and back again, his boots echoing hollowly on the cold stone floor. There was little to distract him in that barren space—a few chairs and some unsmiling portraits of past government officials. Their painted images still looked most disgruntled at being asked to control this wild, barbaric land.

Or perhaps they had just encountered a stubborn ancestor of Eliza Blacknall's.

He glanced toward the door leading to the conference room. The wood panels were stout, so nothing could be heard beyond them. He was just there to get his orders and be about his business.

He remembered life in the islands and how simple it had seemed despite the heat and fevers, with the sporadic, violent bursts of warfare interspersed with the lassitude of long, empty days. It was too humid and languid for passionate firebrands like Eliza and her friends to concoct rebellions. But here in Ireland, that restless spirit of independence ran deep into the earth itself, a longing nothing could extinguish. Perhaps there was even a kernel of it hidden inside himself. But that didn't take away his duty.

The door to the council room opened at last, a footman ushering Will inside. General Hardwick waited there alone, his face gray and tired beneath his neatly powdered wig.

"Major Denton," he said, gesturing to a chair. "Please, sit. I am sorry you were kept waiting. Our work is never done these days. Will you take some wine?"

"No, thank you, General Hardwick."

"Ah, yes. You are eager to hear your orders, I imagine, to get to work, as we all are."

"Waiting takes a toll on the men, it is true."

"But you have been most admirable in keeping your troops busy, Major. Drilling them and putting them through their paces."

"We are ready to march when the time comes," Will said.

General Hardwick tapped at a pile of papers before him, official-looking documents bearing Castle seals. "General Lake is on his way south to take command," he said tightly, as if he did not entirely care for Lake's new command or the man's brutal reputation. As Will did not. Brutality only drove the people closer to the United Irish, away from British rule.

"The Thirteenth is to go to Wexford," the general said. "Tomorrow."

"Wexford?" Will said, his jaw tight.

"Our informers tell us the Catholic Defenders have allied with the United Irishmen and are especially strong there, so trouble is expected any day. A strong military showing will cut them off. I myself will lead a contingent to Carlow."

"I am ready to depart, General Hardwick," Will said. A day was not much time at all, but surely it was enough to persuade Eliza to take her family and leave the country. One way or another.

"Well, that is the thing, Major Denton. I have a different request for you."

"A different request? Am I not to go to Wexford with my regiment?" Will asked, puzzled.

"Of course, eventually. They could hardly do without you. But for now, Lord Camden asks you to go home."

"Home?" Will was thoroughly confused now and angry, too. Was his loyalty now being called into question? Was he being shunted away to keep him out of trouble—and to keep from doing Eliza any good?

"You are from Kildare, are you not?" the general said.

"Yes, sir. My family is at Moreton Manor."

General Hardwick shook his head. "A most dangerous place, Kildare. Full of Foxite families with strange liberal ideas. And the terrain is as dangerous as the populace. The Bog of Allen is the perfect place for rebels to lurk and ambush our soldiers who do not know the land."

Will laughed humorlessly. "I am certainly aware of the bog, General. But my own family is scarcely Foxite."

"Indeed not. Lord Camden has received a request from Prime Minister Pitt himself that Lady Moreton be given a passport to England and a berth on a ship immediately."

"No doubt my mother wishes to join my father in London."

"And be away before trouble starts. Very wise of her. In

fact, I am sending my own wife and daughter to England before the week is out."

"I am sure Dublin will greatly miss their presence."

General Hardwick smiled. "As will I. But I am sure they will return very soon, and Ireland will be peaceful and loyal once more. With your help."

"My help, sir?"

"Kildare is quiet enough for the present, but that will surely not last long. We need you to go there for a time to keep an eye on events."

"To spy?" Will said tightly. "I fear that is not my way, General."

"Nay, not *spy,* Major. Alert us to danger. It will be for only a short time, and then you must rejoin your regiment."

"Where am I to be lodged? In a barracks?"

"We thought you might stay at Moreton Manor. Such a strategic location, it should not be left empty when Lady Moreton has departed."

"And what precisely am I to . . . keep an eye on, General?"

"Whatever seems suspicious, I believe." General Hardwick reached inside a leather pouch, drawing out a thick bundle of papers. "For instance, our soldiers recently raided a home near Kilrush and found an illegal United Irish printing press. They broke up the press and seized these."

He handed them to Will, who quickly rifled through them. Among the leaflets and pages from Paine and Rousseau was a smudged pamphlet. *Proposals for the Prosperity and Independence of Ireland,* written By A Lady Patriot.

"The proprietors of the press were arrested, of course," the general said. "Respectable merchants of the town, no one had suspected them. They claim they do not know the authors of these works. Perhaps a time in Kilmainham Gaol and the threat of execution will sharpen their memories. In the meantime, Kildare can no longer be neglected."

"And so I am the one to remedy this neglect?" Will said, carefully placing the pamphlet on the table.

"You will hardly be alone, Major. Regiments are being posted there as we speak. But none of our other officers know the country as you do."

"I have been away from there a long time."

"Yet they will surely be more likely to trust you than someone like myself." General Hardwick leaned closer. "And it will be a chance for you to take care of your own family and friends, Major Denton. To keep them safe, assure them of their best interests."

Will thought of his mother, no doubt frightened out of her wits. Of the Blacknalls at Killinan Castle. The houses and lands he loved. Of Eliza and her damnable seditious pamphlets that could get her killed. "Then I shall go, of course."

"Very good, Major," the general said, handing him a rolled document. "Here are your orders. You can leave on the morrow with your escort. And now, if you will excuse me, I must go and bid farewell to my own family."

"I hope you will send my best wishes to Mrs. and Miss Hardwick for a safe journey," Will said. "And a swift homecoming."

General Hardwick smiled sadly. "I'm sure they will

appreciate it, Major Denton, especially Lydia. Safe voyage to you as well."

Will made his way slowly from the council room, his fist wrapped around the orders. *Tomorrow*—it did not leave much time at all. But he had to persuade Eliza to give up her work now, to leave Ireland, or at least go back to Kildare with him and stay with her family.

Or he would have to learn to say good-bye to her all over again.

Chapter Fourteen

When do you go?" Eliza said quietly. She stared out
her chamber window at the darkened street below,
but she did not see it, not really. She only knew Will's
words.

He was leaving Dublin.

She had known it was coming, of course, when he left
the card party. But she still felt the cold, wintry chill of
loneliness.

"Tomorrow," he answered.

She looked back over her shoulder to find him by the
fireplace, his arm braced on the mantel as he watched the
crackling flames. She could not read his face at all, the angles of it thrown into sharp, harsh relief by the glow. Yet his
back and shoulders were rigid, his hands curled into fists. It
was as if he was already gone from her.

"So soon?" she said.

"I have my orders. Events proceed apace, it seems."

"Where are you going?"

He did glance at her then, but the smile on his lips held

no humor. "Why, Eliza? Do you want to tell your friends of our movements?"

Was that truly what he thought of her? Eliza flattened her palms on the windowsill, feeling the painted wood pressing roughly on her skin. If only physical pain would take away that blasted ache in her heart!

"I am not a spy," she said.

"Nor am I," he muttered. "But these are strange days we live in. Who knows what we will be forced to do?"

Eliza shook her head, her throat tight and aching. "Are you going far away?"

"I am first to travel to Moreton Manor. My mother is leaving for England and requires my assistance. Then . . . who knows."

"Moreton?" She pushed back from the window, joining him by the fire. They stood merely feet away, yet it felt like miles. "Will you be able to look in on my family, too? I worry about them."

"Of course I will. I'll do all I can for them. But perhaps you could come with me, take care of them yourself."

"Go with you?" Eliza stared at him in astonishment. "To Kildare?"

He nodded solemnly. "It would be safer for you if you had an escort, and I know you must miss them. It would be safer, too, if you were with your family. Your mother is above any suspicion."

"I do miss my family, very much. They are much on my mind of late," she said. She *did* miss them, even her mother, who she had so often quarreled with in the past. Missed them and worried about them.

"Then you will come?"

She shook her head. "I cannot go with you."

"Eliza!" He suddenly cracked his palm against the mantel, making her jump. The books and ornaments rattled. His eyes were dark with frustration, anger, and worry. "I am trying to *help* you. To see you safe."

"Safe? Surely none of us are that, not now."

"But you refuse to see the truth of this situation. You refuse to even try to take care of yourself."

Eliza covered her face with her hands, a fire of her own anger bubbling inside of her. "I have been taking care of myself for a long time, Will. Ever since you left, as a matter of fact."

He laughed bitterly. "And you are doing a marvelous job of it, Lady Democratical." She heard him shove away from the mantel and lowered her hands to watch him stride across the room to where he had dropped a valise on the floor. He pulled out a crumpled, smudged sheet of paper.

"What is that?" she said warily.

"Do you not recognize it?" As she stared at him, he seized her arm and held up the paper before her eyes.

Oh yes, she certainly recognized it. It was a page from her pamphlet. And it could only be an ill omen that he had it.

"Is this not your work?" he said, not letting her go. "I remember your writings from when we were young, your fine satirical style."

"Where did you get that?" she whispered.

"I got it at Dublin Castle," he answered. "A United Irish printing press was raided, and this was among the works."

"No!" Eliza cried out. She reached instinctively for the paper, shocked by the terrible news of yet more arrests. But he tossed it into the fire and seized her by the shoulders, holding her close.

"Eliza," he said roughly. "Look at me, damn it all!"

She raised her eyes to his face, and what she saw there frightened her. Her Will, her beautiful, lighthearted lover, was filled with fury—and dark desperation.

"Eliza," he said, suddenly terribly, terribly gentle. "Matters are about to become very serious. We can no longer escape it."

"I know," she whispered.

"If you are found to be the author of that pamphlet, you will be hanged. If you won't think of yourself, for God's sake think of me. Of your family."

She closed her eyes, swallowing hard as if she could already feel the rough hemp of the rope. "I do think of them." And of him—too much.

"Then let me see you to Killinan."

"I'm sorry, Will. But I can't go. I am too deeply pledged."

Will's lips tightened, as if he held back a spasm of pain. Or was it an angry curse?

She ached, too. Something precious and vital was breaking inside of her, falling into dust and blowing away in the cold wind as if it had never been.

"I am pledged as well. To my family, my work," he said. He raised her hands to his lips, kissing one, then the other, warm and lingering. "I will leave tomorrow. If you change your mind, send me word."

She nodded, but they both knew the truth. Neither of them could change their minds, abandon their course. They had to part, even as what they might have had, might have been, fell into ruin.

"Wait," she said. She hurried to her dressing table, taking a small portrait out of the drawer. It was not new; it had been painted when she married Mount Clare, a miniature of her young self framed in pearls. Maybe if Will had it, he would sometimes think of her, sometimes remember.

She pressed it into his hand, closing his fingers over it. "Take this with you, and . . . don't forget."

He gazed down at it for a long, silent moment before he kissed her lips, hard and desperate. She kissed him back, trying to memorize his taste, the way he felt in her arms. Remember everything. And then he was gone, vanishing out the window for what she knew in her heart was the last time.

Her knees suddenly felt too weak to hold her up, and she collapsed to the floor. She wanted to cry, but it seemed her tears were used up.

Will had been a precious gift in a dark time; she had always known he could not be hers forever. But now she saw that she had become greedy, because his loss broke her heart. It felt as if a part of her own body were torn away, leaving her cold and aching.

"I'm sorry, Will," she whispered.

Slowly, slowly, she took a deep breath and pulled back into herself again. She *had* chosen her path, rocky as it was, and she had to stay on it, moving forward one step at a time.

She rose to her feet, hurrying over to the window to close it against the night. The street was deserted again, silent in a deceptive peace. She drew the curtains shut and turned back to her room.

The pamphlet was mere bits of charcoal in the grate, but she well knew that other problems could never be made to disappear so easily.

Chapter Fifteen

Will's home at Moreton Manor was a handsome, re-spectable house, only a few decades old. Built of redbrick faced with gray stone, it would not have been out of place in London or Brighton. It was not as large as Killinan Castle, nor nearly as grand as Carton or Castle-town. But Will had always liked it and remembered it as welcoming—despite the people inside its walls.

Today, though, *welcoming* was not quite the right word for Moreton. *Chaotic* was more like it.

The front doors were wide open, servants carrying boxes and trunks down the stone front steps to the carts waiting in the drive. Even the windows were agape, maids leaning out to shout new instructions to those below.

It seemed his mother was in a great hurry to decamp, Will thought as he swung down from his horse. He was weary after the journey from Dublin, but there would ob-viously be no rest here today.

He left the horse with one of the grooms, striding past the harried servants and into the foyer. The marble floor was nearly covered by crates, with family portraits stacked along the walls. Even the draperies were gone from the windows.

"No, no! Do not place the box of silver on *top* of the china; it will be utterly crushed," he heard his mother cry, her panicked voice floating out of the drawing room.

Will peeled off his leather riding gloves, slapping them against his palm as he contemplated the shambles of his home. Surely General Hardwick was quite wrong—there was nothing he could do from here. The populace was in flight from a menace that was as yet invisible and thus even more fearsome.

He dodged around the crates, his spurs jangling as he entered the drawing room to find even more confusion. The pastel-green chamber, usually lined with glass-fronted cases full of china figurines, bits of antquities, and miniature portraits, was stripped. Maids were taking down the pale yellow draperies at the windows. The only thing still in place was the painting over the fireplace, a portrait of his mother seated on a bench in the Moreton Manor park, Will and his brother's childhood selves clinging to her silk skirts.

The real lady stood just beneath the painted one, directing the packing. Her blond hair was mostly gray now, strands of it escaping from her cap. Beneath its ruffles, her face was pale and strained, except for two bright spots of red in her cheeks.

"Not like that!" she cried, rushing across the room to grab the offending crate. "Must I do everything myself?"

Will strode across the wooden floor, bare of its carpets, to help the beleaguered footmen slide their burdens into place.

"William," his mother said, pushing back her loose hair as she stared at her long-gone son. "You have returned."

"So I have, Mother," he answered. "And just in time, it would seem. Are you going somewhere?"

Lady Moreton frowned at him. "You are as teasing as ever! Of course I am going somewhere; you are meant to bring my passports. I hope you did not forget them."

"It is lovely to see you, too, Mother," he said, kissing her cheek. "And, yes, I brought you your papers."

"There is not a moment to lose." She cast a suspicious glance at the servants hurrying around them. "Come with me."

She grabbed his hand, leading him out of the drawing room by a side door and along a back corridor. Will followed, curious as to what she was about. His mother had always been a nervous sort, prone to see the worst in situations. As the daughter and wife of staunch Tories, she disliked being in a county of Whig families and seemed to resent Will's father for running off to London without her so often and forcing her to stay behind.

Not that Will could entirely blame his father. He himself had always liked escaping to Killinan when he was young. Eliza and her family, despite their quarrels and disagreements, loved each other so much. Their teasing affection was a balm to a lonely young man's heart.

And when he fell in love with Eliza . . .

Eliza. The memory of their parting burned in his heart. When would he see her again? How could he keep her safe?

His mother led him into the library. Like the drawing room, it was denuded of its possessions, the books gone from the shelves, the paneled walls bare of his father's hunting prints. Canvas covers muffled the carved furniture too heavy to move.

And two of the tall windows were broken, the wall below them marred with black scorch marks.

"You see, William," she said, her voice trembling, "I must get away from here before they kill me."

Will knelt by the dark marks, examining the damage. It still smelled of smoke, the paneling buckled by flames and water. "What happened here?"

"They tried to burn us out, of course. Luckily, I was sleeping in here with some of the maids, and we managed to put out the fire."

Will looked back at her, trying to imagine his fragile mother putting out a fire. "Why were you sleeping in here?"

"There were rumors in the village of unrest. Lady Louisa Conolly and Lady Killinan went there to try talking to the tenants, to reason with them, the great fools. You cannot reason with animals!" Her voice rose. "I have always hated this loathsome place. I knew something like this would happen eventually."

He ran his fingertips over the wall, trying to fathom it. Someone had tried to burn Moreton Manor. Someone hated the Dentons that much.

"I could not sleep in my own chamber," his mother went on, twisting a handkerchief in her hands. "Just lying there in bed like some sacrificial victim. So I stayed down here, watching, and thank God I did or this house would be a ruin. Your brother's legacy, such as it is, would be gone."

Will laughed. He was quite certain his brother Henry would not have cared. He would have just built himself a villa in Italy and stayed there with his mistress forever. But *he* . . . he was furious someone would frighten his mother, threaten this house.

"I am glad you are home, William," his mother said. "You will find those villains and make them pay for their crimes."

Will took her in his arms, feeling her thin shoulders tremble as she sobbed against his chest.

"I was so frightened," she gasped. "They . . . they broke the windows with stones, shouting horrible things. Then they threw in the torches. So much smoke—I was sure we would all be killed."

"Shh, Mother," he said gently, even as his anger grew. "You are safe now. And soon you will be in England."

It was the crystalline crash of broken glass that tore Will out of his shallow sleep.

For an instant, he thought it was just another dream, brought on by his mother's hysterical fears and wild tales. But then he heard it again, the distant crackle of a breaking window downstairs.

He swung out of bed, still fully dressed, and reached for the loaded pistol he kept ready. Eliza's portrait sat next to it on the dressing table, her dark eyes watching him steadily.

"Not this time, Eliza" he muttered, swiping the portrait into a drawer. He could not think of her now. He hurried out of the bedchamber, standing poised on the staircase landing as he listened for any other sound. Less than one day home and it felt like an eternity. At least his mother slept now; tomorrow she would leave.

He had boarded up most of the windows that afternoon, and the house seemed a darkened cave, lit only by one lamp on a pier table outside his door. Obviously, trying to secure the house in any way was a futile endeavor, but the physical activity distracted him as he listened to his mother fretting.

Only when his muscles burned from the exertion and sweat trickled down his spine did he lose himself for a moment. His other work, trying to find useful information for the authorities, was no distraction at all. As he had warned Hardwick, he had no spying instincts, no acting skills. He had not been home in years, and no one would tell him a thing. The servants were all silent, stony, shrugging away all questions.

Which was a relief actually. He was a soldier, not a spy, and he disliked dealing in any underhanded methods. But was his work, his very identity, getting him into too much trouble now?

And trouble in his family's house. He crept lightly down the stairs, holding on to the pistol. All seemed silent now, and there was no whiff of smoke. Had he merely imagined it after all?

But, no, there it was again. The faint music of glass falling to the floor, coming from the library, where they had first tried to burn his mother out. Well, by God, they were not going to burn *him* out. He had as much right to be in Ireland as they.

Carefully, he eased back the library door, peering inside as he held the gun at the ready.

It was very dark, all the windows boarded except the small decorative frosted glass panels at the top. The panels were, or had been, etched with the Denton family arms.

Now they were shattered, as if the attackers were frustrated they could get no closer to the large windows.

Will's senses were heightened as they always were in battle. Now he could hear running footsteps on the gravel outside and could smell the hint of smoke at last.

He took off running down the corridor and through the foyer, under the sway of the crystal chandelier. He threw back the bolt of the front door, rushing out onto the front steps as a strange recklessness took hold of him. He had had enough of waiting, of worrying about Eliza. He needed *action* now.

As his gaze darted swiftly down the driveway, noting every ripple of the shadows, every cloud sliding around the cold moon, he saw they were *not* being invaded by a United army. One bush was on fire near the house, and three or four figures fled into the night.

But it was enough. Filled with that cold anger, Will leveled his pistol and fired after them. One man screamed and stumbled, his companions leaving him behind.

All Will's instincts cried out to capture him now, but the villain's pace was slowed. There were more urgent matters first.

Tearing off his shirt, he leaped off the front steps to beat at the bush. Its summer-dry branches snapped, the flames licking closer to the other trees and shrubbery. It was a small enough fire now, but if he had not been awakened, it would have done its work handily enough.

He knocked the flames out with his shirt, kicking at the last embers with his boot until there was only the smolder of a pile of charcoal. Then he slid his dagger from its sheath and prowled off after the fallen rebel.

He was not that difficult to find. The moon was bright,

the clouds vanished, and thick droplets of blood stood out on the pale gravel. It trailed away into the park, the footprints thick and blurry in the dirt.

Will found him collapsed in a pile of old leaves, moaning softly as he clutched at his shoulder. Will knelt down beside him, and as he turned him over, he recognized him. It was Tom O'Neil, the grandson of some of the estate pensioners. He couldn't be more than seventeen—too young to be out marauding at night, or trying to maraud anyway.

But he wore a white badge on his sleeve, the mark of the radical Catholic Defenders, violent allies of the United Irishmen. A badge now stained with blood.

"I see your friends have abandoned you, Tom," Will said.

The boy stared up at him with burning, hate-filled eyes. "I told them to go on. No sense letting a redcoat like you kill all of us."

Will glanced around cautiously, but it seemed Tom told the truth. He sensed no one else around them, waiting to jump out. But he still held his weapons ready.

"What makes you think I'm going to kill you?" Will asked.

"You shot me!" the boy cried.

"You're alive, aren't you? If you get it seen to soon, it will be nothing. A scar to brag about with your Defender cronies. You're lucky I didn't blast your whole arm off for terrorizing innocent women like my mother."

Despite his dire situation, despite the fear in his young eyes, Tom snorted. "I wouldn't say Lady Moreton is all that *innocent*. Been bleeding her tenants dry for years while you were off fighting for the limeys. But it weren't me who tried to burn her house."

Will felt the chilly night wind on his bare, sweat-streaked back. "I suppose that bush just happened to burst into flames by itself?"

"Don't you ever read the Bible, redcoat? Maybe it *was* me tonight, but that was just a warning. Weren't me the last time."

"Then who was it?"

"Don't know."

"Oh, I think you do, Tom. And I am tired of no one talking to me." Will suddenly tossed his dagger down, the blade's tip sinking in the dirt right by Tom's head.

The boy's eyes widened, and he tried to roll away. He fell back with a grunt of pain. "I don't know, I swear! Could be one of a dozen groups nearby. But it weren't us. We don't hurt women, not even ones like Lady Moreton."

Will glanced over the wound, still seeping blood. "It looks like you're losing more blood, Tom. We need to get you home to your grandmother."

Tom stared at him in suspicious disbelief. "You would take me home? You're not going to finish me off?"

"I just might. But I will take you home on condition that you tell me what I want to know of these dozen groups." Will pulled his dagger from the ground. "Especially any plans they might have for Killinan Castle and the ladies there."

Tom shook his head. "I don't know anything about Killinan, I swear!"

"Oh, Tom, I think you do." Will let the moonlight catch on the blade. "And I think you *will* tell me. Now."

Chapter Sixteen

Part Two, May 1798

I don't know what will become of us. A tithe collector was tossed off a bridge to his death yesterday, and there are nightly raids on local houses by rebels looking for arms. And I have your sisters to worry about! Anna thought someone followed her when she went for a ride last week on our own estate.

Eliza glanced up from her mother's letter, staring sightlessly out her open bedroom window. The spring days had turned hot and dry, with no welcome cool breeze stirring the green leaves. Outside, even now as the sun started to set and the day slid into evening, the sounds of war preparations went on: hammers, the slap of sandbags piling up, the firing of cannons, shouts and cries. It never ended.

She rubbed at her pounding temples with a rosewater-soaked handkerchief. It had been like that in Dublin for months. In March, sixteen United Irish leaders had been arrested at a meeting at Oliver Bond's house, and now only Edward Fitzgerald was free. But surely he would not be for long. There was a reward of a thousand pounds for his capture.

And the city was caught up in the scandal of the upcoming Kingston trial. The spectacle of a wealthy duke being tried for killing his pregnant daughter's seducer, his own wife's cousin, was a vivid distraction from rebellion, from what was happening in counties all over the Midlands and the south.

Martial law had been declared with free quarters—the forcing of private homeowners to give lodging to soldiers—imposed everywhere. There were rumors of the most violent measures to disarm Kildare. Floggings occurred at every crossroads, and in every village center, there were burnings and rape.

A United Irish suspect captured at Wexford had been pitchcapped, a cap of linen filled with gunpowder and tar slapped on his head and set alight, and in his agony had named names. Certainly more arrests would very soon follow.

And now Eliza's own family was caught in the maelstrom, just as she had long feared. Her mother hated to complain; it was beneath the dignity of a lady, she always said. And dignity and position were all to her. If she wrote these things to Eliza now, matters must be even worse than she said.

Eliza turned back to the letter, smoothing the pages on her desk.

So many of our neighbors have gone. Lady Moreton and your husband's mother at Mount Clare. Even

*Lady Conover. No one has yet disturbed the peace
here at Killinan, but perhaps I was mistaken to stay
here, with what happened to Anna. I fear we have
waited too long, though. They say Athey town is already occupied by the rebels.*

*I have visited Killinan village to assure them of
my loyalty to them and to ask for theirs. For have I
not cared for them all these years? Yet so many of
the young men are gone, and some of our own ash
trees have been cut down in the night for pikes. But
I am sure we will be safe here; this is our home,
after all.*

*Oh, Eliza, it has been too long since we have seen
you or had word from Dublin. I pray for your health
and safety. Your ever-loving mama.*

Eliza carefully folded the letter. It *must* be bad at Killinan, she thought sadly. Her mother did so pride herself on
her self-control, her propriety, her duty. She was called the
Angel of Kildare for her goodness and beauty. Between
those neatly penned lines, Eliza saw those traits cracking and falling away. Just like everything else in a world
catching fire.

She closed her eyes, picturing Killinan in her mind.
The green fields, the shelter of the cool woods, the beauty
of the gardens. Her home. But now the fields lay empty,
even as summer was upon them. The woods cleared for
pike handles and the house her great-grandfather had built
vulnerable.

And Will—where was he? What was he doing now?
Such thoughts plagued her over these months apart from
him, returning again and again even as she struggled to

push them away. Remembering and regretting did no good, and yet she could not stop.

She searched the newspapers every day in vain for word of the Thirteenth. Troop movements were guarded, except for the rumors that flew down the streets and around the drawing rooms. Sometimes she had the foolish hope he might write to her.

During the days, she lost herself in writing, in just moving through a fractured life. But at night . . . at night she could not sleep. The heat and her reeling thoughts kept her awake, tossing in her bed. And that was when she most remembered him.

She remembered everything they did in that very bed. Every whispered word, every kiss, the way he smelled and tasted. How very, very alive she felt in his arms.

Sometimes, also foolishly, she would close her eyes and feel again his head resting on her stomach. The long, rough silk of his hair as she ran her fingers through it, spreading it over her skin. His cool breath, the trace of his touch on her hip. The perfect moments there in the dark, when it was only the two of them. There was no army, no England or Ireland, just Eliza and Will. Nothing could touch them in that enchanted spell.

But that all seemed so very long ago. Years, centuries, rather than mere months. Winter had given way to the combustible heat of summer. Peace to war. Certainty to terrible doubt. And she was alone.

Well, not *entirely* alone, she thought as she stared down at her mother's letter.

She reached for her jewel case, lifting the enameled lid. The rosy-gold sunset light caught on the sparkle of diamonds, the glow of pearls, the mellow amber of her mother's hair combs. She lifted away the top tray to reveal the compartment beneath, which held the real treasures.

The pastel portrait of her with her sisters, which she had carefully removed from its frame and rolled up to place there. Her wedding ring, a reminder of where she had once been and would not return to.

She added her mother's letter and replaced the top tray, shutting it all up. As she reached for the bell to summon Mary, a loud noise suddenly tore through the tense, deceptively peaceful evening.

Eliza ran to the window, leaning over the sill to peer down at the street below. A contingent of soldiers, heavily armed, clustered on her doorstep, pounding on the front door.

Her heart pounding in echo, she slammed the window shut, throwing the latch into place even as it felt utterly futile. If they had come to arrest her, she could hardly lock them out.

And what would become of her mother and sisters, then?

She whirled back to the chamber, her gaze darting from desk to dressing table. She had long ago burned all her letters and papers and had even bricked up the hidden cellar doorway. She had never put her name on any of her writings. Even if they did lock her up in Kilmainham Gaol, they would have no evidence.

Not that *evidence* was required, not when all of Ireland was under the iron fist of martial law.

She grabbed her copy of Paine from the bedside table, stuffing it onto a bookshelf between innocuous volumes of poetry. Surely they would not notice it there.

She caught a glimpse of herself in the looking glass,

her pink, flushed cheeks, the curls escaping from her scarf bandeau. Quickly, she tidied them as best she could, straightening the filmy fichu in the neckline of her yellow muslin dress. Did she look like a respectable countess?

Strangely, she felt calm. Removed from the scene, as if she watched it from above herself. Was this how those sixteen men felt when Bond's house was raided?

"My lady!" Mary cried, bursting through the bedroom door. She had lost her cap, her eyes bright with panic. From below, Eliza could hear the pounding on the front door getting louder and louder. "My lady, what shall we do?"

"Have the butler answer the door, of course," Eliza answered, turning away from the glass. "What else do we do when there are callers, no matter how rude they are?"

She took the jewel case from her desk, pressing it into Mary's trembling hands. "Keep this safe for me," she said, hurrying out onto the landing.

She peered down at the foyer as the butler opened the door. He had been summoned so quickly, the collar of his usually immaculate coat was askew. "What is the meaning of this?" he demanded as an officer pushed past him.

"We've been instructed to search this premises for arms," he answered, staring around at Eliza's flagstone floors, her paintings, and her antique statues of Hermes and Athena and the Chinese vases of summer flowers on marble pedestals.

"Do you know whose house this is?" the butler cried. "The Countess of Mount Clare! And her mother is Lady Killinan."

"We have our orders," the officer said, waving around some papers.

"Orders that I have a right to examine," Eliza called,

making her slow, dignified way down the stairs. "I have no arms here. Even my late husband's fowling pieces were sent long ago to Mount Clare."

The officer gave her a small, reluctant bow. "I'm sorry, my lady, but we have information about this house we must examine."

"*This* house?" Eliza took the documents from him, searching the signatures. It was indeed a warrant to look for illegal arms, though she had no doubt they would keep a sharp eye out for other things as well.

Eliza waved her hand. "Be about your task, then. I trust your men will take care with my furnishings."

"As careful as they are able, my lady. We must do a thorough job."

Eliza stepped aside, wrapping her arms around her waist as she watched the troops swarm through her foyer, up the stairs, into the dining and drawing rooms, the morning room, and the library. There was the sound of breaking china, chairs falling to the floor, and ripping fabric.

As careful as they are able, she thought wryly. But she couldn't help but feel frightened as they swarmed over her property. She had thought everything was destroyed or hidden, but what if she had missed something?

She turned to find some of the servants clustered in the corner, staring at her with frightened eyes. Yet she still felt nothing but that strange, icy calm.

"It is quite all right," she told them soothingly. "They will finish their business and soon be gone. Let us go belowstairs and have a cup of tea. . . ."

"My lady?"

Eliza paused in picking up scattered books from the floor of the library, glancing over to see Mary in the doorway. She still clutched the jewel case in her arms.

"Don't tell me they have come back," Eliza said.

"Oh no, my lady."

"Good. They found nothing—they won't bother us again, not once my mother complains to Camden of our treatment."

"They had no right to come here in the first place!" Mary cried, startlingly angry. "Wretched bullies."

"True, they had no right. And they *are* bullies." Eliza left off her task, leading Mary to the settee, which had been too heavy to upend. "Have they caused you some trouble, too?"

Mary shook her head. "But my brother—he's disappeared, my lady. My mother thinks he's run off with the Defenders."

"The Defenders!"

"Aye. I've been that worried about him, and about my parents, all alone in their cottage. If they can raid the house of a countess . . ."

"Yes, I see," Eliza said slowly. "Mary, I have been thinking I need to go back to Killinan to see to my own family and stay with them until matters calm down. I had thought to take you with me, but your parents obviously need you." Eliza could do no more good here if her house was being so closely watched. They had found nothing this time, but the increased vigilance meant they probably would. And her family needed her in Kildare.

"You can't go back to Killinan alone, my lady!" Mary cried. "Traveling is not safe."

"I will take some of the footmen as guards, ones who have kin in Kildare still. It will be safe enough. My mother needs me, just as yours needs you." She took the jewel case, rummaging around in its depths until she came up with a diamond bracelet. "Use this if you need it."

"Oh no, my lady!" Mary protested, shaking her head. "I can't take that from you. It's too valuable."

"It's only for an emergency, if you or your brother need to leave the country in a great hurry." She pressed the bracelet into Mary's hand, closing her fingers over it. "And bring your parents to stay here, if you like. You can keep an eye on this mausoleum for me until I return. Can you do that for me, Mary?"

The maid slowly nodded. "If it will help you, my lady."

"It will." Eliza pushed herself up from the settee, terribly weary. "Now I must make my preparations. I'll leave at daybreak."

Chapter Seventeen

Eliza could smell it long before she saw it. The sour, acrid tang of smoke, thick on the hot summer air.

She pulled up her horse at the sharp curve in the road, pressing the sleeve of her riding jacket to her nose as the two footmen drew their pistols. It had been a quiet enough journey thus far, despite the inns crowded with fleeing people, and they made good enough time. They stayed mostly to the back lanes, away from the villages and the roads clogged with those same fleeing people; the new policy of free quarters meant far too many soldiers about.

They had met with few people that day, stopping only to water the horses at a stream and gulp down a quick meal. But now it seemed their solitude was at an end.

Eliza listened close. She could hear no flames, only smell that terrible lingering smoke and see the dark gray plumes of it drifting lazily into the sky. And then, too, she heard voices, shouts and sobs.

"My lady, we should turn back," one of the men said. She sensed the panic lurking under his words, and she felt the tightness of fear in her own chest. But she knew she could not flee. Though the village ahead was not her own, they were not far from home. She had to help if she could.

"I'm sure whoever did this is gone by now," she said, trying to stay steady. "We should see what we can do."

"But we must see you safe to Killinan Castle, my lady!" the other guard protested. "The longer we are on the road . . ."

The greater the perils. Eliza was all too aware of that. But she urged her horse ahead.

At first, it almost seemed the village was deserted. A few of the cottages were already in smoking ruins, the flames burned away to a smolder. Gardens were violently churned up, the summer vegetable crop destroyed. Two cows lay dead by the side of the road as terrified chickens ran through the dirt and the falling ashes. Their squawks drowned out a more terrifying sound—human screams.

As Eliza listened carefully, she could make out incoherent, shouted words. They seemed to come from the woods stretching behind the village. She urged her horse forward again, her heart pounding.

"My lady!" her guard called. "We should go back."

"I have to help if I can," she answered. But knowing that didn't stop the metallic taste in her mouth.

She dismounted at the edge of the trees, holding tightly to the bridle as she crept forward. As the woods closed in behind her, blotting out the bright, hot sun of the day, the panicked voices grew louder.

In a clearing was what was left of the villagers—and a group of soldiers in red coats. Eliza's gaze swept over the scene, and for an instant, it seemed horribly frozen to her, like an exhibit in a macabre waxworks exhibit. The soldiers' red coats were streaked with smoke and blood, and their faces were written with a grim determination as they faced a distraught, shrieking collection of women.

At the edge of the clearing was a wagon, and three soldiers hauled a young man roughly onto its wooden bed. His bare back was streaked with crimson blood, his head lolling as if he was unconscious. The ropes that held him for the flogging still hung from one of the trees.

"He didn't do nothing!" a young woman shouted, lunging forward to try and catch at the man's naked feet. One of the soldiers shoved her back hard, and as the woman fell, Eliza saw she was very pregnant.

An older woman knelt by her, holding her in her arms. "Hush, Annie! The baby . . ."

"But he didn't do nothing," the girl, Annie, insisted hysterically. "They can't take him away!"

"Oh, but we can," one of the officers coolly replied. "We have the writ here, stating this man is hiding pikes for the United Irishmen. I'm sure a stay in the gaol will make him more cooperative. Perhaps you would care to join him there, miss?"

The older woman clutched the pregnant girl closer. "You wouldn't dare!"

"Traitors must pay the price for their actions," the officer said. He seemed to be enjoying himself. He gestured to one of the other men, who started toward the girl.

Eliza had seen quite enough. "What is the meaning of this?" she called in her best "ladyship" voice, striding into the clearing as she let go of her horse. She stopped behind the two women.

The surprise of her arrival slowed down the soldiers in their grim task, but only temporarily. They finished slinging the poor, unconscious man into the wagon, and the soldier who was bid to fetch Annie paused to frown at Eliza in confusion.

She gave him her haughtiest, most countesslike stare, then turned her glare onto the commander. She was aware of a man on horseback, near the treeline, his red coat dappled in shadows, but as he said nothing, she ignored him for the moment.

"Well?" she said. "What is going on here?"

"And who might *you* be?" the commander said, recovering from his surprise.

"I am Lady Mount Clare, and you are very near my family's estate at Killinan Castle. I demand to know the meaning of this outrage. Is the British Army now in the business of terrorizing innocent women and old people?"

The officer gave her a sneer, but she could see from the shift in his gaze that he would not insult a countess. "These *innocents* have been making and hiding pikes, my lady. Probably meant to murder your own family and neighbors."

"Indeed?" Eliza gave an exaggerated glance around the clearing. "Where are these pikes, then?"

His lips tightened. "They hid them before we arrived. They must have been warned."

"You mean you did not find them?"

"I told you, my lady—they must have been warned of our coming. I am sure you would know nothing about *that.*"

Eliza felt her face flame with a flash of anger. "You mean to say that because your informant was wrong, because these people are innocent of wrongdoing, you flogged a boy and torched their village?"

"These vermin must be made to talk one way or the other. The safety of the country depends on it."

Her gloved hands curled into fists, Eliza took a step toward him. She was brought up short by Annie's sudden scream. She looked down, horrified to see a stain spreading across the girl's brown skirt. Was she losing the baby?

"Jesus, Mary, and Joseph," the older woman whispered. "The baby's coming."

"The baby," Eliza murmured, cold with a new kind of fear. The poor girl couldn't give birth in the dank woods!

"Baby or not, this woman is an accomplice to treason," the officer insisted. "We have to take her in, along with her villain of a husband."

Eliza stepped in front of the girl, her arms held out. As if that would hold back a group of soldiers! "You will do nothing of the sort."

"My lady . . ."

"Leave it," the man on horseback said suddenly, his voice hoarse and rough from the smoke. He sounded amused and . . . and strangely familiar. But Eliza had no time to puzzle it out. Annie let out another scream, and Eliza fell to her knees beside her. Somehow, she felt far more helpless faced with a coming baby than with an armed patrol.

The commander listened to the man on horseback. "Let's go, then," he told the soldiers. "I'm sure the man will tell us all we need to know once he is conscious."

He swung up onto his own mount, leading the soldiers and the wagon with their prisoner from the clearing. The mysterious officer vanished, and Annie was left to her fate.

Eliza glanced back to see her guards hovering uncertainly at the edge of the trees. Some *guards* they were, she thought wryly.

"Will one of you please ride on to Killinan village and bring back a cart and the midwife?" she called, worried Killinan would be in a state much like this one, burned and deserted. "And bring me my saddlebags."

As the confused villagers slowly gathered around, crying or muttering angrily, Eliza leaned toward Annie. The sobbing girl screamed again, shrinking back against the older woman who held her.

"Shh, lass, 'tis only Lady Mount Clare," the woman said soothingly. "Don't you know her?"

Eliza glanced up at her, suddenly recognizing her face. "You are Bridget Riley, yes? I remember—you used to sing at the ceilidhs at Killinan when I was a girl."

"That I did. And you used to dance until daybreak there, my lady."

"That was a long time ago, indeed," said Eliza. "This is your daughter?"

Bridget cradled the crying girl against her shoulder, as if she were a baby herself. "Aye, my Annie. And the young man they took away is her husband, Davey."

"They said he was one of them Defenders, that he made pikes," Annie gasped. "He never did! He was just a farmer."

"Just wait until the Duke of Adair hears of this," Bridget muttered fiercely. "He'll see this right."

"Adair?" Eliza said. She remembered tales of the Duke of Adair, an Irish lord who fought fiercely to hold on to his estates—and who protected his tenants with an equal ferocity. He was an Irish patriot to the core, but far too independent to take the United Irish oath.

"This is his land," Bridget said. "He takes care of his own."

Eliza was almost afraid to know what that meant to someone like Adair. But Bridget would not say more about him, nor was there time. Annie gave another piercing scream.

"Hush, Annie, you've got to lie still," Bridget said. "The baby will come too fast."

Eliza shrugged out of her riding jacket, sliding it carefully beneath Annie. It wasn't much, but it was better than lying on dirt and twigs. One of her guards gave her the saddlebags, and she rummaged through them until she found a container of water and a handkerchief. Soaking the heavy linen, she used it to bathe Annie's face. The girl slowly quieted, sinking into a stupor of pain.

"There now," Eliza murmured. "Just rest now. The midwife will be here soon, and you and your baby will be just fine."

She was not so sure about the baby's father, though. Eliza shuddered as she thought of the young man's bloody back. But she could not help him now. She could only help these people right in front of her.

"'Tis lucky you came along, my lady," Bridget said. "They would have taken Annie, too, no matter that she's about to have the baby."

"I only did what any sane person would do," Eliza answered. Though it did seem as if sanity was in short supply of late.

Bridget shook her head, holding her daughter closer. "They would just say we brought it on ourselves and go on their way."

She meant no one else from an aristocratic family

would help, Eliza thought sadly. Most of them probably huddled in the luxury of their great houses, while the peasants suffered and died.

The truth was, suffering and death could come to any one of them at any moment. No great house could protect them now. As she looked down at the sobbing Annie, she smelled the blood and dirt and smoke—and wondered just what she would find at home.

Chapter Eighteen

Eliza slumped over in the saddle, so numb and exhausted she could only stare up at the house. It was there; it was whole. The pale gray stones were intact, the stern Palladian façade balanced by the romance of the old medieval tower at one end, the only remnant of the original castle. The late afternoon sun gleamed on the many windows, turning them pinkish gold.

But it was also eerily quiet. Usually at this time of day, Killinan was a veritable beehive of activity, especially if her mother was having one of her many parties. Servants rushing to and fro, merchants and caterers arriving. Or, if Lady Killinan was going out, the carriage would be waiting with the liveried footmen. Smoke would be billowing from the kitchen chimneys, and gardeners would be finishing up their tasks on the vast grounds.

Now there were no parties, no outings. But the gardens were as lovely as ever with their rolling, velvety green lawns, symmetrical beds colorful with red and yellow blossoms, shaped topiaries, and gurgling fountains. Those gardens were her mother's great pride, the most famously beautiful in all Kildare County. Today they were deserted.

Eliza studied the blank windows, taking in the perfect stillness. Not even a bird sang. Had her family fled, then?

Her footman helped her from her horse, and for a moment, she held on to the saddle, swaying at the sudden feel of solid earth under her feet. She took in a deep breath, hoping the cool, clover-greenness of home would erase the sour scent of smoke and fear. But the air was hot and thick, and she could imagine the flames followed her even here.

She draped her saddlebag over her shoulder as feeling finally flooded back into her feet. "I will go back to the village later, once the horse is rested," she said. She wanted to check on Annie, who had just been barely settled in the midwife's cottage before her little son arrived.

"Of course, my lady," he answered. "Shall I go with you?"

"No, no, you need to rest. It has been such a long journey." She needed to rest, too, yet she feared it would be a long while before she could sleep. Even though she could hardly put one foot before the other, her nerves felt all a-jangle.

She hurried up the wide marble front steps and into the shadowed foyer. It, too, was silent, as echoing as a cave, the curving staircase with its lacy gilt work soaring up from the black and white tiled floors. Her ancestors stared down at her from their portraits, surmounted by ornate white plaster wreaths that contrasted with their dark sternness. High above, a domed ceiling was painted with a blue sky, curious Greek gods and cherubs peering at the follies of humans below.

It all looked just the same as ever, and even in the quiet,

Eliza blessed its solid reality, its haven of familiarity. She took off her hat, dropping it onto the base of a statue of Artemis, along with her saddlebag. Her curls escaped their net, and she impatiently shoved them back.

And at last she heard a sound, the heavy thud of booted footsteps on the stairs. She spun around to find a man making his slow way down, and at first, she did not know him. He was not very tall but was well muscled, his dark hair tied back tightly from a square face.

And he wore a red uniform.

Eliza shrank back against the statue's stone base, but it was too late. He already saw her.

"Eliza," he said, none too happy. "Your mother said you were in Dublin."

"George!" Eliza answered, equally surprised—and unhappy. George was a sort of distant cousin to her mother, though closer in age to Eliza than to Lady Killinan. When they were children, his parents often came to visit Killinan Castle, which Eliza hated because George often pulled her hair and threw her books into the fountain.

They saw him much less often in later years. The last Eliza heard, he had married some Ulster heiress and joined a regiment there in the north. Yet here he was.

"What are you doing here?" Eliza asked.

"Now, is that any way to greet a kinsman?" he said, leaning on the banister as he smiled down at her. "It has been far too long since we saw each other. Though I see you are quite as lovely as ever, cousin."

"And you are as great a liar," Eliza answered. "I have been traveling for long hours and don't look lovely in the least."

He laughed unpleasantly, coming down the rest of the

stairs. "Nonsense. The Blacknall beauty will always shine through. Perhaps especially with Anna?"

There was a glint in his hard gray eyes as he said her sister's name that Eliza did not care for. "And how is your wife, George?" she said pointedly.

He shrugged. "She does well enough, from what I've heard. I have not been home in a long while; duty has called me here."

"To subdue the discontented populace of Kildare?" Eliza said doubtfully. From the family gossip she had heard, George was best at subduing bottles of brandy.

He scowled at her. "I don't like your tone, dear cousin. We all must do our duty, and mine is to uphold law and order among ignorant, violent Irish peasants who don't know what's good for them."

"We all do what we must, I suppose. But I don't see any violent peasants here in my mother's drawing room, do you?"

His eyes narrowed, and she remembered too well the angry boy who once pulled her hair. "I came here to warn your mother. We *will* disarm Kildare, by whatever means necessary, and that includes her own estate. She is too kind and trusting to see sedition even when it is right under her pretty nose."

"I am sure she appreciates the warning." Eliza started to turn away, but George suddenly grabbed her arm, crushing her linen shirt sleeve and the soft skin beneath.

She tried to wrench away, but he held fast.

"You always were a smart girl, Eliza," he said harshly. "Too smart by half. You never knew your place, and Mount Clare wasn't man enough to take a horsewhip to you and correct you. But you had best tread carefully now, cousin. Rebellion won't be tolerated, even in a Blacknall."

Eliza glared up at him. A horsewhip, was it? She wished she had one right now to wipe that smug look from his face.

Then she smelled it. That heavy scent of stale smoke, thick in his hair and on the red wool of his coat. And . . .

"Is that blood on your sleeve?" she gasped, staring at the long rust-red stain. She remembered the burned cottages, the gash on the old man's forehead—the boy dragged away from his pregnant wife.

She had been too exhausted to see it before, but now it was much too clear. It had been him, the man on horseback at the village. It was George. "You," she whispered.

He let her go, stepping away as he shook his head. "Just remember what I said, Eliza. You are not as clever as you think."

"Good-bye, George. My felicitations to your wife. She is such a . . . fortunate woman," Eliza said tightly, restraining the overpowering urge to slap him. George was nothing. She needed her energy for other battles.

As he finally left the house, Eliza leaned back heavily on the statue. Only when she heard his horse gallop away down the drive did she breathe again. She rushed to the door, slamming it shut.

"Eliza!" she heard someone cry. She glanced up to see Caroline leaning over the balustrade from the landing above, waving wildly. Her spectacles were pushed atop her head, her brown hair gathered in a hasty braid that snaked over her shoulder and down the bodice of her simple white muslin dress.

The sight of her sister's face was like a balm to her injured spirits. This *was* her home, and she was back at last.

"Eliza, you're here," Caroline said, running down the stairs two at a time to throw herself into Eliza's arms. "I've missed you so much!"

Eliza held her close, breathing in her fresh scent of soap and ink, the sweetness of her blotting out the smoke and the coppery blood.

"I've missed you, too, Caro. But I'm sure you've been working too hard to even notice my absence."

"I *have* been working. I'm devising a history of ancient Ireland, which requires a great deal of time and research." Caroline drew back, carefully studying Eliza's face. Eliza tried to smile. "But that never means I don't miss you. Are you sure you're well? You look pale."

"I am tired. It was a long journey. And I just encountered George."

Caroline wrinkled her nose. "Oh, *George.* What a menace he is."

"What was he doing here?"

"Came to frighten Mama, of course. He told her they just cleared out a rebel village and that some of her own tenants were planning to burn Killinan as they did Moreton Manor."

"Moreton was burned?" Eliza cried. Will's home, destroyed?

"No, but they tried. And Lady Moreton went scurrying off back to England. Just like a Tory, Mama said."

"Has anyone tried such a thing here?" Eliza asked, still shaking with shock.

Caroline shook her head. "It's been quiet here. *Too* quiet. It leaves Mama too much time to fuss at me."

"Well, now she can fuss at me instead," Eliza said lightly, but her heart was heavy with worry about Will and his home.

Eliza took her sister's arm as they hurried back up the stairs. Caroline pushed open the door, tugging Eliza into the drawing room with her. Despite the warm, sunny day outside, the heavy satin draperies were mostly drawn, candles lit against the shadows. There was no fire in the large black marble grate, but the room was still stuffy and stale, smelling of candle smoke and the dying flowers in the Chinese vases.

Katherine Blacknall lay on a settee by the fireplace, staring at the portrait hanging there of Eliza's late father with his beloved hunting dogs, Killinan Castle in the background. She did not appear to really see it but merely lay there motionless, the folds of her blue and yellow striped dress spread around her like a cheerful reminder of another time.

Anna sat on a chair beside her, her golden head bent over a piece of embroidery. She tossed it aside when she saw Eliza, leaping up to run over and hug her.

"Oh, Eliza! You're safe; you're here," Anna cried, gathering Caroline into their embrace, too. Eliza held them both close, her precious sisters, laughing with them as they all spoke at once.

Their mother slowly stirred, sitting up to blink at them in the gloom. A whisper of a smile crept over her face, which was pale without her usual powder and rouge, but younger and more vulnerable. "Oh, Eliza dear. Why did you not write us you were coming home?"

"There was not much time, though I did send a note ahead." Eliza hurried over to sit beside her mother on the edge of the settee, kissing her cheek. She smelled of white lilies, of course, as she always did. It made Eliza feel suddenly absurdly young, and she longed to bury her face in her mother's skirts, as she did as a child, to take refuge in Katherine's calm assurance.

But she was *not* a child now, and she had to take care of *them*. She clasped her mother's hands, studying her closely. Katherine was as beautiful as ever; she had always looked as if she was another sister, not their mother. Her fair skin was unlined, her features fine and delicate, her golden hair scarcely threaded with silver. But she looked tired.

"Did my note not arrive?" Eliza asked.

Katherine shook her head. "The post has been terribly unreliable of late. And my cousin has just told us some of the mail coaches were stopped and burned and an officer who was a passenger killed."

The interruption of the mail coaches—the signal for the rising to start. Eliza's hands tightened on her mother's.

"I would place no credence in anything George says," Anna said contemptuously.

"He surely knows more than we do, isolated here as we are," Katherine said. "How are things in Dublin, Eliza?"

"Quiet enough," Eliza said, not mentioning the constant firing of the guns and the troops in the streets. "Crowded. Everyone floods into the city, looking for passage to England."

"England." Katherine sighed. "Everyone leaves. Lady Moreton was one of the first to go."

"Caro tells me there was trouble at Moreton Manor," Eliza said.

"Oh yes. But we have had no such incidents here. We've been left in peace."

"They haven't sent troops to quarter here at Killinan?"

"They wouldn't dare."

"Lady Moreton's son was here as well, but he left to rejoin his regiment," Anna offered.

Eliza glanced at her, startled.

"But we have heard nothing else." A small frown drifted over Katherine's face. "Were you not friends with him once, Eliza?"

"Yes, I was. But you did not like that, Mama," Eliza said wryly.

"I only wanted what was best for everyone." Katherine suddenly dropped Eliza's hands, turning to Anna. "Girls, your sister looks tired. Could you go and ask Cook to send up some food and tea? And have the maids air out her chamber."

Eliza wondered why she did not ring the bell for such tasks. As Anna and Caroline hurried from the room, she watched her mother rise and go to the fireplace. Katherine fiddled with the china ornaments arrayed there on the mantel, moving one, then another, only to replace them again.

"How are things here really, Mama?" Eliza asked.

Katherine took a deep breath, the silk rippling across her delicate shoulders. "I told you, my dear. It is quiet enough. Some trees have been cut in the night, some provisions stolen from the smokehouse, but I have not seen the culprits."

"Yet someone tried to burn Moreton. That is so near."

"That is different, I'm sure. Lord and Lady Moreton never cared for their people as I have. They squeeze what they can from their land and send the proceeds off to London."

Katherine turned back to Eliza, and she saw the bright sheen of unshed tears in her mother's blue eyes. It was the only crack in her dignity. "I have always taken care of our people, have I not, Eliza? I have always made sure that they are comfortable and well rewarded for their work. I have never been severe toward them. I have never let my comforts take away from their prosperity. I have nursed them, helped them whenever I can. I have lived my life among them!" Her voice broke, and she spun away again.

Shocked, Eliza could only nod. "Yes, Mama, you have. Of course." And it was true. Katherine Blacknall had always been a fair and caring landlady, the Angel of Kildare.

"Then how can they think I am their enemy?" Katherine said. "How can they think I would deceive them? I have begged them to confide in me, to turn in their arms and maintain the peace. And yet they turn from me. *You* turn from me."

"I, Mama? No, never! I am here, am I not? I traveled as fast as I could because you said you needed me."

"Yet you always had such strange notions, Eliza, things I could not understand. Such thoughts about the social order, about *Irishness*. Lady Louisa Conolly says you are friends with her nephew, Edward Fitzgerald, and that odd French wife of his."

"I have not seen them in months," Eliza said truthfully. Not since that night she went to the ceilidh with Will and he sang "Cliffs of Doneen." That felt a thousand years ago. "I will help you, Mama, if you will let me."

Katherine wiped at her eyes. "Will you go with me to visit our tenants one more time? They always did like you so much. You were always running off to talk to them when you were a girl."

"Yes, of course."

"I know that you and I have sometimes been at odds, Eliza," Katherine said. She sat back down on the settee, taking Eliza's hand again. "Perhaps we have seen things differently in the past. Perhaps I was wrong to encourage the match with Mount Clare."

Eliza shook her head. "It was a long time ago, Mama. You wanted what you thought was best for me."

"Yes. I always want what is best for everyone I care about. But sometimes I fear I don't know what that is. I feel I know nothing at all anymore."

Eliza feared she knew nothing, either. She leaned her head on her mother's shoulder, letting out a shuddering sigh as Katherine drew her close. She no longer understood anything at all.

Chapter Nineteen

Eliza closed her eyes very tightly, forcing her hands to unclench and smooth over the sheet, making her tense shoulders relax back onto the feather mattress. It did not work—she still could not fall asleep, despite her tiredness. Despite the late hour, deep into the darkest part of the night.

The house was too quiet. Every squeak of the floors, every click of the shutters in the wind, echoed too loudly. They sounded too much like running footsteps, frantic moans.

She rolled onto her side, opening her eyes to stare out over her girlhood chamber. Her windows looked onto the back gardens, those manicured expanses of terraces and flower beds that were her mother's pride. Bathed in the summer moonlight, they looked so peaceful, so wondrously ethereal. But the gardens, the house, and all who lived in its walls were so very vulnerable.

Eliza sighed. Worry was surely her lot now, and as Anna said, the waiting was terrible, especially after she was accustomed to action in her work in Dublin. At least her own worry did not include a baby, like poor Annie, who still waited for word of her Davey. Eliza's courses had been regular since Will left.

But there was also a tiny, foolish part of her who wanted Will's baby. . . .

Impatiently, she kicked back the bedclothes, getting out of bed. She could not lie there another moment, thinking of war and of babies who would never be. It did no good. She should look in on her mother.

As she reached for her dressing gown, a sound even worse than the silence tore through the house. A pounding at the front door, like the one at her house in Dublin when the soldiers came. Loud enough to be a battering ram.

Eliza's stomach lurched, and she pressed her hand hard against it. Was it rebels or troops? Either way, it was trouble. Killinan could be burned, her mother and sisters killed . . .

"Oh, get ahold of yourself!" she said sternly. Panicking would help nothing.

She tied the sash of her gown, hurrying out onto the landing. Anna and Caroline were already there, their arms tight around each other. Caro buried her face in Anna's shoulder.

"I forgot my spectacles!" she whispered. "I can't see what's happening."

"That's probably all for the best, Caro," Anna said, smoothing her hand over Caroline's rumpled hair. The hammering at the door went on, and Eliza peered over the balustrade to see the wood panels shudder. Those new locks her mother had installed would not long hold.

Her mother's chamber door opened, and Katherine emerged still dressed in her gray silk dinner gown. A shawl was tossed over her shoulders, and she held a pistol in both hands.

"Mama!" Eliza cried. "Do you even know how to fire that?"

Katherine glanced down at the weapon, an old dueling pistol that had probably belonged to Eliza's rakish grandfather. "Not really," she said, shockingly calm. "But how difficult could it be?"

"Very," Eliza said. She slid the gun from her mother's hand. "I will see what is happening. You stay here with the girls, Mama, and if necessary, you must run down the back stairs and escape through the garden."

"No, Eliza!" Anna gasped. "You come with us now."

Eliza kissed her sisters' cheeks quickly. "Do as I say for once."

Katherine wrapped her arms around her daughters, hugging them protectively close. Eliza ran down the stairs, suddenly realizing she had no shoes. The tile was cool under her bare feet, but she hardly noticed.

She dragged back the locks, opening the door. For an instant, she was blinded by the glare of a torch and could see only the silhouette of a tall figure against the night sky.

"What is this?" she demanded, despite the fact that her throat was dry with fear. Slowly, her eyes adjusted to the light, but she did not recognize the man who stood there. He seemed very large, broad-shouldered, a monster of the night, with long, wild black hair. His face was half obscured by a dark beard, but his eyes glittered as he watched her. He said nothing.

Eliza drew in a deep breath. He was only one man; surely she could defend her house against one man!

"We have no arms here but this old pistol in my hand," she said. Weren't arms what everyone was after these days? "You may have it, if you leave us in peace."

A deep, agonized moan suddenly sounded at Eliza's feet, and she looked down in growing, icy horror.

"Will!" she screamed, collapsing to her knees, the gun falling to the ground. With shaking hands, she smoothed the tangled, sweat-soaked blond hair back from his face and saw that it really *was* Will. Lying on her doorstep, half unconscious. His coat was gone, his white shirt dirty, the shoulder torn away to reveal a bloody bullet wound.

She cradled his head on her lap, staring up aghast at the dark man before her. Distorted by the torchlight, he looked utterly terrifying.

Will's breath was harsh, his skin hot under her touch. She had never been so scared.

"What is the meaning of this?" she said hoarsely.

"There was a patrol not far from here," the man said in a light Irish brogue. "They were dead when I found them, except for this one."

Found them, or killed them himself? And why had they not killed Will, too? The Moretons were not much liked in the neighborhood.

"Why did you bring him here?" she said, running her hand gently over Will's furrowed brow as he moaned.

"He had this clutched in his hand." The Irishman held out a pearl-framed miniature. Its surface was cracked, but Eliza saw it was her own portrait, the one painted just before she married Mount Clare, the one she gave Will before they parted, hoping he would remember her. She snatched it away, holding it tightly until the pearls bit into her skin.

The dark man frowned grimly. "You and your mother have a fine reputation in Kildare," he said. "No one wants to hurt you, nor none of your friends. But Kildare is 'green' now. We won't stand for the likes of *him,* especially after what happened with Annie and the village. It would be best if he left."

His stare was almost gentle, yet unyielding. How did he know of Annie and the soldiers? What did that have to do with Will? "Left?" Eliza cried in confusion. "He is half dead!"

"The English are being driven out of these lands once and for all," he said. "I brought him here out of respect for your family. I can't say how others will feel. He should leave as quick as he's able." With that, he took his torch and melted away into the hot, dusty night.

Eliza was alone in the silence, except for Will's labored breath as he struggled to hold on to life.

"Eliza," she heard her mother say behind her. "Have they gone?"

"Yes, they've gone."

"What did—oh!" Katherine, too, fell to her knees on the ground, staring down at Will, aghast. "William Denton? What is this?"

"He was caught in an ambush," Eliza said numbly, gently smoothing back his hair until he quieted in her arms. "His . . . rescuer found this on him, so he brought Will here instead of killing him." She handed her mother the cracked miniature.

"Your portrait?"

"They said they brought him here out of respect but that he should leave the county."

"Well, obviously we cannot leave now, can we?"

Katherine said, tucking the painting into her long sleeve. "And they certainly will have killed him if we don't get him out of the night air."

Eliza shook her head frantically. "I don't want to hurt him more by moving him!"

"I know, my dear. But we can't stay here. He needs to be seen to, and who knows if the mob will change their minds and come back again," said Katherine, and in her voice, Eliza could hear the calm echo of the Angel of Kildare. The woman who helped sick tenants all over the county.

"You take his feet, Eliza," she went on. "I will take his shoulders."

Her efficiency and her measured tone shook Eliza out of her own numb shock. She handed Will's head into her mother's arms and went to grasp his booted feet. They were covered with dust and dried blood, though the shoulder seemed his only wound.

"On my count, then," Katherine said. "One . . . two . . . three."

Even though Will was tall, with lean, hard muscles, they managed to lift him in their arms, carrying him into the foyer. They laid him on a backless chaise, set under the unblinking stare of a marble Artemis.

She leaned over Will, examining his ashen face and his pale lips. He was quiet now, but his brow was creased, his jaw clenched as if in fierce, feverish nightmares.

Eliza quickly tore away the blood-matted shirt from the wound. She had helped a few Irish fugitives in her cellar who had wounds, but none this bad. And none of them had been Will. Still, she could tell from gently probing that the bullet was still there under the skin. It would have to come out, or it would fester and he would die.

"The doctor is gone from the village," Katherine said. "The Army conscripted him last week to help with their own wounded."

"There would be no time for him to get here anyway," Eliza said. "I can do it."

"Yes. I will help you."

Eliza looked up into her mother's eyes to see that Katherine Blacknall was back. Whatever torpor she had suffered under the last few weeks was shaken away, and in her blue eyes there was only clear determination.

"I have done my share of nursing in my life," Katherine said. "We can save him, my dear. I'm sure of it."

"So it *was* Will," Anna suddenly said. "I was afraid . . ."

Eliza turned to see her sisters on the lowest step of the staircase, their hands clutched together as they stared at the bloody scene suddenly invading their peaceful home.

"Is he dead?" Caroline asked quietly.

"Yes, it is Will, and no, he is not dead," Eliza answered. *Not yet.* And not for a very, very long time, if she had anything to say about it.

"Girls, you must help," Katherine said firmly, rising to her feet as she rolled up her silk sleeves. "Caro, fetch hot water from the kitchen and a bottle of whiskey. Anna, we need clean sheets, as many as possible, and one of your father's old nightshirts."

As the girls dashed off, Katherine turned back to Eliza. "I will fetch my medicine case."

When they were alone, Eliza took Will's hand in hers, raising his fingers to her lips. He tasted of the salt of sweat, the tang of blood, but underneath there was still the familiar essence of her Will. That hand had caressed her, brought her delight and joy and life. Now it was cold under her touch.

"Don't leave me," she whispered. "Please, please, Will, don't leave me."

His eyes fluttered open. For a moment, they were unfocused, clouded, their usual blue a pained gray. But then he saw her, and they sharpened, his hand flexing in hers.

"Eliza?" he muttered hoarsely.

"Yes, my love, it's me," she said, trying to smile reassuringly. "You're at Killinan now; you're safe."

He shook his head. "Another dream."

"No, I'm not a dream." She kissed his hand, again and again. "I'm here! I'm sorry, Will, so sorry. I'll take care of you."

"No, she hates me now." Suddenly, his back arched, as if in a great spasm of pain. " 'Tis Morrigan!"

Morrigan, the black-cloaked death goddess. "I won't let her find you."

Yet still he cried out, as if at visions far beyond her. His head tossed on the chaise, and his hand tightened painfully on hers.

"Here, I have laudanum," Katherine said, kneeling again beside Eliza with her black leather medicine case. Eliza remembered that case well from her childhood—it had always seemed full of magical elixirs to cure anything. Could they now cure Will?

They had to.

"Hold his head," said Katherine, unstoppering the bottle. Even as she carefully counted the drops into Will's mouth, she directed Anna and Caroline as they rushed in with their burdens of sheets and water.

"We'll have to move him to put the sheet under him,"

Katherine said. "And clean the wound thoroughly so we can find the bullet. I have pincers and scissors and yarrow to stop the bleeding. Girls, tear up this sheet here for bandages, but in the library, please. You should not see this."

Will quieted under the laudanum, enough that they could move him and slide the sheet over the stained brocade upholstery. They cut away the rest of his shirt, and Eliza dabbed at the crusted blood with a wet rag. Cleaned up, the wound seemed smaller, the edges not so ragged, so it was slightly less fearsome. At least his breath was more even.

"You will have to find the bullet, Eliza," Katherine said, taking the pincers from her bag. "Your hands are steadier than mine. But I will be right here to help you."

Eliza smiled at her wearily. "Thank you, Mama."

Katherine gazed down at Will. "I took him from you once, my dear," she said quietly. "I won't do it again."

Chapter Twenty

*I*t's an ambush!"

Will barely had time to spin around at the panicked shout behind him, barely had time to level his firearm before a burning pain seared down his left side. Stunned, he stared down at the charred hole in his coat, at the red blood blossoming on the red wool.

For an instant there was fury, the rush of battle-readiness. Then . . . nothing. A cold numbness that spread over his whole body, his mind. He collapsed to the ground, lying there on the dirt path between the beautiful silvery ash trees.

All around was a nightmare. A sea of pikemen flooded out from the cover of the trees to engulf his men. Screams of agony filled the hot summer air with curses and pleading. The stench of rich black earth, powder smoke, fear, and blood. So much blood.

He reached painfully toward his shoulder, feeling the stickiness there. It was his own blood he smelled, then. His and that of his men, who fell all around him in terrible carnage.

Beneath the sodden wool, he touched a small, flat object, and something about it dragged him from that cold emptiness. Frantically, he clawed open his coat, pulling out Eliza's portrait.

Her painted image smiled down at him, so beautiful. Somehow he always thought he would find her again. That once all this horrible conflict ended and Ireland was at peace again, he could find her. That somehow, despite everything that drove them apart, they could find a way to be together. Now that was gone.

"Eliza," he whispered.

A young captain landed in the blood-soaked dirt next to Will, his glassy eyes staring at nothing. His murderer pulled the pike from his back and turned to Will.

"And what have we here?" the pikeman gasped roughly. "A fancy limey major, from the looks of it."

Will struggled to reach for his gun or sword, to make one last stand for his life, but that paralyzing numbness spread over his whole body now, an icy blanket. With one last desperate surge of strength, he curled his fist around her portrait, holding Eliza in his mind as the last thing he would see. Eliza, Eliza, I'm so sorry I left you . . .

That blood-stained pike touched his chest, piercing just below the gunshot. "Here, now, what's that in his hand?"

"Doesn't matter," someone else said, terribly distant. "Just kill him."

"Will!" Eliza called, her frantic voice drowning out the words of the rebels. "Will, wake up now, please."

His eyes flew open, his hand instinctively reaching for his pistol. A burning pain shot down his arm at the sudden movement, and he fell back with a groan. He could still smell that blood and dirt, but there was something else, too. The sweetness of rose perfume.

Eliza's face swam into view above him, her forehead creased in concern. Her eyes were red-rimmed and exhausted, but she smiled as she smoothed back his hair. Her hands were soft and cool.

This was a new part of the nightmare, one he did not understand. "Are you dead, too?" he muttered.

That crease deepened, but so did her smile. Her beautiful smile. "Neither of us is dead, Will. You were having a nightmare; that is all. But you're awake now finally."

Slowly, he became aware of other things. He lay not on hard, dry-packed dirt but on a bed, amid clean sheets and feather pillows. Above him was an embroidered green velvet canopy, candlelight casting strange, shifting shadows on the flowery patterns. A window was open, letting in a warm night breeze that mingled with her rose perfume and the sickly sweet scent of medicine.

"Where am I?" he asked.

"You're at Killinan Castle. You're safe."

Safe? None of them were safe, not even in their own homes. He clutched at her hand, feeling her fingers curl around his. So familiar, so sweet. He had feared never to feel that touch again.

His Eliza. How she would hate him when she knew of all he had seen since they parted, all the loathsome things he had done. She would not want to touch him again. But for now he held tightly to her, as a drowning man held to a lifeline.

"How did I come here?" he said. "The last thing I remember . . ."

"Was a battle?" she said hoarsely.

"An ambush. I was shot right away, could not even fight back as my men died around me. I thought I was dead, too." Dead . . . and holding her in his mind as his last thought. His beautiful, fierce Eliza, who believed so fervently in her idealistic freedom. Her Ireland. What did she think of it now?

"My portrait was found with you," she said. "You were left on our doorstep. At first, I thought you *were* dead."

Will tried to picture the scene. Eliza opening her door to find him bleeding all over Killinan's pristine marble steps. "I'm sorry, Eliza," he said, kissing her hand. "I never wanted to bring any danger to you. Not a single moment of fear."

She laughed wryly. "We have had more than a moment of late. I came home because my mother was scared to be alone in her own home, and yet I have been able to do nothing of use. Just wait and worry, like a bacon-brained ninny."

"I think saving my life was of use. At least to me."

"That was mostly Mama's doing. She is an excellent nurse."

"I daresay it was not *all* her doing," Will said, watching as Eliza eased her hand from his and reached for a basin of water. She soaked a cloth in it, gently bathing his warm brow. The water smelled of lavender, which added sharpness to her sweet roses and slowly washed away the last stinking vestige of blood and dirt from his dreams.

"I take it Lady Killinan has forgiven our youthful romance," he murmured, closing his eyes to revel in her touch. To convince himself it was real at last.

"That was a long time ago," she said softly, tracing the cloth over his cheekbones and along his throat. That cool caress seemed to restore life to his nerves, his blood, his heart, wherever she touched. "I am finding that even Mama can change."

And Eliza herself? Did she change, too, in the face of these terrible events? "Why did they bring me here? Why not just kill me?"

Her touch stilled for an instant before moving on. "They said Mama had been kind to their families. When they saw my portrait, they knew you were connected to Killinan."

"But that was not all they said to you, I'm sure."

"It is all you need to know right now. You should rest."

Will opened his eyes, staring up at her. Her gaze met his, and for a moment she was unguarded and vulnerable to him. And she looked so very young and unsure. Not the revolutionary countess, not Lady Democratical, just Eliza. The girl with the shining ideals. But now so sad. What *had* she seen the night they brought him here? What had she done since they parted in Dublin?

But then she smiled, a veil coming down over her eyes, hiding that sadness from him.

"I don't want to rest," he said. "It's been too long since we were together, Eliza. I just want to look at you, be with you."

She laughed. "William Denton, you *are* a charming rogue! But I don't think you are quite in any condition—"

He suddenly reached up, threading his fingers in her hair to tug her down to him. He claimed her lips in a kiss, hard, frantic, full of the dreams, fears, and memories of their months apart. She tasted of cool water and mint, of Eliza. Of *life,* glorious life that was his again.

For an instant, she stiffened, tried to pull away, but then she seemed to feel it, too, that connection between them, unbreakable even when they parted. She moaned, kissing him back, their tongues touching and clashing as they tried to be ever closer.

Will arched up but then fell back to the bed, gasping at the sudden pain.

"Oh, Will!" she cried. "I am so sorry. I shouldn't have gotten so carried away."

"I'm not sorry," he managed to say, laughing through his gritted teeth. "I've been dreaming of just such a kiss for months."

She laughed breathlessly. "So have I, I confess. But this hardly seems the time for amorous activity, does it? Here, let me look at your wound."

"Are you sure that is *all* you want to look at, Eliza?" he teased.

She set her lips in a stern line, drawing back the bedclothes and unlacing his nightshirt. "No flirting, William Denton. You don't want to distract me from my nursing duties. I might inadvertently pay attention to the wrong pain, you know."

"And now who is flirting, Nurse Blacknall?"

"I am not as good at it as you." She pulled the shirt away from his shoulder, and Will glanced down to see bright spots of blood on the stark white bandage.

A vision flashed through his memory of the dead young captain, red blood on red wool. The bitterness of knowing it was the end, and there were so many regrets left behind.

He swallowed hard, forcing himself back into the present, to Killinan and Eliza. He watched as she peeled back the bandage to reveal a neatly stitched wound, blood seeping around its edges.

She frowned as she examined it. "You see, the bleeding has started again."

"I don't care. It was worth it to kiss you, Eliza. I would do it again. In fact, I might do it again right now."

He reached his good hand toward her, but she seized it and forced it back down onto the mattress. "Don't you even think such a thing. You will lie still while I clean this up."

"Aye, my lady." He settled back against the pillows, watching as she reached again for her basin. "Who did the stitches?"

"My mother did," she answered, dabbing carefully at the blood. "After I dug out the bullet."

He stared at her in surprise. "You removed the bullet?"

"Of course. Do you want to see it? And you needn't look so surprised," she said with a little smile. "All that embroidery my mother made me practice wasn't for nothing. I have a delicate touch when needed."

He snorted. "I doubt you've embroidered an hour in your life."

"Not if I can help it, certainly. There are so many more interesting things to do. But every lady learns to sew a fine seam, and those old lessons we put to good use. We used the last of my father's best brandy to clean the wound, too."

"Such a waste."

"Indeed so. But at least it did not putrefy, and your fever is almost gone."

"I had a fever? That would explain it."

"Explain what?"

"The dreams. They're so . . . vivid."

She glanced up at him. "What are the dreams like?"

"More like memories, I suppose."

"Memories of what?"

Death and blood, burning homes, screams. A lash flashing through the air. But how could he tell her that? Let her not hate him, just for a little longer. Let him not discover what *she* had been doing, either.

Those rebels had dumped him at Killinan. There had to be a reason for that, a reason she held things back from him. But just for now, he only wanted to be with her again. To remember something that was good and beautiful, not death and violence.

"I don't know," he said. "It is gone when I wake."

She nodded. "I have dreams, too. But they're never really gone." She reached for a bottle of whiskey on the bedside table, soaking a fresh cloth with the sticky brown liquid. "This may smart a bit."

She pressed the cloth to his shoulder, and hundreds of fiery little devils leaped onto him with hot pincers.

"Saint's blood, woman!" he shouted. He convulsed up off the bed, but she firmly pushed him back down. "Are you trying to kill me?"

"Yes," she answered. "But first we dug out the bullet and stitched you back up again. Just for the merriment of it."

She took away the cloth, and the pain faded to a stinging prickle. She wound a clean bandage around his shoulder, tying it off before drawing the nightshirt back into place.

"And on top of other indignities, you make me wear a nightshirt," he muttered as she fluffed the pillows. "I haven't worn one to bed in years."

Eliza laughed. "Oh yes, I know. But my younger sisters are here, and they do insist on looking in on you occasionally."

"Since when did you become so concerned with the proprieties, Lady Democratical?"

"Oh, I am concerned with many things," she said, tucking the sheets around him. "Such as making sure you rest and regain your strength. What do you need? Besides a kiss, that is."

"Well, if you will not indulge me in my greatest wish . . ."

"I will not. I don't want to bandage that wound again."

"I wouldn't say no to a dram of that whiskey."

"Now that I can do." Eliza rose from her chair by the bed, taking the bottle to a table where there were tinctures and jars, a tray of untouched food, and piles of bandages. She reached for a glass, her back to him as she poured out the whiskey.

She wore a plain blue muslin dress and no corset or fichu. Her back was an elegant line through the thin fabric, her hair carelessly upswept and tied with a scarf, curling at her vulnerable nape. Will imagined standing behind her, caressing that curve of her spine, kissing her neck softly as she trembled. Tracing his lips along her shoulder, tasting her, feeling her . . .

She suddenly spun around, and a pink flush spread over her cheeks, as if she read his thoughts. As if she, too, remembered their long, lustful winter nights in Dublin.

But she said nothing. She merely slid her arm gently under his shoulders, helping him sit up against the pillows as she held the glass to his lips.

He wanted to protest that he was not *that* much of an invalid, that he could bloody well drink for himself. But she smelled so sweet, her body so soft against him, that he could not give up her nearness. So he drank, letting the rough, hot liquid spread its forgetfulness through his veins.

Eliza settled him back, smoothing his hair gently from his brow. "There. You can sleep now."

"Will you stay with me? Just until I fall asleep," he said.

"Of course." She took his hand in hers, holding on to him as the night closed in around them. "I am here."

"Damn it all, Eliza!" he said, his voice slurred. "You drugged me, didn't you?"

"Just a tiny drop of laudanum to help you sleep," she answered. "Sleep will help you mend. You'll be stronger in the morning."

"And then you'll be sorry for plying me with your potions," he said, or tried to say. His words felt thick as he was dragged down deeper, deeper into those dreams again.

"I'm sure I will." He felt her hand on his forehead, cool and gentle. "Sleep now, Will. I'll stay here with you."

His hand slipped from hers as oblivion dropped heavily onto him, but still he felt her presence near him, holding the darkest nightmares at bay.

Eliza sensed the instant Will dropped into sleep, his breath turned heavy and regular, his hand limp in hers and then falling to the bed. She tucked the sheets around him, kissing his lips once more before she slumped back in her chair.

A soft knock sounded at the chamber door, and Eliza turned to see Anna peering in. "Is he asleep?" she asked.

"Yes," Eliza answered. "A true sleep at last, not a feverish stupor."

"May I sit with you for a while?"

"Of course. I'll be glad of the company. But you should be asleep, too."

Anna shook her head, coming over to sit in the chair on the other side of the bed. "I can't sleep. I just lie there, listening for them to come back."

"Them?"

"Whoever left Will here."

"They won't be back," Eliza said with far more confidence than she felt.

"Will we have to leave Killinan?"

Eliza had thought of all that, over and over as she sat there by Will's bedside. "Them," as Anna called Will's rescuer, had said they were taking over all of Kildare. She had thought someone as beloved as her mother would be safe to stay in her home, but now she knew that was not so. The danger increased every day for families like the Blacknalls, and they should all be away—Will, her mother, and her sisters—and she had to go with them. They were her chief responsibilities now.

"Yes. As soon as Will can go."

Chapter Twenty-one

He looks better," Katherine said, setting down a tea tray on the bedside table as she examined Will's sleeping face. In the morning sunlight streaming from the open window, he looked bronzed again, not chalk-white. His breath was even, too, deep and rhythmic.

Eliza nodded happily. "He ate a bit of breakfast, too, which is a good sign."

"Indeed. I fear I have seen too many wounds fester in hot weather like this, but William has made a remarkable recovery."

"Thanks to your nursing expertise, Mama."

"Thanks to your own tireless efforts. But I don't want *you* to become ill now." She poured out a cup of tea, pressing it into Eliza's hand. "Drink this. You haven't been taking enough sustenance, and you can't afford to grow any thinner."

Eliza laughed, but she did take a long sip. "I know I am quite unfashionably tall and bony, Mama. I cannot help that now."

"You look like my own mother. She was tall, too."

Katherine sat down in Anna's empty chair, watching thoughtfully as Eliza tucked the blankets around Will. "You know, Eliza, I never really loved your father."

Eliza stared at her in shock. Of all the startling events of the past few days, surely her mother's sudden, calm confession was one of the most strange! Katherine Blacknall always kept her own counsel, and she never admitted she was wrong about anything at all. "Mama? How can you say that? You and Father were always most courteous to each other."

"I never said I did not like him," Katherine said. "He was a good man, a dutiful one. And I was dutiful, too. That was why I did what my parents required and married the man they chose when I was barely fifteen."

Eliza had never heard her mother speak of such things before. As far as she knew, Katherine had sprung from the earth as the dignified, reserved Angel of Kildare and had never been fifteen at all. "Did you not want to marry Father?"

"I didn't want or not want anything. I had no choice. I did what my parents had done before me—married who they were told. And it was not so very bad. Your father was kind, much better than my own rakish father, and I loved Killinan Castle from the first day I saw it. It has been my home."

She paused, gazing down at the sleeping Will with unreadable eyes. "I know you will understand, Eliza, when I say your father and I had little in common. He liked to hunt and ride, simple country pleasures. He laughed at my books, my friends and parties, my amateur theatricals. We did not have much to talk of together, and there was never much . . . passion in the bedroom."

"Mama!" Eliza cried, feeling her cheeks burn. Even a grown woman did not want to know such things about her parents!

"I regret nothing, Eliza," Katherine said calmly. "I have my home; I have you and your sisters and brother. But I know I have never looked at a man the way you look at William Denton. And I probably never shall. Time is so short, my dear. We have to discover what is really important to us."

She came around the bed to kiss Eliza's cheek and added, "Drink your tea, dearest, and get some rest. You need all your strength now, as do we all." She leaned close to Will, sliding Eliza's portrait under his hand. "I am sorry for the mistakes I made all those years ago."

Eliza stared up at her, bemused by all she had heard. It seemed that, like so much else of late, her mother had changed. But what had really wrought such a transformation?

"Mama . . . ," she began.

"Shh," she said. "I think Will is waking. I have some things to see to downstairs. Make sure he takes his medicine again."

That would be a hard task, indeed. But she smiled at her mother and settled in to wait for Will to wake up. She did not have to wait long.

"Good morning," he muttered, opening his eyes to give her that grin that always made her heart pound. "Did I miss much when I was asleep?"

"Nothing at all, unless you count my sisters' constant arguments. They're never quiet."

"Well, then, it sounds as if you could use a mediator." Before Eliza realized what he was doing, he shoved back the bedclothes and swung his legs over the edge of the bed. He rose swiftly, if a bit shakily, holding on to the bedpost. His jaw clenched with the effort, but he stood straight, taking one step, then another.

"Will!" she cried. "Get right in bed this moment. I won't let our hard nursing work go to waste. You need to rest at least one more day."

"I am vastly tired of resting," he insisted, almost to the door by now.

"You are a stubborn man, William Denton. But I can be more stubborn than you on your best day, so you had best not argue with me anymore." She seized his arm, and despite his protests, he swayed toward her. "Come, sit down by the window. It's a fair day, and the sunshine will do you good."

"I *am* better, Eliza," he said, but he did go with her to the armchair by the window, sitting down heavily on the brocade seat. "I can travel; I am sure."

"Yes. Very soon." Eliza perched on the arm of the chair, resting her hand on his back. He was warm, but with life now and not fever, his muscles taut and strong under her touch. She swept aside the tangled length of his bright hair, leaning close to inhale his scent, his essence. How very close she had come to losing this.

He covered her hand with his, drawing her closer as he stared out the open window. The gardens of Killinan were magical in the summer light—lush, bright green rolling lawns with beds of brilliant yellows and reds. They wilted a bit under the heat and lack of care, but from a distance, their beauty was intact, and it seemed eternal.

Will turned his head suddenly, capturing her lips with his as he wrapped his arm around her waist, pulling her down onto his lap. She tangled her fingers in his hair, feeling its silken coolness on her skin as his tongue touched hers, tasting, savoring.

Their kiss was rough, desperate, tender, full of need, full of the words they could not say. She knew his kiss, his touch, so well now, yet it seemed all new and sweet. She was hungry for it, starved. She framed his face in her hands, longing for more and more, for all of him.

But she forced herself to draw away. "We shouldn't do this yet, your wound . . ."

"Other parts of me hurt far more," he said hoarsely.

She laughed, drawing her hands away and clambering off his lap. But she was none too steady herself, her head whirling with hot desire and need, with the ache of having been months without him in her bed.

She leaned on the windowsill, feeling the warm breeze on her damp skin. "I'm quite certain we should not be doing *that* yet."

"Even if I lie very still and you were on top?"

Eliza drew in a shuddering breath at the erotic image suddenly so vivid in her mind. Their naked bodies entwined as she rode him. "Even then."

"Ah, well. I see my powers of persuasion have failed with you, Eliza." He smiled ruefully, adjusting himself carefully through the thin shirt. She turned her head away, trying not to stare at the hard outline of his penis under the cloth.

They were silent for a long moment, the only sound the rush of their breath and the pounding of her heart in her ears.

"It was all I thought of every night while we were apart," he said, breaking the quiet.

Eliza tried to laugh. "Being spurred on like a wild stallion? I'm sure it was."

"Only by you, Eliza," he answered, laughing back at her. "It sounds ridiculously lustful, I know. But I would lie there in the darkness, that horrible, tense darkness, not knowing if we would be attacked at any moment, if death waited just around the corner. Yet none of it mattered, because I had you. I had our nights in Dublin, and I remembered every moment of them. Every kiss and touch, the way you smelled and tasted and looked. The way your eyes watched me as we made love."

Eliza swallowed past the dry lump in her throat, fearful she would cry. "I remembered all that, too. I have never wanted anyone as I want you, Will. I never imagined it could be like that."

"I've missed you."

"I've missed you, too," she admitted.

Will leaned his head back against the chair, closing his eyes. "I know our reunion now is hardly ideal, Eliza. But I am grateful for it nonetheless."

"Grateful you were shot?"

"I suppose so, for it brought me to you, for a while anyway." He suddenly opened his eyes, that bright blue gaze that saw too much piercing her to the heart. "I thought I was dying there in those woods, that I would never see you again. That we are here now is a miracle. I only wish it was a miracle the other men in that patrol could share. When I think of them . . ." His voice broke, as if it was much too painful to say more.

A miracle, yes—but for how much longer?

Chapter Twenty-two

Eliza sat with Will as the sun sank below the horizon and darkness blanketed the gardens in an illusion of safety. She knew all too well it was *only* an illusion, though.

He cradled her hand in his, raising it to his lips for a tender kiss. "Come, walk with me in the garden for a while," he said, pressing her hand against his cheek.

"Are you not tired?" she answered. "You should—"

"I cannot face yet more rest. It is such a fine evening, one we may not see again for some time. Please, Eliza. I won't take you far from the house."

A time they may not see again. Eliza feared that was all too true. They had to leave Killinan right away. But she could sense what he meant, for she felt it, too—that yearning to be young and free again, just for a while. To be as they once were. "Very well, for a few minutes."

Holding hands, they made their way down the stairs and onto the stone terrace at the back of the house. The gardens were quiet under the silvery moonlight, the sparkle of the stars scattered across the dusty black sky.

The dry heat of the day had dissipated, leaving only a

fresh green coolness. The only sound was the crunch of their shoes on the white gravel paths as they walked past the silent, still fountains, the looming sentinels of the topiaries, and the blank-eyed statues.

Eliza saw where he was leading her—to the enclosed garden where they parted all those years ago. The marble bench was still there, where once she sat and waited for him with all the yearning excitement of her young heart. All the foolish ideas that love would conquer all.

Love, she knew now, conquered nothing. But being near him still made her shiver.

She sat down on the bench, just as she had then, and he braced his booted foot on the marble seat beside her. He leaned his elbow on his bent knee, his hair falling forward in a golden curtain to hide his expression from her.

"Do you remember that night?" she asked. "The night when you told me of your commission?"

"Of course I remember. You sat right there in your pretty white gown."

"And you were in your new red coat." Eliza folded her hands on her lap, thinking how very long ago that all seemed. And yet, in one of those tricks of time, it also seemed to be only yesterday. She feared she was no wiser now than she was then. "If you could talk to that Will now, what would you say to him?"

He smiled down at her. "I would tell him to purchase more mosquito netting. The islands are full of the annoying creatures."

Eliza laughed despite herself. "Is that all you would tell him?"

"Are you asking if I would warn him not to join the Army?" He sat down beside her, not touching but close.

As close as he had been before they parted that night. "I felt I had no choice then, Eliza. I wanted to make my way in the world, and it seemed the best path to do so. I had no calling to the church, no aptitude for politics or the law. The military seemed an honorable career for a younger son."

"Seemed?"

He looked at her, his eyes shadowed with pain and secrets. "I am not so sure of anything any longer. I have had to do things as my duty that were . . ." His words trailed away, as if he could not bear to voice them, could not yet tell her those secrets. Just as she could not tell hers.

"I know," she said quietly. "Things have not turned out as I imagined, either. As I once foolishly hoped."

"What would you say to that past Eliza, then, if she were also here now?"

"I would tell her to kiss you and not part in anger. To cherish every moment together because life is fragile and precious."

"Would you tell her not to marry?"

Eliza laughed. "Oh, she told herself that every day! But she was young and heartbroken from first love. She let herself be guided by her family and not her own instincts. She vowed never to do that again."

"And has she kept that vow?"

"She is trying," Eliza whispered. "But it is not always easy."

Will reached over and took her hand again, twining his fingers with hers until they were palm to palm. She could feel the thrum of his pulse, the beat of his lifeblood that flowed against hers. "Then kiss me now, Eliza. We can be that young, foolish pair again, just for a moment."

She leaned toward him, softly touching her lips to his. She closed her eyes and remembered the first time they kissed. Her heart had been pounding then, too, with excitement, fear, and the blossoming of passion.

Now she knew him, knew the taste and feel of him, the full, volcanic force of that lust between them. And also knew the dark depth of the gulf between them. They had parted twice now, and the next farewell would surely be their last. But for now she had to take her own advice—kiss him and never part in anger.

He groaned, his tongue seeking hers hungrily as that flame again soared between them. All-consuming.

He tugged her muslin bodice and thin chemise lower, baring her breasts to the cool night. Softly, enticingly, his hands skimmed over her naked shoulders and arms. His lips pressed kisses to the corner of her mouth, the line of her jaw, and her throat as her head fell back.

Eliza closed her eyes tightly, reveling in the feel of his kiss on her skin, the touch of his tongue to the sensitive spot just where her neck met her shoulder. He licked at the pulse beating frantically in the hollow of her throat, his long, skillful fingers caressing her aching nipple, tugging at it gently as it hardened under her touch.

"Will," she whispered roughly, tangling her fingers in his hair. Whether to push him away or draw him closer, she hardly knew. Her mind was wrapped in that golden haze of desire. "We should not . . . your wound . . ."

"Bother all that," he growled. "I've been waiting for too long for this, Eliza. I won't give it up now."

She had been waiting so long, too. All those lonely nights. She pulled him closer, moaning as his mouth closed over her nipple, warm and wet.

His hand reached for her skirts, dragging them up until her thighs were exposed. His palm skimmed over her stockinged calf, the curve of her knee, to caress the naked skin of her thigh.

"So beautiful," he muttered, kissing her other breast, the arc of her ribs. He circled her waist with his other arm, trying to drag her onto his lap, but his breath caught painfully.

"No, Will," she whispered, backing away from him. But his arm tightened, holding her close.

"Don't go," he said, capturing her lips in a deep, frantic kiss.

"I won't hurt you," she insisted. She shook her head, trying to clear it of that mist. It was very hard to do with his hand on her thigh!

"I am not hurt. I need you, Eliza." He tilted back his head, his eyes dark as he stared at her. "What about my offer to let you be on top?"

An enticing vision of riding him as if he were a sweaty stallion flashed through her mind, and she laughed. "Will, no . . ."

"Then you would not hurt me. I couldn't open my wound if I just lay there, could I?"

"Somehow, I suspect you would not just lay there," she said.

"Upon my honor."

Honor surely had nothing to do with it, Eliza thought. But she went along as he stood up from the bench, drawing her with him. Her clothes fell to the ground, leaving her clad only in her stockings there in the moonlight.

For an instant, a strange jolt of modesty struck her. Perhaps her younger self, curious but still frightened, was haunting her. She tried to cross her arms over her chest, but he took her hands, holding them to her side as he kissed her. She opened her mouth, reveling in the hot, pure *life* of him. The essence of all he was, all they were together—at least in rare moments like this one, out of the world and all its terrors.

She snatched at the hem of his shirt, dragging it up over his head, leaving his chest bare to her. The bandage was stark white against his lean, bronzed flesh, and the blond, coarsely curling hair sprinkled there gleamed like gilt. Fascinated, she trailed her fingertips through that hair, over his warm, damp skin. Her nail scraped lightly over his flat, pebbled nipple, and his breath caught.

Her touch skimmed lower over his taut abdomen, unfastening his breeches. His penis was erect, hot velvet over iron under her caress. A tiny drop of moisture glistened at its tip, and she spread it along his taut length.

"Eliza," he growled. Seizing her around the waist, he drew both of them down to the soft, green grass. True to his word, he fell onto his back, letting her straddle his hips.

She shook her hair free of its pins, leaning down to kiss him hungrily as the dark strands fell around them in a concealing curtain. She braced her hands to either side of him, rising above him, drawing her damp cleft along his length as he groaned against her lips.

"Eliza!" he whispered. He reached for her hips as if to roll her beneath him, but she arched away.

"You promised," she said. "Just lie there, sir."

She reached between them, guiding him inside of her as she slowly lowered herself. The slide of him against her sensitive, swollen tissues was utterly delicious. It had been so long, so long . . .

She threw back her head, closing her eyes to concentrate on every sensation as she found her rhythm, as they learned each other again.

The salty-sweet musk of their joining, the fresh green of the grass crushed under them combined in a heady perfume that drove her onward. Their moans and incoherent love words echoed on the wind, and it was as if the night was theirs alone. The stars, the moon, all theirs, a treasure that could never be taken away.

Their rhythm grew faster, more frantic, his hands tight around her waist as she rode him. Then, deep in her very core, she felt that pressure expanding, growing. Behind her closed eyes, brilliant lights exploded in the darkness, red and white sparks.

"Will!" she cried out, her back as taut as a bowstring as her climax washed over her.

He, too, shouted, her name. His head thrashed on the grass as his hips arced beneath her.

She collapsed to the ground beside him, their legs still entwined as they tried to catch their breath. Will kissed her shoulder, resting his forehead against her as she trembled.

She thought she would weep from the sudden force of her emotions, and she curled her fist into the earth to try and hold those tears back.

"You see," Will muttered against her hair, "I kept my promise."

Eliza laughed shakily, turning her face to look at him. A cloud obscured the moon for a moment, wrapping them in the welcome concealment of darkness. "So you did."

"How I have missed this," he said, drawing her closer into the curve of his body. "Missed you."

"I missed you as well. Dublin was dull without you."

"Somehow I doubt your life could ever be *dull,* my lady."

"I would welcome a bit of dullness just now, I confess." She caressed the arm he wrapped around her waist, running her fingers down the corded muscle to hold his hand close against her. From far off, in the perfect silence of the night, she heard the howl of a bird. Long and mournful, eerie like an omen in some old Irish tale. A banshee, perhaps, the harbinger of death. It made her shiver.

"Are you cold?" Will asked, kissing her shoulder. "Come, we should go inside."

"It does grow late," Eliza answered. "But I hate for this to end."

She rolled over, pressing her lips to his in one last, lingering kiss. A kiss that had to say all she could not. "Thank you, Will."

He gave her a bemused smile. "For what?"

"For giving me this night."

Will laughed, reaching for his rumpled shirt and her chemise and gown. "Surely I should be the one thanking you. You have been a most excellent . . . nurse."

Eliza pulled her chemise over her head so he could not see her face. He should not thank her for nursing him back to health when it was her own ideals and work that helped wound him in the first place.

She stepped into her gown, pulling the sleeves over her shoulders. He stepped close behind her, fastening the tapes of her bodice. His fingers brushed the bare skin of her nape, brushing her tumbled hair aside to press his lips to that sensitive spot. A shower of sparks danced down her spine again, and she swayed back against him.

Will wrapped his arms around her waist. "I should have

done this all those years ago, when we last met in this garden. Maybe then we never would have parted."

Eliza laughed raggedly. "Or we would have gotten into even more trouble with our families!"

"Isn't trouble worth it?"

"I used to think so." Suddenly, far off on the horizon, Eliza glimpsed a strange silver gray snaking along the black sky. Smoke, just like that that had lingered over the destroyed village. "Look," she said, pointing.

He went very still. "Come inside now, Eliza."

She ignored him, pulling away to run along the garden paths, up a hill that afforded a better view of the surrounding countryside. That ominous cloud looked thicker there, hanging over a neighboring estate like a warning.

Kildare is green now, the man had said. Was this what he meant?

"Eliza," Will said, tugging insistently at her hand. "Come inside *now!*"

"We have to go," she whispered. "Now."

Chapter Twenty-three

W ill checked the cart one more time to be sure all was in readiness for the journey ahead. The horses, stolid farm animals, stood placidly in the dawn light. In the back, a mattress was covered with old quilts, Lady Killinan's jewels sewn into their seams. Caroline had even slipped in a few books, tucking them under the bedding. Eliza tucked her pistol into a canvas knapsack she would keep with her at all times.

They had to look like an ordinary farm family, taking an ill daughter, played by Anna, to find a doctor somewhere. No detail could give them away.

He stepped back, tugging his plain wool cap over his brow. It hid his newly shorn hair, but he feared no garb could truly disguise him. It was a perilous journey they embarked on and impossible to tell what they would encounter on the way.

He could hardly believe that only hours ago they had been making love in the garden.

"Will!" he heard Eliza call out, and glanced up at the

house to find her leaning out a window. She wore a boy's shirt and coat, but her hair fell over her shoulders. "We're very nearly ready."

Will looked to the horizon of the night sky, which was now pale gold at its edge. "Hurry! We need to make as much distance as possible today."

She nodded and drew back into the house, slamming the window after her. In only a moment, he heard the squeak of the front door opening, and she emerged into the dawn.

She had pinned up her hair, covering it with a woolen cap. With her tall, thin figure and her breasts bound, she looked quite passable in her male garb—unless someone looked closely at her smooth, pretty skin and her buffed nails. She *was* a fine lady, no matter how she tried to hide it!

She grinned at him as if she read his thoughts, pulling out a pair of old leather gloves. "Will I do?" she asked, drawing them over those pretty hands.

"If no one studies you too near." If they *did*, Will would surely feel compelled to hit them. Eliza looked strangely alluring in her new clothes, with her long legs encased in snug wool.

"It feels quite delicious, I must say. I never felt I could move about so freely, with so many petticoats and skirts!" She patted the horse's neck, checking its bridle. "But I suppose I should not become accustomed to it. We'll be in Dublin before we know it, yes?"

"We certainly shall. It may take a bit longer than usual, because we aren't in a fine carriage and because we'll have to use back pathways and hidden roads. But I vow I will get you there as fast as I can."

"Oh, Will. So heroic." She smiled sadly. "I just wonder what we will find along the way."

She strolled to the edge of the drive, staring off over the gardens of Killinan. They were blanketed in morning mist, pale silver like a quiet, peaceful fairyland. He wanted to know what she thought as she took one last look at her home, but her face was as pale and still as the marble statues around them.

He came up behind her, sliding his arms around her waist to pull her close to him. "We will return soon."

"I know," she said, covering his hands with hers. "Yet it won't be the same. It will never be the same, I think."

"It will always be your home. You must always remember that." He gave her a teasing smile. "And also maybe you could remember what we did in the garden?"

A faint blush actually stained her cheeks. "Will! You are—"

"My dears, we are ready," Katherine called, emerging from the house with Anna and Caroline in tow. They all wore simple muslin dresses and knit shawls, plain caps over their hair. But, just as with Eliza, their disguises could only go so far. They looked quite worrisomely as if they were on their way to a masquerade ball.

"I will remember Killinan just as you said, Will," Eliza whispered. "At least we will always have that."

She kissed him quickly before going to help her mother and sisters into the cart.

"I feel rather like those wild, bloodthirsty creatures one reads about in France," Katherine said wryly, settling her skirts around her as Anna covered up in the quilts, pretending to be ill. "I should have some knitting with me, as they say that terrible Madame La Farge did in Paris."

"I fear you look more like the poor French queen, Mama," said Caroline. "Here, Anna, wrap this blanket around you tighter. You're meant to be an invalid."

Will climbed up onto the cart seat beside Eliza, gathering up the reins. "We'll go as far as we can before finding a concealed place to rest for the night."

"Yes, of course," she murmured.

"Are you ready to leave?" he said gently.

She glanced back one last time at the house, so serene and beautiful in the sunrise light. "Yes. I am ready."

And Will flicked the reins, setting the cart into creaking motion as they rolled inexorably away from Killinan—and into they knew not what.

Chapter Twenty-four

W ill!" Eliza laid her hand on his arm, forcing him to rein in the horses. "Do you smell that?"

It was the same; she knew it was. The same as that thick, sour miasma that hung over the ruined village on her way home—smoke. Smoke and charred decay, rotten in the warm weather.

Will's eyes narrowed, becoming a stormy gray as he quickly scanned the woods on either side of the narrow track. "I certainly do."

"Something is burning."

"*Was* burning, I think. It smells stale."

"Fighting last night?"

"Perhaps. The town of Rossmorland is not far ahead, and there's said to be a store of weapons from Dublin there. It could easily have been raided."

From the cart behind them, Katherine stood up, balancing herself against the rough wooden slats next to the sleeping figures of Caroline and Anna. Like all of them, a sleepless night hiding in the woods had left her pale and disheveled, her golden hair straggling from beneath her cap.

"Do you think we should go back?" she asked. "Find another route?"

Will rubbed at his stubbled jaw. "Surely it is just as dangerous behind us, Lady Killinan. It seems quiet enough now. If Rossmorland *was* burned, they would have moved on by now. We can go around the town, though, just past the bridge ahead."

"Mama?" Anna mumbled, slowly sitting up as she blinked at the light. "Why have we stopped? Is it nightfall?"

"Not nearly, my darling," Katherine answered. "I fear we have a long way to go before we rest."

A bird suddenly screamed in the distance, a haunting echo that pierced Eliza to the core. Or was it just a bird, not an omen? She hardly knew any longer. Reality had become distorted, unreal. There was no Killinan, no Dublin, either, only the five of them trapped in an endless uncertain purgatory.

"We can't stay here forever," Eliza said.

"Indeed not." Will slapped the reins, urging the horses forward.

The hot sunlight pierced through the trees, dappling the dusty roadway under the horses' hooves to dark emerald spotted with black. It seemed an enchanted place, like in the old Irish tales Eliza loved so much as a girl. The realm of fairies and elves, hidden beneath the verdant leaves only to emerge at night to dance and make merry—and make mischief on unsuspecting humans.

But even the world of the fairies could so quickly turn dark and violent. Fairies were so jealous and changeable, and heartless, too. They destroyed men who displeased them with scarcely a thought, laid waste to their dreams.

Gradually, the light grew brighter as the trees became farther apart, the roadway wider. They were emerging from the fairy world of the woods into that of the river, the realm of mischievous naiads. There was a bridge there that led to Rossmorland and then curved in two directions, either to Dalkey and the coast or to Dublin. If they could make it past there, certainly their way would be open to the city.

The smell of smoke grew stronger as the woods thinned, a thick, cloying scent that stuck in Eliza's throat. Was this the smell of the whole country now, the stench of destruction?

Anna coughed, pressing her hand to her face as Katherine gently urged her back down beside the still-sleeping Caroline.

"What does this mean?" Anna whispered.

"It only means we will have to find a path around the town and avoid people still," Eliza answered. "That is all."

Even as she prayed her words were true, Eliza very much feared they were not. A terrible sight greeted them as they emerged into the light, the river just ahead. The bridge was blocked by slack, broken bodies clad in bloodied red uniforms, a cloud of smoke hanging over all in a dark gray pall.

"Mama, get down!" Eliza cried. "Don't look."

Katherine, though, had already glimpsed the carnage. She caught Anna in her arms, bearing her all the way to the bottom of the cart, holding her daughter's face close to her shoulder.

"What is it?" Anna sobbed brokenly.

"Shh, darling, we must be quiet," Katherine whispered.

Will slowly climbed down from the cart, his face a frightening blank.

"Will, no," Eliza said, lunging forward to catch at his sleeve. But he was already gone from her.

"It's all right, Eliza," he said, not looking back. "The battle is obviously done. I have to see if anyone lives."

How could anyone possibly be living, she thought in horror, staring at the scene of perfect, terrible stillness. The only things moving, the only sounds, were those shrieking birds wheeling overhead.

"Stay here with your mother and the girls," he said, looking back at her at last. His eyes were dark gray, flat and hard. Her Will, the tender, passionate Will from the garden at Killinan, was gone, the cold warrior now in his place.

It made her shiver, despite the heat of the sun and the smoke.

"If anything *does* happen," he said, handing her the reins, "run back into the woods, as far and fast as you can, and don't return."

Eliza wrapped the reins tight around her fist, watching as Will drew his pistol from inside his coat and made his way to the bridge. The whole world seemed at a perfect standstill, the river frozen in its flow, the birds caught in midflight.

"Mama," she said. "You heard what Will said." And she, too, climbed down from the cart, taking her pistol from the knapsack.

"Eliza, no!" her mother cried. "You must not. Stay here with us."

"I have to help Will if I can," she said. "Who can hurt me there now?"

As she moved closer to the bridge, the stench grew thicker and more pervasive. Smoke, blood, the stinking odor of fear. There were not so many dead as she thought from a distance, perhaps a dozen or so. But that was surely quite enough.

Eliza swallowed hard past the sour knot in her throat and knelt down beside Will as he examined the first body.

It was a young man, his eyes wide in startled horror. His boots were gone, his coat and bloodied shirt ripped open as if he had been searched for valuables.

Her hand shaking, she reached out and closed his eyes.

"I told you to stay at the cart," Will said quietly.

"I . . . I want to help, if I can."

"Help?" He glanced at her from those terribly dark eyes.

She turned away from him, from that cold stare, and looked at the other men on the bridge. There was not a stir of movement, only the sprawl of broken limbs, broken lives, among broken pikes and torn flags. The green of the United Irishmen mingled with the red and blue of the regiment's standard, as if they were all doomed together now, no matter which side they chose. Ireland was doomed.

"I fear we cannot help any of them now," she whispered.

"No, we can't." Despite his empty eyes, he took her hand, helping her to her feet. Together they made their way from man to man, making sure none yet lived even as they knew it was futile.

But the soldiers were not the only ones who lost their lives there. At the middle of the bridge dangled a thick rope and a hanged man, clad in the cheap garb of a farmworker. Eliza turned away in a rush of cold nausea, but not before she glimpsed the proclamation pinned to his chest—the order for Kildare to disarm and come back to the rule of the Crown.

"They must have come here to hang him," Will muttered. "And been surprised in their turn."

"Yet the attack came too late, if saving this man was their aim," Eliza said. "And why did they not take the body away?"

"Who has time for such civilized niceties as burial in times like these?" Will said bitterly. He drew his dagger from the sheath at his waist, as if to cut the man down, but then his gaze caught on the crumpled body at the end of the bridge.

As Eliza watched, confused, he walked slowly to the man, kneeling down. She followed, even though her instinct told her to stay where she was, to run back to the cart. She had become quite adept at ignoring her instincts of late.

It was not one man but three, a red-coated officer and two Irishmen. From the bloodstains on the stone, she judged there had been a most ferocious battle between them.

"Who is it?" she asked quietly.

"General Hardwick." Will gently rolled over the man's stiffening corpse, and Eliza saw to her horror that it was, indeed, the genial man she had last seen at Dublin Castle, laughing with his wife.

And she remembered the general's pretty daughter, smiling shyly at Will as he led her into the dance.

"He was your friend, I think," she said.

"He was a brave and honorable man who should not have been in the field at his age," Will answered hoarsely. "He said Kildare was a most dangerous place."

"And his family?"

"He sent them to England months ago. They won't hear of this for some time, I fear."

Suddenly, a burst of gunfire exploded from the trees lining the river, a flash of deadly sparks that shattered the eerie stillness. Will grabbed her hand, dragging her down the bank and shoving her under the pilings of the bridge.

"Stay there!" he shouted. "And for God's sake, Eliza, bloody well do as I say this time."

"Will!" She reached for him, but he was gone from her, disappearing back up the muddy bank. He knelt there just at the rise, firing his pistol in response. ·

Holding on to the jagged stone of the piling with one hand, Eliza drew her own firearm, taking in a deep breath to steady her nerves. She was surely caught, with the unseen attackers ahead and her vulnerable family behind. The river flowed on beneath her, unconcerned at all the violence it witnessed that day, not caring that Will's blood and hers might join its waters, too.

But their blood would *not* flow that day, not if she could help it! Eliza was sick of death, of fear, of the terrible end of dreams. And she was angry, too. Angry with a fiery passion that made her want to howl with it all. To rush into battle and be done, once and for all.

The sunlight glinted off the barrel of a gun, deep in the shadow of the trees. A mere flash, but that was enough. She leveled her gun at that spot and fired. The deafening explosion, the kick of that hot metal in her hand, was deeply satisfying.

"Eliza!" Will shouted, firing off his own weapon. He fell with his back to the riverbank, reloading. "What are you thinking, woman?"

"I'm thinking two shooters are better odds than one," she said. "I'm thinking I will not just sit here and die, and I won't let you die, either."

He stared at her, and she was sure he would push her farther under the bridge, shout at her to run away. But he just handed her his gun, taking hers as she reloaded.

By the time they ran out of ammunition, the hail of gunfire from the woods had ceased, as if their attackers fled. Eliza slumped down in the dirt next to Will, her eyes shut as she listened closely for any sign they were still there. Waiting. There was nothing, not even the rustle of leaves, the snap of a twig. Even the birds were silent.

Long, taut moments crept past as she thought of her mother and sisters and prayed they had fled. The rush of pure, hot energy was drained away, and she was exhausted.

"I think they've gone," Will whispered, a strange, tight sound to his voice.

Eliza turned to him, opening her eyes to find that his wound had reopened in the fight. Blood spotted his shirt, and his lips were pressed together in a white line.

"Oh, Will," she groaned. She quickly unlaced his shirt, peeling it back from his shoulder.

Some of the stitches were torn, the flesh around them red and angry, blood oozing through. She pulled out her handkerchief, pressing it against him to stop the flow.

"Why didn't you say something?" she said.

"It hardly seemed the right time to pause during a gunfight and say, 'Excuse me, Eliza dearest . . .' "

"We'll have to find a place to mend it." She stooped down to dip the cloth into the river, wiping away the blots of fresh blood. "You're not hurt anywhere else, are you?"

"Not at all, thanks to you, my warrior goddess."

"I doubt any goddess was ever so frightened out of her wits!"

"You didn't seem frightened at all."

"I wasn't." Eliza dragged in a ragged breath. "Not until now. You could have been killed!"

"Eliza!" she heard her mother say, and she glanced up to find Katherine peering down at them from the bank above. Her hem and shoes were stained with mud and dried blood. "Has William been shot?"

"Mama, you should have stayed away," Eliza protested.

"Nonsense. The villains are quite gone. I saw their shadows creeping away, like the bloody cowards they are."

"Mama!" Eliza cried, almost laughing at the ridiculous sound of that curse in her mother's cultured voice. "No, he's not shot, but he opened his wound again."

"Such a nuisance. Here, let me see." Katherine scrambled down the bank to kneel beside them in the dirt, peering beneath Eliza's handkerchief.

"Ladies, really," Will said, trying to draw his shirt over his chest.

"Oh, William," Katherine said sadly. "If you think the sight of a bit of bare male flesh is going to give me the vapors after what I saw on the bridge, you are quite mistaken. We'll have to fix those stitches, but we can't do it here."

"We can't go into Rossmorland now," Will said. Despite Katherine's words, he managed to pull his shirt and coat back into place, wincing as the cloth slid over his shoulder.

"Indeed," Katherine said. "But Houghton Court is not far. I heard that family fled weeks ago. Hopefully the place is deserted, and we can stop there for the night."

"Can we afford to lose the time?" Eliza asked.

"No, we cannot," Will said. "I vowed to get you all safely to Dublin."

Katherine peered down at his shoulder. "William, I fear we have little choice in the matter. Eliza, help me get him back to the cart."

"I can certainly walk," Will insisted, shaking them away. "I tell you, it is nothing. We have to press on."

He scrambled up the riverbank, hurrying back over the horrible bridge as Eliza and Katherine ran to keep up with him. They went back to the cart where Anna and Caroline waited, watching them with white, tense faces. Caroline sat in the back while Anna held on to the horses' bridles.

"Where do we go now?" Anna asked, her voice subdued and sad. How much had she seen? She always did seem to be watching just at the worst times.

"To Houghton," Katherine said. "We can rest there for the night."

"No, toward Dublin," Will insisted. "We should be to the next town soon after nightfall."

"Denton stubbornness," Katherine said, shaking her head. "I tell you, William, you will be no good to us if you faint from blood loss."

"Denton stubbornness is nothing at all to that of the Blacknalls," Will muttered. "And I never *faint*."

Chapter Twenty-five

Despite her deep tiredness, Eliza could not sleep, even in the perfect stillness of the deepest part of the night. They had taken refuge for a few hours in the woods, near a burned-out farmhouse on the road to Dublin. There her mother had repaired Will's stitches, and they had all fallen into fitful sleep, but Eliza was too wary to join them. She was alert to every birdsong in the trees, every twig crackling.

Will could not sleep, either, she knew. He lay beside her on a pallet of blankets under the cart, his breath quiet as he stared out from their meager shelter. It was so hard now to think of the past or future, or anything more than that one, single moment.

"Will?" she whispered. "Are you asleep?"

"No," he answered. "But you should be. We'll have to cover many miles tomorrow."

"I'm not the one injured and needing rest."

"My shoulder is fine; I promise. Your mother is an excellent physician."

"But will it be fine if we meet with another gunfight?"

"We won't, and if we do, I will be very careful." He turned his head to smile at her in the darkness. "I don't want your mother to scold me again."

Eliza laughed despite herself. "Nor do I." She propped her head on her arm, gazing down at him in the lacy patterns of moonlight. "Will?"

"Yes?"

"I am very sorry about your friend General Hardwick."

He just nodded, as if he could say nothing.

"Earlier today you said we all have regrets."

"Of course we do," he said. "We're all forced to see the truth of ourselves in times such as this, even when we would rather not."

Even if they would rather hide and pretend? Surely that would be the prudent course, the course that would allow them all to go on with their lives. But hiding had never been in her nature. Nor had it ever been in Will's.

"I do regret that a dream that seemed so wonderful has turned terrible in so many ways," she said.

"But you can't regret what led you to those convictions."

"No, I can't regret that. Freedom should be every human's right. But are convictions, abstract ideas, worth pain?" She frowned. "I don't know."

"Is duty worth it?"

She glanced down at him, puzzled. "What do you mean?"

"I spent all my life hearing of duty," he said, turning his face back to the night. "Duty to my family, to England, to our estate. It seemed everything."

And that was the tale of their whole Ascendancy world,

the one Eliza had fought against. Had imagined she *could* fight against, underestimating the strength of its hold. "Do you think that still?"

"It was all I knew, until I met you."

"Me?"

"I loved the way you spoke of Ireland, Eliza. You made me see my home in a new way, the true beauty of it that was all around us. You made me think it a source of pride to be part of it all, not something shameful to deny, as my family does."

Had he really thought that, when her younger self peppered him with tales and lectures, fired by her own youthful enthusiasm? She laughed softly, lying down beside him again. "I thought you were just trying to steal kisses."

"I was, of course. But I also listened, more than you could know."

"Yet you still went off with the Army."

"Well, duty is a tenacious thing, after all. We're all bound to it—even you, Eliza."

And so she was. "Yes. I did marry Mount Clare when I was told to, and I tried to live my life as I was told I should. Perhaps it would have been better if I simply went along with that life and all it entailed."

"And perhaps it would have been better if I had rebelled," he said in a bitter tone.

Eliza's head was spinning, so she hardly knew what was up or down, right or wrong. "Oh, Will. What really happened to you while we were apart?"

"I saw a man flogged," he said flatly.

"What? But that is nothing, surely. I saw such terrible things myself."

"But you did not order it done, did you?"

Eliza sat up in shock. "You . . . ordered it?"

"Yes. Soon after I rejoined my regiment after leaving Moreton, we captured a man suspected of being a Defender, of knowing some of their strategy in Wexford. He refused to give us the names of his cohorts, and the order came that we were to publicly flog him as a warning. To show no mercy. I said such a thing was likely to make the populace even *more* recalcitrant, not less, but the order was repeated."

"You . . . you did not flog him yourself?" she whispered. She shook her head hard, but the image of Will wielding a bloodstained whip would not be dislodged. That was just the sort of brutality and injustice she fought against.

"Of course not. But I sent the order through, I had the proclamation read, and I witnessed the punishment. The man nearly died, and the next day in retaliation, an Anglican bishop's house was sacked and burned."

"So your warning was quite right. It made the rebels more recalcitrant."

"I took no comfort in being right."

What *was* right? Eliza did not know any longer. She lay flat on her back, staring up at the slats of the cart as she felt Will watching her. She thought of the burned village, of pregnant Annie and her missing husband. Of her mother and sisters, forced out of their home, of General Hardwick and his family. So much pain on all sides, and the divisions between them blurred.

His hand touched hers in the darkness, the merest light brush. She curled her fingers around his, holding on to him. They said nothing else. What *could* they say? They just lay there, so close, but so very, very far apart.

Anna lay very still in the darkness, huddled beneath a tree not far from her sleeping mother and sister. She could hear Will and Eliza whispering under the cart, indistinguishable words that blended with Caroline's soft snores, but she could not rest herself. Her thoughts raced through her mind, one after another, and would not be quieted.

Once when she was a child, her father gave her a kaleidoscope from Italy, an enameled tube containing bright shards of colored glass. With one twist of the wheel, the mosaic's patterns shifted into something entirely new, the old picture never to be found again. That was what the whole world was like now. They were all trapped in an ever-moving kaleidoscope, where nothing could ever be familiar or comfortable again.

She closed her eyes, shifting on the hard ground. The heroines in the novels she loved were in danger all the time, menaced by villains, their lives and virtue at risk. They usually reacted by swooning or running away in the midst of a rainstorm.

Anna doubted swooning would solve their problems, and there were no rainstorms on the horizon. Their danger was all too real. Those dead men on the bridge were all too real. And sleep still would not come, would not give her forgetfulness for even an hour.

She sat up slowly, sliding off the edge of the blanket. Caroline sighed and rolled over, but she did not wake as Anna tiptoed from the clearing. The farmhouse nearby was a burned-out shell, but she had seen the stable just behind, a space with two walls still standing. Maybe if she sat there for a few minutes, away from the others, she could breathe again and find one moment of solitary peace. Then she could think straight again and not be sucked down into blind fear.

She crept into the ruins of the stables, two standing walls and two that were crumbled onto piles of scorched hay. It smelled of smoke rather than the comforting scent of horses, but there were no moaning ghosts. There was no sound at all. She leaned her elbows on an intact stall railing, wondering what would happen tomorrow. Where would the next turn of the kaleidoscope take them?

A rush of wind swept through the stable, startling her and making her spin around. Her skirt hem caught on a loose nail, causing her to stumble into the railing. It collapsed beneath her, sending her tumbling into a loose pile of moldy hay. She gasped in surprise, her hand shooting out to catch herself as she fell to the floor.

But she did not land in soft, yielding hay. She fell onto something hard, something that shouted and grabbed her by the arms.

Fear seized her by the throat, an icy, strangling grip that killed her terrified scream. The hay-monster pushed her to the floor, holding her down hard as warm breath touched her cheek.

Was *this* what those novel heroines felt, then, as they were menaced to the point of death? Cold, tingling, terrified, yet so strangely removed from the whole terrible business? It was most odd.

"Who are you?" the monster rasped. "What are you doing here?"

Certainly monsters should not have human voices. That irrational thought somehow gave her a burst of new strength, and she kicked and pounded at him, trying to break that steel-trap grip.

"Who are *you*?" she shouted. "How dare you frighten me! Let go of me at once."

"Cailleach," he said, gasping as her booted foot connected with his shin. His *human* shin. "Quit fighting me. I mean you no harm, if you mean me none."

"What, I'm supposed to believe that just because you say so?" Anna cried. "You're probably a marauder!"

"A marauder?" A strange hint of laughter crept into his voice, and it was oddly familiar. His voice was deep and rough, tinged with an Irish brogue. "Someone is an over-educated English colleen."

"I am not English—I was born here in Ireland, which by my calculation makes me Irish," she insisted, twisting in his grasp. "But I know a marauder when I meet one."

"I am not a marauder or a rapist," he said, tightening his grip on her even more. "I merely sought refuge here for the night, as I suspect you did."

"And maybe you planned to steal our horses in the morning?"

"I hadn't planned anything at all."

Anna twisted her head, biting at his shoulder. She felt the barbarically satisfying give of his flesh under her teeth.

"Cailleach!" he shouted again. "Witch." He rolled over, carrying her with him. A stray beam of moonlight from the window landed on his face, illuminating the harshly elegant features, the dark stubble of beard along his square jaw. Long black hair was tangled over his brow, but she still recognized him.

The Duke of Adair. The dark, brooding man she met

on her way to Killinan. She remembered him all too well. And now she was in his power.

"You," she whispered, frozen with fear for Will, for all of them.

"Ah, so it's the fairy trespasser," he said, his hands loosening on her arms. "I thought I hadn't seen the last of you."

She wrenched angrily away from him, sitting up in the tumbled hay. Her head was spinning so wildly she wasn't sure she could rise yet. He watched her far too warily, glittering perception in his dark green eyes. "What are you doing here?" she whispered.

"I told you, taking refuge here for the night," he answered, sitting up stiffly beside her. He did not come too close, but she could sense him there in the darkness, the heat and power of him. It was unlike anything she had ever known before. "Believe me, I had no more desire to encounter an English witch than you had to see me."

"But why are you not at your home?" she asked, trying to distract him, to turn that penetrating stare of his away from her. "Or did your cousin seize it from you again?"

"So you heard that tale, did you?"

"Kildare County is a small place."

"And a gossip-ridden one, especially among you Ascendancy folk, who have nothing better to do. As it happens, I have business in Dublin I must see to. Not that it's any of your concern." He stretched his leg out in front of him, gasping as he straightened the knee.

Anna glanced down to see a dark stain on his doeskin breeches. "You're hurt!" Yet somehow that thought gave her no comfort, no surcease from her fear—or her strange excitement. Even a wounded Adair was a powerfully strong one.

"A scratch, that's all," he said tightly. "You may have noticed it's not the safest time to be traveling, *cailleach*."

She scrambled to her feet. "I will fetch my mother's supplies; she has medicines, bandages. . . ." And she could warn them, too, so they could flee.

"Nay!" He grabbed her skirt in his fist, holding her still. His fingers brushed her bare legs, sending a shiver over her skin. "No one must know I'm here."

"But you're wounded."

"I'll be fine. I told you, it's nothing. I've had worse." He smiled up at her, a teasing, white grin in the darkness. "And you tried to wound me yourself not five minutes ago, English witch. You ruined my shirt with those sharp teeth of yours."

"That was before I knew who you were."

"And now that I'm a rogue Irish duke, everything is safe and well?"

Far, far from it. She had never felt less safe in her life than she did at that moment, staring down at him as he held her fast. She couldn't breathe, couldn't think. *Run, you fool!* she thought frantically, but still she stayed. Perhaps he had her under a magic Irish spell, after all.

His dark eyes narrowed as he stared up at her, a muscle in his jaw flexing. Slowly, slowly, his fist tightened in her skirt, drawing her closer to him. His stare was intensely focused on her parted lips, his breath warm on her throat as she landed half on his lap.

Yes, it *was* a spell. That was the only explanation for not running away; she knew that. His palm flattened on her leg, and she moaned at the new, delicious sensation.

"Cailleach," he whispered, just as his lips met hers, soft at first as he explored her taste, her texture. He rubbed slowly back and forth, his own lips rough, his long hair brushing her skin like silk. She had never imagined a kiss could be like this at all, could make her feel all hot and cold at the same time, frightened and yet . . . yet she wanted to scream out with joy.

Then his tongue touched her lower lip, licking, and that joy vanished. This was an Irishman, a rebel, a man who had almost killed Will! Still not thinking clearly, not at all sure what she would do, Anna jerked herself out of his arms, falling back onto the hard floor.

He watched her, breathing hard. For an instant, he looked as stunned as she felt.

"Who are you really?" he whispered.

"I . . ." Her hand touched the edge of something hard, a piece of wood, and in a flash she caught it up. She brought it down on the back of his head, and he tumbled heavily to the floor. His hair covered his face.

"Oh!" She clapped her fingers to her mouth, holding back a shriek. Had she just done that? Kissed a man and then knocked him unconscious? Reeling with the suddenness of it all, the sick feeling in her stomach, she leaned over him. Was he dead?

No, he still breathed. *Thank God.* She wasn't yet ready to have that sort of thing on her conscience.

"I'm sorry," she whispered, backing away. "I had to protect them."

She took off at a full-out run, not stopping until she dove under the cart where Eliza and Will slept. She shook her sister's shoulder. "Eliza! Eliza, wake up."

Her sister sat up immediately, nearly hitting her head

on the cart's wooden slats. "What is it? Will finally fell asleep. . . ."

Anna sucked in a sharp breath. "We have to go! Now!"

"Why, what happened?"

"I went to use the necessary in the woods and . . ."

"And?"

"We're not alone here, I fear."

Fortunately, Eliza seemed to understand at once. She gave a quick nod, bundling her loose dark hair back into her boy's cap. "Go get Mama and Caro. I'll wake Will."

"No need," he said hoarsely. "I am quite awake now with all your female whispering, my dears. Come on, let's go. It's nearly dawn anyway."

Chapter Twenty-six

A re you quite sure you feel well, William?" Katherine asked for the eleventh time since they left their wooded sanctuary in such a hurry. The afternoon sun was now high overhead, blazing hot, and still she persisted.

Eliza almost laughed. She must be exhausted, suffering the effects of their hurried, dangerous journey, to feel such an urge to giggle! But the sternness of her mother's voice, the long-suffering look on Will's face, struck her as oddly comical.

She did not laugh, though, but merely faced forward toward the road ahead, that road that never seemed to end.

"I assure you, Lady Killinan, I am quite well," Will said again. "Your nursing skills are most effective."

"I still wish you would let me examine the stitches again," Katherine persisted. "We did leave in such a hurry this morning—"

"Mama, he said he felt very well!" Anna said. She and Caroline slumped against the sides of the cart, too tired even to read or bicker.

"And we can hardly stop now," Caroline added. "We

have a long way to go before nightfall. Isn't that right, Will?"

"Quite right, Lady Caroline," said Will.

Katherine opened her mouth, but there was no time to argue anymore. Shouts and cries suddenly erupted from the trees around them, men swarming out from their cover onto the road as if conjured by an evil magician.

Eliza went cold, every trace of hysterical humor vanishing as their cart was surrounded. She pressed close to Will, staring around them frantically. There were only about ten of them, men and a couple of women, clad in tattered clothes with ragged green bands tied around their arms. But despite their ragtag appearance, the guns and tall pikes looked deadly enough. Were they the ones who killed the patrol on the bridge yesterday and fired at Will from the riverbank? Or perhaps they were the people Anna saw in the woods before dawn? Had they been following them the whole way, and Eliza all unknowing?

And her gun was tucked away in her knapsack.

One of the men, the tallest of the group, stepped forward, smiling at them menacingly. "Well, now?" he said. "What have we here?"

Suddenly, Anna gave a bloodcurdling shriek, tumbling from the back of the cart to land in a heap on the ground, her skirts artfully tangled around her pretty legs. The man's grin faded as he stared down at her.

"What's wrong with *her*?" he said, as if a lady fainting at being accosted on the road was a strange thing.

"Must have been shocked by your handsome face," one of the women mocked.

Katherine leaped down beside Anna, kneeling down

in the dirt to gather her into her arms. "Me daughter is very ill," she said in a flawless Irish brogue, a distressed tear trickling down her cheek. Anna lay limp against her. "We're trying to find a doctor somewhere, but there's none about. None that will treat a poor girl."

The man still stared, as if caught by Anna's fragile beauty. But the others surrounded their cart, weapons at the ready.

"What's wrong with her, then?" one of the men repeated.

"She's . . . delicate," Katherine answered, a sob in her voice. "My sons and daughters and I just want to find her help before it's too late. She needs rest more than anything."

Anna lay perfectly still, the consummate actress. But Eliza hardly dared breathe.

"We've been on the road for days and days," Katherine continued. "Chased everywhere by those nasty soldiers. I fear so for my poor little girl."

The man knelt beside them, staring at Anna as if enchanted. Eliza almost laughed again, despite the terrible danger. Her sister's prettiness could enthrall even hardened rebels!

Very carefully, he reached out to touch one of her golden curls. Anna moaned as if in pain, her eyes fluttering open. "Oh, Ma," she whispered brokenly, her accent as flawless as her mother's. "I'm so very tired. . . ."

"We'll help you," the man said decisively.

"Liam!" the woman cried. "We've no time to play nursemaid. We have to meet up with the others by nightfall."

"It's all right, Molly," he said. "They're in trouble just

like us. Come on, we'll take you with us. She can rest there for the night."

"You're so kind," Katherine said, her gaze meeting Eliza's over Anna's head. *Play along,* she seemed to plead.

As if they had any choice.

Chapter Twenty-seven

The whole world has gone mad," Eliza murmured, clutching the knapsack containing their guns on her lap.

Will glanced at her from the corner of his eye, not taking his attention from their newfound companions. "You just discovered that?"

"I suppose I've known it for a while," she said. It was just that their surroundings now seemed particularly dreamlike and unreal. Like a nightmare come to life.

The rebels had taken them to a deserted manor house where, as far as Eliza could tell, they were meant to meet with another group who had not yet appeared. The only people who waited for them were two hard-faced men who seemed to look none too kindly on Eliza and her family. Now, as it passed midnight, they all waited together in the small drawing room, the only sound the snap of flames in the grate, the whispers of the rebels as they knelt by the fire.

A little dried-out bread and a few bottles of brandy seemed to be the only provisions in the house, and the rebels made use of both. The bottles seemed to be getting steadily lower, the murmurs angrier. And as the whispers grew harsher, the atmosphere became more tense as the moments ticked onward.

Eliza especially did not like the way the two new men, who hovered in the doorway like guards, watched them. Their eyes glittered with suspicion.

She tugged her cap lower over her brow and stared at the floor. Will sat next to her on the settee, and she could feel the coiled tautness of his muscles. Under the folds of her long coat, he touched her hand, as if trying to reassure her, but she still feared she might scream and leap up from her seat. As if she could run, as if there was anyplace to escape to. She had been lucky to hide the guns in her sack before Will left the cart in the shelter beside the house.

Eliza glanced at Anna, who lay on a chaise near the half-open window, away from the smoke of the fire. Her eyes were closed, her hair tumbling loose from her cap, and she did look convincingly pale. But her fingers were tense where they lay against her skirt. Katherine hovered over her watchfully, and Caroline observed the whole scene in thoughtful silence. Perhaps she thought to write it down in her history of Ireland someday.

If they ever got away, that was. If they could keep Will's identity secret.

Eliza sneaked a glance at the men in the doorway again, only to find that one of them watched her very closely. His eyes were narrowed in suspicion, and she hastily looked away again.

"What's wrong with that boy there?" he muttered to his companion, pointing at Eliza.

"Molly says she thinks he's a mute," the other man said.

"He hasn't said a word at all; he doesn't even seem to know what's going on around him, poor idiot."

Eliza felt the burn of the man's stare on her skin. She tried to be like Anna, to summon up her acting skills and pretend not to notice.

"I don't like it," he said. "The way they just brought these people into our hiding place—they could be anyone at all."

"Oh, Bill, surely they're harmless! Just some poor refugees like everyone else. Isn't that the point of fighting? To help such people?"

Before Eliza could eavesdrop on them any further, the man who was their rescuer suddenly knelt down by Anna's chaise, distracting her. He held out a bottle of brandy, his gaze still full of infatuation as he looked at Anna. The woman Molly glared at them from beside the fire.

"Maybe something to drink would help revive her," he said.

"How kind you are to my poor girl," Katherine said, sliding the bottle from his hand. She pretended to take a sip from it. " 'Tis fine stuff."

"No rough homemade whiskey here," he answered. "A fine girl like this shouldn't ever taste such rubbish. It's sad she's so ill."

Katherine sighed. "It *is* sad. She's always been delicate, but so sweet. I fear all this turmoil has only made her illness worse."

Anna moaned softly, turning her face to the window.

"The fire is too warm for her," Katherine said.

"Perhaps she should lie down in one of the chambers upstairs," the man said. " 'Tis cool and quiet there." He glanced toward Molly, who still glared at them. "No one will bother her there; I promise you."

Anna's fingers tightened on her skirt. Katherine covered her daughter's tense hand with her own. "What a good thought," she said quickly. "My son will carry her upstairs."

Will took the hint, leaping up to gather Anna into his arms before the rebel could do the same. Wincing only the merest amount, he carried her past the two men in the doorway, Katherine and Caroline close behind them. Eliza followed, trying to remember to appear empty-headed. The sharp-eyed man watched their progress up the narrow staircase.

Katherine opened the first door on the landing and found a small bedchamber. Moonlight streamed through the small window, illuminating a rumpled bed, open doors on an empty wardrobe, and a dressing table in disarray. It appeared the house's occupants left in a great hurry, but there were candles on the table.

"Put her in here," Katherine said. "We can surely sit here and wait until all is quiet."

"Better than having everyone stare at us like exhibits in a menagerie," Caroline muttered.

As Will laid Anna on the bed and Katherine lit the candles, Eliza heard a sudden commotion downstairs. Keeping carefully to the shadows, she peered over the balustrade to the foyer below.

It seemed the new people had arrived at last. A group of about eight men, dressed in threadbare clothes and green armbands like the others, poured through the door. They carried several crates with them.

The tense silence cracked at their appearance. "We thought you'd been captured!" Anna's admirer called.

"We're too wily for that," one of the newcomers answered, putting down the crates on the dusty floor. "But when we found this stashed in the woods, we knew we couldn't leave without it."

"What is it?" Molly asked.

"Just this." One of the men pried off the top from a crate, revealing piles of ammunition. Eliza almost gasped, remembering how all of their shot was used up at the bridge. There were ten crates down there; surely they could spare just a bit and never miss it.

If she could just find a way to borrow it without letting them know.

"It's beautiful," Molly said, as if the crates were full of jewels and silks.

"There's food and blankets, too," one of the men added. "Some patrol in a hurry had to leave them behind."

The sharp-eyed guard crossed his arms over his chest as he surveyed the stash. "They left them behind? As easy as that?"

"Maybe not *that* easy, after all," one of the other men said.

"Eliza." Will suddenly touched her arm, making her jump in surprise. She had been too wrapped up in what happened downstairs to pay attention to her own surroundings—a big mistake. Anything at all could be lurking around every corner.

"You should come into the bedchamber now," he muttered, "where they can't see us."

"There is more of them now." She gestured to the foyer, where a few of the men still examined the crates. Molly had led most of them back to the drawing room, where laughter and talk now floated free.

"All the more reason to come in here," Will said. "We'll slip away as soon as it's quiet."

Eliza cast one more longing glance at the crates. She had to find a way to steal some of that ammunition and perhaps discover more of what those people were doing. But one look at Will's steely expression told her he would stop her from putting herself into even more danger. She nodded and followed him into the chamber. He closed the door behind them, shutting them into a quiet, stuffy, candlelit world.

Anna sat up against the headboard of the bed, ready to slide down into a faint again if needed. "If I can't marry a duke, perhaps I could turn to the stage," she said. "I thought I did that quite well."

"You did very well, my dear," said Katherine. "But I do hope we don't have to call on your acting skills again any time soon. I'm quite sure my nerves could not bear it."

Eliza unlocked and pushed open the window, letting the night breeze into the warm room. The newcomers' wagon stood just below, one of the men busy unharnessing the horses. How long would it be before they could sneak away?

"I wish we had something to eat," Caroline grumbled. "My stomach is quite empty."

"Perhaps there is some food left in the pantry," said Eliza, turning away from the window. They shouldn't go hungry, after all, if they all needed their strength to get away. She could surely find food and snatch some ammunition while she was at it. "I'll slip down and see."

"No, I'll go," Will said. "You should all stay here."

"Of course not," Eliza argued. "I am much more inconspicuous than you, a mute besides. They won't even notice me."

Before he could protest, she hurried from the bedroom, closing the door softly behind her. If he followed her now, he would only attract more attention. Once she was sure no one remained in the foyer, she tiptoed down the stairs. She turned not toward the drawing room, where voices still echoed, but to the stairs leading down to the kitchens. She would find Caroline some food, and if she happened to snag a bag of that shot while she was at it . . .

She did find a few withered potatoes left in the pantry, as well as two bottles of cider that had been left behind in favor of the brandy. But as she tried to leave the dark, dusty kitchen, she was brought up short by heavy footsteps on the stairs and the sound of masculine conversation.

Holding her breath, she ducked behind a cabinet, tucking her feet close under her.

"You're sure, then?" someone said. She thought it was the suspicious guard, but she couldn't be sure. "Fitzgerald is dead?"

Dead? Eliza's hand tightened on the bottle she held. Oh, but surely there were many Fitzgeralds. It was not Edward. Yet he had been wounded and captured soon before she left Dublin. Everyone had been quite certain his powerful family could secure his release, but what if they were too late?

She pressed herself tightly against the cabinet, biting her lip to hold back her fear, listening closely.

"Very sure. We met a messenger coming from Dublin just yesterday," another man said. "After he was shot, the bastards just threw him in Kilmainham Gaol, no doctor or anything. His aunt Lady Louisa Conolly finally persuaded the Lord Lieutenant to let her see him, but it was too late.

They buried him in the middle of the night at St. Werburgh's, thinking no one would notice."

"A sad day for our cause. He was a born leader. But we have to go forward! It's what he would want."

There was a long silence, a rustling noise as if they rummaged in the pantry. At last they found what they sought and left the kitchen, still talking of Edward Fitzgerald and his sad sacrifice.

Eliza drew her knees up to her forehead, closing her eyes tightly as she let the grief flow over her. Edward had been her friend, her comrade in the Irish cause. And now he was gone, senselessly murdered before he could see his beliefs made reality. What would become of his wife and children now, of everyone who depended on him?

She remembered the night she took Will to the ceilidh, when they danced and sang "Cliffs of Doneen." How very alive the world seemed that night, so vital with wondrous possibilities!

Now Edward was dead, and she and her family were on the run. It was up to her, to all of them, to keep that dream of Ireland alive, however they could.

She wiped at her eyes and pulled herself to her feet. If she didn't return soon, surely Will would come looking for her no matter what the danger. She hurried out of the kitchen, clutching at her provisions as she listened for any sound.

Everyone was in the drawing room talking of Edward Fitzgerald. Two of the crates still stood in the foyer, and she took the chance to scoop up two bags of shot. Any more might be missed, but two was better than none. Hopefully it would last them until they reached Dublin.

She hid the bags inside her coat, running up the stairs before anyone decided to leave the drawing room.

"I found some food," she said, diving into the bedchamber. She smiled at them, hoping they could not see her damp eyes, the grief she pushed down deep inside. But Will stared at her closely, as if he could see something was amiss. He said nothing, though, and just took the potatoes and bottles from her arms. "Was it quiet downstairs yet?"

"Not yet, but soon I think."

"We can leave after we eat, then. I think there's some fuel in the fireplace still."

Chapter Twenty-eight

Eliza held up a candle, leading Will and her mother and sisters down the stairs. The tiny flame barely cast enough light to show them the way through the house, which was pitch-dark now in the predawn gloom, but it had to be enough. They dared not wake the people sleeping inside, or especially anyone who might be lurking outside. They had to be very far away before anyone realized at all.

But it was too late. As she pulled back the door latch, a voice called out, "What's this? Leaving, are you?"

Eliza spun around to find the leader of the little rebel band, tousle-haired and bleary-eyed, standing in the dining room doorway. One of the women lurked behind him. The two of them might not be so very frightening, but the guns they held certainly were. There was little trace of the congenial companions of the night before.

Without a word, Will swept Anna up into his arms. She drooped against him in a seeming faint, and he didn't even wince as her head hit his wounded shoulder. Katherine slid in front of them, her face written with a barely repressed panic Eliza feared might not be entirely feigned.

"We have to find a doctor now, no time to waste!" Katherine said with a sob in her voice.

The man's face softened, but the woman had no such sympathy. With an exclamation of disgust, she grabbed the pistol from his limp hand.

"We'll go with you," she said, scowling at them. "There's bound to be a doctor at Rossmore, and we're supposed to meet up with the rest of our friends there anyway."

"We're sure you must have . . . other things to look after now," Katherine answered. "We've put you to so much trouble."

The woman gave her a bitter smile. "'Tis no trouble, not for *friends*. Not for fellow Irishmen."

Eliza exchanged a long glance at Will. Was this some sort of a trap? But, then, what choice did they have but to go along even if it *was* a trap? Their guns were hidden in her sack, and she couldn't risk a fight with her family so near anyway.

We have to continue to play our roles, Will seemed to say. *And hope we can get away from them soon.*

Eliza nodded and pulled back the heavy door. It was near daybreak now; the stars were fading overhead. Will laid Anna gently into the back of the waiting cart, which Will had prepared for them earlier, and she moaned to great effect.

"I just hope it's not too late," Katherine fretted, climbing up beside her and pulling Caroline with her.

Will swung onto the seat, gathering up the reins as Eliza took her place beside him. The others tumbled out the door, looking as if they would relish a fight despite the restless night behind them. The waning moonlight glinted on the metal pikes they brandished.

"So we go with them to Rossmore?" Eliza whispered to Will. "What then?"

"I'm sure they'll soon find other distractions in a town, and we can go our own way." He gave her a reassuring smile. "Think of it as a scenic detour."

"I think I prefer the direct route," she muttered.

Will smiled, setting the tired horses into motion. It was a slow progress as the sun crept up over the horizon, spreading burned-yellow light and burning away the cool night. It would be another hot summer day.

Their escort was quieter today, quarrelsome among themselves, but somehow that only made them more fearsome. What were they planning? What could possibly happen next on this surreal journey?

There were few signs of life along the rutted, dusty road. Trees were cut down; stone walls enclosing fields chipped away, their rocks and mortar taken; grain crops unharvested and going to waste. There weren't even any cows grazing in those dry fields or smoke curling from distant chimneys. It was a deserted land, far too quiet for her peace of mind.

Or for Will's, either, it seemed. His narrowed gaze was constantly moving, taking in every detail of their surroundings. His jaw tightened at every sound.

Eliza longed to scream, to break the tension building inside of her however she could. Will seemed to know how she felt. As he flicked the reins, his hand brushed secretly against hers, a warm, reassuring touch. "Battle itself is never worse than waiting," he said. "We'll be rid of them soon and on our way to Dublin again."

Perhaps they would—but *then* what would happen? She smiled at Will, trying to hide her worries, and twisted around to check on her sisters. Katherine held Anna's head on her lap, slowly smoothing back her daughter's golden hair as Caroline stared out at the countryside.

Eliza felt a protective rush of emotion and a strange sense of pride. They were strong, her mother and sisters, far stronger than she had given them credit for. She would never underestimate her family again.

Will drew the cart to a halt at the crest of a hill, and Eliza turned to face forward again. The town of Rossmore lay just ahead, but it was not the sleepy village she remembered. It was now surrounded by a hastily built, rough wooden wall and a shallow trench. Soldiers guarded the closed gates, far more of them than a place like Rossmore surely required.

"What do you think is happening there?" Eliza asked. "I would have thought it would be half-deserted, like all the other towns, not fortified like an armed camp."

"I have no idea," Will answered, frowning as he took in the heavily armed guards, the walls. "It seems the government is preparing to take back County Kildare."

"From here?"

"We're very near the county border. Where better to store their weapons and gather troops." He slammed his fist down on the seat. "Damn it, Eliza, we never should have come here!"

"You could not have known. This must have happened very fast."

"I *should* have known. We should have kept to our plan to avoid towns."

"We hardly had a choice." Eliza glanced back over her

shoulder to see their rebel escorts scrambling up the hill on foot. They could not yet have seen the walls and the soldiers, but they looked grimly determined to find a fight, one way or another. Perhaps that had been their intention to come to Rossmore in the first place, not to "meet up with friends."

But it was all too late. They came over the crest of the hill, glimpsing the armies at last—and the soldiers saw them, too. With a blast of warning trumpets and a great shout, they poured out of the gates and the guardhouse, charging over the ditch and up the slope of the hill. The rebels, taken by surprise, charged back with a gathering roar.

Will pushed Eliza off the cart seat. "Run, now!" he yelled, reaching for his gun. The horses whinnied in panic, pawing the dust as if they, too, wanted to flee.

Katherine jumped down, pulling Anna and Caroline with her. Will took shelter behind the cart, bracing his forearm on the splintered wood rail to focus his pistol. He did not yet fire, though, just watched to see which way the action would go, covering their retreat even as he placed himself in the forefront of battle.

Eliza longed with all her might to stay there with him, to fight with him, but she had to think of her family and get them away first. There was no place to take cover on the bare hillside, no sheltering woods.

"We have to hide in the barley fields we passed earlier," she cried, urging them toward the unharvested stretch of dried grain in the distance. This might give them some disguise. They took off running, but it was too far, too late. The two forces clashed in a deafening roar of shouts and screams, the metallic ring of pikes and swords, the blast of guns firing. People fell and were crushed underfoot, but she could not tell who. It was massive confusion, smoke and dust and noise.

They were surrounded and could not run.

"Get down!" Eliza shouted over the chaos, pushing her mother under the cart. The three women crawled beneath its meager shelter, Katherine covering her daughters with her own slender body.

Eliza drew out her pistol, ducking low as she ran back to Will's side. He didn't even glance at her, but, just as they had at the bridge, they automatically moved in unison. He handed her his spent gun, taking hers as she reloaded.

Much to her surprise, her hands were steady, her mind clear. The taut worry of waiting faded with danger and purpose. She had to survive, to save Will and her family— and then find a way to send word to the United leaders about the new fortifications at Rossmore.

If she could stay alive. That was the crucial point at the moment. Surrounded by the roar of bullets and a thick, acrid cloud of smoke, survival was a bit doubtful.

"You have to tell them who you are!" she shouted to Will.

He exchanged guns with her again. Their shot was getting perilously low. "It hardly seems the time to say, 'Wait a moment, I'm a British officer!' "

"After, then."

"We have to make sure there *is* an after."

One of the rebels, the one infatuated with Anna, suddenly lurched out of the smoky fog, his face half torn away. He collapsed, dead, just beyond the cart, and Caroline cried out. Will knelt and snatched up the gun from his dead hand, standing and firing again in one smooth motion.

Distracted, Eliza did not see the soldier come around behind them until she heard Anna scream. She whirled around to see that a burly man in a red coat, his face blackened by the smoke like a devil, had caught Anna by the leg, dragging her out from under the cart. She kicked and flailed, Katherine and Caroline screaming, but to no avail. It was obvious that battle lust was upon him, giving him a superhuman strength, and he shoved the women away without breaking his hold on Anna. Katherine fell hard against the wheel, striking her head.

The rebel's woman suddenly leaped on Will's back, knocking him to the ground. Her blade arced down toward him, but he rolled over and held her off. It was obvious he was quite distracted, even as he won control of the skirmish. Eliza whirled back toward Anna, leveling her gun at the attacker even as she prayed the overheated firearm wouldn't explode in her hand.

The soldier had Anna pinned to the dirt, ripping at her skirt until her leg was completely bare as she screamed and writhed. She flailed around so much, Eliza could not get a clear shot without the risk of killing her sister instead.

It felt like terrifying hours passed, but surely it was only seconds. Anna blindly grabbed a dagger from the man's belt, a swift move he didn't even notice as he loosened his breeches and tried to drive himself into her. She stabbed at him wildly, until at last she sank the blade deep into his shoulder.

He reared up with a shout, a movement that gave Anna the leverage to pull the dagger free and plunge it in again, three stabs to his chest. He collapsed on top of her, his blood pouring out onto her torn dress, her body.

"Get him off! Get him off!" she screamed hysterically. Eliza leaped forward to grab the man's thick arm, tugging at it ineffectually. He was enormously heavy.

Katherine, who had a large bruise on her forehead from falling against the wheel, snatched up his other arm, and together they finally pushed him aside. Anna lay on the ground, her legs sprawled, her gown bloodstained as she stared at them with wild eyes. She still clutched the dagger.

If the man wasn't already dead, Eliza would have happily killed and scalped him herself. She had never hated anyone more in her life.

"Anna, darling, it's done," Katherine murmured softly, leaning over her daughter. "He is dead; he can't hurt you now. Can you give me the dagger?"

Anna shook her head frantically. Behind them, the cacophony of battle was fading. Soon the fighting would cease, and the soldiers would take stock. They could not find Anna with the bloody knife, the dead redcoat. They couldn't find her at all. Surely they would kill her in the blind fury of war—but first they would finish what the dastardly dead man started.

"Anna, please, give it to me," Katherine coaxed. But Anna was sunk too deep in terror.

Caroline crawled from under the cart, kneeling down by her sister. Calmly, she reached out and smacked Anna across the cheek. "Give Mama the knife. He can't hurt us now, thanks to you, but the others can if we don't get away *now*."

Something in Caroline's brisk voice got to Anna, breaking through the haze of fear. She dropped the knife as if burned and leaped to her feet. She caught a glimpse of her bloodstained hand, but Caroline grabbed it, holding on to her tightly.

"Forget him now, Anna," Caroline said firmly. "He was an animal who deserved to die. We have to try and get away."

Eliza glanced back at Will.

"Yes, go now, Eliza!" he shouted. "I'll cover your retreat."

"Will, come with us!"

"I can't, not yet. Don't worry—I'm an officer, remember? Go!"

Eliza nodded, trying desperately to tell him with one last look what she could never say. *I love you. Stay alive. Come back to me.*

She grabbed Anna's arm, running with her family as fast as she could away from the waning battle. They didn't stop until they had climbed over the crumbling wall into that barley field, burrowing into the sun-scented earth below the swaying, dried-out stalks.

She could still hear the fighting, but it was muffled, muted, like in a nightmare. She held on to her sisters, keeping them down as the hot sun beat on their heads. The smell of powder, smoke, and blood was thick in her throat.

"I murdered someone," Anna whispered, as if coming to some sudden, horrifying, life-changing realization.

Eliza couldn't bear that pain in her sister's voice. She never wanted this, not for lighthearted, sweet Anna. She raised her head to look into Anna's cloudy blue eyes. "You had no choice at all. You had to save yourself, save all of us. You were very brave."

"When I felt his hand on my . . . I was so *angry*. I couldn't see anything. I just had to . . ."

"Hush now," Katherine murmured. "Eliza is right—there was nothing else you could do. It's all right now; you will see."

The four of them lay there in the dirt for what seemed like a very long time to Eliza. The sun started to sink again, and the air grew mercifully cooler. A silence settled over the land.

But where was Will? Had he been killed or captured?

Eliza's worry threatened to tip over into panic, but there was no time for wild fear or desperate thoughts. Anna had done what she had to do; Eliza had to do the same.

"We need to leave as soon as it gets dark," she said quietly. "We can start toward Dublin."

"I need a fresh gown," Anna said. "I can hardly wander about the countryside looking like Lady Macbeth."

Eliza glanced down at her to see that her sister was still pale, but her eyes were clearer, her shaking ceased. That was a good sign, surely.

"I have clothes in the cart," Katherine said. "But . . ."

But who knew where the cart—and Will—were now.

"I will go look soon," said Eliza. But in the end, she didn't have to go searching. Will found them.

The sunset had turned the barley around them pink and orange when they heard soft footsteps in the dirt. Eliza sat up straight, drawing out her gun again in case it was the soldiers come to find them. Then she saw the gleam of his golden hair, and her arm fell back to her side. Her heart pounded in sudden relief.

He looked dirty and tired, his coat gone and his shirt torn, but he was *alive*. Alive and whole and beautiful.

In front of her family, Eliza jumped up and ran to him, throwing her arms around him to hold him close. She buried her face in the crook of his neck, inhaling deeply of the warm, precious life of him.

His arms came around her, too, just holding her there for a long moment.

"We were going to leave as soon as it's dark," she said, drawing back to examine his shoulder beneath the blood-streaked shirt. The stitches held firm.

"I think we should go *now*," he answered. "I left the cart on the road. One of the horses is dead, but the other should get us as far as Dublin."

"And the soldiers?"

He gave her a bitter little smile. "I did as you said—I told them who I am. I told them I had been on my way to rejoin my regiment when I was captured by the rebels. The Rossmore soldiers heroically rescued me."

"And they believed you?"

"I can be persuasive enough when I try."

Oh, Eliza knew *that* all too well.

"But they should not see you or your family here, especially Anna," he said. "We need to leave now."

Eliza nodded. On to Dublin—and whatever they might find there.

Chapter Twenty-nine

H alt! Let me see your pass."

The soldier strode out of the guardhouse, his weapon at the ready as Will drew up the cart. They had reached Dublin at last, all of them in one piece. Sanctuary was just beyond those walls. Eliza swept an exhausted, longing glance over their dark stone ramparts, at the curious faces that stared down at them, and she felt the burn of irritation that anyone would block them now.

She was tired to her very core, dirty and hungry, and worried about her mother and sisters. Anna had said scarcely a word since the battle in the woods, just staring off into the distance. They needed food and sleep, not guards leveling guns at them and demanding passes!

Her shoulders stiffened, but before she could say anything, Will laid a warning hand on her arm. He looked just as tired as the rest of them, his eyes lined with purple shadows, but he sat up military-straight and swept the cap from his head to focus the full force of his bright blue gaze on the man.

"I am Major William Denton," Will said sternly,

drawing a paper from inside his coat. They must have given it to him in Rossmore, for the rest of them certainly had no passes. "And I am escorting the Countess of Killinan and her daughters to safety. They are most eager to reach home."

The guard hesitated, his glance sweeping over Katherine's dignified mien, Anna's pale, pretty face. He gave the papers a quick glance. "I'm sure that's all in order, Major. We've had many families fleeing into Dublin these last days. But we have to make sure they aren't the rebels. Hard to tell now."

Will gave him a terse nod, urging the exhausted horse forward. Eliza leaned against his shoulder, suddenly aware of just how very tense she had been. She had been balanced on a sharp edge of fear ever since they left Killinan, never entirely sure they would reach Dublin at all. Even now, as they rolled slowly along the familiar streets, she could hardly believe it.

Those streets, usually so crowded and bustling at that time of day, were silent and almost deserted, the heat shining on the cobblestones and the blank windows. Houses were shuttered, many with doors draped in black mourning; shops were shut. But there was the constant echo of marching patrols in the distance.

"I'm glad to see Dublin is so well guarded," she said wryly.

Will gave a humorless laugh, urging the horse to go marginally faster. "You can't imitate such military bearing as mine, Eliza. It is entirely bred in the bone."

"You're teasing me," she said uncertainly.

"Just a bit, my dear." He looked around at the silent dwellings. "This place needs a bit of joking. But the signature of the commander at Rossmore seems to be an influential one."

At last they turned down Henrietta Street, rolling to a halt before her own front steps. The marble was unswept, and the curtains were drawn over the windows. "I would say it definitely needs some humor, among many other things."

Will swung down from the cart, reaching up to help Eliza to the pavement as her mother and sisters climbed out of the back. Anna leaned on Katherine, her mother's arm going around her waist to hold her upright.

And Eliza held on to Will for a moment, reluctant to let him go. It was as if she could feel him slipping away from her, slowly but inexorably. Slipping back into Major Denton as the city closed in around them.

"Thank you," she whispered, "for bringing us back here."

He briefly pressed a kiss to her temple, chuckling. "I think it's entirely due to chance that we're here at all."

"Oh no. If it was up to chance, we would all be dead long since."

He let her go, turning to take Katherine's medicine case from the cart as Eliza made her way up the steps and through the unlocked front door. Much to her surprise, the vast, drafty place looked just the same as when she left. Had she really been gone only a few weeks? She felt like an entirely different woman than the one who departed here.

"Oh, my lady! You've returned!"

As she dragged off her cap, Eliza looked up to find Mary running down the staircase.

"I am returned, Mary," she answered, turning to take

the valises from Will as he stepped into the house. He watched her in solemn silence, that brief flash of humor vanished. "And I've brought my mother and sisters and Major Denton with me, as you can see. I hope there is someone still here to make up guest chambers for everyone?"

"And a bath," Katherine added, her arms around her weary, drooping daughters. "I feel like I'm covered in acres of dust!"

"Of course, my lady," Mary said. She stared at their party with round eyes, as if astounded and scared by their sudden appearance. "Most of the servants are still here."

"Indeed?" said Eliza. "I thought we would find the place deserted, as most of Dublin seems to be."

"Some people have gone, my lady," Mary said. "But mostly everyone just stays inside, waiting for news."

"Is there any news to be had?" Eliza asked.

Mary glanced nervously at Will. "Not much, my lady. They say ten thousand men are on their way from England, but no one knows for sure."

"Well, whatever news there may or may not be," Katherine said, "we need sleep and food. I'll just take the girls upstairs if you will send a bath to us, Mary."

"Of course, Lady Killinan. At once," Mary said, bobbing a hasty curtsy. She looked to Eliza, her eyes wide and pleading, as if she had some secret to impart.

"I'll send for the maids, Mama," Eliza said. "You take the girls upstairs." As Katherine led Anna and Caroline up to their chambers, Eliza glanced at Will. He watched her carefully, as if he expected—or suspected—something. She smiled at him. "You go upstairs, too, Will. I know you're exhausted, and I need to speak to the servants for a moment."

"I should leave," he said, gesturing toward the front door.

"Where will you go?" she answered, studying him across that vast marble silence. How very strange it was to be here with him again, in the very house where their affair began. How long ago that seemed. "No respectable landlady would take you in looking like that!"

A smile flickered over his lips. "Perhaps you are right. I do somewhat resemble a scarecrow."

"And you're about to fall asleep where you stand. Go on—I will be up soon."

He nodded and slowly made his way up the stairs, his boots clicking on the cold marble. Eliza waited until she heard her bedroom door close above before she turned back to Mary.

"All right, then, Mary," she said briskly. "Tell me what is happening."

"I . . . oh, my lady! I did something terrible while you were away."

"Something terrible? Did you steal the silver?"

"Worse."

Eliza was tired, and she feared her patience was in rather short supply at the moment. She crossed her arms and said, "You had best tell me, then. It can't possibly be any worse than anything else I've seen in the last few days."

Rather than answer, Mary turned and led Eliza through the green baize servants' door and down the narrow stairs. There was the murmur of voices from the servants' dining room, but Mary slipped past them and went even farther down, through the wine cellar. The doorway to the secret room was unsealed, barrels rolled in front of it for concealment.

"I'm so sorry, my lady," Mary whispered, tears thick in her voice. "I just didn't know what else to do."

Eliza frowned as she studied the door, the secret space where she herself had hidden so many people. "I think you should show me, Mary," she said gently.

They pushed back the barrels, and Mary unlocked the door. Inside, the small room was dim, lit only by one low-burning lamp. A tray of half-eaten food sat on the table, and a man lay on the rumpled cot pushed up against the brick wall. Despite the hot summer day, it felt cold and damp in there, the air sweet with the smell of medicine, wine, and coppery blood.

"Mary, what . . . ," the man said, his words heavy with panic. He sat up quickly, the bandage wrapped around his chest stark white in the shadows.

"It's all right, Billy," Mary cried, leaning over to urge him back down to the pillows. "It's only Lady Mount Clare."

He resisted her gentle push, glancing at Eliza. "You said she was in the country, that no one would know. I won't put you in danger anymore, Mary!"

"She just now returned. You know she won't give you away."

Eliza stepped forward, her hands held out as if to show she meant no harm. "Mary is quite right. I won't turn you in. I only want to help, if I can. You are Mary's brother, yes? The fisherman?"

Billy cautiously lay back, his feverish gaze never leaving her. "Aye, or I *was* a fisherman. Not much work now, especially for an Irishman."

"Especially an Irishman who joins the Defenders?" Eliza said.

"I had no choice! I've tolerated their abuse for too long," Billy cried fiercely, trying to break away from Mary's soothing hands. "We had to fight back, to get justice."

"Oh, I know," Eliza said. "Believe me, I do know."

Billy finally lay back down, Mary smoothing the sheets around him. But still his eyes burned with the fervor of his cause, of fury too deep for any words.

Yes, she knew very well indeed how that felt.

"How were you injured?" she asked, sitting down in one of the old wooden chairs.

"He went off to Wexford, the fool," Mary said. "That's why we couldn't find him before."

"Wexford?" Eliza frowned, thinking of the town the United armies had seized, only to be run out again in a bloody battle by the British. "You fought there, and yet you managed to escape when the town was retaken? I heard they killed everyone they could find."

"He went there to find his sweetheart, Sarah," Mary said quietly. "To try and rescue her."

"Mary!" he growled.

"No, Mary is right," Eliza said. "I can be trusted, I promise." Even with the officer upstairs, waiting for her. She wouldn't betray an Irishman.

She remembered how she felt when Will was left on her doorstep, broken and bleeding. She remembered that sensation of her heart cracking, of losing part of herself. She leaned forward, bracing her hands on the edge of the bed. "You were injured trying to save someone you love."

Billy studied her face carefully. Something there must have reassured him, for he nodded, the fire in his eyes crumbling to ash. "We had captured the town; it was in Irish hands. It seemed safe. But in the end, I couldn't save her at all." He took in a deep breath before he could go on. "I was fighting outside of town when we saw the smoke. We knew then that the soldiers had broken through, that they would take the town back and show no mercy to anyone there. I ran all the way . . ."

"She had been . . . violated," Mary whispered.

"Killed like a dog in the street!" Billy shouted, beating his fist against the bed. "My Sarah. But I found one of the men who did it."

Eliza closed her eyes tightly, afraid she would start crying. Tears never did anyone any good. "That's how you were injured?"

"He stabbed me, aye," Billy said with grim satisfaction. "But he got it much worse in the end."

Eliza could imagine. What would she have done to the man who left Will at Killinan, if Will had died?

"I managed to escape and find Mary," Billy said. "But I know they'll find me eventually. People who could do such things to an innocent woman—raping her, leaving her for dead—they'll surely hunt down an Irishman like me and tear me to bits. It's what they've done to our kind for years, with none to stop them. But I won't put Mary in danger any longer. I would have left a long time ago, if she hadn't locked me in here!"

"I told you, you're in no condition to be running," Mary scolded. "Think of how Ma and Da would feel if you died."

Eliza sat back, watching them argue. So many thoughts whirled in her tired mind—her own siblings, all the blood and violence they had seen in the last few days, Will, and her love for him. The whole world, burning away in flames, along with her hopes for freedom.

And she also remembered *why* she worked and fought so hard. For Ireland, and for people like Mary and Billy and his poor, dead Sarah, abused and kicked aside like trash for too long. She had worked for the ideal—a foolish one, perhaps, but a glorious one—that everyone deserved justice. That Ireland and all her people should be free.

She could not give that up now, even in the face of bloody defeat. Even in the face of losing Will.

"I will help you get away," she said. "But for now, you must rest, as Mary says, regain some strength. You're going to need it."

And she had to decide what her next move would be.

The house was silent when Eliza made her way up to her bedchamber, her mother and sisters asleep and the servants vanished. But they had obviously been busy while she was in the cellar; a bath sat steaming by the empty grate, and food was laid out on her empty desk. And Will stood at the window, staring down at the street.

"I must promote Mary to housekeeper at once. She is terribly efficient in ordering the servants about," Eliza said. She stood by the closed door, uncertain if she should approach Will or what she should say to him. He stood so very still, she feared he knew what she was up to downstairs. "Is the ivy still growing there?"

"Abundantly," he said quietly. "I told you to have it trimmed back."

"Why would I do that when it is so very useful? Come, we should take a bath while the water is warm."

"You go first."

"Certainly not." She knelt down by the tub, testing the temperature with her fingertips. If he knew, if this was indeed the end for them, she wanted just a few more hours with him. Something to remember. "There is plenty of room for two."

As he watched her, she shed her coat, slowly unfastening her shirt and drawing it over her head. She took off her boots and breeches, until she stood before him in only the strip of cloth wound around her breasts to flatten them for her disguise.

"I'm afraid I need some help with this bit," she whispered, turning around.

There was a soft footstep on her carpet, then the gentle brush of his fingers over her bare shoulders, the nape of her neck, sweeping away the wispy curls that lay there. His lips followed, a soft kiss on her skin that trailed down her back to the line of the muslin. Eliza sighed, her head falling forward.

He loosened the knot, untwining the cloth slowly as she spun around. Faster, faster, until she landed in his arms, naked, laughing helplessly despite her worries.

Will laughed, too, kissing her on the lips. "Beautiful Eliza," he whispered.

"Grubby, tired Eliza," she answered. "But I'm happy to be safe here with you." For however long it lasted. She feared it might be only a few hours.

She pushed his coat back from his shoulders, removing his shirt and breeches as she had her own. The bandage was white against his skin, still in place after everything. She carefully untied it, examining the repaired stitches.

"You see," he said. "I don't need a doctor."

"I think you do, just to be sure. If one can even be found in Dublin. They've probably all been taken over by the Army."

Will shook his head. "All I need is *this*." He kissed her again, softly, tenderly, as if in wondrous greeting—or farewell.

His tongue traced the curve of her lips, and she opened to him, savoring the taste and feel of him, the ways their bodies knew each other now, so intimately. Even when they parted, surely he would always be a part of her. She would always remember this moment when they belonged to each other.

She slowly drew back from the kiss, greedily taking one more, then yet another. "Come," she whispered, clasping his hand. "The bathwater grows cold."

He frowned as if he would protest, would drag her back into his arms, but then he nodded. He climbed into the tub, lowering himself stiffly into the water. Eliza slid in behind him, wrapping her legs around him as he leaned back into the curve of her body. Their skin was slippery, pressing them close together.

"Tell me something good," she said, reaching for the bar of soap. Its rose scent mingled with the steam of the water, sweet and heady. She lathered it between her hands and ran the white froth over Will's shoulders, down his arms. His taut muscles relaxed under her touch, and he closed his eyes with a deep breath, his head resting on her shoulder.

"Good things?" he muttered. "I fear I can scarcely remember any."

"Oh, come, Will. Surely there is still something good in the world. Such as . . . scented soap." She held up the bar, wafting it under his nose until he smiled.

"Rose scent, of course. I always think of you when I smell roses. So warm and sweet."

"Sweet?" Eliza laughed, tracing a light, soapy pattern along his chest. "That's the first time anyone has said that of me."

"But you are." He caught her wrist, inhaling deeply of the soft spot where her pulse beat. "It was like I was numb, until I came here and found you again. You felt like life to me."

Life—in the midst of so much death and despair? Yet she knew it was true, for when she was with him, she, too, felt alive. Alive and happy, full of hope, despite everything.

"What else is good?" she said hoarsely.

"Hmm, the gardens at Killinan. I like it there. Black-faced sheep on green hillsides. Shakespeare."

"Romeo and Juliet?" she said, remembering that night at the theater.

"Except for the ending."

"Quite right. I have had my fill of sad endings." But she feared there were still more ahead, for all of them.

"And I like your littlest finger," he said, holding up her hand as if to study it.

Eliza laughed. "My littlest finger?"

"It's very elegant. Just like all of you." He slid the tip of that finger between his lips, nipping at it lightly with his teeth.

Eliza gasped at the sensation. "Sweet *and* elegant. It is a day for flattery."

"Or a day for truth-telling?" He took the soap from her, rubbing the rose-scented bubbles along the soft inside of her arm. "Now you tell me of a good thing."

She could scarcely think at all with him touching her like that. "Books. Those are good."

"Even the dangerous sort?"

"Such as Paine and Rousseau? I am not sure now. Perhaps we should all read novels as Anna does."

"Some would say those are even more dangerous."

"Only for people of a romantic turn of mind, like my sister."

"Are you not romantical, Eliza?"

"I am beginning to think I might be," she murmured as his caress brushed against her breast. "Anyway . . . oh yes, books. The seaside. Family."

"Family is important, indeed."

"I am starting to think so. My mother and sisters are magnificent, don't you agree?"

"Troupers of the first order. No one else could have made such a journey so valiantly. I wish they were *my* relatives."

"Do you worry about your own family?" she asked.

"My family has always been most adept at looking after themselves," he answered. "But I have always done my duty by them. I'll keep on."

Duty—always duty. "Food is also a good thing," she said, trying to shrug away doubts and fears. "And I think we should have some. I feel rather faint with hunger."

She slid out of the tub, reaching for one of the folded towels. She wrapped it around herself, listening to the slosh of the water as he shifted in the tub. He watched her as she sliced the bread and cheese and poured out soup from the tureen.

He slicked the wet hair back from his brow, rubbing his hands over his face as if he, too, ached with tiredness. "You need sleep as well as food, Eliza. You must be completely exhausted."

"I'm sure we all are. It's been a long journey. And believe me, I intend to sleep for days and days! As should you."

A frown flickered over his face. "You know I have to go to the Castle first thing in the morning."

"What will you tell them?" she said, staring down into her teacup.

"That I was injured. That the men in my patrol were killed."

"And about General Hardwick? The battle at the bridge?"

"Yes, though I'm sure they already know."

Eliza reached for another towel. "The water must be chilly now. Come, Will, you need to eat. Everyone needs their strength before facing the drafty corridors of the Castle." And she needed to make her plans—now.

Chapter Thirty

Will watched as the rose-gold light of day slowly crept across the chamber floor, over the bed, finally touching Eliza's face as she slept. That light was a formidable foe, indeed, he thought, for there was no force to stop it. It covered everything in its path, throwing all things that would stay hidden into plain sight.

Even love.

He had long known he loved Eliza, ever since the first time he saw her, when they were so young and foolishly romantic. He spent years trying to forget it, denying it, but some things simply refused to be denied. His heart was Eliza's and would be until he died.

To know that she loved him, too, despite everything, despite all he had done in the name of duty, was the most precious of gifts. The bonds between them would never entirely break, no matter what happened. Or what he had to do now.

He reluctantly got out of their warm bed, dressing quickly. Mary had found him some old clothes that belonged to Lord Mount Clare, and though they were too large, they were of fine cut and cloth and were better than appearing at the Castle in his traveling rags. The fine garments, as well as the bath and a shave, at least made him look semirespectable.

There was nothing he could do about his hair, though. He ruefully ran his fingers through the short blond strands. He looked a proper "croppy" now. At least a hat would cover it on the streets.

Eliza murmured in her sleep, her fingers twisting at the sheets.

"Shh," he whispered, leaning over to gently kiss her forehead. "Go back to sleep now."

She went still again, sinking back against the pillows. Purplish shadows under her eyes, dark against her pale skin, showed how very tired she was. The weight she had carried for so long.

"Just rest, my love," he said. "I will make sure that you are safe." No matter what he had to do to accomplish that.

Eliza still slept as he quietly left the chamber, making his way down the stairs in the still-silent house. The city itself was just as quiet. Not even coal carts or milkmaids were about, as if the nighttime curfews extended into the morning—or as if everyone was too scared to stir out of doors. Windows were closed, despite the gathering heat, and the shop displays were empty.

Walls were plastered with posters and broadsheets, with cartoons of barbaric-looking "Paddies" piking old men and looting houses.

Will ignored those, stopping only to read the sheets that seemed to promise news. MASSACRE AT SCULLABOGUE! screamed one black headline. A killing of two hundred loyalist prisoners, mostly women and children, piked and burned alive in a barn in Wexford. Another massacre, of ninety, at Wexford bridge. County Down overrun and then recaptured. Possible sightings of a French fleet to the south.

Will frowned as he read the hysterical reports. It seemed nothing much was known for sure; fear and hysteria still held sway. Battles were fought where neither side gained, and no one surrendered. Arrests and hangings, both of United leaders who fought and of people merely suspected of rebellion.

He turned away grimly, setting his path toward the gray fortress of Dublin Castle.

He wasn't sure what he had expected to find in those cold corridors—panic, noise, piles of guns. But once past the locked gates and the guards and the grim barred windows of Kilmainham Gaol, there was none of that. The place was eerily silent. The old Lord Lieutenant was gone, the new one not yet arrived, and it seemed everyone was keeping their heads down. Waiting.

A footman in red and gold livery led him along the corridors, past all the closed doors. At last they came to a room that was oddly familiar—the small private office where once he had found Eliza hiding at the queen's birthday ball.

"Wait here, please, Major," the footman said. "Someone will be with you very shortly." Then he was gone, leaving Will alone behind the closed door. He went to the one window, staring down at the Castle courtyard. It, too, was deserted, the flagstone shimmering under the hot sun. So different from that winter's night, when the space was full of revelers and frost covered the ground.

Will glanced back at the desk, at the tiny space beneath

where he and Eliza had hid, pressed close to each other in tense fear, anticipation, and desire. The desire had not faded, despite everything they had faced. In fact, it burned hotter than ever.

Papers were piled haphazardly atop the desk, awaiting someone's signature or seal. Once, Eliza had found them so important she risked her life. Now they seemed an insignificant pile of kindling.

Idly, Will shuffled through them, scanning troop orders already made obsolete by new battles. Letters from angry landowners that made him laugh bitterly. Appointments for new officials, men sent by the government at Westminster to restore order. But how could order possibly be restored when war still raged?

And then, at the very bottom, a creased list that appeared to have been passed through many hands. Neat columns of names, people Will recognized as liberal lawyers and writers, Catholic shop owners and shipping merchants, book importers. Pamela and Lucy Fitzgerald, their names crossed out after they left the country. In the margin was scrawled, *People to be watched closely. Questioned?*

The last name on the list was Lady Mount Clare.

Will's fist came down on the paper in fury, rattling the desk. Eliza was being watched, just as on that night he found her at the coffeehouse. And he could certainly guess what "questioned" meant. Arrest. Kilmainham. A hanging?

But he would never, ever let that happen. Even if he had to fight the whole British government to stop it. The door suddenly opened, a flustered-looking secretary appearing there with another stack of papers in his arms. Will swept the list beneath the other documents, forcing his fist to uncurl.

"Oh, Major Denton!" cried the secretary. "I am so sorry you have been kept waiting. General Fitch is on his way now to speak to you. . . ."

"Eliza, my dear, you are awake at last! Come, have some breakfast," her mother said as Eliza made her way into the dining room.

Katherine, Anna, and Caroline were already making progress through the meal, with racks of toast and pots of tea scattered over the polished mahogany table amid jam jars and spoons. Anna seemed pale and preoccupied, Eliza thought, but Katherine was determinedly cheerful.

They all wore borrowed gowns from her own wardrobe, Eliza saw, which lent a faintly comic air to the scene, considering how much taller she was than everyone else.

"Mary tells me it has grown difficult to obtain things such as milk and butter of late, as the roads into the countryside are mostly closed," Katherine said as Eliza sat down. "There is little meat as well, but plenty of toast and jam and some tea."

"No chocolate, though," Caroline said. "Which I'm sure has Anna quite disconsolate. She drinks an inordinate amount of it at home."

Anna made a face at her. "Tea is quite all right with me, I assure you."

Eliza was happy to hear her sister speak again, even if she did look distracted and pale.

"But you're not eating," said Caroline.

Anna glanced down at her plate, at the toast nibbled at the edge. "I'm not very hungry."

Caroline shook her head. "You'll never fit into your fine gowns again if you don't eat."

Eliza knew just how Anna felt; the thought of food made her slightly queasy, too. But she reached for the pot of jam and a piece of toast. "Caro has a point, I think. We need to keep moving forward, think of the future."

"Even when it comes to something as frivolous as gowns?" Anna said quietly.

"Yes, even then." Eliza firmly spread a smear of strawberry jam over the bread, trying not to think of how its sticky redness looked rather like blood. "Has Will had breakfast?"

"Mary said he was gone long before we came downstairs," Katherine answered gently. "I'm sure he had a great deal of work to do, now that we are back in Dublin."

"Of course," Eliza said. Will was gone now. Would he return? "I may have to go out later, too."

"Are you sure that is wise, my dear?" Katherine said, passing Eliza a cup of tea. "Mary says everyone has been asked to remain indoors unless absolutely necessary."

"Wisdom, Mama, has never been one of my virtues." Eliza took a sip of the tea, even though she was still not at all hungry. "I won't be gone long."

Katherine frowned, but she did not argue. "The girls and I will set about altering these gowns, then. Even if no one sees us, we can't go around like this." She tugged at the sleeve of her borrowed black silk dress.

"I would rather read, Mama," Caroline protested. "Eliza's dress looks quite well enough for me."

Anna, who could usually be trusted to have an opinion on matters of fashion, merely stared thoughtfully into her tea.

"You cannot go about looking like a ragman's child, Caro," Katherine said. "But I suppose it does not signify now. I think we have all earned a respite from doing things we would rather not. Now, Eliza dear."

"Yes, Mama?" Eliza said, setting aside her half-eaten toast.

"I have been thinking. Perhaps, after all this awfulness is ended, the girls and I might stay here in Dublin for a bit. I haven't had a taste of town living for some time, and I'm sure Killinan can go on without us for a while."

"Yes, of course, Mama. You can use this house as long as you like," Eliza said in surprise. She could scarcely imagine her mother away from Killinan, or Killinan without her mother. The two had been synonymous for so long. But she had certainly learned that all things change, sometimes in the mere beat of a heart.

"No, we can always take a house nearby," Katherine said. "You won't want us constantly underfoot, especially as Anna is going to be so busy with her Season next year. You must be accustomed to great independence now."

"Not at all. You *must* stay here. There is plenty of room in this vast old mausoleum," Eliza said. "But I thought you were going to England?"

"I see no need for that," Katherine answered with grim determination. "Ireland is our home. We can't leave it; we can't let anyone drive us away."

"Oh, how grand! I didn't want to leave," Caroline exclaimed. "When will the bookstores and lending libraries open again, do you think? I am terribly behind on my studies."

Eliza smiled. It seemed Caroline, at least, was recovering from her experience on their journey! She would lose herself in her studious pursuits.

Anna looked to be another matter, though. She still seemed quiet and preoccupied, despite the mention of her Season. But Eliza didn't know what could distract her from all that happened.

"I will see if any of the shops are open when I go out," Eliza said.

"I still wish you would stay in, my dear," said Katherine. "You need to rest."

"I don't think I could sleep if I tried, or even sit still," Eliza answered, sipping at the last of her tea. "I won't be gone long. Perhaps I can find some news of what is happening."

"I'm sure there is no good news to be had," Anna murmured.

"Even so, it is surely better to know," said Eliza. And she had to arrange for Billy's safe passage out of Ireland. She wondered if she should arrange her own passage while she was at it.

Chapter Thirty-one

Eliza sat in the drawing room after sunset with her mother and sisters, sewing and half-listening to Caroline complain about it every moment. Her thoughts were far away, though, wandering and worrying. Where *was* Will? What happened at Dublin Castle?

Anna had been right—there was little enough good news to be found or reliable news of any sort at all. But there were rumors aplenty. The United armies had seized towns and barracks; no, the Crown forces had taken them back. United leaders were captured and hanged; no, they had escaped and were marching on Dublin. There was nothing certain known.

"Caro, dear," Katherine finally said. "Why don't you read to us for a time, if the needle is so onerous?"

Caroline happily tossed aside her stitchery. "At last. My fingers are all bruised from this horrid work."

"You shouldn't be so clumsy, then," Anna said, examining her sister's puckered stitches as Caroline hurried to the bookshelves.

"Something cheering, if you please," Katherine called

after her. "A comic novel or some poetry. No ancient Celtic battles tonight." She glanced at Eliza, who tried to smile at her.

"I am quite all right, Mama," she said. "I'm sure I won't faint away at a tale of warfare, no matter how violent."

"I think we have all had quite enough violence, don't you?" Katherine looked at the clock, ticking away on the marble mantel. "I'm sure William will return very soon."

Eliza nodded. "I'm sure he will."

They stitched on in silence, Caroline reading from Mrs. Burney's *Camilla* as the minutes ticked away on that clock. Only when Eliza was quite sure he would *not* return that night, that he had been dispatched to fight in Wexford or Antrim, did she finally hear the knock at the front door.

She jumped up from her chair, the sewing falling to the floor, as the butler came into the drawing room.

"Lord William Denton, my lady," he announced, as if at some formal reception.

"Will!" Eliza cried. She ran to him and flung her arms around his neck. He lifted her off her feet, holding her close. "Oh, Will, I thought you weren't coming back."

"I promised I would, didn't I?" he said, his face buried in her hair.

As he lowered her to her feet again, she stepped back to examine him carefully. He had shed his borrowed coat and loosened his cravat, the white linen stark against his tired, tight smile.

"You must be terribly hungry, William," Katherine said. "I'm sure there is some of that mutton stew left from supper. Come, girls, help me see what we can find in the way of provisions."

"Why should we . . . ," Caroline began, but Anna grabbed her hand and dragged her out of the room.

"Don't argue, Caro, for once," Anna said, her words muffled as Katherine firmly closed the door behind them.

"You do look as if you could use some sustenance, Will," Eliza said. "Here, sit down. I'll pour you a whiskey."

"No laudanum this time?" he said with a grin, lowering himself wearily onto the settee.

Eliza laughed. "None at all, I promise. You look quite tired enough without it." Despite the fact that she ached to know what had happened at the Castle, she took her time at the sideboard, pouring out two tumblers of whiskey. She handed him one as she sat down beside him. *"Fad gaol agat."*

"Agus bas in Eirinn." He took a deep swallow of the fiery, fortifying liquid. "Not very good, is it?"

"Ungrateful wretch," Eliza said, lightly kicking him on the leg. "One of the Killinan tenants makes it in his own still. It's healthy for you."

Will sighed, knocking back the last of the "healthy" brew. "Why are so many things that are good for us so bloody unpleasant?"

"Are you going to tell me what happened, then?"

"The Castle is in an uproar. Camden is being replaced as Lord Lieutenant by Lord Cornwallis, who will be arriving any day now."

"Indeed?" Eliza said, surprised. "Well. Who would have thought one could change horsemen in the midst of Apocalypse?"

"They think Camden has been too soft, that a firm

hand is needed to bring the heathen Irish to heel once and for all."

"They think the United army is defeated, then?"

"Not entirely. No one is a more fiery, or more stubborn, warrior than an Irishman—or woman. But General Lake is hacking his way brutally through Wexford, and McCracken was captured in Antrim. It's only a matter of time. Then they will set to pacifying the country any way they can."

Eliza stared down into her glass. "And you, Will? Where will they send you now?"

"Nowhere at all. I have resigned my commission."

"What?" She sat straight up in shock. Whatever she expected, whatever she braced herself to face—separation, arguments, parting forever, Deirdre's sorrows—it was not that. He held his duty much too highly. "You left the Army?"

"I had a very good reason." He carefully set his empty glass on the table, giving her a terribly gentle smile.

Eliza did not trust that smile. It was the way one person looked at another just before they delivered terrible news. She folded her hands tightly together, bracing herself. Had Billy been intercepted as he left, smuggled out in a France-bound boat?

But, no. Will could not know of that. She took a deep breath, waiting.

"When I arrived at the Castle, I was taken to that office where I found you at the birthday ball."

"Indeed?" she said carefully. "That was most careless of them."

"But most fortunate for me. I was there for only a few moments, but I did learn from your example."

"You looked at the papers there?" she said. She could scarcely believe it! Will, snooping? She almost laughed aloud.

"Of course. And I found one I did not like at all." He reached for her cold hand, cradling it between his.

Eliza swallowed hard. "What sort of paper?"

"A list of people to be watched, questioned. Arrested."

"And I was on it, yes?" Or . . . no. It could not be Anna. No one could know what happened there in the heat of battle.

Will just nodded.

"I should not be surprised," she murmured. "I've long known I was suspected, of course, but, damn it all!"

How could she help anyone now, go on with her work, if she was watched and followed at every moment? Everyone she talked to would be suspected along with her, even her family.

Even Will.

"Eliza," he said firmly, his hands tightening on hers, not letting her go. "Eliza, listen to me now. I have a plan."

"A plan?" Plans so often came to naught; she knew that now.

"Yes. You must know now it is not safe for you to stay here. I say we leave."

"Leave?" she cried. She had not expected him to say that. To leave Ireland? How could she? But then again, how could she stay when she could no longer do anyone any good? "But . . . where would I go?"

Will laughed. "Not just you, my dear. We. We should leave for the time being, as soon as possible."

"You will go with me?" She stared up at him, a tiny, fearful hope just barely touching her heart. Will loved her enough to leave Ireland again, to stay with her? Even with everything he knew about her? Everything that had happened?

"I hardly think you could be trusted abroad alone. You would get involved in a revolution in Turkey or something like that."

"Very well, then. If not Turkey, where?"

He sat back, watching her carefully as if to gauge her reaction to his words, to forestall protests. "I have thought about it, and I say it should be Hamburg. It is a free port; there will be no passport troubles there. I heard Pamela Fitzgerald went there after her husband's arrest. There will be friends to welcome you. And from there, we can go wherever you like."

Her head spun wildly. After the endless day of waiting, now all this at once. Danger, imminent arrest, questioning. The possibility of giving away her United friends. Will declaring they had to run away together. "It seems you have considered everything."

"It does not have to be Hamburg, if that doesn't appeal. We can go anywhere you like. Vienna, Venice, Bonaparte's armies be damned! Or America." He crooked his finger gently under her chin, raising her gaze to his as he smiled at her coaxingly. "I am quite sure we could find some Indian tribes to live with there. You could teach them of Voltaire and Paine, and I could fish for our supper."

She laughed despite herself, catching his hand in hers. "I'm sure Hamburg is quite far enough; I do not need to go to the American frontier. Not yet. But my family—how can I leave them?" But even as she spoke, she knew she had to. Her presence put them in danger. If she was gone, the Angel of Killinan could hold them off. They would never find out about Anna and the soldier she killed.

"It won't be forever, my love. Only until things calm down here at home."

"Will they ever be calm?"

"Not for a Blacknall, perhaps. You all do seem to have a knack for finding trouble. But I am sure your mother would urge us to go as well. It's not safe here. Once they finish with the United military leaders . . ."

"They will look to others ruthlessly," Eliza whispered. "Yes, I am sure that is so."

She rose from the settee on unsteady legs, going to stare out the window. The whole city was blanketed again in night, in silence that seemed to wait and watch and fear. This was her home, everything she knew. Her work was here, or had been. It seemed she could help no one now.

Will came up behind her, his reflection wavy in the glass. He gently touched her shoulder, drawing her back against him. Eliza sighed and leaned into him, feeling his kiss on her hair.

"We *will* come back to Ireland," he said. "And while we are gone, perhaps you could write."

"Write what?" she said with a laugh. "One of Anna's romances?"

He chuckled. "I think you would be an excellent author of horrid novels. But perhaps you would prefer a memoir of 1798, a treatise on all that has happened and the ideals of freedom. You can tell the world what happened here, what it was all for."

Tell the world what happened. Yes, that was one way her work could go on. And there would be others, if she could stay alive to find them. "I could write about freedom, the rights of all people. One day."

"When you are ready, I will be here to help you. If *you* will do something for *me*."

Eliza smiled. "Of course. There is always a price."

His hand slid in front of her eyes, holding up an emerald ring. "Before we leave, you must marry me. Tonight. Will you, Eliza? I know it will be difficult to give up the title of countess to be mere Mrs. Denton. . . ."

Eliza stared at the ring, at the way it gleamed, as fresh and green as an Irish summer against the endless night. For the first time in that dark day, she saw a glint of hope. "I might be persuaded to the demotion, if the offer was tempting enough."

"I offer you my heart—but you have had that for years. I offer you love and devotion for as long as I live. I will never leave you again, Elizabeth Blacknall. *You* are my family now, my duty, my life. If you will have me."

If she would have him? She had dreamed of such a thing, of having Will for her husband, since she was fifteen. Even when they were apart, when she thought never to see him again, she had never forgotten. Their coming together now was not entirely as she imagined. It was flawed by the past, by war, by the end of ideals.

But it was wondrously sweet nonetheless. Perhaps even sweeter for all the obstacles they had faced, all they overcame to be together. And she would grab on to their love, their life together, with all her might. She would never leave him again.

"I will marry you, then," she said, holding out her hand to let him slip the ring over her finger. A bit of green she would carry with her as a reminder of home, until they could come back again.

Will laughed, lifting her in his arms as he twirled her

around and around. "At last! I have been waiting for this for years and years. You will not escape me now, Eliza."

"Will, your shoulder!" Eliza cried dizzily, holding on to him tightly as the room blurred. She wasn't sure if she laughed or cried, or both all at once.

"I feel no pain at all," he said, but he did lower her to her feet, the two of them swaying with the giddiness. The one transcendently happy moment born of all the chaos. The one thing that stayed strong and lasted—love. "I will be much happier when we are safely away."

"But do you really know what you are getting into?" she warned. "Even if we are on the Continent, you will still be part of my family. They won't ever let you forget that."

"And I always wanted sisters. We'll be as one family, Eliza, as we should have been a long time ago. . . ."

As if to prove his words, the drawing room door flew open to reveal Katherine, Anna, and Caroline, poised there in anticipation.

"Well, William?" Katherine said sternly. "What have you to say for yourself?"

"Lady Killinan," Will said, turning to her with a formal bow. "May I have the honor to ask your permission to marry your daughter?"

"It seems my daughters have never needed permission for anything at all." Katherine came to him and kissed his cheek, smiling up at him. "But I give my blessing, most heartily. It takes a special man, indeed, to deserve one of my daughters, and I think you may prove worthy after all."

"Let me see your ring!" Anna cried, the first sign of emotion she had shown since the battle. She rushed forward, grabbing up Eliza's hand to examine the emerald. "It is lovely, indeed. Just like you, Eliza."

"I am glad you approve," Eliza said, laughing.

"How can I not? He is a fine man. I only hope I may find such a man someday."

"I thought you were set on marrying a prince, Anna," said Eliza.

"Princes are rare. But even rarer, I fear, is true love," Anna said sadly.

"Not so rare as all that," said Will, sliding his arm around Eliza's waist and pulling her close for a soft kiss. "Sometimes love is right before you all the time."

AUTHOR'S NOTE—
LAUREL McKEE

I've wanted to write a book with an Irish setting for a very long time! My own family is of Irish descent, and I grew up with tales of "the green shamrock shore" (as well as stories of all the magical creatures, like faeries, gods, and gnomes, who live there). But I always knew it would have to be just the right story, with the right characters. It took a while for me to "meet" the three Blacknall sisters and their heroes, but as soon as I did, I fell in love with them and had to discover what would happen to them.

I also found just the right setting for them, the tumultuous year of 1798 and its aftermath (which goes on to this day in Ireland). I read Stella Tillyard's great book *Aristocrats: Caroline, Emily, Louisa, and Sarah Lennox, 1740–1832* (and watched the lush Masterpiece Theater adaptation) and was hooked on the story of these beautiful, intelligent, headstrong sisters, two of whom married Anglo-Irish noblemen and spent their adult lives in Ireland. One of them, Emily, Duchess of Leinster, was the mother of twenty-two children, among them Edward

Fitzgerald, whose story led me to look deeper into the 1798 rebellion.

I loved doing the research for this time period. Be sure and visit my website, http://www.laurelmckee.net, for Behind the Book research notes, a list of sources, excerpts, and photos of sites in Ireland I used in the story (as well as hints about Anna's and Caroline's stories!).

The Daughters of Erin Trilogy

continues in
Laurel McKee's

next captivating romance!

Please turn this page
for a preview of

Duchess of Sin

Available in December 2010.

Chapter One

Dublin, Autumn 1800

She really should not be doing this. It was a terrible, imprudent idea.

But had that ever stopped her before?

Lady Anna Blacknall drew the hood of her black cloak closer over her pale gold hair, which would shimmer like a beacon in the night and attract unwanted attention. She pressed her back tighter to the stone wall, peering out at the world through the eyeholes of her satin mask. Her endeavor to become invisible seemed to be working, as everyone hurried past her without even a glance.

But where was Jane? If she turned coward and refused to appear, Anna couldn't get into the Olympian Club on her own. Jane was the one who was the member, and the club had a strictly enforced "members only" policy. It wasn't likely Jane would abandon her, though. Jane, the widowed but still young Lady Cannondale, was the most daring woman in Dublin, always up for a lark or a dare.

She was also Anna's new bosom bow, much to her mother's chagrin. Katherine Blacknall, Lady Killinan, feared Lady Cannondale would run Anna into scandal and ruin.

It was fortunate Katherine didn't realize most of their pranks were Anna's idea, just like the one tonight.

Anna pressed her hands tight to her stomach, where a nervous excitement fluttered like a hundred drunken butterflies. This had seemed like such a fine idea when she first heard about the exclusive, secretive, scandalous Olympian Club and found out Jane was a member. Tonight the club was holding a masked ball, the perfect opportunity to see what went on inside its hidden environs. Something so secretive must be worth exploring.

Strangely, though, Jane had tried to put her off, to laugh away the invitation to the ball. "It is sure to be quite dull," she insisted, taking the engraved card from Anna's hand after she found it hidden in Jane's sitting room. "The club has such a reputation only because it restricts its membership. There's just cards and a little dancing, like everywhere else in Dublin."

Anna snatched the invitation right back. "How can a masked ball at a secret club possibly be dull? I've been so bored of late. Surely this is just the excitement I need!"

Jane had laughed. "You have been to parties every night this month. How can you be bored?"

"All anyone talks about are the Union debates in Parliament," Anna said. Those endless quarrels for and against Ireland's Union with England, rumors of who had been bribed with titles and money to switch sides, who had come to fisticuffs over the matter in St. Stephen's Green. She was so vastly tired of it, tired of everything.

It did not distract her from memories, either, from the

old, terrible nightmares of blood and death. Only dancing and wine and noise could do that, for a few hours
anyway.

She had finally persuaded Jane to take her to the
Olympian Club's masked ball. Anna crept out of her
house at the appointed hour, in disguise, to wait on this
street corner. But where was Jane?

She tapped her foot under the hem of her gown, a borrowed frock of Jane's made of garnet-red satin embroidered with jet beads and trimmed with black lace. Her
own gowns were all the insipid whites and pastels of a
debutante, but this gown was much better. The beads
clicked and sang at the movement, as if they, too, longed
to dance, to drown in the sweet forgetfulness of music and
motion. But if Jane did not hurry, they would have to leave
the ball before it even started! She had to be home before
dawn if she didn't want to get caught.

At last, Jane's carriage came rattling around the corner. The door opened and Anna rushed inside, barely falling onto the velvet seat before they went flying off again.
Those nervous butterflies beat their wings even faster as
they careened through the night, and Anna laughed at the
rush of excitement.

"I thought you changed your mind," she said, straightening her skirt.

"Of course not, A," Jane answered, tying on her own
mask over her piled-up auburn hair. "I promised you an
adventure tonight. Though I do fear you may be disappointed, once you see how dull the club really is."

"I'm sure it can't be as dull as another ball at Dublin
Castle," Anna said with a shudder. "Terrible music, endless minuets with stuffy lordlings. And Mama watching

to see if I will marry one of them and cease my wild ways at last."

Jane laughed. "You *ought* to let her marry you off to one of them."

"Jane! Never. Just the thought of one of them touching me . . . that way. No."

"It lasts only a moment or two, A, I promise. And then you have freedom you can't even imagine now. My Harry was a terrible old goat, but now I have his money *and* my Gianni, who is quite luscious." Jane sighed happily. "It is a marvelous life, truly."

"But you are Harry's widow, Jane. You no longer have to endure his . . . attentions." Anna stared out the window at the city streets flashing by, a blur of gray-white marble, austere columns, and black-painted doors. She thought of old Lord Cannondale before he popped off last spring, his yellow-tinged eyes that watched Jane so greedily, his spotted, gnarled hands. And she thought of someone else, too, that crazed soldier who had grabbed her in the midst of battle. . . . "Not even for my freedom could I endure sharing my bed with someone like that."

"Well, what of Grant Dunmore, then? He is young and so very handsome. All the young ladies are in love with him, yet he wanted to dance only with you at the Overton's ball last week. He would not be so bad."

Yes, there was Sir Grant Dunmore. Not so very old at all, and the most handsome man in Dublin, or so everyone said. If she had to marry someone, he would make a fine enough choice.

"He's all right," she said neutrally.

"Oh, A! Is there no one in all of Dublin who catches your eye?"

Anna frowned. Yes, once there had been a man who caught her eye. It felt like a hundred years ago, though in fact it had not even been two. When she closed her eyes, she could still see him there. The carved lines of his dark, harshly elegant face, the glow of his green eyes. The way his rough, powerful hands felt as he reached for her in that stable. . . .

The Duke of Adair. Yes, she did still think of him, dreamed of him at night, even though they had not met since those fearsome days of the uprising, when she was on the run with her family and he was intent on his own unknown, dangerous mission. He would not want to see *her* again, not after what she did to him.

She shook her head hard, trying to dislodge him from her memories, to shake free any memories at all. The past was gone. She had to keep reminding herself of that. "No, there is no one."

"We shall just have to change that, then," Jane said. "Oh, look, here we are!"

Desperately glad of the distraction, Anna peered out the window to find a nondescript building. It could have been like any other house on Fish Street, a square, harsh, classical structure of white stone. The only glimmer of light came from a leaded, fan-shaped window over the dark blue door. All the other windows were tightly muffled with dark drapes.

Anna smoothed her black silk gloves over her elbows, taking in a deep, steadying breath as a footman opened the carriage door.

"Are you quite sure this is the place?" she said. "It doesn't look scandalous at all."

"I told you it might be disappointing," Jane answered,

stepping down to the pavement. "But then again, the most delicious forbidden places are adept at disguise."

Just like herself? Anna had found she, like this house, was very good at putting up facades and pretending to be what she was not.

Or maybe trying on different masks to hide the terrible hollowness inside. But that would require far too much self-introspection, and that she did not have time for.

She followed Jane up the front steps, waiting just behind as her friend gave her invitation to the unsmiling butler who opened the door.

"Follow me, if you please, madame," he said, letting them in after examining them carefully. As two masked footmen stepped forward to take their cloaks, the door swung shut with an ominous, echoing clang. Now that they were really in that strange, cold, silent house, Anna wondered if Jane was right—maybe they should not be there.

But if she was not there, she would be alone in her chamber, with nothing but Gothic novels to distract her from her own thoughts.

She caught a glimpse of herself in a mirror as the butler led them up the winding marble staircase, and she scarcely recognized the woman who stared back. In that sophisticated red gown, with her face covered by a black satin mask and a beaded black lace net over her blond hair, she looked older than her eighteen years, as mysterious and cold as this very house.

That was good. Sometimes she did not want to be herself at all, didn't want to be Anna Blacknall, with all those duties and expectations and memories. And she didn't want anyone else to recognize her, either.

If anyone discovered she was here, she would be quite ruined. She would disappoint her mother and family yet again, in the worst way. But on nights like this, it was as if a terrible compulsion, almost an illness, came over her, and she had to run away.

They turned at the landing on the top of the stairs, making their way down a long, silent corridor. Medieval-looking torches set in metal sconces flickered, casting bronze-red shadows over the bare walls. At first, the only sound was the click of their shoes on the flagstone floor. But as they hurried farther along, a soft humming noise expanded and grew, becoming a roar.

The butler threw open a pair of tall double doors at the end of the corridor, and Anna stepped into a wild fantasy.

It was a ballroom, of course, but quite unlike any other she had ever seen. The floor-to-ceiling windows were draped in black velvet; streamers of red and black satin fell from the high ceiling, where a fresco of cavorting Olympian gods at an Underworld banquet stared down at them. More gods, stone and marble, stood in naked splendor against the silk-papered walls. The air was heavy with the scent of wax candles and exotic orchids and black lilies, tumbling over the statues in drifts of purple and black and cream white.

A hidden orchestra played a wild Austrian waltz, a sound strange and almost discordant to Anna's ears after the staid minuets and country dances of Society balls, but also gorgeous and stirring. Masked couples swirled around the dance floor, a kaleidoscope of whites, reds, blacks, greens. It was a primal scene, bizarre and full of such raw energy.

That nervous feeling faded, replaced by a deeper stirring of excitement. Yes, this Dionysian place was exactly what she needed tonight.

Jane took two glasses of champagne from the proffered tray of another masked footman, handing one to Anna. "Cheers, A," she said, clicking their glasses together. "Is this more like what you expected?"

Anna sipped at the sharp, bubbling liquid, studying the dancers over the golden rim. "Indeed so."

"Well, then, enjoy, my friend. The card room is over there, the dining room that way. They have the most delectable lobster tarts. I think I will just find myself a dance partner."

"Have fun," Anna said. As Jane disappeared into the crowd, Anna finished her champagne and took another glass, making her way around the edges of the room. It was decidedly *not* a place her mother would approve of. It was too strange, too dark—the dancing much too close. One man leaned over his partner, kissing her neck as she laughed. Anna turned away from them, peeking into the card room, where roulette and faro went on along with more intimate card games. There seemed to be a great deal of money, as well as piles of credit notes, on the tables.

No, the Olympian Club was assuredly not Dublin Castle, the seat of the British government; not some stuffy Society drawing room. And that was the way she wanted it. There was no forgetfulness in staid reels and penny-ante whist.

She took another glass of champagne. The golden froth of it, the rich scent of the flowers, was a heady combination. For a moment, the room swayed before her, a gilded mélange of red and black and laughing couples, and she laughed, too.

"You shouldn't be here, *beag peata*," a deep voice said behind her, rough and rich, touched at the edges by a musical Irish accent. Though the words were low, they seemed to rise above the cacophony of the party like an oracle's pronouncement.

Anna shivered at the sound, the twirling room slowing around her as if in a dream. Her gloved fingers tightened on the glass as she glanced over her shoulder. And, for the first time since she stepped into the alternate world of the club, she felt a cold frisson of fear trickle down her spine.

The man stood far enough away that it would be easy for her to run, to melt into the crowd. Yet something in his eyes, a fathomless, burning green behind a plain white mask, held her frozen into place, his captive.

He was tall and strongly built, broad shoulders and muscled chest barely contained in stark black and white evening clothes. And he was so dark. Bronzed, almost shimmering skin set off by close-cropped raven-colored hair, a shadow of beard along his sharp jaw. Dark and hard, a Hades in his Underworld realm, yet his lips seemed strangely sensual and soft.

They curved in a wry smile, as if he read her fascinated thoughts.

"You don't belong here," he said again.

Something in that gravel voice—the amusement or maybe the hint of tension—made Anna prickle with irritated anger. He did not even know her; how dare he presume to know where she belonged? Especially when she did not even know that herself.

She stiffened her shoulders, tilting back her head to stare up and up, into his eyes. He really was cursed tall! She felt like a delicate little elf beside him, when she wanted to feel like a powerful goddess.

"On the contrary," she said. "I find this all remarkably amusing."

"Amusing?" His gaze swept over the room before landing on her again, pinning her as if she were some helpless butterfly. "You have strange taste in amusement, *beag peata.*"

"You should not call me that. I am not *that* small."

One dark brow arched over his mask. "You know Gaelic?"

"Not a great deal. But enough to know when I am being insulted."

He laughed, a harsh, rusty sound, as if he did not use it very often. "It is hardly an insult. Merely the truth."

Before Anna could tell what he was doing, he grabbed her wrist, holding it between his strong, callous fingers. Though his touch was light, she sensed she could not easily break away. That eerie fascination, that hypnosis he seemed to cast around her, tightened like a glittering web.

Unable to breathe, to think, she watched as he unfastened the tiny black pearl buttons at her wrist, peeling back the silk. A sliver of her pale skin was revealed, her pulse pounding just along the fragile bone.

"You see," he said quietly. "You *are* small and delicate, trembling like a little bird."

He lifted her wrist to his lips, pressing a soft kiss to that thrumming pulse. Anna gasped at the heat of that kiss, at the touch of his tongue to her skin, hot and damp.

She tried to snatch her hand away, but his fingers tightened, holding her fast.

"You should not be here among the hawks, little bird," he muttered, his gaze meeting hers in a steady burn.

There was something about those eyes . . .

Anna had a sudden flash of memory. A man on a windswept hill, his long, black hair wild. A man who held her close in a dark, deserted stable, who kissed her in the midst of danger and uncertain fates. A man all tangled up in her blood-soaked memories.

A man with green eyes.

"Is . . . is it you?" she whispered without thinking.

His eyes narrowed, a muscle in his jaw clenching. "I told you, *beag peata*. You should not be here."

"I go where I please," she said, an attempt at defiance even as her head spun.

"Then you are a fool. Everyone should be most careful these days. You never know who is your friend and who is your foe."

"I am not stupid, sir." Angry and confused—and, she feared, aroused by him—she tried again to twist away.

He would not let her go. Instead, he drew her closer, his other arm coming around her waist and pulling her up against him. His body pressed to hers, warm and hard through the slippery satin of her gown.

"Since you insist on staying, then," he said, "you should have a dance."

Before she could protest or even draw a breath, he lifted her up, carrying her into the whirling press of the dance floor.

She stared up into his eyes, mesmerized as he slowly

slid her back down to her feet. He twirled her about, her hand held over her head in an arch.

"I don't know the steps," she gasped.

"We're not at a Castle assembly," he said roughly, dipping her back in his arms. "No one cares about the steps here."

As he spun her again, Anna stared around in a dizzy haze. He was quite right—everyone seemed to use the dance merely as an excuse to be close to each other. *Very* close. The couples around them were pressed together as they twirled in wild circles, their bodies entwined.

She looked back into his eyes, those burning green eyes that saw so very much. He seemed to see all the fear and guilt she tried to keep hidden. That mesmerizing light in his eyes reeled her closer and closer.

She suddenly laughed, feeling reckless and giddy with the champagne, the music, and being so close to him, to the heat and light of him. Well, she had come here to forget, had she not? To leave herself behind and drown in the night. She might as well throw all caution to the wind and go down spectacularly.

Anna looped her arms around his neck, leaning into the hard, lean strength of his muscled body. "Show me how *you* dance, then," she said.

His jaw tightened, his eyes never wavering from hers. "You should go home now."

"Ah, no. The night is young. And you said I should dance."

In answer, he dragged her tight against him, his hands unclasping hers from around his neck as he led her deeper into the shifting patterns of the dance. Even as the crowd closed around them, pressing in on her, she could see no one but him. The rest of the vast room faded to a golden blur; only he was thrown into sharp relief. He held her safe in his arms, spinning and spinning until she threw back her head, laughing as she closed her eyes.

It was like flying! Surely any danger was worth this. For one instant, she could forget and soar free.

But then he lifted her from her feet again, twirling her through an open door and into sudden silence and darkness. She opened her eyes to see they were in a conservatory, an exotic space of towering potted palms and arching windows that let in the cold, moonlit night. The air smelled of damp earth, rich flowers, of the clean salt of his warm skin.

There were a few whispers from unseen trysts behind the palms, the ghostly echo of music. But mostly she heard his breath, harsh in her ear. She felt the warm rush of it against the bare skin of her throat. Her heart pounded, an erratic drumbeat that clouded all her thoughts, obscured any glimmer of sense.

And, for the first time since they started dancing, she felt truly afraid. She was afraid of herself, of the wild creature inside that clamored to be free. Afraid of him, of his raw strength and strange magnetism that would not let her go, of who she suspected he was.

Afraid he would vanish again.

He set her down on a wide windowsill, the stone cold through her skirts, his hands hard as he held her by the waist. Anna braced herself against his shoulders, certain she would fall if he let go. Fall down and down into that darkness that always waited so she could never find her way out again.

"You should listen to me, *beag peata*," he said, his

accent heavy and rich like whiskey. "This is no place for someone like you."

"Someone like me?" she whispered. "And what do you know of me?"

"You are too young and innocent for the likes of these people."

"*These* people? Are you not one of them?"

His lips curved in a humorless smile that was somehow more disquieting than all his scowls. "Assuredly so."

"And so am I—tonight. I am not so innocent as all that." Innocents did not do what she had done, seen what she had seen. They did not commit murder.

"Oh, but you are," he whispered. "I can see it in those blue eyes of yours. You are a lamb among lions here."

She laughed bitterly. "But I can be a fierce lamb when I need to be."

"You're very brave." He took her hand in his, sliding his fingers over the silk of her glove until they completely circled her wrist and then tightened.

She gasped. His hold wasn't painful, but she was all too aware that she could not break free from him, could not escape. The pulse at the base of her throat fluttered, and she couldn't speak. She just shook her head—she was not brave at all.

"Brave, and very foolish," he said hoarsely, as if he was in pain. "Don't do this to me."

"What . . ." She swallowed hard, her throat dry. "Do what to you?"

"Look at me the way you do." He leaned into the soft curve of her body, resting his forehead against hers. She closed her eyes, feeling the essence of him wrap all around her. She felt safe, safer than she had in so very long, and yet more frightened than ever. This had to be a dream, something not real. *He* could not be real.

He let go of her wrist, bracing his hands on the window behind her. Slowly, she felt his head tilt, his lips lower toward hers. The merest light brush, a tantalizing taste of wine and man. His tongue swept across her lower lips, making her gasp at the hot sensation. The damp heat of it was like a drug, sweetly alluring like laudanum in wine, pulling her down into a fantasy world. He bit lightly at that lip, soothing it again with his tongue.

She felt his hands sliding over her shoulders, bared by the daring gown, trailing a ribbon of fire over her collarbone, the hollow at the base of her throat, and the sensitive skin just at the top of her breasts.

But then he was gone, pulling back from her, his arms dropping away. She cried out involuntarily, her eyes flying open. He stood across from her, his back turned, his shoulders stiff.

She would wager that was not the only part of him that was *stiff,* either, but he would not turn to her again.

"Go home now," he growled, his hands tightening into fists.

Anna knew she might be foolish, but she also knew when to cut her losses and retreat. She leaped down from the ledge, her legs trembling so she could hardly walk. But she forced herself to turn toward the door, taking one careful step after another.

"And don't ever come here again!" he shouted after her.

She broke into a run, hardly stopping until she was safely bundled into a hackney carriage, racing toward home. She ripped off her mask, burying her face in her gloved hands. But that did not help at all; she could smell him on the silk, on herself, taste him on her lips.

Damn him! How could he do this to her again? Or rather, how could she do this to herself? He had drawn her into his strange world once before; she couldn't let him do it again. She *wouldn't* let him.

Chapter Two

"A igh se," Conlan McTeer, Duke of Adair, muttered.
He rubbed his hands hard over his face, resisting the urge to drive his fist into the stone ledge where *she* had just sat. Even though she had finally shown a glimmer of sense and fled, her presence lingered—a whiff of lilac perfume, a drift of warmth and softness in the air. He flexed his hand, trying to shake away the imprint of her skin there.

It *was* her, Anna Blacknall. He knew as soon as he saw her there in the ballroom, the candlelight shining on her pale gold hair. Despite the risqué red gown and the satin mask, she could not hide her ladylike bearing or the bemused wonder in her blue eyes as she watched the dancers.

Yet even then he could scarcely believe it. Lady Anna, daughter of Protestant aristocracy, toast of the Society Season, sneaking into the scandalous Olympian Club? Wandering alone amid hardened rakes in her scarlet dress? For one instant, he was sure it must be a trap, something meant to lure him and his work out into the open.

But even as the thought flashed through his mind, he dismissed it. No one knew he owned the Olympian Club. And no one knew his connection to Anna or what happened between them two years ago in the midst of the failed Uprising.

Sometimes in the bleakest hours of night, nothing could ease the memory of her beautiful face, her fierce anger, and her fiery spirit. No woman could substitute; no amount of whiskey could drown her out. She stubbornly refused to leave him.

It was easy enough to push her away come the light of morning, because their paths never crossed. He sometimes glimpsed her riding in St. Stephen's Green or sitting in the visitors' gallery at Parliament with her friends during Union debates. And he certainly heard gossip about her. But he never went to Society balls, and she never came to *his* sort of parties. Until tonight.

Conlan braced his palms against the ledge. It was mere hard, cold stone now, with no vestige of her heat. He could finally think, without her intoxicating presence so close. The party whirled on beyond the glass conservatory doors, louder and wilder, but he was removed from all that revelry—as he always was.

He tried to think coldly and rationally. If Anna was not here at the behest of someone trying to close the Olympian Club, why *was* she here? He had heard rumors she was a most daring young lady, the toast but also the talk of Dublin for her exploits. Card-playing, horse racing in the park, lines of suitors trailing behind her. Perhaps she had slipped into the Olympian Club on some kind of dare.

But how could she get in? His staff was well trained to scrutinize invitations, to let in only members and a very limited number of their guests. The exclusive nature of the club was one factor in its great success. People always wanted to be *in* where others were *out,* and they were willing to pay a great deal for that.

Someone, then, had brought her as their guest. And he intended to find out who that was, to make sure Anna found out nothing at all on her little visit. She wasn't stupid. She might be able to convince all of Dublin into thinking her a fluff-brained Society beauty, concerned with nothing but ball gowns and games of chance, but he knew better.

He rubbed at the scar just beneath the cropped hair at the back of his neck, feeling the raised ridge that was a constant reminder of just how quick-witted and brave Anna Blacknall could be. And how he had once played the fool for her. She was the only person who managed to slide beneath his defenses during the dangerous days of the Uprising, the only one who brought him down.

That would *not* happen again.

Conlan frowned as he stared at the faint shadow on the window where her head had pressed. *Is it you?* she had whispered. Did she remember, too?

A moan echoed through the conservatory, followed by a rustle of silk. He was not the only one to lose his wits in passion amid the plants, then. Good, that was what the Olympian Club was designed for, to wrap people up in hedonistic delights, make them forget everything else in pleasure, so they gave up all their power. All their secrets.

Its allure was not meant to work on *him,* though. Pleasure could hold no snares for him any longer; he learned his lesson when he was a careless young man and nearly lost everything for it.

Silently, he pushed away from the ledge and crept around the banks of towering palms and heavily scented flowers. There were a few couples hidden amid the shadows, engrossed in each other, but one pair lay entwined on a wrought-iron chaise just under the moonglow of a skylight. The woman's head was thrown back, her gown slipping from her white shoulders. The distinctive auburn hair revealed her to be Lady Cannondale.

The man who knelt over her, kissing the curve of her neck as his hand slid beneath her skirt, was Sir Grant Dunmore. Conlan's cousin—and most bitter enemy. Once, years ago, Grant tried to enforce the Penal Laws that declared a Protestant could claim a Catholic relative's property. Conlan's ancient title saved his estate, but it was a hard-fought battle and not one he would ever forget or forgive.

Conlan smiled. It had been a long road trying to lure Grant into the web of the Olympian Club. And yet, in the end, all it had taken was Lady Cannondale's charms.

"Oh," she moaned, hooking her bare leg around his hips, tugging him closer against her. "You *are* being terribly naughty tonight, Sir Grant."

He laughed hoarsely, bracing himself on his forearms to gaze down at her. "Not nearly as naughty as I can be, my dear Jane."

"Then why are you holding back?" She threaded her fingers through his bronze-colored hair, dragging his lips back down to hers.

Conlan had a sudden vision of Anna sighing as he kissed her, her mouth opening to him. What would she have done if he laid her back on one of those chaises, spreading her legs and tugging down her dress as Grant did with Lady Cannondale? A little daredevil Anna might be, but he doubted she would welcome him with moans and sighs, her lithe legs wrapping around him tightly.

But a man could always dream.

THE DISH

Where authors give you the inside scoop!

♥ ♥ ♥ ♥ ♥ ♥ ♥ ♥ ♥ ♥ ♥ ♥ ♥ ♥ ♥ ♥

From the desk of Larissa Ione

Dear Reader,

"Family" is a word that means something different to everyone. Your family might consist of those who were born into it, or it might be made up of the people (or pets) you choose to bring into the fold. Your family members might be tight, or they might be estranged. Maybe they fight a lot, or maybe they get along beautifully. Often, family dynamics exist in a delicate balance.

So what happens when something happens to throw off that balance?

In ECSTASY UNVEILED, the fourth book in the Demonica series, I explore that question when the assassin hero, Lore, is forced to go up against his newfound brothers in a dangerous game of life or death.

In previous books, the conflicts each hero faced brought the demon brothers together to battle an enemy. In ECSTASY UNVEILED, the conflict is more internal, their bond is put to the test, and they become their own worst enemies.

Can love and trust overcome suspicion, tragedy, and an old enemy bent on tearing them apart?

When Idess, an angel bent on thwarting Lore's mission to kill someone close to his brothers, begins to fall for the coldhearted assassin, family ties are tested, betrayals are revealed, and a dark shadow falls over Underworld General Hospital.

Fortunately, "family" can also be a source of hope, and with Idess's help, Lore may yet find the family he gave up hoping for so long ago.

For more about the Demonica world and the families that make it come alive, please visit my website at www.LarissaIone.com to check out deleted book scenes, sign up for the newsletter, and enjoy free reads.

Happy Reading!

Larissa Ione

♥ ♥ ♥ ♥ ♥ ♥ ♥ ♥ ♥ ♥ ♥ ♥ ♥ ♥ ♥

From the desk of Laurel McKee

Dear Reader,

When I found out I had just a few days to come up with something for The Dish, I froze! There were just so many things I *could* write about that I couldn't decide. Should I talk about the rich history of late eighteenth-century Ireland? The beautiful Georgian architecture of Dublin? The gorgeous fashions? Irish music? The inspirations behind the characters? Or maybe a cautionary tale of my one attempt at Irish step dancing (there were head injuries—that's all I will say about that!).

I confessed my dilemma to my mom, who suggested we throw an Irish party with lots of Irish food and some Chieftains CDs, and then I could write about it (though there would be no dancing).

"Great!" I said. A party is always good. "But what are some Irish recipes?"

"Er—there's your grandmother's soda bread recipe," she said after some thought. "And, um, I don't know. Something with potatoes? Fish and chips? Blood pudding?"

"And Guinness," my brother added. "Every Irish party needs Guinness. And maybe Jameson."

I happily agreed. Fish and chips, soda bread, Guinness, Irish music, and you have a party! Blood pudding, though, can stay off the menu.

It was lots of fun to have what we called a "halfway to St. Patrick's Day" party. I just wish my characters, the Blacknall sisters and their handsome heroes, could have joined us. And if you'd like to try the soda bread recipe (which is supereasy—even I, officially the "Worst Cook in the World," can make it), here it is:

  4 cups flour
  1½ tsp. salt
  1 tsp. soda
  2 cups buttermilk

Preheat oven to 375 degrees.
Grease a round pan. Mix the ingredients
    thoroughly before kneading into a ball.

Cut a cross in the top, and bake for 50–60
  minutes.
Serve with fresh butter and a Guinness!

And for some background on the history and
characters of COUNTESS OF SCANDAL and the
Daughters of Erin series, be sure to visit my website at
http://laurelmckee.net.

Enjoy!

Laurel McKee

♥ ♥ ♥ ♥ ♥ ♥ ♥ ♥ ♥ ♥ ♥ ♥ ♥ ♥ ♥

From the desk of Lilli Feisty

Dear Reader,

For those of you who have read my previous book,
Bound to Please, you may have noticed I have a bit of
a thing for music and musicians. My latest novel,
DARE TO SURRENDER, is not about a musician,
but it's still related to music. It's about a woman whose
emotional release is to dance. She won't dance in
public; she's much too shy for that. But she dances by
herself. A lot.

And it's not just any sort of dancing; she prefers to
belly dance. She's quite good at it, better than she

thinks. In fact, Joy is better at a lot of things than she gives herself credit for, and it was great fun helping her realize that. Because don't we all have our hang-ups? And working our way through them can be quite an exhilarating release.

If you read DARE TO SURRENDER, I'll tell you right now that there are a lot of similarities between the heroine, Joy Montgomery, and myself. She's a red-head. She's not necessarily comfortable with her curvy figure. She's totally disorganized. Her handbag is the size of a small suitcase.

There's more. She works in an art gallery—I owned one. She's very spontaneous, to the point of getting herself in crazy binds because of it. I do that. A lot. She drives an old Mercedes. So do I.

So you can see we have a lot in common. Except the dancing in public thing. To put it simply, I love to dance. Am I any good at it? Probably not. But I simply can't help myself. If I'm out, and I hear a good beat, I'm lured to the dance floor. In fact, I tend to dance at any opportunity, however inappropriate. It was quite pathetic, but just the other day, I was reprimanded at the grocery store for doing the Wang Chung in the frozen-food aisle.

However, let me tell you, belly dancing is not as easy as it looks. To be good, you have to be able to move separate parts of your body at varying speeds and rhythms. For some people (me), it's not easy. But that's irrelevant—it's fun, and once you let yourself go, it really doesn't matter how good you are. You feel the music take over your body and you want to shimmy. To undulate. To dance! I think belly dance is one of the sexiest, most feminine, mesmerizing forms of dance there is.

Some people assume belly dance was created for the sole purpose of entertaining men. In fact, this is not true. It was invented by women, for women. I think that's why it's such a sexy form of dance. When you belly dance, you're celebrating being a female. You use your hips, your arms, your waist. And, of course, your belly. And you don't need to worry if your belly is a bit round because it's about having fun and using your body to express yourself. And let's not forget the costumes. Belly dancing costumes are pretty darn gorgeous.

So this is Joy's hobby. And it's mine, too. The only difference is that Joy is too shy to do so in public so she only practices in her own bedroom. (Also Joy is way better at it.) Of course, when she meets Ash Hunter, he slowly begins to chip away at Joy's inhibitions. But does he get her to dance in public?

Well, I won't give away the ending. But I will say, by the end of their story, Joy is ready to take the dare to surrender everything, even if it means embracing every facet of her femininity.

I hope you enjoy their story.

XXOO,

Lilli Feisty

Want to know more about romances at Grand Central Publishing and Forever? Get the scoop online!

GRAND CENTRAL PUBLISHING'S ROMANCE HOME PAGE

Visit us at www.hachettebookgroup.com/romance for all the latest news, reviews, and chapter excerpts!

NEW AND UPCOMING TITLES

Each month we feature our new titles and reader favorites.

CONTESTS AND GIVEAWAYS

We give away galleys, autographed copies, and all kinds of fun stuff.

AUTHOR INFO

You'll find bios, articles, and links to personal Web sites for all your favorite authors—and so much more!

THE BUZZ

Sign up for our monthly romance newsletter, and be the first to read all about it!